Porta M

By A A Spectre

For the lovely Rachey, for her never-ending support.

This book contains explicit language.

Copyright 2025. A A Spectre

Book One

One

'Are you excited?' Saskia asked.

Ayesha screwed her mouth up in thought. 'Not yet.'

'I don't believe that you're ever going to get excited,' Saskia stated. 'You'll just continue to wear that focused, steely look, and scare away all the customers.'

'That's why we're employing staff! So that I don't get the chance to scare away customers.'

'Don't you want to get your hands dirty now and again?' Saskia said disappointedly. 'Sell the odd Tang Dynasty Horse.' It was a conversation they'd had before; several times; Saskia still did not know if Ayesha was being serious.

'No, not even if we had one. Would I scare away the customers?' Ayesha frowned.

'Ayesha,' Saskia smiled, relenting. 'I believe there are men out there who would willingly pay for your steely look.'

'Hmm, I wonder what else I would be being paid for. Don't worry, the steely look will be gone by the official opening next week. I'll keep it up for the staff interviews this afternoon, with the addition of spectacles.'

Saskia looked interested. 'Those sexy little black designer ones. You've yet to wear for me in bed.'

'Dream on Saskia!'

'You! are cruel,' Saskia said disappointedly.

'Yes, I know. But not as cruel as you would like me to be.'

They were across the street from their newly established business premises. The sign above the double display windows read: Challoner-Shah Antiques and Fine Art. The creation of it had consumed them for four months. Ayesha was dressed in a fitted navy-blue suit with a grey waistcoat and black stilettos, Saskia in an open black waistcoat over a loose white shirt, skinny black jeans, and ankle boots. She was sporting a new hairstyle, a stylishly hot messy bob; cut into being that very morning and revealed to Ayesha less than ten minutes earlier. The look had been her ambition since she had discovered Parisienne chic in a glossy magazine eighteen months previously; just a week after she had had her hair cut; she was grateful she had chickened out of her plan to have it cut dangerously short though, in a misguided attempt to look like Sinead O'Connor. Ayesha had studied the new look with cool appraisal as Saskia strode jauntily along the pavement towards her. Saskia had given her a heads up on her mobile that she was on her way. Ayesha had handed her a chocolate mocha in a disposable cup; she removed the lid as they turned to review their premises. Ayesha drank some of her own coffee, a dark chocolate mocha. She had waited, allowing disappointment to build; knowing that Saskia would feel quite crestfallen at her lack of enthusiasm for her hair. It had been intended as a surprise, and it had been. Saskia had disappeared with an excuse as soon as they had arrived in York; it was not unusual; she had a habit of disappearing. Ayesha had sensed the despondency deepen. In her mind's eye she could see Saskia's white teeth grip the side of her under lip, and her green eyes grimly fight the threat of tears.

'You look gorgeous little mantis,' she told her softly.

'I know,' Saskia responded, feeling satisfaction. 'Have you been inside? I see the shutters are up.'

'Yes. I haven't put the main lights on though.'

'Shall we go in?' Saskia inquired.

'It's nice standing here in the sunshine. Can we finish our coffees?'

Saskia nodded, content to be there with Ayesha. It was nice to stand there in the sunshine, she thought; surrounded by the impersonal hum of people. She closed her eyes and went elsewhere for just a little while. She opened her eyes and gazed down at her empty cup. Ayesha took it from her and smiled.

'Away again?' she said.

'Yes.'

'I wonder where you go?'

Saskia sighed. 'I wish I knew, it's nice though.'

They crossed the street, threading through the crowd. Ayesha fished the keys out of her bag and let them in; they closed the door behind them on the sound of humanity. Saskia drew in the smell of newly refurbished space, paintwork, and bamboo laminate flooring, polish, and the lingering trace of adhesive. She allowed in the feel of the place, taking pleasure in the structured eloquence of the interior; their narrative, though admittedly it was mostly Ayesha's narrative, of stylish free-standing shelves and glass cabinets, and skilfully located lighting. They had priced and displayed a good percentage of their stock, and the character of the place was beginning to take shape. It was Ayesha's vision primarily and Saskia had embraced it, taking on the role of assistant. She had given where she could; it was her idea to include upright cabinets among the displays and to make the big upstairs space into a bespoke gallery, though there was plenty of art on display on the walls of the main showroom too. Saskia was certain Ayesha would have come up with the idea eventually, though she did suspect that she had and was simply being kind to her by letting her propose the idea.

'I like it more every time I see it.'

'We're a good team.'

'Yes, but you're the architect.'

'Saskia, it's shelves and a bit of lighting.'

'It's a lot more than that and you know it.'

'Yes, it is. It's marvellous objects and wonderful Art. Much of it provided by you for free. I'm getting the best of the deal.'

'We've spent a lot of money between us too. I thought that I was getting the best of the deal myself. All my stuff cost me nothing. You've forked out for the lease and the refurbishment and the fittings.'

'It still doesn't compare. Anyway, we've had this conversation before. The one thing I can say for certain is that I have so much enjoyed finding the things that we've bought together. And I really do not want that to stop.'

They had reached the transaction counter, it's polished birds-eye maple top equipped with card machine, phone, and computer screen; there was a secure till housed underneath.

'See there's another thing,' Saskia pointed out determinedly, 'the hours you've spent entering stock lists and describing stock on the computer. There have been times when I've had to drag you off to bed, you've been shattered and determined to carry on.'

'You've had a couple of serious tongue lashings in return for your pains, haven't you?' Ayesha looked conscience stricken and she threw Saskia a glum look.

'They were brutal.'

'I'm sorry.'

'I loved them.'

'You're odd.'

'Would you have me any other way?'

'God no!'

'No sign of the business cards yet!' Saskia indicated the empty card holder.

'I'll get onto it. I'll pay them a visit in person, it's only a few streets away.'

'That should do the trick. Are you really not going to help in the shop? I know that you can handle people, I've seen you do it. Look how you took care of me.'

'But I fancied you like crazy! Of course, I will, I was only yanking your chain; if you're prepared to do it, so am I.'

She glanced through the doorway into the tiny office; she frowned, and she pushed out her under lip.

'It's barely a cupboard! We can't conduct interviews in there.'

Saskia shrugged indifferently. 'I never thought that we were.'

'Didn't you? We should use the flat I suppose, like we said.'

'It's okay, too intimate though. No.' Saskia spoke firmly. 'Let's strip the polythene off three of the client chairs, drag them together to the middle of the floor, next to the Indian temple wood carvings; re-locate a couple of lamps; the big Anglepoise for one and conduct the interviews there.'

'Brilliant!' Ayesha surprised her with instant approval.

'You're nervous, aren't you?'

'Yes, I'm nervous.'

'Why?'

'I don't want to get it wrong.'

'Ayesha, you will not get it wrong. It's not all on you anyway; unless you believe that I'm just here to make up the numbers.'

Ayesha appeared mildly shocked by the idea; she fixed Saskia with a long penetrating stare.

'You don't really think that do you?'

Saskia tilted her head on one side, she compressed her mouth into a small gentle smile; her eyes were sympathetic. She leaned into Ayesha and kissed her tenderly on the lips. They breathed one another's scent and the smell of coffee. Saskia withdrew though not entirely and searched the beautiful anxious face with warm eyes that were full of amazement.

'Never in a million years,' she replied.

'Why are you looking at me like that?'

'Because I never cease to be surprised by the realization that you're mine.'

'I see.' Ayesha's smile compressed into pleasure. 'We could go up to the flat. We've got an hour.'

Saskia experienced the velvet clawing of desire. She was about to lean into Ayesha again but at that moment Ayesha's mobile phone rang inside her bag and someone began to bang loudly on the glass door of the shop. Ayesha shrugged and gave a disappointed little smile.

'There's always tonight, I'll answer this, you go and tell them we're not open yet!'

'It might be the man with the business cards,' Saskia suggested, though she was not hopeful; she turned, and frowning, stalked away to answer the door.

It proved not to be the man with the business cards. But it was Amber and Pearl Shalako. Amber was on her mobile and Pearl was pressed up against the door with her eyes crossed. Saskia grinned as she opened the door to them. Saskia and Pearl hugged and swayed.

'It's been weeks!' Pearl said.

'I'm sorry.'

'It's okay, we know you've been busy.'

Saskia disengaged and moved toward Amber as the older twin came through the door still talking into her mobile. She threw an arm around Saskia's neck.

'It's okay Ayesha,' she said smiling into her phone, 'the idiots let us in.' She shut down her mobile and slipped it into a red faux snakeskin shoulder bag.

The twins looked incredibly smart Saskia thought. Pearl was in a grey dress with a pencil line knee length skirt, and a matching bolero style jacket and red stilettos. Amber was in a suit of the same colour with a waist length jacket and double row of buttons; her pencil skirt was knee length, and she was wearing identical red stilettos to Pearl's and carrying an identical shoulder bag. Typically, Amber was wearing her shoulder length hair, down, whilst Pearl's was pinned up. They gazed admiringly about as Saskia closed the door and dropped the catch.

'This is fabulous!' Pearl said quietly.

'You two look good! Don't they Ayesha?' Saskia complimented as she turned toward Ayesha who appeared between the displays. She smiled and nodded, agreeing; her dark eyes flitting from Pearl to Amber

'Amber, Pearl, it really is nice to see you!' Just a few weeks ago that was something she would never have imagined saying to them, less still meant it, she thought, as she gave herself to easy hugs. 'But you're going to think I'm a cow. We've got staff interviews starting in an hour. Otherwise, we could have taken you out for lunch.'

'We know!' Amber replied, she glanced sideways at Pearl, a hint of uncertainty in her expression.

'That's why we're here,' Pearl smiled brightly.

Ayesha continued to smile but directed a puzzled frown in her direction.

'We've come to ask for a job! We only found out an hour ago, that you were interviewing for staff today,' Amber said.

'Aunty Claire told us,' Pearl revealed.

'We were making our weekly report on Amadeus,' said Amber.

'She asked if we were going to your opening event,' said Pearl.

'We told her that we wouldn't miss it for the world!'

'She said she hoped you'd find the right people today; she actually said young ladies at first but changed it to people...' Pearl said.

'Because she didn't want to sound sexist,' said Amber. 'But I said bullshit! a nicely edited chick, will always outperform a guy in a high-class retail environment, in my opinion.'

'So long as she is informed and chatty not like the snooty cows in T...' Pearl began to vent.

'We wouldn't let you down,' Amber rested a calming hand on Pearl's.

'And you know that we live literally a ten-minute walk away,' Pearl said.

'Do you need the money?' Ayesha asked.

'No, we need the purpose,' Amber stated. 'We'd even work for free.'

'I think everyone should take a breath,' Ayesha suggested.

'You've no reason to like us, Ayesha,' Pearl said glumly, 'I don't blame you if you simply blow us out of the water.'

'Well, that might have been true once.,' Ayesha replied. 'I admit I wasn't the easiest person in the world to like, and I did myself no favours, in fact I actively sought to...'

'Ayesha,' Saskia closed Ayesha's hand in hers, pausing her.

'Yes. Sorry. Saskia, please will you make us all a cup of tea?' Ayesha turned pleading eyes to Saskia.

'Pearl, Amber will you give us a moment?' Saskia said.

They nodded; they looked as anxious as Ayesha, Saskia decided as she took Ayesha by the arm and drew her away; she relayed a tight and hopefully reassuring little smile to Amber and Pearl.

'What are we going to do?' Ayesha asked.

'You must be really stressed, or you wouldn't have asked that,' Saskia said. 'Let's hear what they have to say. I've no intention of writing them off, have you?'

Ayesha screwed her face up in intense thought, indication of a fierce inner battle. Her expression relaxed; she smiled suddenly. 'No, I haven't.'

'Right, in that case.' Saskia turned to regard the twins. 'Pearl, Amber will you help Ayesha to take the polythene off those chrome and white leather chairs that are dotted about and help her get the four of them into the middle of the room. I'm going to make us all coffee; its quicker, and then we'll sit down and talk seriously about this.'

'We didn't even think about it until a couple of hours ago,' Amber said.

'Then it just made perfect sense,' said Pearl.

'This is our pitch. We don't have another. We're us,' Amber smiled.

'Please, please, consider us, it really is important to us,' Pearl looked intense, it was obvious that she was passionate.

'We absolutely will not let you down,' Amber stated.

The Anglepoise and another lamp, a Gino Sarfatti multicoloured floor lamp created an intimate area of illumination in the middle of the expansive showroom. A plate glass hospitality table was centred between them for their drinks.

'You've admitted that it's a spur of the moment decision.' Ayesha said.

'It doesn't make it any less valid,' Amber insisted.

'It's been staring us in the face for weeks,' said Pearl.

'And you know what you'd be getting with us,' said Amber.

'We do! And it worries me,' Ayesha said quite gently.

'Yes, but you know that we'd be loyal!' Pearl declared.

'I can't argue with that,' Ayesha admitted. 'What do you know about selling?'

'God Ayesha, we're finding it difficult to even sell ourselves right now,' Amber declared.

'You aren't doing a bad job,' Saskia said.

'We've no experience, we know,' said Pearl.

'We've never worked,' said Amber. 'It's not a great start, we know that.'

'Neither have I,' Saskia replied.

'I know this though,' Pearl asserted, 'I know how a customer should be treated, and how they shouldn't.'

'You would be taking jobs from two people,' Ayesha said.

'Would they be the right people though?' Amber asked.

'For you and Ayesha,' said Pearl.

'There are always other jobs for pretty girls,' Amber insisted. 'Because that's what you are looking for aren't you?'

'Pretty girls who can sell themselves and sell a product,' said Pearl.

'But they come with experience,' Ayesha pointed out.

'They aren't our problem,' said Amber.

'And we would work for free,' Pearl announced.

'We couldn't let you do that,' Ayesha said. 'Suggesting that is not exactly a recommendation.'

'Fair enough,' said Pearl, avoiding her twins stare. 'It's wrong of us...me to attempt bribing you with that. But we would each be twice as committed as any one of them.'

'Why?' Saskia said.

'We've already told you. We need a purpose. Why else are you opening this place other than that; you must be driven.' Amber said.

'Yes, what inspired you to go into business with Saskia?' Pearl said. 'Neither of you needs the money. And neither of you comes across as wanting a lavish lifestyle.'

'It fulfils a need,' Saskia responded thoughtfully.

'Exactly! it gives you that purpose,' Amber declared.

'Yes, but it's our purpose,' said Ayesha.

Pearl gave a little huff. She looked away. She had not touched her coffee.

'Do you think we would have come here like this, if you were opening a dress shop or homewares, or a Jewellers?' Amber said, not giving up.

'So, it's the nature of the business then?' Saskia moved forward in her seat, interested. Her elbows were on her knees, her cup between her fingers. She looked intently from Amber to Pearl.

'Of course, it is!' Pearl proclaimed. 'We looked through the windows the day before yesterday, in the afternoon and saw what was taking shape in here. It wowed us; it really did.'

'You should have knocked or phoned.' Saskia felt a little rush of gratification at the recognition.

'We couldn't see you,' said Amber. 'So, we didn't bother, we assumed you'd gone off somewhere.'

'There's a gallery upstairs,' Ayesha said, by way of explanation. She recalled that they had not yet remade the ruined bed in the flat.

'Look it's obvious that you're doing something that means a lot to you,' Amber said. 'Well, it presses the right buttons for us too.'

'Yes, do you think we sit in our apartment painting our toenails all day, dreaming about our next holiday in the Seychelles?' Pearl was quietly defiant, but Saskia could see she was working hard to deny tears of frustration.

'We don't go on holiday to the Seychelles,' Amber pointed out.

'I know we don't,' replied Pearl. 'I said it for dramatic effect.'

'Go on then Pearl, tell me?' Ayesha invited, there was no audible inflection in her voice and her face was open. She wanted to know. Pearl stared into her dark questing eyes. She tugged at a stray strand of hair that had fallen in front of her ear. She was about to let someone into a closed world. It was not an easy thing to do.

'We buy some Art.' Pearl shrugged; she felt the statement was rather lame. She rallied. 'You've never been to our apartment, so you don't know. We collect Art Deco face masks. Amber collects micro mosaics.'

'Pearl collects medieval coins, and muff and pocket pistols,' Amber said smiling affectionately towards her twin. 'She can restore them too. And she can strip down anything clockwork and make it work again. She's restoring an old automaton of an acrobat presently.'

Ayesha exchanged looks with Saskia, she looked almost taken aback; Saskia tried to remain stony faced in response, but her compressed mouth slowly surrendered into a smile.

'You said that you intend to come to our opening event,' Ayesha addressed Pearl with a cool tone.

'You'll let us know then? That's fair enough,' Pearl replied, she nodded; she looked crestfallen.

'No. What I'm saying is that you had better get here an hour early, because staff are expected to welcome guests.'

Pearl's eyes rounded in sudden disbelief, and her face lit up in pleasure. 'Ayesha! I promise you won't regret it. You know I never believe any of the bad stuff people say about you. Thank you so much Ayesha!'

'God what have I done? Right! You come to work every day looking as polished as you do now. Got that?' Ayesha said sternly.

Amber and Pearl nodded, grinning.

'Isn't she fierce?' Amber smiled.

'Start to familiarize yourselves with the stock.'

'Absolutely. Use us in the meantime,' said Pearl.

'What do you mean?' Ayesha said.

'Amber can lift and sweep up, make tea, we both have IT skills, I see that you've got a computer.'

'You have IT skills?'

'Yes. Why, are you doing something that involves it?' said Amber.

'Nothing complicated but it's time consuming. I'm making a fact list of all our existing stock including price paid. I've given each item a number so it can be searched quickly. I create a description stroke price label and print it out. They're peel off labels to stick on the display cards and tags, there are a several boxes of them on the shelf in the office.'

'We can help with it. Pearl can build you a web site, she has the skills.'

'Are we to call you Ayesha or miss Shah?'

'Are you tak…' Ayesha looked suspiciously at Pearl. 'Ayesha will do just fine. First names.'

'Do you mind if we look at what you've done so far on the computer?' Pearl asked.

'Feel free.'

'Can we do it now and hang around. We'll stay in the background, at the counter, by the computer, or in the office.'

'Erm! Okay.'

'How many more staff are you hiring?' Amber inquired.

'One more now. We have five interviewees.' Ayesha's eyes fixed on Saskia. She scowled. 'I don't know why you're grinning like an idiot. We've got the first scheduled interview in five minutes.'

'It'll be a walk in the park,' Saskia smiled. When the twins were out of hearing, she said softly: *'thank you.'*

'Number fives not arrived,' Amber chanted; she and Pearl had taken it upon themselves to escort the applicants to their interviews, taking it in turns. She screwed up her mouth and put her head on one side, she peered inquiringly at Ayesha waiting for a response. Saskia compressed her mouth and indented her brows hard; she glared at the floor for a moment. She was correct, she had confirmation, right there in front of her; Amber and pearl had already, even this early on, assumed the existence of a hierarchical order in the management of Challoner-Shah. Saskia doubted if it was even a conscious recognition of authority. Ayesha was considered head honcho. Saskia gave a mental huff, then she too deferred to Ayesha, peering expectantly in her direction.

'Give her five more minutes,' said Ayesha. 'We've all been late in our lives.'

'If she arrives after that?'

'Tell her that the interviews have been conducted.'

Amber went away nodding. Thoughtful. So far, she had been unimpressed.

'What do you think of them so far?' Ayesha asked Saskia.

'Nice hair, nice nails, boring.'

'They are the types you get in high end retail. Did any one of them stand out to you?' Ayesha said.

'None,' Saskia admitted. 'Maybe they aren't the types for our kind of high-end retail.'

'You didn't like any of them.' Ayesha peered over the tops of her glasses at Saskia, her gaze searching. Saskia shrugged.

'I'm sure they could all do the job,' she responded unenthusiastically.

'So, what do we do, put their names in a hat and pick one out?' it came out more tartly than she intended.

Saskia cleared her throat. 'We don't snap at our business partner,' she replied. Ayesha glowered back at her, she was determined not to say anything, but she also was feeling decidedly underwhelmed. Ten minutes passed, mostly in silence. Then Amber returned. Ayesha peered at her inquiringly. Saskia smiled.

'No one?'

'Actually, there is an odd little creature across the street. She's been there for about ten minutes; she keeps pacing up and down, then she stops and stares intensely at our door.'

Ayesha and Saskia exchanged looks. Ayesha looked taut Saskia thought. Ayesha shrugged, do what you want, her body language said.

'I'll go,' Saskia said.

Saskia crossed to the other side of the street; to where the girl stood. she watched her approach; staring at her through sixties style winged retro spectacles. She was in her early twenties and not very tall; maybe five one tops, Saskia decided; her mousey brown hair was styled in a pleasing bouffant that increased her height by another four inches. She was wearing a plum-coloured trouser suit; over this she had on an open black trench coat, her hands thrust into the pockets; Saskia thought of these as spy coats. Her ankles were bare, and she was wearing plum coloured Mary-Janes on her feet.

'Nice shop, isn't it?' Saskia said as she took up position next to her, turning round so that they both faced the shop. She pushed her fingers into her jean's pockets.

'It's wonderful,' said the young woman.

'Would you like to work there?'

'Very much.'

'Well, someone hasn't turned up for their interview for a job there. Would you like to take their place?' Saskia said.

'It was my interview,' said the young woman disappointedly.

'Why didn't you have it?'

'I bottled it. I've had lots of interviews for jobs I didn't want. I want this job, and I didn't want not to get it.'

Saskia puzzled at the skewed logic; then realised that it could make sense in a funny sort of way.

'Were you so worried that you wouldn't get the job, that you didn't dare come inside for the interview?' she asked.

'That about sums it up,' was the reply.

'What's your name?'

'Hattie Dillinger.'

'That's a good name. I'm Saskia Challoner.'

'That's a good name too.'

'Well Hattie, I'm inviting you to come and have your interview. I'm going back inside now; if I get through that door and close it, you've lost your opportunity. I'll let you into a secret. I did not like any of the other applicants. I'm not yet sure I like you, make me.'

Saskia set off back across the street. It was late in the day there were not so many people about. There was less of a hum. She was halfway across when she heard footfalls, running. Hattie caught up with her, glancing across at her as she walked beside her having to hurry to keep up with Saskia's long lithe strides. Saskia did not return her look. Amber opened the door for them, she was grinning; Saskia winked at her.

'This is Hattie Dillinger, and she's come for her interview.'

'You're very late Ms Dillinger,' Ayesha said, her stare uncompromising. Pitiless, Saskia thought.

'We've been through that Ayesha. I've given Ms D... Hattie the chance to sit her interview. Give Amber your coat Hattie. She'll look after it.'

'I...' Hattie slipped out of her trench coat and passed it to Amber. 'Thank you.' Amber floated discreetly away.

'Take a seat.'

Hattie perched, hands in her lap. She stared at Saskia and Ayesha as they sat opposite. She looked anxious; she had grey eyes, and they stared, piercing and bird like, on the edge of flight. She was pretty, Saskia decided, but you had to look hard to see it. Her makeup was wrong, mostly it was the shades. Her lipstick was too pale. It was not that she was wearing too much makeup either, she was not; it was that she was wearing more than the hint that she should have been wearing, or far and away too little; she had that sort of face.

'I have your CV Hattie,' said Ayesha.

Hattie's eyes fixed on Ayesha. 'Pathetic, isn't it?'

'You worked for an auction house for eleven months, the rest of your experience is voluntary work, mostly for museums; I can see that you're willing to put in the hours though.'

'I liked my work at the auction house. And I was good at my job there,' Hattie affirmed solemnly.

'I'm sure you were. Why did you leave if you liked working there?'

'I loved working there; I was among antiques. But I was unhappy there too.'

'You can't be both surely!' Ayesha said, but she realised one probably could.

'You can, if people don't like you, and bully you, and just won't leave you alone to get on with things. My face didn't fit. The men that I worked with weren't kind. I handed in my notice.'

'I'm sorry that you had that experience. This is a totally different environment though. It's retail; what would you bring to Challoner-Shah?'

'Dedication. I'm willing to learn. It's more than retail though surely.'

'She's right,' said Saskia softly, she had remained quiet and watchful until then.

'I don't disagree,' Ayesha responded.

'I know what you're thinking,' Hattie's anxious eyes were still fixed on Ayesha; they were quite relentless.

'What am I thinking?' Ayesha felt vaguely uncomfortable under the force of the gaze.

'That I've only got GCSE's.'

'What else am I thinking?'

'That I got eight of them and my grades were excellent. And why didn't I stay on for my A levels?'

'I was thinking that!' Ayesha admitted, she could feel her tension soaring even across the space between them; it was almost tangible and quite intrusive.

'I know, yes, I'm stressed. Mum left us when I was eleven. Dad got ill when I was fourteen. I needed to work. Now you're thinking what sort of work because I haven't listed it in my CV.'

'That is what I'm thinking, naturally.'

'Alright, I stacked shelves in Tesco's, I worked in a newsagent. I sold Burgers from a stall. And you're right I'm ashamed of it and I shouldn't be. But I can't help it. I'm proud like you. I'm nervous and anxious, you're right. But no...no I'm not all wrong for your business!' she was suddenly insistent as though responding to a comment. 'I'm like this because I'm desperate for the job, and I'm worried that I won't get it. I know that I won't get it now. You think I'm unsuitable. You don't like the colour of my Mary Janes! Yes, I should have put black shoes on! Please don't pity me. Her!' Hattie's eyes flashed behind her spectacles to Saskia and quickly back to Ayesha. 'Not you! You're as hard as nails; or maybe you aren't, you just hide it well.' Hattie's voice had risen.

'Get out of my head! She's in my bloody head! And she's lost it! Calm down!' Ayesha's nails sank into the arms of her chair, and she glared fiercely at Hattie and conjured Aspis to repel Her incursion.

'Hattie! Do you possess magic?' Saskia rose out of her chair.

Hattie stood quickly she appeared to recoil from Ayesha, her expression confused and scared. Her eyes darted from Ayesha to Saskia. Amber and Pearl appeared as if from nowhere; both watched Hattie with cautious readiness, sensing the vibe from her. Saskia could sense her fear, like nettles brushing her skin. Hattie stared round frantically as though looking for a way of escape.

'Shit she's readying intent!' Pearl said.

'Put it away!' Amber snapped, 'we've all got intent here; don't worry.' Amber's face relaxed and her voice mellowed suddenly. 'You don't want to damage the antiques, do you?'

'No. I'd never do that.'

'Hattie, you do know that you are a magician, yeah?' Saskia asked cautiously.

'No...I mean Yes. Dad was one. I don't know any others!' she was drawing fast shallow breaths; still very much on the edge of panic.

'You do now; we're all magicians here.'

'I should go. I'm sorry.' Hattie looked about, scared, surprised, intrigued.

Ayesha eyed her darkly; it was a chilling look. She dismissed Aspis and folded her arms, drumming with her fingers elegantly on the sides of her elbows. Hattie's eyes darted frantically over her angry beautiful face; she backed away a couple of steps on shaky legs. Suddenly her eyes became still, and a little bit of defiance crept into them. She stared back; quite bravely Saskia thought; her expression said: *I won't let you quell me.* She lasted thirty seconds; all the power of Ayesha's gaze had launched itself at her, in hammer blows that shattered her resolve to fragments. Her eyes dropped, then her head fell, and she cried.

Amber began to take a step towards her, then prevented herself. Pearl felt sympathy but it was not her place to intervene; she found herself looking at Saskia, it was her call, but she was watching Ayesha, with her poker face on, the one Pearl coveted.

Ayesha studied the sobbing little figure of Hattie unmoved, for almost a minute. Then she stalked across the gap between them and stood directly in front of her. She put a single elegant index finger under Hattie's chin and lifted it up, to gaze at her distressed face. Hattie tried not to meet her gaze.

'Look at me,' Ayesha commanded. Hattie's eyes lifted and gazed back at her miserably.

'You have one month,' Ayesha told her. 'To prove to me that employing you was not a mistake.'

'Thank you for today.' Ayesha's voice emerged from the en-suite. She had switched off the shower some time ago. Saskia knew that she would now be engaged in conducting essential maintenance.

'Why? What did I do?' Saskia replied.

She had showered in the en-suite attached to her own room. Dried her body and serviced any personal requirements. Then she had relocated to Ayesha's bedroom; here they habitually slept and conducted much of their frequent lovemaking. She had called to Ayesha making her presence known. Then she had laid out her yoga mat and naked she began a short routine. Saskia considered herself to be a work in progress. She had increased the strength and endurance of her lithe body which was becoming progressively more toned; she was flexible, but she desired to be much more so. She had taken up yoga and wanted to achieve advanced level Asanas. She considered those poses to be beautiful and some of them to be exquisite. She knew that as she progressed, because of her possession of magic, as a matter of course she would awaken the kundalini force one day: the sex serpent. But she was prepared for that event, and to draw its spiritual venom, which belonged to the great liar; then exploit the serpent for her own magical ends, maybe for a little erotic pleasure too.

'For reminding me that I'm not an ordinary. That we don't have to play by their rules,' Ayesha replied.

Saskia smiled. She was holding Eka Pada Rajakapotasana pose, or one-legged king pigeon pose; enjoying its shaping; she released her foot, lowering it with considered elegance and straightened her arched back; she rested her fingertips on the mat on either side of her. She practised Pilates and Callanetics in the gym; her yoga in the solitude of her room, or occasionally in Ayesha's bedroom while she waited for her, as now.

'I'm proud of you,' she called.

'Careful, knowing that, might go to my head.'

'I doubt it. Hattie's odd: what was it like having her inside your head?'

'It wasn't like that; it was like having bits pulled out!' Ayesha replied.

'Well thank you for giving her a chance.'

'You had already decided. Soft touch!' Ayesha accused, laughing.

'I've a good feeling about Pearl and Amber,' Saskia said.

'That was so totally out of the blue. Fancy Pearl restoring a Victorian automaton!'

'I think it's wonderful. I want to see it.' Saskia rose to her feet and rolled up her mat. She stood it by the door.

'So, do I. Here I come, ready or not,' Ayesha announced.

Saskia faced the door of the on suite; her eyes lit up with pleasure as Ayesha appeared through it and she gasped. Ayesha was dressed in just an oversize white shirt, which was unbuttoned. Unusually, she had pinned up her luxurious hair; most importantly though, she was wearing her black framed spectacles.

Two

'I am so impressed with what you two have achieved with this place,' Claire remarked. She gazed appreciatively around the interior of Saskia and Ayesha's premises.

'We are so grateful to you, for letting us know that this place was coming vacant, and for the business you've put our way.' Saskia looked completely relaxed. Inside she was bubbling. Background music played from concealed speakers, a selection of soft chants and early instrumental music. Saskia had firmly refused to play a set on her lute. Pearl and Amber were discussing some last-minute details with the young man and woman on drinks duty. In a few minutes they would take up position at the door, to greet arriving guests; a duty Ayesha had asked them to perform; which had been courageous of her, she thought. Hattie Dillinger was making minute adjustments to the trays of nibbles laid out on the banquet tables with fixed intensity. When she had finished, she would revert to her usual habit of peering anxiously about. An atmosphere of calm had descended, and it felt sophisticated and professional and impressive, Saskia thought proudly. Claire had arrived early, as requested.

'I thought that you were taking on too much, but now I see how you've transformed the space. I get it; I really do! I wish you every success.' Claire raised her flute of Champagne to Saskia and drank. Saskia sipped a little of her own; she was under strict orders from Ayesha to pace herself. At that moment Ayesha emerged from the little staff kitchen; the doorway was concealed behind one of the displays; she arched her brows as she approached them. She was wearing a coral-coloured ruched midi dress with asymmetric neckline and hem, with nude stiletto heels. Her long hair was straight and newly layered. She wore a slender red gold torc around her throat and several red gold bangles on her left hand. Saskia was reminded of that first day when they had been thrown together. She remembered watching the sliding movement of Ayesha's bangles as she drove; when she was not watching Ayesha that was.

Saskia was wearing closely fitted ruched black silk trousers, with strappy red stiletto heeled sandals and a fitted red silk jacket; it had a daring, plunging neckline and was secured at the waist by a black glass buckle. In her left earlobe she wore a single black pirate pearl suspended on gold; it was her only jewellery.

'Hello Claire,' Ayesha said. She smiled warmly. 'Thank you for coming early. And thank you for the last two referrals. We did so well out of them.'

Claire returned her smile, she looked relieved. 'Don't be so generous in future,' she advised. 'Both families were cock-a-hoop.'

'We'll do alright out of it,' Saskia assured her.

'It's business. There'll be more, and it goes with the territory. Ayesha, you'll know, you've seen it. You too Saskia, as a beneficiary.'

'Roger Lavery was part of a syndicate; they would buy house contents after someone died,' Saskia continued the theme. 'He found it lucrative. We'll have you on commission Claire.'

'Are you still using Cardray-Adams as the go to auction house?' Ayesha inquired.

'We have to Ayesha. I control the firm, but I don't want to fall out with Daniel Wuddery; their families go back a long way. I'm sorry, I know I protected her, and I know that I really behaved stupidly at the beginning. Is that why you haven't visited?'

'We've been busy, you can see that,' Ayesha said.

'Is that really the reason?' Claire said, dubiously.

'You'll be sick of the sight of us soon I promise,' Saskia laughed.

Claire gave Saskia a little grateful smile, but she continued to stare at Ayesha. It was not an anxious sort of stare but rather an "I'm prepared to take it on the chin sort of stare".

'I told you I've forgiven you,' Ayesha said.

'Have you really?'

'It's behind us; things are okay between us I promise,' Ayesha tried to reassure her. 'Why do you think I asked you to come early? I want to show you what we've achieved. Anyway, I would have thought hard about this place and not accepted those referrals if I was at odds with you. And Saskia wouldn't either she's too loyal to me.'

Saskia gave them a little smile, glancing happily from one to the other; but her thoughts were her own. 'Come on, we'll give you the escorted tour before people start arriving,' she said.

'What you've done for the twins, I am grateful you know,' Claire told them.

'Amber and Pearl are standing on their own merits. I was impressed with their intensity,' Ayesha replied. 'I have to admit that I see them in a new light.'

'Well, they think that you are ferociously wonderful, Pearl's words. As for you,' she turned her gaze on Saskia, 'they call you Kali, goddess of destruction. They say that you arrived and blew everything 'to hell' and everybody got a kick up the arse. I believe I know where they are coming from. Kali is also goddess of time change and creation.'

'Are you complimenting me?'

'Saskia you've shaken me awake. I'm not one to dramatize but I've come to believe that the twins would die in the dust for you, as would this one.'

'I don't want anyone to die for me,' Saskia said.

'Then the answer is to keep them safe dear.'

'And how do I do that?'

'I'm sure that you'll find ways. Ah this is the one. By John Piper, he died last year you know.' Claire was referring to a small modernist painting, located on the wall next to a display of Benin bronze plaques. 'I remember seeing it at Mocking beck; I wondered if you were going to sell it; I brought my cheque book with me.'

'We should present it to you as a thankyou gift,' Saskia said, Ayesha nodded.

'Nonsense. And I don't want discount. Just make this place work.'

'I'll put a sold notice on the painting, and we'll deliver it in person next week,' Saskia promised.

'That sounds good to me!' Claire fished inside her bag and produced a cheque book contained in a leather folder, and a gold fountain pen.

'You don't have to pay for it now!'

'Why not?' Claire crouched down to rest the cheque book on her thigh. She was dressed in an elegant, embroidered suit in blue and black silk with skinny fit trousers. It had sheer strips down the inner and outer sides of her legs and arms and around the curve of her breasts. Saskia thought it quite daring, and not for the first time realised what a pretty woman Claire was. Claire stood again and presented the cheque to Saskia with a flourish. She grinned.

'There! I know that Holly Penn is bringing her cheque book too! And a guest, Felix Malek; he's wealthy by the way and a serious collector. Are you keeping the Lucien Freuds and the Hockney's?'

'Yes. Ayesha advised me to keep them. I've retained a select body of work as an investment.' Saskia felt quite pleased with herself just saying it. 'Although I had to like it too; most of it anyway.'

'Come up to the gallery,' Ayesha's hand closed instinctively over Claire's wrist, and she led her towards the stairs. It was a gesture that meant more than any words to Claire. Smiling, Saskia followed them.

'They are beautiful!' Claire's voice was lowered in admiration.

The gallery was softly lit; with downlights illuminating each picture. The bamboo floor of the main showroom was repeated here, and the atmosphere was still, and again sophisticated, with the chilled background music emerging from concealed speakers. Two long, aligned bespoke screens occupied the central floor space, with several pictures suspended on both sides of them. Claire had browsed the pictures with Saskia and Ayesha, feeling a familiar sense of enjoyment take over her. She loved Art and it had been several years since she had dedicated some of her time to admiring it or buying it for that matter; acquiring the Piper had given her a real buzz. She felt relaxed and she was enjoying the company of the two young women. But now she had stopped to gaze at the contents of a glass cabinet mounted on a stand; it occupied the space between the two screens. It contained only two items; the only pieces in the gallery that were not paintings or drawings. An ancient Attic black-figure Kylix occupied the lower section of the cabinet, a thing of rarity and beauty. The upper glass shelf supported a stunning Minoan Rhyton in the shape of a bull's head, the collar was decorated with black figures, a naked man wrestling with a bull, succeeded by a naked girl performing an acrobatic leap over a bull's horns.

'I'm surprised that you aren't keeping those,' Claire added.

'That's why we haven't priced them. We're not sure. We thought that we would have them on show until we decided. Ayesha's torn; I'm not to be honest.'

'We've spent such a lot of money, I know that we've bought some beautiful objects, but we must begin to earn something back,' Ayesha was aware that her words came across as a lame defence of her position. 'These came from the last referral from you.'

'There's a fortune in this place. I saw that you have an alarm system and that you have shutters.' Claire spoke with a level of concern; she gave them both a searching stare.

'Most of it couldn't be got away easily,' Saskia said reasonably.

'That might be, but are you taking any other precautions just in case? I'm thinking about 'Snuggles' or similar.'

'We're keeping 'Snuggles' at Mocking beck for the time being,' Ayesha replied.

'We leave Ayesha's itsy-bitsy spider on the loose here overnight!' Saskia said.

'Very droll! That thing is hideous!' Claire responded.

'Yes, it gave me a bit of a shock when it crawled out of her first edition of 'Night Spiders': I was reading it at the time. She thought it was funny.'

'Yes, she's capable of a questionable sense of humour,' Claire nodded.

'I...We have been wondering if you will do a making with us and create a Guardian for the showroom,' Ayesha said. 'The Spider is a weapon not a Guardian, so it's only a temporary solution.'

Claire felt genuine pleasure at Ayesha's request. She knew it was Ayesha's way of saying that things were back as they used to be between them. They were now close friends with Holly Penn after all, and she was easily her equal in a making.

'Let me know when. Us?'

'I want to be involved in the making,' Saskia said.

'You don't surprise me. You're feeling your power Saskia, Has Ayesha taught you all her skills?'

Saskia bit her lower lip and smiled with a hint of conceit. Claire was standing between them, and Saskia peered across her to Ayesha.

'She's very strict. I get away with nothing. And she plays rough! I've been covered in bruises for weeks. I'm sick of nose bleeds, we thought that she'd broken it once.'

'She's loved every minute of it,' Ayesha said. 'She can energise all the basic intents except Grim, which I don't have either, she can deflect and discard, she has Aspis too. It won't be long before she can unleash vis ultima, then we'll know if splitting five tons of rock was a one off or not. But I know that she's serious about advancing; it's important to her, and with everything that's happened it's made me reassess my situation. I wish that I'd had that sort of compulsion at her age or younger! I've no excuse, I used magic for convenience and self-indulgence.'

'There's nothing wrong with that, most magicians do. Fucking hell Ayesha, you're only twenty-four! I wasn't as powerful as you when I was your age.'

Saskia gurgled with laughter at Claire's uncharacteristic obscenity, but Ayesha scowled at her and remained intense and resolute.

'I was content, but now I'm not. I can't afford to be if Saskia and I are to share our lives. I wasn't unhappy before though, you know; I was just never driven.'

'Perhaps you were on hold. Waiting!'

'For what?'

'For whom. Someone to come along and kick over your sandcastles. Saskia destroyer of complacency.'

Claire regarded her with affection. Her eyes searched Ayesha's face. She loved her like a daughter, and she had been there for her during that temporal shift in her early life when Hal had exploded her world, and afterwards as she had grown into adulthood. She saw no reason for that relationship not to continue. She saw no reason why it should not extend to Saskia. But Saskia seemed at ease presently. It was Ayesha who needed counsel.

'Saskia.'

'Yes Claire.'

'Would you mind if I stole Ayesha away from you for a couple of hours tomorrow? say around one o'clock.'

'Not at all,' Saskia smiled.

'I can't. We'll be open. I'll be needed!' Ayesha protested.

'Why will you be needed?' Saskia demanded.

'Stuff! Make decisions!'

'Crap! And you know it. Pick her up at one, she'll be ready!'

'I can hear people arriving,' Ayesha remarked.

'I arrived with a guest. But I've mislaid him,' Holly Penn announced after an exchange of genuinely affectionate hugs and kisses.

'You're not that careless,' grinned Saskia.

'Actually, I've known him for years. He's made disappearing into an artform. He can vanish in an empty room.'

Ayesha high arched her brows; she was feeling half relaxed and happy. She had been looking forward to this moment, to show Holly what they had accomplished; she wanted her approval as much as anyone's; despite that, she narrowed her eyes a fraction and indirectly sent Holly a curious look. What did they say? Hide a truth in a lie, or in a joke.

'I need a drink,' Holly announced. 'Oh, bubbly! You're not stinting either.'

Saskia had grabbed a crystal flute of Champagne from a passing tray and transferred it to Holly's waiting hand. Claire had gone to mingle. Saskia and Ayesha had been about to separate and fraternize with guests when Holly had found them.

'Claire informed us that your guest is quite an Art collector,' Ayesha said.

'Ayesha Shah your mind's on money! Felix is a collector of Art and Antiquities; I'll introduce you if I get the opportunity. He has deep pockets. And tonight, so do I.'

'Is that Felix Malek, the entrepreneur?' Ayesha asked.

'You've been doing your research. Yes, I've known him since my first exhibition. He bought two pictures then and a dozen more in the intervening years. He has business interests in various parts of the world and he's never in the country for more than a few months in the year. I like his company, and we meet up when it's feasible. Tonight, he's my gift to you.'

Holly peered at her empty flute. Saskia dived away and returned with an opened bottle of Champagne in an ice bucket. She set the bucket down carefully on the top of a small antique lacquered Chinese table. She refilled

Holly's glass; ignored her own glass and offered Ayesha a top up. Ayesha shook her head, amused.

'Amber and Pearl.' Holly's eyes twinkled. 'I had to do a double take at the door when I realised it was Amber who'd greeted me.'

'If it wasn't for them and Saskia, I think that I would have been running on empty now. But you know, I feel quite chilled.'

'It's hard persuading Ayesha that she doesn't have to do everything,' Saskia commented.

'That doesn't surprise me at all,' Holly chuckled.' Look I'm going to explore this wonderful place of yours and take in all these treasures; I know you two need to smooch your guests, so leave me to it. Let's meet up again in say an hour.' Looking very much in her element, she wandered off, clutching her flute of champagne. She surprised Hal with a high five and a 'Hi Hal,' as she passed him heading in Saskia and Ayesha's direction.

'She's chilled,' Hal grinned, coming to stand between them, holding a glass of red. He leaned to the side for a kiss on the cheek from Saskia. He looked surprised when Ayesha took his hand and pulled him down so she could plant a kiss on his other cheek. 'I'm seriously impressed,' he said. 'So is Amelia; though I have to say, we aren't surprised. She's got her eye on a piece of Jade, and we're both seriously attracted to a Georg Jensen coffee set.' He was dressed in a nice designer suit in blue, and a white shirt with an open collar. He looked smooth, tanned and lean.

'I've heard some things you might be interested in,' he announced. 'I've been hearing whispers about Nathan Xavier.' They both pricked up their ears. They knew that when Hal said whispers, he meant hard facts, not rumour.

'What have you heard?' Saskia asked.

'Hopefully something grisly,' Ayesha said, looking mean.

'Nothing like that I'm afraid,' Hal replied. 'It seems he's taken up with Bernadette O'Hare full time. He needed a natural home for his talents, and she appears active again, so she must have settled her differences with Pandemonium. It was only a matter of time. But that isn't all.' Hal paused to drink some of his wine. 'I heard more whispers. This time concerning the night Amelia and I were called to help you when Nathan came to scoop you up Saskia. With the help of the ghost. What's he called?'

'John Pickering. Docker John,' Saskia supplied.

'Yes him. I know who recruited him and acted as go between; so, Nathan and the people from the Kadman Order could communicate with him, when they were going after you.'

'Who?' Ayesha said, darkly. It was a question that had puzzled both her and Saskia, and one filled with angst for herself; she had been treated cruelly that night and but for Hal's intervention, she would have been killed.

'Tell us Hal,' Saskia said. She saw and could communicate with ghosts; she knew no others that could.

'Her name is Rachel Zimpara. She locates people who are hiding, among other things. calls herself a facilitator. She's basically for hire. She's a demonic from Pandemonium who's lived in our society for nearly forty years. She found you Saskia, for Nathan Xavier. Though to be fair she did think she was working for Claire. Apparently, she has done quite a bit of work for my sisters firm in the past.'

'I've heard of her,' said Ayesha. 'I've never met her. She's never been into the office, not while I was there. Thanks for this Hal. It answers a few things for us.'

'Saskia.'

'Yes Pearl.' Saskia was between conversations. Hal had chatted for a while and then gone to find Amelia. Saskia and Ayesha had split up for a while to circulate. She wrinkled her nose in a happy smile at Pearl. Pearl grinned back.

'How's it going. Are you okay?' Pearl was in an understated oyster coloured dress and ivory stiletto heeled sandals. She looked graceful Saskia thought, even a little ethereal in a necklace of moonstones and matching earrings.

'I'm fine,' Saskia said. 'I've found that if I don't understand what someone's talking about, or I want to scream, I simply look over their shoulder and wave, and say I'm being summoned! What about you are you okay?'

'Couldn't be better and Amber's made up because she got to meet that actress, you know, the one who's always getting her kit off. Anyway, I came to tell you that someone's looking for you and Ayesha. A mister Malek, he arrived with Holly Penn.'

'Claire told me about him,' Saskia said. 'Point me in his direction will you; I'll find him.'

'He went upstairs to the gallery.'

'Will you tell Ayesha that's where I'll be. From what Holly say's he intends to spend a lot of money on her say.'

'Nice one!' Pearl grinned. 'You can't miss him, he's...hello here's trouble.' Hattie crept hesitantly towards them; her expression was even more anxious than usual.

'What is it, Hattie?'

'A man with a long fancy chain hanging round his neck wants to buy the lignum vitae wassail cup; he wants twenty percent off!'

'Screw him!' Pearl scowled.

'You go and sort it out Pearl,' Saskia smiled. 'I'll find our mister Malek.'

'Okay Saskia. And I won't forget about Ayesha. In fact, Hattie, you take me to chain man and then find Ayesha and tell her that she's wanted in the gallery.'

The staircase began at the centre of the showroom floor; it was supported on cylindrical iron columns, surfaced to look like pondweed with newts crawling among it; the staircase was broad and curved, with polished wooden treads; the supports were made of cast iron and shaped like giant dragonflies and sinister frogs; these stood upright and peered out from behind bullrushes. Saskia adored it and wanted to own it. She emerged at the top of the staircase and paused beside a table, on which stood a tray of crystal champagne flutes and two ice buckets, each containing a stoppered bottle of champagne. Saskia's eyes searched the still calm of the gallery. She could see no one. She had been convinced that she had heard a couple in conversation as they mounted the stairs behind her, but when she looked round the staircase was empty, and she assumed they had changed their minds and gone back down. She moved onto the gallery floor and peered down either side of the central display on the off chance that Malek was bending low to examine a detail of a picture. Both aisles proved empty. She glanced behind her in the direction of the rear wall. There were two doorways leading out of the gallery, some distance apart and with rows of pictures to either side of them and a row between. One door led to a stock room, the other to the flat. She toyed with the idea that Malek had passed through one of them, in search of a toilet perhaps, or simply out of curiosity. She recalled that both doors had been locked; but in her world that stood for very little. She discarded the idea that he might have gone back down to the showroom, instantly. With a little shrug she went to gaze into the cabinet at the Kylix and the Rhyton, a smile playing on her mouth. 'I know you aren't shy Mr Malek,' she said. She waited then; counting in her head, almost to a hundred, before she felt a strong sense of presence directly behind her.

'Magnificent,' he said.

'Yes, it's beautiful,' Saskia agreed.

'Ancient.'

'I know. Is this when you say that it belongs in a museum? You are referring to the Rhyton?'

'Of course. I own several such pieces; in my opinion none of them belong in a museum; that would be a fine addition to my collection; have you a price in mind for it?' It was a deep male voice, rich and dark. Polished. She found it enamouring. His cologne was heady, not overpowering.

'At present it's here for display only; Yorkshire television is doing a piece about both artefacts; it will be great free publicity for the business; then Ayesha must decide if we sell it. She collects antiquities, statement pieces, and I'm a fan. I would keep it. But it's her turn to decide.'

'Perhaps I can persuade her,' he said.

'Perhaps. I've sent for her; she should be here any moment.'

'Then I will continue to enjoy your sole company until she arrives,' he said.

'Apart from the Rhyton, has anything here seduced you to the point where you must have it?' Saskia said, she turned around; she found herself looking up at a mountain of black skin in a silver-grey Savile row suit and hand-crafted leather shoes. She took a pace back in surprise and felt her back press against the glass cabinet.

'Good evening mister Malek.' She smiled recovering quickly; she extended her hand in greeting, the heel almost resting against her breastbone, he was so close. 'Saskia Challoner.'

She watched as her hand disappeared into his. His grip was warm and pliant, but she felt he possessed the power to break every bone in her hand with the pressure it could exert, and easily. He raised her hand and leaned down into the kiss he applied to it; slightly unsure, Saskia allowed the gesture. Her eyes fixed on a huge gold ring set with a large carnelian on his second finger; it flashed with a lazy sensuality in the soft lighting.

'You're elusive for someone of your size.'

'So, I've been told.' He released her hand.

She was enthralled by his large gold-coloured eyes; she thought that they were strange and beautiful. They were set in a large face which jutted forward; the upper part of his head was squarish and covered with a matt of closely cut hair. His wide mouth lifted at the corners in a frugal smile that hinted at condescension. He looked like a bull, she thought. The head of a bull, the shoulders of a bull. Almost the size of a bull standing on two legs, and height wise, she speculated, nearer to seven than six feet. His gold-coloured eyes generated entitlement. They were calm, and confident of acquisitions. Saskia found looking at him quite erotic. His eyes tried to acquire her, then withdrew quickly, surprised as her own eyes came for him like wolves.

'To answer your question...' Malek paused, his attention was captured by Ayesha as she appeared at the top of the stairs. She smiled as she saw them and advanced towards them. Malek watched her approach, his smile became slightly sardonic as he finished his reply. 'One or two,' he said.

Saskia slipped from between the cabinet and Malek and made space between them. She had passed the point of mere attraction; she was feeling desire, and she wanted distance.

'Ayesha Shah; Felix Malek,' she introduced them a little breathlessly.

'I'm very pleased to meet you mister Malek.' Ayesha extended her hand, which Malek accepted and as he had done with Saskia's; he raised it and kissed the back of her fingers below her knuckle.

'Likewise, miss Shah.'

Ayesha withdrew her hand. She flashed her dark eyes at Saskia as if amused.

'Would you like a drink mister Malek!' she inquired looking pointedly at Saskia.

'I'll get them!' Saskia said. She strode away, her fists clenched at her sides, convinced Felix Malek had bewitched her. She was angry and sexually aroused. But she decided, if he spent fifty grand, she would take it with a smile. She deliberately popped the cork of one of the bottles of champagne, narrowing her eyes in satisfaction as it ricocheted off the ceiling. She returned with three flutes of Champagne and a coy smile.

They raised their glasses but refrained from chinking them together, in the tradition of magicians, so as not to attract unwelcome spirits. Saskia had become familiar with a couple of dim shapes lurking furtively about the building, both female; one was a barely extant memory; the other hinted at physicality, it exhibited curiosity and seemed to want to approach; it had watched impassively a couple of times as Saskia and Ayesha had made love in the bed, in the flat. Saskia had decided to name her Gertrude. She had not told Ayesha about her, she did not want to disturb her lover, and Saskia being

Saskia had decided that she quite enjoyed being observed.

'Will you walk around the gallery with us mister Malek?' Ayesha asked; she was intimately close to him Saskia thought, gazing up at him with expressive eyes.

'Please call me Felix.' Malek offered her his arm, and she took it, curving her arm under his; her slim fingers emerged and rested on his sleeve; her red nails shifted with gentle movements on the expensive cloth. Saskia scowled in disgust; she followed them, listening enviously as they discussed twentieth century British Artists with an easy fluency and discerning knowledge. For the next half hour Ayesha laughed and flirted overtly with Felix Malek; watched by Saskia with, increasing contempt.

They halted in front of a painting of oddly shaped figures inside what looked like a shored-up cave. It was not to Saskia's taste, though there was something about it she liked; it was cool, self-aware. She positioned herself next to Ayesha, and watched her lover's body language, her tells; it was evident that she was enjoying herself, she was excited, but to Saskia it was obvious that she was also very turned-on. Saskia stared at Malek and Ayesha, barely concealing her annoyance.

'You have a couple of celebrities here tonight,' Malek remarked conversationally to her; Saskia deemed this somewhat patronising, as it seemed to assume it was pointless including her in the conversation about Bacon, Freud, and Co. Which she had to admit, it probably was, considering her knowledge at its present level. 'I am personally acquainted with them.'

'Holly tells us that you are very wealthy; fame and wealth attract each other I'm sure,' Saskia responded, she half smiled, concealing resentment.

'I am wealthy, yes.'

'Do you intend to spend some of it with us?'

'If I can!' Malek laughed appreciatively, his teeth were very white Saskia thought; smaller than she had thought they would be. His canines were elongated, she noted, not in proportion.

'Please excuse Saskia's rudeness!' Ayesha said, but she was smiling all the same.

'No. No. It's refreshing.' Malek grinned and shook his head. He focused his gaze fully on Saskia. Her sense of desire had piqued and diluted, but the sexual energy was still at large, and she felt excited, ready to spar or flirt, and give Ayesha a run for her money.

'I admit I have a fat cheque book. But I like what I like. I am hard to please.' His smile slowly withdrew from his eyes, he frowned becoming suddenly curious.

'You are the one who was assassinated and came back aren't you?'

'That's me!' Saskia responded brightly.

'I heard it from Holly Penn; she told me it was a true mortality. Not some near-death experience.

'My death was imprinted in the place apparently. I'm waiting to meet my own ghost.' She chuckled. 'Joke. Apparently, joking aside, it's not as rare as you'd assume.'

'Then I shall not assume. It was a Shee that killed you I understand!'

'And I killed that Shee. You are not a friend of the CaolShee are you, by any chance?'

'I've no love for any Shee,' he said, with conviction. 'I like this David Bomberg however, and I will pay your price.'

Ayesha grinned with pleasure; she pinched her under lip between her teeth. 'More Champagne Felix?' Saskia smiled.

Some of the guests had begun to arrive up in the gallery and there was more of a buzz of occupation in the space. Ayesha smiled at Saskia and then squeezed Malek's arm.

'We should go down to the showroom,' said Ayesha, 'would you like to continue browsing Felix?'

'I think I'm finished here, but only for the present,' he said. 'I'll come down.'

He stood aside and let them go ahead of him onto the staircase; he followed; Saskia listened to the stairs creaking under him; she could feel his weight compressing them. At the bottom he parted company with them.

'Thank you, it's been a most enjoyable experience meeting you both. I'm going to say hello to Helen; she's obviously beguiled by your cabinet of silver. Sometimes she needs a little prompt.'

He smiled, his eyes roving between them. He looked smug Saskia thought. Entitled. She smiled warmly back at him. They watched him join a fair-haired woman; Saskia recognised her from the TV, she liked her, and she wanted to meet her; Claire who regarded her as a personal friend had promised to introduce them; she was absorbed in the contents of one of the silver cabinets. It contained icons and Judaica. She smiled up at Malek as he appeared at her side, with an easy familiarity.

Saskia stared at Ayesha, widening her eyes, and giving her a funny little smile. Ayesha frowned and peered at her.

'Why are you simpering?'

Saskia ran the tip of her tongue along her upper lip then pinched her underlip between her teeth; she tilted her head to one side and smiled at her ingénue.

'What is the matter with you?' Ayesha demanded.

'That's the way you flashed your eyes and flirted with him!'

'Was not.'

'Was so, it was obscene,' Saskia spoke with pretence at contempt.

'What about the way you jumped away from him when I turned up,' Ayesha narrowed her eyes. 'That was guilt if ever there was!'

'I was putting space between us! He was arousing me with some sort of intent.'

'And what do you think he was doing to me?' Ayesha's eyes widened questioningly. 'I accepted it. Learn to take it Saskia! there'll be a lot more of that sort of thing during this life that you've elected to live. It goes with the territory.'

'He isn't human either, is he?' Saskia said.

'No, he isn't, at least not in part.'

'What is he?'

'I don't know specifically. Some sort of demon,' Ayesha replied, frowning.

'Is he dangerous?'

Ayesha huffed. Saskia loved it when she huffed. She would tell her one day. 'We're all dangerous. You're dangerous, I'm dangerous. He's probably no more malign than you or me. I don't think he's malevolent. He spent eighty thousand pounds in any case. Don't get so jealous.'

'I'm not jealous!' Saskia grinned. 'I'm yanking your chain!'

'Sometimes you go too far!' Ayesha snapped keeping her voice low; her black eyes had turned into onyx.

Saskia's face became expressionless, she studied Ayesha with eyes that she allowed to moisten.

'I didn't mean that. I was only yanking your chain for a change,' Ayesha told her quickly, suddenly worried.

'I know that' Saskia said. 'You really do need to be mean to me more often, you know.'

'You are so bloody odd!'

'That, from the girl with silver pain thorns buried inside her!' Saskia said satirically. 'There's Hal and Amelia. Let's go and prize some dosh out of them for that Georg Jensen coffee set!'

They stayed together for the remainder of the evening after getting a cheque out of Hal. Acquiring

Amelia with whom they had relaxed into an easy friendship. She seemed to know every other person there and it came as no surprise to discover that she had connections to various museums and galleries.

Holly found them, she was with Amber who was dressed in a red and black jacquard suit and red Russian Amber jewellery.

'I've got a big fat cheque for a Bomberg, and a couple of others. You wooed him well bosses!' Amber told them, grinning.

'She's got a cheque from me too,' smiled Holly, 'not as fat though.'

'I've got a little wad of cheques in my pocket!' Her eyes lit as Saskia handed her Hal's, for the Jensen. 'I'm off to put them in the safe. Just thought I'd let you know. God he was so big!' She exclaimed over her shoulder as she danced away.

'She has a dozen cheques,' Holly informed them. 'You've done well tonight. And Felix might not have finished; I know that he's interested in at least one more painting; he simply needs to see if they pull him back to them. He's in the UK for two more weeks. Then I believe he's off to the far east; he has business interests in Hong Kong and Thailand. But you actually never know when he's just going to disappear.'

'You kept him hidden!' Saskia remarked.

'Did I?' Holly directed her an unsoftened look.

'Not easy to achieve.'

'Implying?' Holly's voice had gained an edge.

'Just that he's so immense.'

'Really. We go back years. I brought him along as a favour to you. He will prove a regular and very valuable client.'

Saskia had a sense of needles inside her, and nettles stings on her skin, displeasure.

'Have I offended you?'

'A little bit. I still love you.'

Saskia was feeling ill willed, she almost replied with a sarcastic: *That's good to know*, but she pulled herself up in time. Ayesha had almost stepped in, intending to suggest more drinks, but Saskia was suddenly contrite.

'I'm sorry, he's intriguing and unexpected,' she said. 'And sometimes I don't know how to behave as Ayesha will tell you.' She felt the needles relent and the nettles tingle away.

'Who are we talking about?' Amelia inquired curiously.

'Felix Malek,' said Ayesha.

'Oh, is he here? You know I haven't laid eyes on him!'

A little reluctantly Ayesha went with Amelia to fetch more Champagne, leaving Saskia and Holly together.

'Are you really that nosey?' Holly asked when they were out of hearing.

'You know I am. He's magnificent.'

'And you know what he is?'

'He's a demon.'

Holly compressed her lips and studied Saskia with an enigmatic look. 'At least you'll know we'll have something interesting to talk about when you and Ayesha come to dinner on Wednesday.'

'We always find something interesting to talk about.'

'This will be personal to me.' Holly laid her hand on Saskia's arm, showing everything was okay.

'You don't have to you know. I was being a little cow,' Saskia said.

'I know that I don't; I don't do anything that I don't want to do. But I suppose it's only fair given what I know about you. There must be a balance. And I know something lit your blue touch paper tonight.' Holly's brows indented and she peered at Saskia quizzically.

'There's something else. I can see it in your face. Are you and Ayesha okay, you must have been under a lot of stress in recent months.'

'Never better!' Saskia said a bit of unexpected shyness revealing itself.

'What about Khalid, have you heard anything from him?'

'He's furious with us.' Saskia was amused. 'And next week he's handing an enormous sum of money to Ayesha, so he'll be even more furious!'

'I'm pleased that he's out of your hair. Take care, he's cunning.'

'Are we invited to stay over?' Saskia asked.

'You only want a go with my bow. Bring your own.'

'I will bring my own.' Saskia was smug. She had taken to bow-work during their visits, practising with one of Holly's bows. On the last occasion she had hit the target by design.

'I want you to stay over. I've a favour to ask you both...one that might last until cockcrow.'

Saskia frowned, puzzled by Holly's vaguely archaic term; she was about to press her for more information when Ayesha and Amelia came back with Champagne; Ayesha was relieved to see Saskia and Holly at ease with each other.

'I want to see what you've bought Holly,' she said, her dark eyes were sparkling.

'Come on. I'll show you.'

'Holly Penn brought a demon with her tonight and he's probably fucking her,' Saskia said.

'Why are you surprised? Where do you think she gets her kicks? there could be other benefits too.' Ayesha gave a tiny shrug.

'Imagine Holly Penn with him; she's tiny, he must weigh about two hundred and fifty kilos!' Saskia looked intrigued at the thought.

'I'm sure she can handle it,' Ayesha said confidently.

'You laughed at the idea of Claire's sister being fucked to death by a demon,' Saskia responded. 'Which I thought at the time was incredibly mean of you; yet you're saying that it's no big deal, having sex with a demon.'

'It isn't! Helen took it to an extreme. You must never mention that to the twins; promise me!'

'I'd never do that. They are too fragile. Have you?'

'Have I what?' Ayesha asked, puzzled.

'Had sex with a demon.'

'Not to my knowledge.'

'Would you have sex with a demon?' Saskia screwed up her mouth and peered at Ayesha with playful intensity.

'If I wanted to. You've had sex with entities; you've admitted it.'

'It doesn't seem quite the same.'

'Yet it is, if not marginally odder,' Ayesha countered. 'Would you have sex with a demon?'

'Probably.' Saskia formed a cynical darkly comedic smile. 'What a marvellous night!'

Ayesha was tired, it gathered around her eyes, but she wanted her lover's touch before she slept. Everyone had departed by eleven; and they had opted to clean up the restrained debris of the party the following morning. They had decided to spend the night in the flat; they kept clothes there and it was a much easier option than driving to Leeds and then back again the following day. She turned her back to Saskia, which was an indication to unzip her dress and remove it from her. She felt the tug of the zip and the fall of the dress. Saskia's fingers caressed her shoulders and upper arms, she felt her hair moved aside and the kiss applied to her neck.

'I love your hair like this.'

Ayesha smiled contentedly. She felt Saskia's fingers glide over her skin, moving to undo the fastening of her red lace strapless bra. She was wearing delicate red lace panties too, often she did not wear any; she knew that Saskia would leave them for the present, preferring to remove them during lovemaking. She slid elegantly onto the bed, sitting on the edge to watch Saskia, in turn, undress.

Saskia regarded Ayesha with smoky amorous eyes; she studied Ayesha's own dark eyes as they followed her actions and enjoyed her transition to nakedness. She knelt on the floor in front of Ayesha and removed her shoes and began to squeeze and caress her pretty toes. Ayesha sighed in pleasure.

'You looked exquisite,' she said. 'I love the single black Pearl.'

'I thought you'd tell me off for that!'

'Noh! It's delightful,' Ayesha insisted. 'And you chose so well with your outfit.'

'It was brave of you to give me carte blanche.'

'I totally approve, then and now.'

'I stepped out of line though, I'm sorry.'

'No, you didn't, that was play, it was a game; seeing you jealous and fizzing, and when you made fun of me; I loved it.'

'Did you?'

'And you showed…oh that is so good…judgement when Holly called you out; she is a very private person little mantis. I think you surprised her when she saw how much respect you have for her.'

'She must have felt guilty afterwards; because she intends to tell us some personal stuff when we go over; including about Felix Malek.'

'No way! Why?

'That's what she said. Maybe it's quid pro quo; she knows so much about me, presumably about you too, and we know so little about her; at the same time, we have a very real friendship with her.'

'I can't wait!' Ayesha chuckled.

'She asked us if we would stay over. She wants a favour.'

'Did she say what?'

'No, and I didn't have opportunity to ask. She said it might last until cockcrow.'

'Sounds like magic,' Ayesha frowned, but only in a puzzled way. She shrugged. 'Interesting.' She drew a long breath and allowed herself a satisfied look.

'We took a great deal of money tonight. Even without Malek's cheque it's a lot of money. Also, if he comes back and buys another picture, and there's the Rhyton and Kylix, who knows!'

Saskia kissed her toes and delicately licked their tips, then progressed to insteps and ankles. Ayesha sighed in pleasure and scrunched the bedcover in her fingers.

'Make love to me little mantis,' she said. 'But be gentle with me tonight please.'

Ayesha luxuriated in the tenderness of Saskia's lovemaking, as she was kissed and caressed with increasing intimacy. Ayesha reached for Saskia, but she disallowed, kissing her fingertips as she brushed them away from intended intimacy. Saskia shook her head her eyes warm with desire, content to be the instrument.

'This is my pleasure,' she told her.

'Aren't you aroused?'

'Of course, I am.'

Ayesha raised her hips as Saskia removed her panties and passed a pillow under her. She made little pleasure noises as the touch of Saskia's tongue and fingertips excited her. Her upper body was propped against pillows which enabled her to watch. She stimulated her own suffused nipples with her fingertips; unaware of Gertrude watching from the doorway of the en-suite. Her lower body undulated into sensual orgasm. Saskia listened to Ayesha's descending pleasure vocals and raised her face; she stared from between her lover's upright thighs, she smiled, pleased with herself.

'I don't want us to sell the Rhyton, or the Kylix. I want to keep them,' she announced.

'Okay my darling little mantis; oh, you really are a little bitch.' Ayesha was still in after bliss. Her lower body made tiny pleasure movements. Saskia kissed her very tenderly on the satin like softness of each of her upper inner thighs, then repeated the action.

'We'll find a nice place in the apartment or the house to display them.' She studied Ayesha's face, watched as her teeth pressed into her underlip. She placed the most delicate kiss she could at the top of Ayesha's exposed labia minora.

'If that's what you want darling,' Ayesha sighed.

Saskia smiled tenderly as she met Ayesha's weary post orgasmic stare.

'Again?' she asked.

'Mmh!' Ayesha whimpered.

Three

Claire came to collect Ayesha the next day. They found one of York's establishments with atmosphere and an old-world look; it had an upstairs restaurant in which to have their lunch.

'You're missed at the office,' Claire told her.

'No, I'm not and you know it. Jamie will be lusting after someone else by now and the rest of them couldn't care less.'

'Very well. I'm missing you at the office.' Claire heaved a deep sigh. 'Okay I miss you, period.'

'I've missed you.'

'Sometimes I feel annoyed that Saskia is Saskia you know; the twins are right about her!'

'You don't resent her, do you?' Ayesha's eyes searched Claire's face. the revelation surprised her and amused her.

'Part of me does,' Claire admitted. 'Because she turned up and changed everything. Don't look at me like that, I know that I was searching for her. That's not the point. You can laugh. I love you both you know that. You two look so good together. Is the relationship as strong as it looks? I hope so.'

'God yes! I'm rattled at present with everything that's been going on, but being with Saskia has kept me grounded. I've never been so certain of anything.'

'No regrets about your old life?'

'Probably. I enjoyed being me you know. Doing my work, enjoying my sex, and indulging in my pain.'

'You are still you. Do you regret becoming involved with Saskia?

'I used to, occasionally. But now not at all. It's just that I was safe in my own little world, almost hidden away. And now I realise that's what I was doing, I was hiding away from myself.'

'A lot of us do, hide from ourselves I mean. And I'm to blame for bursting your bubble. I gave you Saskia.'

'I couldn't go back Claire. The ride has been astonishing, like walking in cool fire. It feels exquisite every day. She's edgy and a little twisted, but I'm that too; I know she's self-centred. I know she's manipulative, I don't mind that about her. even when she drives me up the wall, and she's infinitely capable of doing that; the sensation is delicious. And I think she feels the same. In fact, I know she does.'

'Then you are two very lucky young women,' Claire stated. She peered searchingly at Ayesha. 'I was so pleased when I heard that you'd severed links with Khalid Taharqa. You have, haven't you?'

'Yes, I assure you I have. Not without reservations though.'

'About selling him your part of the business you mean?'

'No, I think that was one of my better decisions; on a personal level.'

'Do you care about him? Love him I mean? You can love two people.'

'No Claire, I don't love him; I never have felt anything for him other than lust. He fulfilled a need and I'm finding it hard to compensate; my compliance of thorns fascinates Saskia, but it scares her too; she'll come round eventually.'

'You can't blame her for being cautious. But you're worried about something I can tell. I know you, Ayesha.'

'Yes, I am,' Ayesha replied. Claire was surprised by her lack of reluctance to admit to it, she knew how fiercely independent she could be, and how self-dependent. This insular little being was undergoing an evolution.

'It's no mystery. I might be Saskia's champion, but I believe she might outclass me! And she won't be content with just that.'

'You really think that's the case?

'I'm convinced of it and it's that that's rattling me. She's powerful Claire, but inconsistent at present. She's driven, she aspires to be an Adept though she hasn't couched it in those terms yet, and it scares me because I don't want to be left behind to gradually become detached from her.'

'I don't think that would happen. Do you think it could happen?' Claire looked doubtful.

'Neither do I if I look deeply, but I'm paranoid that it might, and I won't give it a chance to happen. I'll take whatever measures I need to.'

'Fair enough. But are you being entirely honest with yourself?'

'I don't know what you mean!' Ayesha became defensive, puzzled.

Claire raised her teacup and found it was empty; she gazed into it, disappointed. She replaced it on its saucer before responding to Ayesha. 'It's good to admit the real reason for wanting a particular thing or for taking a particular course of action; it puts the partial reason in perspective. It clears your head, and darling you need clarity. Self-deception can obscure the path, don't let it.'

'In what way do you believe that I'm deceiving myself?'

Claire drew a long breath, readying herself. 'Has it occurred to you that you might be jealous?'

When she was of a mind to, Claire Bosola was capable of real perception. Ayesha was aware of that. She was close to her. She had worked closely with her. True, Claire had experienced a blind spot where Nathan Xavier was concerned; sex had a way of obscuring and Nathan had always kept an alternative persona for her consumption. But if she needed to, she was able to get to the truth, she saw things that other people missed, often hidden in plain sight. So, Ayesha did not automatically dismiss what she suggested to her, or rail against it. She considered Claire's words with acuity. She considered her own motivations with equal acuity.

Claire watched as the skin of Ayesha's neck cheeks and ears suffused to red. It was quite endearing, Saskia would have loved it, she thought. Ayesha's eyes rounded and she confronted a sudden shocking possibility.

'Shall I say it for you?' Claire inquired.

'I think I'm capable of saying it for myself. I can't allow Saskia to outshine me!'

'Then don't let her. Make the journey with her.'

'I don't know how to Claire!'

'Then first ask yourself this: What will Saskia do?'

'She won't dodge the bullet. I think she would do anything.'

'So, what would you do?'

'Whatever I must!'

They came to the end of their open sandwich lunch and Ayesha excused herself to visit the loo. After she had peed, she washed her hands and gave her beautiful teeth attention. She inspected her appearance in the mirror; she was in a blue collarless shirt tucked into tight jeans. She narrowed her eyes at her reflection. Her face shifted into a look of contempt. Sometimes she wondered who the haughty person was that stared back at her. She unfastened her top button and turned abruptly away. She re-joined Claire who had ordered more tea.

'How did you advance Claire?'

'Grief and despair I suppose,' was Claire's immediate answer causing Ayesha to direct her a hesitant look.

'My mum and dad passed within a few weeks of each other, my dad from illness and my mother from grief, I believe anyway. I entered a very dark place. When I emerged from my grief, I was angry and needed distraction. I chose heroin and magic.'

'Heroin?' Ayesha went wide eyed in surprise.

'I had used it before recreationally. I was never an addict. Have I shocked you?'

'You've amazed me.'

'My intent which, was around your level to begin with began to increase as my anger decreased,' Claire told her. 'After about a year I was the me, you know. No anger, lots of intent. By that time, I'd acquired making and a bit of elemental magic from Holly Penn's mother, and Evocation. I taught myself psychometry and Scrying. The energised intent came easily to me, it was like a dam slowly bursting. It felt good. But my ascension was alternative, peculiar to me, so no use to you or Saskia.'

'And Hal?'

Claire smiled enigmatically. 'Naturally high octane our Hal. He didn't gain energised intent until he was eighteen. He entered at my current level. Impressive I know. He's way beyond that now. Hal and Amelia were fortunate to acquire each other. They are in accord psychically; their energised intent comes from sex magic; Astral stuff in the Boundless Edge. Those sexual pathways are the quickest routes after all, though they can be beset by risks. Hal has advanced further than Amelia, it's how he acquired cockatrix. You saw him raise the Wyrm in my garden. He never aspired to it. It was accidental. He spat feathers when it first happened. It's one of the holy grails of magic too.'

'Are there many magicians capable of it?' Ayesha asked. 'I was in the dark about it until then.'

'I don't know if there are any in the UK or anywhere else. Maybe Theodor Bacchus: but I really don't know. I know how important this is to you Ayesha. I'm not being particularly helpful. You could consult Theo Bacchus, he stands head and shoulders above everyone else, including Hal. And he likes both of you.'

'Does he?' This came as a surprise to Ayesha.

'He is on cordial terms with Hal; apparently Saskia impressed him, as did you, he refers to you as miss intensity.'

Ayesha smiled sardonically at this.

'It's no good consulting Hal. He'd just avoid you; he hasn't got the patience. I haven't the knowledge. The obvious go to is Holly Penn. Why not use her knowledge; she's the savant.'

'I have already come to that conclusion myself,' Ayesha admitted.

'It would surprise me if you hadn't. Shall we talk about ordinary things?'

'Why not? We need to catch up.'

'Business first. There will be another referral for you soon. You can spend some of that money you took last night,' Claire smiled.

'I'm still on a high after that. So is Saskia. It's money in the bank. Everyone's wages for a year and working capital. I still think I'm dreaming. But the business must pay for itself from now on.'

'I'm sure it will,' Claire said confidently.

'I'm still shocked that I'm saying it, but Amber and Pearl, if they carry on like this, are going to be real assets to the business. We've developed a real friendship with them too. I never thought I'd be saying that either!' Ayesha shook her head.

'They experienced something last year that caused them to take a hard look at themselves,' Claire said.

'They've mentioned an encounter with Svarts a few times, in Derbyshire,' Ayesha frowned.

'Svarts are Norse stuff. Old world, and that might be it. I'm sure they'll tell you eventually. The events in Mocking beck wood they shook them to the core. But I think it was the night of the Pandemonium attack that they suddenly found themselves part of something. They like Saskia and they like you. Though Pearl did say you were like trying to melt an iceberg with a blow torch.'

'They managed it, I'm pleased to say,' Ayesha admitted.

'They miss Helen you know, as do I.' Pain had entered Claire's voice.

'Saskia believes that they are emotionally fragile.'

'I wouldn't disagree. But they possess nerves of steel. Thank you for doing this for them.' Claire smiled suddenly, changing the mood. 'Now, tell me about the strange young woman you've taken on. The one that creeps everywhere; does she ever not look anxious?

'Hattie Dillinger. She knows her antiques. She has intent and compellence.'

'Does she indeed?'

'At her interview she used it to read me; her problem was she was so stressed she was in emotional meltdown. We confronted her; she was petrified when she realised that we all had intent. You should have seen her face.'

'Poor little thing. You probably terrified her; it's a wonder she didn't bolt,' Claire replied solemnly.

'That's what impressed me, she was courageous,' Ayesha asserted. 'She cried but that was because she wanted the job so badly and was convinced that she had blown it.'

'You're certain that she's not an agent of Bernadette O'Hare's then?'

'Yes, we're certain. Vigilance is our middle name.'

They conversed for another hour and made small talk and re-established their customary familiarity. Then it was time for them to part company.

Claire paid, leaving a generous tip. Ayesha watched her draw on her tweed jacket and get her things together. She stood and put on her own long designer jacket. They went out together and walked side by side along the sunny pavement.

'It's your birthday soon. I know that you'll be spending it with Saskia.' Claire glanced and smiled at Ayesha. 'But I've a dinner party in planned and I want to hold it in your honour. Family and friends. You know that you are family.'

'I know I am.' Ayesha had been preparing for the moment when they parted company. She had something to say, and it was long overdue. She drew a deep breath. Prepared, began.

'Claire, there's something I must tell you. I've been meaning to tell you for a long time, but I've never been able to say it until now.'

'You can tell me anything you want to Ayesha.'

'You know I was angry with you.'

Claire looked uncomfortable.

'Even though I was, I never stopped caring; I want you to know that. I love you as my friend, but I need you to know this: I love you as my mum too! I hope that's okay.' Ayesha's voice tightened with emotion.

Tears spilled from Claire's eyes. She reached out to take Ayesha's hand.

'It's more than okay,' she said.

Four

The drive up to Holly's house, Larkspur, was reached via a narrow track through the wood; it was edged in bricks, which were sunk at a slant, so the corners made points. It curved around a broad expanse of lawn, where mist often gathered at dusk to thread between ornamental conifers and rhododendrons. In the mornings it was populated by rabbits, squirrels and blackbirds; it often had mole hills. The drive widened enough to accommodate several vehicles in front of a colonnaded entranceway. Larkspur was built of patterned brick, in different shades of yellow, red and some black; a band of herringboned brickwork ran around its middle. A double garage was attached to the house. It had quarters above where in an earlier age a chauffeur would have lived. Other buildings were situated behind, including Holly's studio.

The early evening sun shone between the trees, the mellow light slanting down onto a section of lawn. It was quite a shaded garden, in parts dark, where sunlight never reached. There was birdsong; the morning and evening chorus had a surreal quality they were so intense; Saskia had experienced both. She climbed out of the passenger door of the BMW and went to get their shared case from the rear. Ayesha joined her, she was smiling and lazily relaxed; Larkspur was a place she loved to visit. They were to stay for two nights and tellingly the day between; a few days ago, the idea of entrusting the business to Pearl and Amber Shalako and Hattie Dillinger would have given Ayesha nightmares; Saskia expected her to 'have kittens' when the idea was passed by her; instead, she had smiled and nodded. 'It will be nice spend a bit of time with Holly,' she had remarked as she framed her face in her hands and leaned her elbows on the Birdseye maple countertop. She was absorbed by the sight of Pearl at the time, who was flirtingly engaged with a customer at a cabinet filled with antique Japanese lacquers; Ayesha had smiled sublimely, knowing there would be a sale without her intervention, in fact aware that her intervention might have been counterproductive. Bliss!

Holly came out to greet them with smiles and kisses. 'Was it a nice drive over in the sunshine?'

'It was lovely,' said Ayesha.

'What's for supper Holly?' Saskia grinned.

'I hope you like dumplings?'

'God yes!'

Holly gave a little shiver in the autumn air. She was wearing jeans and a pink polo shirt with flour down the front, and a pair of moccasins. Saskia retrieved their case from the back of the car, while Ayesha took care of their coats. Holly grabbed their shared toiletry bag.

'It's going cool. Are we eating on our knees in front of the fire tonight?'

'Sounds good,' Ayesha responded for them both. She was in jeans a loose denim shirt and black suede ankle boots. Saskia was in a drop shoulder tennis jumper with a wide V neck, light blue jeans, and brown leather lace up oxford brogues over socks.

Holly led them inside; she deposited the toiletry bag in a chesterfield, brown leather, night porters chair, which stood to the right side of the door. 'I suggest you join me in the kitchen, for a chilled glass of Chardonnay and sort your stuff in a bit.'

Wine glugged seductively into Saskia's glass; she was anticipating the crisp chilled taste, and she watched the flow of liquid almost spellbound. With a head start, Holly set aside the empty bottle when she had filled their glasses. The kitchen was filled with the smell of beef stew cooking in the pot on her range. A small platoon of uncooked suet dumplings stood on a medium size blue and white Adams Charger, waiting to be added to the stew. Saskia suddenly became aware of how hungry she was.

'Now the business is open, will life get back to something like normality?' Holly inquired.

'Hopefully,' Ayesha said. She drank some of her wine appreciatively. She watched Saskia savour her own wine, retaining it in her mouth briefly before swallowing. Ayesha's gaze continued to follow her as she moved to rest her back against the granite worktop. Ayesha returned her full attention to Holly.

'Sometimes it's been fraught; I just wanted everything in place,' she confessed. 'I've probably been a real pain in the arse.' She looked at Saskia again as if for confirmation of the fact or possibly hoping for a contradiction or at least a sympathetic glance. Neither was forthcoming. Saskia shrugged.

'You've been a driving force,' she commented.

'So, I have been a pain in the arse. I don't want us to fail at it. We've put a lot of money and time into it, a lot of our selves too, and now it must stand on its own merits.'

'It must be fun too. I don't want to lose sight of that,' Saskia said firmly.

'I know.' Ayesha positioned herself next to Saskia, wanting the contact, the pressure and warmth of her. 'I'm relying on you to maintain my sense of proportion.'

'It's a great layout, you have fabulous stock,' Holly remarked, she gazed at Ayesha's intense, worried expression, she shifted her gaze onto Saskia; her brows furrowed slightly as she realised that Saskia was withholding compassion, indulging in a little mild psychological cruelty. Holly found herself wondering, not for the first time, if this was how they teased one another.

Saskia relented. 'We will make a go of the business,' she said. 'I feel it in my heart. But if by some remote chance we did not, it wouldn't be because of Ayesha. She is amazing. Don't forget that she's had my emerging powers to contend with too.'

'I have been brutal with her,' Ayesha supplied, 'I'm not a natural teacher.'

'I've hurt you too.'

'Recently yes. I haven't got through Saskia's defences in the last couple of weeks. She needs vis ultima though.'

'I haven't forgotten your promise to teach me elemental intent Holly,' Saskia said.

'The offer stands when you're ready to take me up on it.'

'Does the offer extend to me?' Both Saskia and Holly turned surprised looks in Ayesha's direction. Saskia's eyes fused with pleasure.

'It does,' Holly assured her. 'Nothing would give me greater satisfaction.'

'Ayesha! What a force we'll be!'

Ayesha searched Saskia's expression for validation of her exclamation. Saskia's face expressed only excitement and unreserved enthusiasm. Holly smiled, pleased. She picked up the charger of dumplings and moved them next to the range.

'Room temperature,' she said, 'never in the fridge, or they don't cook evenly through.' She removed the lid from the orange enamelled le Creuset and began to distribute the dumplings into the hot stew.

'About half an hour,' she told them.

'I am an acclaimed artist. So, what! That person is not me. I leave that person in my studio. They exist for eighteen hours a week maximum. The rest of the time I'm Holly, who doesn't see enough of her friends. I don't know the person in the studio. I don't recognize them. Do you understand what I'm saying?'

Saskia thought that she might in essence. Holly's words evoked glimpses of feeling that resonated.

'I think so. I'm a musician of sorts. But I don't feel like a musician and frankly I don't want to, I'm not that interested. My musical skill enabled me to busk for money.' Her mother had given her musical craft; she taught her to play the Mandolin, the Banjolele and the violin with versatility, the Lute with brilliance.

'That's a bit cynical, isn't it?' Ayesha said revealing doubt. 'You've created some lovely pieces, including the piece you dedicated to me.'

'I can't write music to order. It's a bit arcane, but that piece and others like it emerged fully formed from somewhere within my psyche! I don't write pieces intentionally, I can't!'

Ayesha frowned; this was a revelation to her. It accounted in some way, for the reason Saskia so rarely practised on her instruments.

'So, you really don't like to play.'

'It's not that; sometimes when I busked, I didn't feel like me. It was like somebody else was playing. When I played at Claire's party I can't remember playing, it's a blank.' She reached and touched Ayesha's knee. 'It was different when I played for you, it was intimate, sensual, I'd play for you any time you asked me to and with joy. I'm saying I know where Holly's coming from; that music doesn't define me at all, not in the way that I feel magic does.'

They had eaten their meal in front of the fire in Holly's main living room, where her flock of Martin brothers Wally birds looked on from their roost in the cabinet. Holly had slid from her armchair onto the thick rug, her upper body rested against the front of the chair, the v of her arm on the seat; she held her wine glass in her free hand. Ayesha was curled into a corner of the couch, her wine glass stood next to Saskia's beneath a table lamp on a rosewood table. Saskia lay on the couch legs slightly drawn up; she rested the side of her face and head on Ayesha's thigh. They had discarded their footwear and were comfortable in socks. They talked about Claire and about the Shalako twins, and the business and general trivia. At some point the conversation had moved onto the subject of motivation, and Holly began to open up on a more personal level, as she had inferred she would.

'I love my paintings. Don't get me wrong! But Holly the artist is an act of imagination. I know that magic defines me! I am my magic. I know that I put a bit of it into my paintings. It's probably why they sell.' Her last words were spoken with a note of derision. Ayesha and Saskia smiled at this.

'You don't mean that,' said Ayesha.

'Don't I? There are better artists out there than me who have never sold a single canvas!'

'Surely it isn't about that.'

'There's no formula for success,' Saskia said, she stroked Ayesha's knee.

'Exactly,' Holly said.

'Same as in the pop industry,' Saskia continued, 'Overloaded with talented people who never get a look in. She's saying it's the luck of the draw.'

'I am. I'm not great. I'm not a genius. I'm exceptionally good at what I do. I see the idea inside things and people, and illustrate it, beautifully if I say so myself, and imaginatively. But I don't believe that I deserve the acclaim that I have. Though beyond these walls I would deny that I ever said that. My success wasn't down to luck though, it was by design.'

'What happened?' Saskia's eyes widened with interest.

'First I fucked a demon who happened to like Art.'

'Felix Malek!'

'At the time I was twenty-one; I was ill; I had been for years; unstable; then I lost my mum whom I loved! I was dismantled. For months when I looked in the mirror, I saw a hollow-eyed ghost staring back. I had just inherited Larkspur. I wanted to make a go of selling my Art. I didn't want to work for anyone, I wanted to work for me. I wanted to be an acclaimed artist; I was young, I was convincing myself. I had money; not a great deal, I needed to make more, I needed a purpose too. I could just afford a couple of my own exhibitions and to self-represent. I had intent; on a par with yours, though I was desperate for more, and I had basic elemental intent; I wanted to be a powerful Adept; I was my mother's daughter after all. I financed my first exhibition. I sent out invitations to critics, to everyone I knew including my mother's friends, I had very few of my own. I asked them all to bring guests; anyone who might appreciate original art. I was wound up for days, a wreck, I barely slept. But on my opening night plenty of people attended and most of them had intent; I think most of them came in memory of my mother. One of them was Archie Bosola, Claire's father; he brought a close friend, and he bought a picture, the one you now own as part of your inheritance Saskia. I didn't recall his name from the event, but I now know that it must have been Trevor

Challoner. When Hal and Amelia arrived, they brought Felix with them. It was synchronicity. They introduced him; he proved to be highly intellectual, well-travelled and extremely wealthy; he collected among other things unusual Art. I've never been green, and I live and breathe my craft; I knew he was a demon. To be honest he scared me, but that turned me on. He bought two pictures and tried to buy my self-portrait from Trevor Challoner, but he had no interest in selling. I followed Felix around like a little dog all evening. I made it obvious that I was available. He had me that same night. On a rug on the floor of the studio with the shutters down and the lights on, surrounded by my art. Believe it or not I was a virgin; my first sexual encounter was with a demon, a Lalyt to be exact, who went on to initiate me in radical aphrodisia, demonic sex magic. I had never had an orgasm until that night either, though I had tried very hard. It was the single most erotic and frightening episode of my life. We were frequent lovers for the next three months. We are still infrequent lovers.

'Felix told his wealthy friends and business associates about the edgy new artist he had discovered; he had critics in his pockets, and they were impressed; he entered two of my paintings in a New York Fine Art auction for me; then he lit the fuse. I thought it would be a waste of time, but six weeks later I was a celebrity artist. Those paintings didn't sell for millions, but I've never looked back.' Holly grinned brightly, then she frowned as she did look back, and her eyes darkened.

'I was paper thin emotionally. It wasn't just losing my mum. It was me; it was several years in the making. I was this close to not being anymore. If events hadn't happened as they did...' she left the thought unfinished. She sighed, a deep sigh.

'My magic has always been more important than my painting, and when you're in a place as dark as I was then, magic has the capacity to hollow you out. It can feed on you if you allow it until there's nothing left but pieces of emotion and personality, and the overriding force of all those things that we want and above all need; that is called Desiderata. The fragments of us that survive are the blocks which we use to rebuild ourselves if we can. I believe that those fragments which have the strongest ability to survive are our true selves, stripped to the bone; its why certain traits are accentuated in us; by that I mean magicians; deviance, obsession or cruelty are examples. Magic is glamorous in the dark or the light. It gleams in our thoughts. It can create and destroy. It is never false. It is beautiful and frightening. Sleek, cool, hard, brutal, cruel, sexy, jealous. There have I described magic to you?'

'No, you've described magicians,' replied Saskia, smiling enthusiastically. 'I see pieces of all those things that you've mentioned in me. At least I hope that part of me is perceived as sleek and cool. I see all those pieces in you Holly, in different quantities and in Ayesha too.'

'She's right,' Ayesha said. She was combing Saskia's hair with her fingers and tracing the edge of Saskia's ear with their tips, tenderly teasing the lobe and the white pearl, which was suspended from it.

'She most certainly is,' Holly affirmed. 'We are what we are, we walk among ordinary people, but you could never call us ordinary. We are Sorceresses for the modern era. We wield a sort of designer magic that has thrown off a hundred old suffocating traditions. I discovered then, as many must have discovered before me, that apart from incredibly rare exceptions, the path to power is gained by design and need, and how much we want it and what we are prepared to do to achieve it.

'I was in the darkest space from which I saw no way of escape. Until I had radical aphrodisia with a five-hundred-pound sex demon. Afterwards the dark space became less and less dark every day, until after a few weeks it didn't exist anymore, and one day I was the real Holly Penn, and I cried with joy. At the same time my intent grew exponentially. Channels opened inside me; I was gleeful; I could feel them! I embraced them! and you know my centres hummed like hives of bees.'

'You're the second person within the space of a few days to tell me that they had come back from despair with massively increased intent,' said Ayesha. 'I believe that she was one of your rare exceptions.'

'You mean Claire, of course.'

'Felix Malek, you called him a Lalyt?'

'Yes, a male Lilith.'

'In the Hebrew Bible Adam's first wife was called Lilith,' Ayesha said uncertainly. 'The two aspects merge somehow. It's as much as I know, which might be worse than knowing nothing at all, which is shameful.'

'Don't beat yourself up, you had to be interested or see the knowledge as useful.' Holly said reassuringly.

Saskia who was paying close attention eased herself into an upright position, she drew her legs under her, remaining close to Ayesha. She laid her outspread hand on Ayesha's thigh where her head had been supported. It was still warm from the pressure of the side of her face. Ayesha glanced at her and smiled at the imprint of the seam of her jeans in the skin of Saskia's cheek.

'Lilith wouldn't lie under Adam, she wanted to be on top when they had sex,' Saskia said. 'She left Paradise in a rage. Yahweh sent Angels after her, but she wouldn't come back. Not even at the threat of a hundred of her children dying every day. Which is a bit of an enigma.'

'Bernadette O'Hare?'

'Local library on a wet day. We are genuinely interested.' She glanced at Ayesha for confirmation. Ayesha's gaze flickered from Saskia's face to Holly's; she nodded, sincere.

'I think we might infer that Lilith was a demoness. Some ancient world stuff can be rationalized. So much is lost in translation though, mostly by ordinaries or kept deliberately ambiguous. The Greek Lamia, the Jewish Lilith and the Babylonian Lalytu are the same thing. Lalyt are an order of demons that walk with and have sex with humans, awake or asleep. But they can be much more than that. Things have moved on since ancient times. There are a great many more people in the world. A great many more magicians in the world, and a great many more demons too. And most of them are fit for purpose in a modern era. Sex with a Lalyt can be just that, great sex. Or it can be sex and a feed for the Lalyt on the released sexual energy of its chosen partner. Or it can be a quid pro quo with the benefit for both parties greatly multiplied. Radical aphrodisia, cold little term isn't it; means incredible otherworldly sex and a fast track to Keraunos.'

'Keraunos?' Ayesha's brow furrowed; it was not a term with which she was familiar.

'The ancient energy of the thunderbolt,' Holly said. 'Zeus. Thor. The ultimate expression of what we call vis ultima. Keraunos is the source of our intent and its ultimate aspiration. There are lots of benefits, but it does have its dangers. Fascinating, isn't it? I can see by your expressions that I've shocked you.'

'I'm not shocked; I am enthralled!' Saskia said, her eyes smouldered as they searched Holly's face.

'I'm a little bit shocked,' Ayesha admitted. 'But I find it spellbinding.'

'I was unaware of what was happening to me, and Felix didn't explain for a couple of weeks. Even I wasn't born genned up,' Holly grinned. 'I still had plenty to learn. I'd never heard of Radical Aphrodisia or demonic sex magic. I just knew that I wasn't feeling broken anymore; and my intent was increasing. Felix liked me you see. He's not malevolent. He functions in this world. He might be a demon. But he loves beautiful women, and great wine and good food. Art and Antiquities are his passion. And of course, cricket; a day at Lords or the oval; nothing would give him a better buzz than England being two hundred and fifty for one at tea! I've been candid with you. You two are the only true friends I have. I believe you know that you can be equally candid with me; just putting it out there.'

'Hal and Amelia brought him to your exhibition! Did...' Saskia was animated, her eyes were beginning to relish her thought.

'Sorry to disappoint,' Holly quelled Saskia's excitement. 'Hal and Amelia and Felix are colleagues, maybe allies, nothing more.'

Dubiously Saskia turned her gaze on Ayesha. She frowned. Ayesha shook her head. 'No little mantis. I told you what Claire said, Hal and Amelia worked their sex magic in the Boundless edge.'

'Felix is unequivocally straight too,' Holly smiled. 'Wherever he might be, he hits on the most beautiful women in the room and excites them. He is what he is after all. There were lots for him to choose from at your launch.'

'Wasn't he with you?

'I met him in town. I drove myself home. He was into you two.'

'He made that clear, but I believe he preferred our Rhyton to either of us,' Saskia grinned.

Holly emitted short, amused laughter. 'His other obsession.'

'He wants to buy it. But we want to keep it.'

'Then don't sell it to him! He won't hold it against you.'

'At the launch Pearl told me that he was looking for us and that he'd gone up to the gallery' Saskia remarked.

'When I followed him, I couldn't see him. I looked for him, he wasn't there. Then he appeared behind me out of nowhere.'

'Had he gone back down to the showroom floor?' Ayesha asked curiously, this was the first Saskia had mentioned these details to her. 'You'd have seen him had he been hiding in plain sight.' She was referring to Saskia's ability to see the invisible.

'Yes, and he didn't emerge from the stockroom or the flat either. I'm certain,' Saskia said.

'He was there! you weren't looking hard enough,' Holly told her. 'He's tougher to see than a Shee! But you'd have seen him if you'd tried. He enjoys sliding between. He was amusing himself with you.'

'He caused me to feel desire, it was deliberate. And I felt jealous when Ayesha arrived, and he devoted most of his attention to her,' Saskia said.

'He lit your blue touch paper.' Holly smiled. 'You do know that you have one.'

'You do Saskia,' Ayesha smiled mildly amused. 'You slow burn, it's like you could turn into fireworks at any moment. He caused me to feel desire also you know.'

'You were all over him, giggling and flirting.'

'I couldn't help myself and I don't giggle.'

'That smoky chuckle you have.'

'It's still not a giggle.' They grinned affectionately at one another. Ayesha abruptly switched her attention back to Holly. She looked at her intensely. 'Holly, what did you mean about Felix sliding between?'

'I was going to ask the same thing,' Saskia said, her eyes fell on Holly with equal interest.

Holly laughed. 'Ooh! Creepy girl looks. I thought it had gone over your heads.'

'It sounds like something we need to know about,' Ayesha said.

'You know that Place exists between,' Holly said,

'Yes,' they said together.

'Do you know what between is?'

'Sub space,' Saskia said.

'The emptiness between dimensions,' Ayesha said. 'What Saskia said.'

'Okay, but it's not emptiness. How would you respond if I told you that between is elastic, but when crafted into form it is extremely stable.'

'I would say that you're describing Place,' Saskia said.

'In fact, what you're saying is that between is composed of Place,' Ayesha said, insightfully.

'I am, and Felix possesses the ability to slide in and out of it, at will. I would love the ability, but I haven't been able to persuade him to teach me the skill; yet.' Holly knelt to replenish their wine glasses and her own, from the open bottle on the table.

'The etheric realm is the shadow of Place, of between,' she continued, conversationally. 'So, we can partially access between, but not with all of our physical beings. Though it is possible to access between physically, obviously, in a limited sense.'

'How?' Ayesha said, absorbed.

'By opening a portal without a destination, to craft a Place. That's how a Place is made; then other factors come into the reckoning; volume, contents. The portal is bespoke, though; its limited to those who crafted it, or were party in some way to its crafting; it's after all in some way a part of them. Some Places are crafted with the same criteria in mind, though most Places are accessible to anyone with the ability to access Place.'

'How often do you see Felix now?' Saskia asked. The conversation had moved on from Holly's revelation about the nature of Place.

'Not often. As a lover a couple of times a year; it's like a casual habit. Socially maybe two or three times, which suits me. He's always in and out of the UK on business. He marches to the beat of his own drum.'

'Is he resident here in the UK then?' Saskia inquired.

'He considers himself English, he's a UK citizen. He owns a rather chic apartment in Knightsbridge, over his restaurant. And a mansion on the Humber, a great concrete, Brutalist thing.' Holly moved onto her knees again.

'I'm going to have a whisky,' she announced. 'Then nothing more until tomorrow. Would you like anything?'

'What brand of Whisky?' Ayesha inquired.

'Dalmore.'

'I'll have one. No ice.'

'Saskia?'

'I'll stick with my wine.'

Holly rose smoothly to her feet and went to pour two large whiskies from the decanter on the drinks tray; happy that she did not have to get ice from the kitchen.

'What are we helping you with?' Ayesha asked as she accepted her drink. 'Saskia said it might take to cockcrow.'

'I want you to help me raise something. I'll understand if you say no.' Saskia felt her heartbeat accelerate and the skin around her fetter scar tingle all the way up into the nape of her neck.

'God, I hope nothing chthonic,' Ayesha remarked.

'Nothing from beneath I promise.'

'Something or someone dead, or of the underworld,' Ayesha said by way of explanation to Saskia; she arched her brows at her and smiled smugly. 'Saskia would feel really at home.'

Saskia tilted her head on one side and holding Ayesha's gaze presented her with a non-smile. She wondered if Ayesha was aware of how unattractive her smirk was.

'Nothing like that. You're acquainted with the demonic I want to raise. Sort of.'

'What is it?' Ayesha frowned, puzzled.

'The owner of the Pandemonium dagger I bought from Saskia for a pound. It is an artefact, ancient and will be very personal to her. Connection will be innate. I am hoping she will be unable to resist coming for it.'

'The cat girl! You want to raise that cat girl!' Saskia became gleeful. 'Brilliant!'

'Why?' Ayesha demanded.

Holly did not resume her place on the rug but sat in her chair; she leaned back resting her whisky glass on the arm. She flashed her brows and smiled a little derisively, biting her underlip.

'I need to ask her something.'

'What?' Saskia inquired, fascinated.

'If she'll let me paint her.' Holly widened her eyes at them a little mischief shining in the copper-brown; her gaze shifted back and forth between them, an amused smile played around her mouth.

'Neither of you are phased, are you?' she remarked, pleased.

'Can't you paint her from memory?'

'Nope. It doesn't work like that.'

'What time in cockcrow?' Ayesha asked. She was referring to the third watch of the night.

'Two a.m.'

'What do you suggest we do for the next three hours?'

Five

'I only know that I will never play kerplunk with you again!' Ayesha growled. Saskia responded with a stony look.

'My conscience is clear,' she replied.

'Only because you haven't got one.'

Holley shushed them. 'Quiet now, a little decorum.' She had led them from the back of the house along the gridwork of brick paths that intersected her walled garden. She unlocked the door of the building next to her studio and went inside. A couple of lamps had been left on; the forty-watt bulbs shone a subdued light into the room. Saskia and Ayesha gazed about. It was a room neither had entered before then. It contained solid pine cupboards and shelves, and iron hooks along the walls, a couple of saddle stands with drawers stood down one side. Obviously, an old tack room; much of it remained, but harness and saddles had stayed in another age. The rear half of it had been transformed into a laboratory complete with glass freezer cabinet. There was a narrow window quite high up in the wall, being clawed at by a tree branch. The floor was tiled in smooth oblong terracotta cobbles. In the centre of the floor Holly had prepared a circle, eight feet in diameter, of alchemical salt, divided into three equal triangular sections. Holly walked around the edge of the alchemical barrier and stepped over it into the section furthest away. She faced Ayesha and Saskia and indicated with a little nod of encouragement that they should join her in the circle, which they did. Holly, with easy poise and balance raised each of her legs, bending them at the knee, and removed her socks. She stood barefoot on the cobbled floor. She began to remove the rest of her clothes. Ayesha had removed her socks with a nice elegance and was unfastening her jeans before Saskia realised that Holly intended that they all undress. She calmed the little bit of uncertainty that she felt and made herself undress with studied poise; she was the last to lay her panties on her folded T-shirt and jeans.

It was cool in the room and the floor underfoot was cold. Saskia gave a little shudder, but it was not caused by the cold; for the present she found that enjoyable; it was induced by her sense of nervous excitement.

'Are you okay with this?' Holly inquired in a soft voice.

'God yes!' Saskia grinned. 'Just nervous.' She gazed at Holly's nude body and gave a little gasp. Holly was toned and lithe and beautiful, but what caused Saskia's little audible exclamation were her tattoos. They extended from her smooth mons pubis over her abdomen, to finish beneath her small high breasts; others swept round her slim hips disappearing behind them. They were tattoos of bees in flight; Saskia thought there were between fifty and sixty of them visible to her; on the wings of each bee were tiny occult symbols. Saskia did not know what they meant but in time she determined to find out. She became aware of Holly's indulgent smile and the copper-brown eyes making a study of her reaction. Ayesha too looked fascinated. Holly had looked at her compliance of thorns with interest. She had heard of it; to see it added dimension.

'Sorry for staring!' Saskia said.

'That's okay. Wait till you see my back!' Holly stretched out her hands to them. Saskia gave a little smile of gratitude for the spoken indulgence and took Holly's right hand in her left. Ayesha took Holly's left hand and extended her free hand to Saskia, she looked amused, her eyes gleamed and a small smile played on the line of her mouth; Saskia took her hand, completing their circle.

'Holly Penn!' Holly announced her name, surprising Saskia. Then she chanted her couplet:

'In the leaven of the stars and the cradle of the rain

I laugh with my lover in the arrows of the moon.'

'Ayesha Shah!' Saskia thought that Ayesha announced her name almost with joy. Ayesha too chanted her couplet; haughtily, smiling:

'I stare at the sun, and I dance in the hail.

I know myself I am tooth and nail.'

Saskia grinned. 'Saskia Challoner!' she said boldly. Then chanted:

'It's all my fault yes, it's all my fault.

And I don't give a damn cos I am what I am.'

It was irreverent, her couplet, she knew that it was. And Claire inwardly probably shook her head and sighed in mild despair when she first heard it chanted by Mocking beck waterfall, when they had set a keeper on the gate to the Wild. She could have been more deferential and more poetic admittedly; she had the ability, but it did define her, Saskia decided; just as Ayesha's absolutely defined her.

'Come magicians; protections are in place.'

Holly released their hands and turned and stepped from the circle. Saskia stared at Holly's back; she could not help it. She even felt as if she had been invited to. The bees swarmed across Holly's hips and tight buttocks, becoming smaller and more densely portrayed as they covered her lower back; the swarm eventually disappeared through the aperture of a hive in its traditional form, the skep. The apex of the skep's dome finished at the central point between her shoulder blades. Tattooed on her left shoulder blade was an upright arrowhead in traditional form, with a partial shaft, and on her right shoulder blade a scarab.

'I want to dance in the hail with you,' Saskia whispered to Ayesha as they stepped from the circle and followed Holly, who had crossed the room to a door, in the wall on the left.

'It stings,' Ayesha replied.

'I hope so.'

'Serious faces ladies,' said Holly.

Holly unlocked the door with a heavy antique iron key that was already lodged in the lock. She opened the door and led them into another room. A single low bulb, no more than sixty watts burned among the beams, spreading meagre light. The floor was tiled in the same terracotta cobbles as in the tack room, and the room was of similar size. There were a couple of narrow windows in the outer wall, these had bars on them, the glass in them was obscured. The walls were bare brickwork, and the ceilings were beamed; iron hooks were sunk in the beams. Saskia thought that the room might have previously been used for hanging game. The heady smell of alchemical incense lay on the air, it came from an ancient Chinese bronze burner from which the flavoured smoke trailed into the air in tiny whisps. Saskia felt slightly giddy as the scent penetrated her senses. She ignored the slight disorientation and concentrated on the thing that dominated the space, dividing it into two roughly equal halves. A gridwork of finger thick tendrils spanned the room; they intersected each other like a giant abstract cobweb from wall to wall and ceiling to floor; they were the colour of dark red wine, and they resembled exposed veins; they stirred restlessly occasionally. They emerged from a mass of about the size of a football, which had compressed into the angle of the ceiling and wall to the right. Eight small round black protrusions formed a circle on its surface. Cold little beady eyes, Saskia thought; not for the first time. It was Holly's house guardian. She recalled when she had first been made known to it on her second visit to Larkspur. She thought it looked like the spider from hell, and she was not keen on any spider at the best of times. Looking at its current form it obviously had the ability to alter its shape. Holly had taken her hand by the wrist and pressed the underside of her fingers to one of its legs. Saskia had almost recoiled and pulled away, but she had steeled herself to the contact; it had felt cold to the touch and pliant. 'Friend', Holly had said in a clear voice. That had been a few months previously and she had not encountered it again on any of her visits until then. It lived from choice in an old, galvanized bath in the space above the garage. It possessed physicality, unlike their guardian, snuggles, so it remained visible. Ayesha had been introduced to it a couple of years before, on a visit with Claire. On the floor in the middle of the partitioned part of the room beyond the barrier, Holly had placed a shallow stoneware bowl containing a clear liquid, which bubbled quietly to itself. Across the rim of the bowl lay the silver Pandemonium knife which Saskia had reclaimed from Claire's Garden; and with which she had killed the CaolShee, Lachaen. Afterwards she had intended to give it to Theo Bacchus as a gift, and he would have appreciated it, but Holly had asked her for it and Saskia had given it into her keeping. She saw that a cord had been attached to the knife, made from some sort of woven fibre, this had been coiled around the knife, and its two ends immersed in the liquid. Saskia felt her heart rate increase and her skin prickle as she saw the knife and felt the atmosphere of expectation in the room.

'Are you okay?' Holly inquired, as if sensing her reaction. Saskia felt Ayesha's arm enclose her waist; her slim fingers pressed into the skin of her abdomen and the pleasant cool pressure of her nude skin felt good against her side. She could smell the scent of her hair, confusing in the smell of the incense.

'I'm fine! I want this!'

'Okay. If either of you feel odd compulsions or a strange presence make me aware; it's unlikely but we don't want to pick up something unexpected, do we? Ready…good!'

Holly's expression became gleeful; for the first time Saskia saw in her look the face of the little, naked, female demon, sitting on the well in the self-portrait, which had hung in the bedroom but now hung in the living room at Mocking beck. Holly chuckled as if reading her thoughts;

she took her hand and reached for Ayesha's. She led them right up to the grid; another inch and it would brush against them. Saskia smiled knowing that she was born for this. Ayesha and Holly, Amber and Pearl, Hal, Amelia, and Claire; they were her kindred and with her fetter gone she was part of their world. She summoned her intent; Ayesha would be calling on her own. She held it; she felt it coil inside her, wanting release; she denied it like checking an orgasm. Holly had prepared them; they were her reservoirs of intent. The operation was a breaching of within, of Place, as she now understood it to be; the raising was an invitation to retrieve what was without doubt, precious. It might be declined. Saskia truly hoped that it would not be. She gasped in surprise as she felt her suspended intent sucked from her; she heard Ayesha's own little exclamation as she experienced the same thing. It did not end there, the flow of intent continued as Holly drew on the intent gathered at her centres. After thirty seconds or so Saskia felt her central pillar turn to cold fire; it was exhilarating; her heart rate and breathing elevated; she felt excited, and the start of sexual arousal. Tiny bursts of static sparked across her naked skin. After a minute, disappointingly it ended. Holly released her hold on their hands and moved her own hands to in front of her body; she kept them about nine inches apart; they were curved as if she held an invisible ball between them. She began to form elemental intent between her fingers and palms. Dozens of silver tendrils had formed in the space between her hands; like threads of mercury, they wove in and around each other, never touching.

Enviously, fascinated, Saskia watched Holly's manipulation of the elemental realm. She raised her eyes, suddenly aware of scrutiny, and found Ayesha studying her with calm curiosity. She met her stare solemnly, her mouth an expressionless line. Ayesha moved and came to join her, moving from the other side of the consumed Holly Penn. She took Saskia's arm, holding it at elbow and wrist, and kissed the cool skin of her shoulder.

'We're redundant,' she commented. 'Just observers now.'

'I envy her,' Saskia told her.

They continued to watch Holly. Her face had become fiercely focused on the silver threads which had drawn together at a single point, they waved and undulated like the tentacles of a sea anemone.

'I can see that,' Ayesha replied.

'I want more from my magic. I'm discontented,' Saskia told her.

'I know!' Ayesha said. 'I intend to keep you on a leash in case you run off.'

'I won't do that. Though I like the idea of a leash.'

Holly had formed the silver threads into a sphere; it pulsated, suspended, attempting to contort. Static spat around her fingernails and the ends of her hair. She released the sphere, causing it to dart away from her hands, between the strands of the barrier; her fingers twitched once, and it became stationary above the Pandemonium dagger on its bowl of fluid. They closed inwards the merest fraction, and the sphere descended to rest on the dagger. As this contact was made the atmosphere in the room became unsettled and quickly became more agitated. The air seemed to paw at them and appeared to be filled with movement. Saskia could see darting shapes, probably invisible to Holly and Ayesha; they were only just visible to her; insubstantial asymmetrical structures, aligning and realigning. They winced at sudden pain in their eardrums and a shrill ringing. The world inside the room felt like stretched elastic, so tight it might break. The sphere shrank to nothing, and the structures had imploded with a speed Saskia could not follow. They had formed a single structure hovering metre or so behind the dagger, like an Olympic ring, over a metre across; it rotated slowly. Saskia blinked, and unfocused; the structure shifted from her vision, merging with the air like a disappearing wraith.

'You can see it, can't you,' Holly said, her eyes were gleaming at present, more copper than brown. She studied Saskia's face, mostly watching her eyes.

'If I try. Not that clearly now.'

'Keep watch.' Holly returned her attention to the room.

'What if she snatches her dagger and legs it,' Saskia said.

'She won't. She can't, it's too dangerous.' She called out loudly then, making them jump. 'You in Pandemonium, come and get your dagger!'

'Is that the tomb I can smell?' Ayesha said.

'Don't be mean,' Saskia told her. They waited, for perhaps five- or six-minute-long ages; before Saskia thought she saw movement in the vicinity of the dagger, as if a small section of the room had gone out of focus.

'I think she's there,' she said.

'Pax! Pandemonium,' Holly announced. 'Tell her!' She said to Ayesha and Saskia.

'Pax!' they said, almost together; cautiously.

An abstract formed in the middle of the room, an undefined twist of presence; it shaped as though emerging into view in a distorted mirror, becoming structured. It leapt suddenly into focus. A thread of tension tightened through the room.

'Pax,' she replied in a softly uncertain voice. She approached; stopping in front of them, she assumed an elegant stance. She folded her arms and peered at them. She did not appear confrontational, her large yellow eyes contained curiosity more than anything else, accompanied by caution. Saskia admired a silver bangle on her wrist, it was beautifully crafted, and hand beaten, its surface was concave, and it was set with a single huge cut pale yellow Citrine in a high collar. The cat girl followed Saskia's gaze.

'It is an heirloom. I recall you all; why have you summoned me?' She spoke precisely; her voice had a strange little inner tremor; her accent was akin to polish with a slight lisp. She rotated at her slim hips, to gaze at her dagger.

'That too is an heirloom. To replace is beyond my purse.'

She turned and approached the dagger, her body possessed supple grace, with a ballet dancer's poise. She was barely taller than Holly. She was dressed in a tabard of silk that tapered at both front and back to a point between her knees; it was held by a tie at both hips; it was coloured dusky pink; it moulded to her firm pointed breasts. She was wearing velvet ankle boots on her slim feet, of a similar colour to her tabard. She crouched down over her dagger, on the balls of her feet, and rested her forearms across her knees, her hands hanging loosely between them; her fingers were tipped in pearl-coloured nails.

She gave two little sniffs in the direction of her dagger. 'I cannot...would not risk touching that,' she remarked. 'I thought we had a truce. *Come and get your dagger!* I heard. I was almost thrown from my bed my room was in such a turmoil; I covered quickly and came. I almost didn't.' She paused gazing at their faces, her large eyes fixed on Holly. She tilted her head to one side and frowned, holding Holly's gaze, as she finished her sentence.

'You're the one that spoke. Am I mistaken?'

'No, I'm the one, and I'm merely being cautious,' Holly replied. Her eyes never stilled, they darted over every inch of the cat girl, a relentless appraisal.

'Because I come from Pandemonium. I am not trustworthy. I am not honourable.' She rose and approached them again, she stood with her hands on her hips, her fingers spread out, her expression affronted, though it was obvious that she was mocking them. She was pretty; Saskia had thought that in Claire's Garden. Most of her body was covered in fine white fur, about the length of the short fur on a cat's face. On some parts of her body, she had no fur, just pale human skin toned by muscle. Her pretty face was hairless and mostly human with elements of cat; it was triangular in form, the jaw was slightly long, she had a snub nose, retroussé they called it. She had blond, almost white hair, messy and short. Her large eyes were as yellow and as sad as Saskia remembered; and she had a thin, fine, pale mouth. She had large upright furry ears, and a slender neck. She was elegant, odd; delightful, Saskia thought.

'You wounded me with iron. It made me sick.'

'I'm sorry! but you were coming for me.'

'I was tasked with taking you. Others failed,' she seemed briefly amused. 'Though in their case you were where you were not expected to be.'

'But you're better now? My friend wanted to kill you! I refused to strike you with the sword,' Saskia said, she thought reasonably.

'Aah! You expect my gratitude!' She said in a mocking tone; she gave a little shimmy of her slim shoulders.

'I was flogged for my failure!' She laughed, a soft hacking sound.

'I'm sorry,' Saskia said.

'Then I was starved for a month and flogged again.'

'That was cruel.'

'Shit happens. Life is harsh in Pandemonium.'

Saskia shivered. Ayesha raised her hands to her upper arms and stroked the skin, feeling goose bumps.

'I'll get our clothes,' she said, she glanced at Holly for confirmation. Holly nodded.

'I've been wondering who you remind me of,' Saskia said. 'It's just struck me. Brigitte Bardot.'

'Who is this, Brigitte Bardot?' the cat girl asked.

'A famous actress. Very beautiful. French.'

'I'm told the French are beautiful,' the cat girl remarked, surprising them. She grinned showing pointy canines. 'Who killed the Shee? I could smell its death even through all that shit close to my knife!' She peered, with suspicion, at Holly whose eyes were still evaluating her. 'Not you.'

She shifted her gaze to Ayesha searching her dark eyes. 'I believe you are capable of almost anything; though it was not you.' Ayesha smiled contemptuously and freed her gaze; she turned away and went to fetch their clothing.

'You killed the Shee!'

'I killed the Shee,' Saskia responded quietly. 'But it killed me first.'

'A good kill,' said the cat girl her eyes going distant; she ignored the rest of Saskia's response, perhaps considering it to be enigmatic. 'What must I do to regain my knife? What do you want? I have little money. You want me to perform some act for you? Do you want someone dead? Consider it done!'

At that moment Ayesha returned with their clothes, she distributed them supporting them like some sort of offering. Saskia accepted hers from the top of the neat stack and began to put them on.

'I don't want you to kill anyone,' Holly said. She took her clothes from Ayesha; she and Ayesha began to dress. The cat girl watched from behind the barrier; she eyed their clothing with interest, their jeans got most of her attention.

'Were these clothes made for you? The breeches, trousers.'

'They are called Jeans,' Saskia told her.

'The fabric is it a twill?'

'Yes, it's called denim.'

'I like them, the black most!' she pointed to Ayesha's Levi jeans. Ayesha zipped and fastened her button over her board-flat abdomen. She was not keen on being scrutinized by a stranger whilst she dressed, particularly one who was a denizen of Pandemonium.

'My name is Luca,' the cat girl told them unexpectedly.

Saskia peered at her from just a couple of feet away. 'You know that I'm Saskia.'

Luca nodded. She directed her gaze at Ayesha. 'Her, the mean one,' she said. Saskia smiled as Ayesha reacted on cue with a dark look.

'Ayesha's not so bad when you get to know her.'

'And her! what is the name of my gaoler?' Luca glared fiercely in Holly's direction. Holly frowned back at her, she looked uncomfortable; then her expression hardened and became defiant.

'I'm called Holly. I have a purpose for you; when I'm through with you, then you get your knife, and you can go home.'

'So, you invite me, and you make me a prisoner! With or without my knife I cannot leave!'

Holly shook her head. 'The portal I made is a form. It locked when you came through; Only I can re-open it.'

'This is my prison! Iron at the windows! An elemental monster my keeper!'

'Yes, you are temporarily a prisoner, just for a few days.'

'And this is my worth? This room!' Luca railed angrily; she waved an arm around in an agitated gesture.

'Do you think I shit in corners?' she demanded angrily.

Holly frowned again. 'Of course not! through that door is all you need. A bed, a comfy chair, and a room for your sanitation. I'll bring you food when you tell me what you want to eat.'

'What do you want from me? What is this 'purpose''?' Luca demanded.

'I want to paint your picture.'

Six

'You've brought a bow with you!'

Holly grinned a welcome; she had turned and lowered her bow when they came out of the house behind her. Saskia was carrying the forty-five-pound recurve bow she had purchased a month before. She practised in the garden at Mocking beck when they were there, and she and Ayesha had spent hours in the woods searching for arrows at first, but not so much recently. Ayesha was carrying a tray of drinks. Fresh orange. She set it down close to them on top of the low brick wall that ran between the garden and the house.

'It was in its case in the car. I want to try a few shots in this lovely atmosphere.'

'It's nice in your garden at mocking beck,' Holly said, 'with all that woodland around, and the sheep!'

'It is! I fire in the opposite direction to the sheep by the way after the Millie incident with the sundial, I don't want to risk anything unfortunate. But it's special here.'

'What time did you get to bed?' Ayesha inquired.

'About an hour after you. Did you sleep alright? Go on, I've just reclaimed my arrows.' Holly indicated for Saskia to take a shot at the empty target. She took a stance and drew an arrow from her side quiver.

'Like logs,' She replied to Holly's question. She smiled affectionately at Ayesha. They had fallen asleep almost as soon as they had got into bed. A rare event for them. Saskia had kissed Ayesha awake that morning, but they had resisted intimacy and gone downstairs to join Holly instead. It was almost midday, and they had found her where they anticipated. The sun peered through high cloud, but it was mild enough for T-shirts. Saskia was wearing a snugly fastened leather wrist guard and a three-finger archery glove. She released an arrow at Holly's habitually small target; it went above it by six inches and struck the straw filled sacks that were piled behind.

'Close!' Holly commented, 'for a warmup. Try another.'

'How's your guest?'

'I haven't seen her since last night. I thought I had better leave her to cool off. She told me I could paint her fucking arse and that was it, and to stick my offer of some food up my own arse. And to stick the censer there too because the stink of it was giving her a fucking headache.'

'Not a happy bunny,' Saskia said grinning.

'Would you be?'

'I would be incandescent,' Ayesha remarked.

'I'm not the wicked witch here!' Holly smiled her protest. 'Luca is not an innocent; she was part of a company of otherworld mercenaries sent to destroy our covenant and take you Saskia. Now she stands to regain something of immense personal value to her; an artefact that she thought was lost forever.'

'I know. I can't help being sympathetic to her that's all. But I am on your side.' Saskia released another arrow. She experienced a glow of pure satisfaction as it lodged an inch away from the centre of the target.

'Good shot!'

'I'm going to eat with her.' Saskia set down a big modernist wooden tray with brushed steel inset handles at the end of the kitchen table. She poured two cups of coffee and a little jug of milk which she added to the tray.

'Bacon and eggs and crusty bread,' Ayesha said drily; they got their own breakfasts; it was almost one o'clock, but breakfasts felt right; she was having boiled free-range eggs with Holly; she paused, bread soldier immersed. Holly eyed her Georg Jensen steel cutlery dubiously; it lay neatly wrapped in napkins. Ayesha noted the little pile of glossy magazines, Harper's Bazaars, under one of the plates.

'Do you want me to open a tin of Tuna and give her a choice?' Saskia said, more tartly than she intended. She set two aluminium plate covers over the breakfasts.

Ayesha shrugged and looked away. Saskia frowned at them both. 'Will someone get the door for me. I'll manage at the other end.'

Holly got up from the table and held the door open for her.

'Be careful,' she said to her; Saskia nodded.

'Hi Luca! are you feeling, okay? Stupid question I'd be thoroughly pissed off! So, I get it.' She closed the door behind her with her heel and set the breakfast tray down on the floor in front of the protective gridwork of vein like tendrils; she was used to them now, she ignored them. She lowered to the floor and sat cross legged. It was cool and hard through her jeans. She shrugged inwardly. She could take a bit of discomfort. She raised her face and looked directly at Luca which she had avoided doing until then. Though she was aware of her.

Luca had moved a large tan leather armchair on castors into the room and placed it a safe distance to the right of her dagger; the 'comfy chair' Holly had mentioned. It was a heavy chair, and she would have needed to put it on its side to pass it through the doorway. Saskia presumed that the demonic had probably accomplished it without much difficulty, despite her small frame. Luca was sitting in the chair, legs folded in front of her, knees turned to one side. She was barefoot and elegant, waiting. Her yellow eyes gazed at Saskia with cold emptiness. If she was surprised to see her and not Holly, she did not reveal it.

'I've made us Late breakfast. You must be hungry. I am. And coffee.' She could have played it with an element of dizziness, but she decided against it; she settled for direct friendliness, no frills. To her surprise Luca unwound from the chair and approached. She lowered herself with supple fluency to mirror Saskia's posture. She was wearing her tabard, but it was untied at the hips.

'Show me.' she peered at the tray; her expression had not changed. Saskia removed the covers from the plates and set them aside, revealing the breakfasts. Luca gave several delicate little sniffs. Saskia heard a little growl emerge from the direction of Luca's stomach; she suppressed a smile as she realised that pride was about to be kicked into touch in the face of hungriness.

'It smells good,' Luca said.

'Are you familiar with bacon?' Saskia inquired.

'We eat all manner of foods in Pandemonium.'

'Of course, you do, you're not going to tell me to stick it are you?'

'No, I think I will eat it,' Luca said.

'They're both the same, food nothing else,' Saskia told her in case Luca should think that there might be a toxin or a tranquilizer present; though she suspected that she might be able to tell. 'Pick which one you want.'

Luca shrugged, staring. Saskia passed her a plate through a scalene gap under the grid; she slid it over the floor; she had placed utensils and napkin on the side of the plate.

'Would you like milk in your coffee? I prefer black.'

Luca slowly shook her head. She began to eat, breaking an egg yolk with bacon held between her fingers. She had unwrapped her utensils Saskia noted. Saskia pushed a mug of coffee under the gap.

'You're much calmer.'

Once again Luca shrugged a response; she continued to eat, and to stare into Saskia's eyes. Saskia refused to lock gazes, she kept up a continuous sequence of looking and glancing away.

'I brought you some glossy magazines.'

'Glossy magazines,' Luca repeated.

Saskia indicated the magazines on the tray with her fork 'Harper's Bazaar. You can look at the pictures.'

'Are they without words?'

'No,' Saskia looked puzzled.

'Why would I not read the words?'

Saskia gasped in dismay. 'I'm sorry. I've insulted you,' she said, she flushed in embarrassment.

Luca shook her head; Saskia got the impression that she was amused by her faux pas. 'No, you haven't. I am hard to insult,' she said. Saskia concentrated on her food, and they ate quietly together. Luca finished her bacon continuing to eat it with her fingers; her manner was precise, unhurried. She cut up her eggs with the knife and scooped them into her mouth with the fork. Finally, she mopped up the yolk with the bread. Saskia wondered if she would pick up the plate and lick it clean and felt a further surge of embarrassment.

'I'm sorry about this. I know you're being detained, but you will get your knife,' Saskia assured her.

Luca nodded. 'She wants to paint my picture.'

'It's what she does, she's a professional Artist,' Saskia said.

'She could have asked. The people of Pandemonium have been painted before.'

'You'd have said, yes?'

'Probably. Maybe.' Luca shrugged. 'I've missed my watch; I'll be punished. If I miss another I'll be flogged.'

'Flogged? Are you in the military or something?

'I'm not a common soldier. I'm indentured to Satran Saradina. For criminality as a child, and for debt accrued for my keep, and for my armour and my sword and my net.'

'But not for your knife?' Saskia said, fascinated.

'My knife is an heirloom. In Pandemonium heirlooms are honoured.'

'I found your knife where you dropped it in the garden after the fight. It was lucky to survive. The Cockatrice destroyed everything else, including your net I'm afraid.'

Luca sipped her coffee; tasted it. She nodded. 'It's not bad,' she commented. 'Tea is better.' Keeping hold of her mug she stood with a single fluid motion. She went to the wall to Saskia's right and sat down again with her back against it, her knees drawn up in front of her.

'Join me,' she invited, 'Side by side is less formal. You won't have to keep avoiding my gaze.'

Saskia stood, also in a single supple movement. She went to join Luca; she felt a slight regret, because now her bottom would need to warm another area of cold floor.

'You've been an hour!' Ayesha called across the garden as Saskia emerged with her tray into the daylight. Ayesha was on her way to the tack room, a little on edge. She smiled in relief when she saw her. Saskia walked along the gridded paths to coincide with her route. She spoke to her without breaking her jaunty stride, passing her.

'She'll sit for Holly! I like her! She prefers tea, I'm going to make some. I left her looking through the May edition of Harper's Bazaar.'

'You cocky little cow!' Ayesha called after her. Saskia gave a burst of mocking laughter over her shoulder in reply, and Ayesha grinned and shook her head; she turned to follow her back to the house.

    The following morning Saskia went to see Luca before they left. Ayesha went with her; which was odd, Saskia thought; she had not accompanied her the previous day on the now three visits she had made to Luca. Saskia decided she was simply being nosey or maybe a little jealous. Luca was in the chair peering through the copies of Harper's Bazaar; a pose possibly assumed when she heard them coming. Saskia went to sit on the floor near the wall where she had sat on her previous visits; Luca walked unself-consciously over, her tabard loosely sliding between her thighs; she sat down next to her; their shoulders were only inches apart, only the strands of the barrier separated them. Saskia slid a mug of tea under the barrier to her and sipped her own.

    'We're leaving soon. Don't be too hard on Holly.'

    'She came with food an hour ago. We didn't speak, though she did to find my eyes with hers.' Luca smiled and shrugged. The sadness in her eyes was a little more on display. She brightened suddenly.

    'She acts like your mistress?' Luca nodded towards Ayesha who had positioned herself next to the door; she leaned with her back to the jamb, arms folded, one leg bent at the knee and crossed over the other.

    'Are you, my mistress?' Saskia asked her amused.

    'I don't own you!' Ayesha snapped.

    'I believe that sometimes you want her to, yes? Just for a while.' Luca's eyes gleamed mischievously.

Saskia chuckled and lifted her thumb automatically to rest its nail against her lower teeth, sharing the humour with Luca, but she made no verbal response.

'She is compliant to you. I smell alchemy in her, barbs under her Art,' Luca said mischievously.

'That's my business!' Ayesha hissed. She stepped forward from the door. She glowered at Luca; she had folded her arms more tightly; her frame had become rigid.

'Don't talk about me! I don't want the likes of you talking about me!'

Luca shrugged and nodded in acquiescence, she looked down, away. Saskia frowned up at Ayesha, forming a question in her expression.

'I'll wait for you outside,' Ayesha said grimly.

'The likes of me,' Luca said with quiet bitterness when she had gone. 'A twisted little halfling bitch; scum from Pandemonium she meant.'

'She didn't mean it, I know her. There are other things going on.' Without thinking Saskia reached out and laid a reassuring hand on Luca's arm, passing between the strands of the guardian. They both tensed. Saskia resisted the temptation to withdraw her hand; she felt her heart rate elevate. Luca felt warm, her fur soft, the underlying muscle firm. Saskia knew that she was taking a chance; she knew that the halfling, Luca, citizen of Pandemonium, possessed the strength to tear her arm away, despite Saskia's energised intent.

'Even if there was no Pax between us, I wouldn't harm you,' Luca said. 'I'm not a fiend, though in

Pandemonium there are many. I hope we meet again, though it's unlikely.'

'I hope so.'

'Go to your woman; she won't be feeling good about herself,'

'Be kind to Holly. She's nice. Give her a chance,' Saskia pleaded.

Ayesha was walking the brick paths in the sunshine; her fingers were thrust into the rear pockets of her Levi's; her attention was lost in Holly's flower beds. She looked very alone Saskia thought; there was a slight haziness in the sunlight and insects buzzed everywhere; she was receiving attention from hoverflies, but she did not appear to notice them.

'That's a very judgemental face,' she said, as Saskia came up to her, there was a hint of defiance in her expression.

'That was hurtful, more by what you implied than what you said.'

'She was pushing the boundaries,' Ayesha claimed defensively.

'Don't we all? Aren't we now? We've helped Holly to imprison her! You should apologise to her.'

'I've no intention of doing that,' Ayesha said defiantly. 'She's just a halfling. She intended the same for you!'

'But she failed. She's a young woman like you or me,' Saskia said reasonably. 'God knows what goes on in her life.'

'I don't care! she's a snidey mocking little bitch!'

'And Pearl and Amber are capable of that, and me, and you are too Ayesha. And yes, you do care. I know that you do.'

'Are we going?'

'Not yet,' Saskia said, 'I want to walk in this lovely garden for a while longer with a very beautiful lady.' She bumped Ayesha affectionately. Ayesha reached out a hand and their fingers curled into each other as they walked.

'I love this place,' Ayesha said.

Seven

Luca pretended not to notice when Holly came into the room. She was seated in the tan leather armchair; she paged through a magazine and did not look up. She had not been in the chair; she had adopted her pose when she heard someone entering the building, she knew that it would not be Saskia; she had said her goodbyes. Luca had been pacing, frustrated; behind the chair to avoid accidental contact with the bowl and its alchemical contents. She had already, almost walked onto the bowl by accident, her mood angry and distracted at the time; she had stopped herself in the nick of time; that had scared her; she had no idea what she would release or what the substances would do to her if she got any on her. She had taken care since.

Holly gazed through the elemental gridwork at the elegant Luca. She sat straight, poised; one knee crossed above the other, ankle boot extended; her face an expressionless mask as she studied the magazine. Holly knew that she was being given the ice treatment.

'Luca, can we put our last conversation behind us and start again?' she asked quietly.

Luca paused her page turning and looked up; the Harper's Bazaar magazines had given her great joy. When she had first looked at them, they had filled her with excitement, the pictures, and the people in them, to her, were wonderful to behold, their clothing and appearances delicious. The magazines fascinated her and excited her. On Saskia's second visit on the previous day, she had fetched her more issues and had explained them to her, and she thought that she understood what was at play here, within the limitations of her experience and her realistic imagination. What they had shown her alone was worth the flogging she would receive when she eventually turned up for duty, on her watch in Pandemonium.

To Holly's surprise Luca's expression was not hostile; the large, beautiful, sad yellow eyes fixed calmly on her and stared. When Luca spoke, there was no edge to her voice.

'Tell me what you want me to do Holly.'

'Thank you, Luca,' Holly showed relief.

'Thank Saskia, she told me that you are nice. She has left by now, I presume.'

'They, have. I am nice, I think; at least I think I'm a decent person.'

'Yet, you keep me a prisoner under Pax; do you intend to paint me from the other side of this barrier?'

'If I explain...I was betrayed under Pax by one of your...'

'One of my kind,' Luca said.

'I didn't mean it like that.'

'I have honour. Many of us have honour.'

'I came close to death,' Holly explained. 'I'm cautious now that's all.'

'Could you not read their real intentions?'

'I didn't look. I believed.'

'You could look in me,' Luca suggested. 'Then you'll believe me.'

'I'm sorry. I'm sorry for summoning you. Saskia said that you'll be punished if you miss your duty on the watch again.'

'That is already a given I'm afraid,' Luca shrugged resignedly.

Holly drew a deep breath. She felt guilt rise inside her. She looked down; she did not want to meet Luca's gaze right then; she did not know what to say. Luca watched her in silence for a time. Then she got out of the chair and put the Harper's Bazaar aside, onto the seat. She crossed the floor avoiding the bowl and stopped as close to the grid as she dared and peered intently at Holly as if seeing her for the first time, her slightness, and her prettiness. She noted her clothing; kitten heel sandals showing her feet, skinny jeans, a white camisole top under a short snug fitting blue velvet jacket. The neat brown hair, the makeup darkened lids of her downcast eyes. These looked up as she sensed scrutiny, beautiful and copper brown, questioning.

'I didn't know. How could I? Go home Luca. You can have your knife; I'll make it safe for you.'

'You don't want to paint me after all?'

'Of course, I do; you're amazing! But I don't want to see you harmed!' Holly's eyes lit with intensity. The need had smouldered inside her since the night in Claire's Garden. The images of the creatures from Pandemonium under the yellow sky had stayed with her. She intended to paint them. A sequence of paintings. A furious Satran Saradina. Luca with her net coming for Saskia. All from memory. Then Saskia had produced the knife. And the idea had risen in her. It would not be the first time she had painted a demonic or a demon, using a live subject.

Luca peered at Holly's animated pretty face. She saw something of what her project meant to her. And she saw compassion there too, and her willingness to set aside her own needs and sacrifice them. Luca was not used to selflessness or decency; it was not that it did not exist in Pandemonium, it was simply that it was rarely revealed by the few that possessed it. Luca was tempted to take the offer of her knife and run and not look back. Would Saskia be disappointed in her? she knew that she would not blame her if she took the offer. But the mean one, the incredibly beautiful one, Ayesha, she would look smug, and she would smirk.

'In two days If I do not fulfil my duty, they will come to find me. They will come to my flat and break down the door. They will kill my cat if it's there, I share it or does not have the sense to run away over the rooftops, which I think it would. Can you do what you need to do with me, in under two days?'

'Yes, I can!' Holly replied, more than surprised. 'Are you sure about this Luca? Why would you?'

'Waywardness and curiosity. How do we begin?'

'Like this!' said Holly; she clapped her hands together twice.

Instantly the elemental guardian began to dismantle; the vein like tendons withdrew in sets of two or three. They melded and took on a new form, gathering in the upper left angle of the ceiling and wall around the red mass.

'You are no longer a prisoner,' Holly said.

'Why did you lock me up? Were you scared of me? Three Sorcerers and you a mistress of form.'

'To keep everyone safe. Now it's unnecessary,' Holly replied. She nodded determinedly at Luca and smiled. 'I'm going to photograph you. I'll need images of you in studio lights.'

'Photograph,' Luca repeated; she frowned in thought. 'In the Harper's Bazaar glossy mags, I've read many times: photographs by, then a name. Is this the way you will paint me?'

'No. Photographs are a living record of you, They're Images of light, captured in time like the ones in Harper's Bazaar. They'll help me with my painting of you.'

'These photographs?' Luca frowned again, puzzled. 'They are not drawn, not painted?'

'No, they're images captured in a box, a type of instrument called a camera, on a thing called a memory card.'

'A camera obscura?' Luca was trying to grasp her meaning.

'No, not really, you'll see. I'll show you!'

A thought leapt into Luca's eyes, and she smiled in pleasure.

'Will you make me look like those women in the photographs in Harper's Bazaar?' she said jokingly; she felt nervous, it sounded like magic to her; but she was beginning to feel excitement too.

Holly grinned. She shook her head. 'You transcend them Luca, you put all of them in the shade. You would grace any fashion show.'

Luca grinned back, showing her small teeth and her pointy canines, suddenly she was shy and disarming.

'I'll show you my favourite photograph then.' Luca turned, eager to fetch her magazine. She forgot the bowl in her enthusiasm and kicked it with her foot. She cried out in fear as the bowl rocked and slid across the floor grating on the tiles; Luca's knife too tumbled to the floor and some of the alchemical fluid spilled out and was splashed across the tiles and ended up on Luca's left boot. Alchemical agitation began at once and the chemicals hissed and spat in a vitriolic reaction, sizzling on the floor and Luca's boot like acid. Holly felt a sudden barb of fear, instinct told her to get out, the room had become an incredibly dangerous place. She had a cool head though and she was not inclined to bolt. She acted swiftly. Avoiding the sizzling liquid, she ran at Luca and thrust her backwards into the chair. At first Luca thought she was attacking her, and she prepared to fight, but she watched as Holly tore off her jacket and crouched to wrap it around her boot; the instep had begun to blacken and flicker like burning soot in the back of a chimney. Holly yanked away the boot inside the jacket and flung them both away. Vapour from it streamed into her eyes but she held her breath so as not to draw any into her nose or lungs. Through stinging eyes, she saw that Luca's upper foot had begun to blister. She straightened. She fixed Luca with a frantic look.

'Come! quickly! Watch where you put your feet!' She grabbed Luca's hand. Luca did not hesitate; her foot burned, it hurt, the alchemy piercing the melamic barrier almost instantly; she quickly realised that Holly meant to help her. She recalled the conflict in the garden when she had been wounded; it was Cedile the Spider Scorpion, who had prevented it from being fatal, by countering the toxic iron getting inside her skin and getting into her blood, with her secretion.

'You speak extremely good English,' Holly remarked.

'The common language of the spheres for the last two hundred years. Dravidian, Punic, Latin, English in that order,' Luca responded.

'The first language of Pandemonium is lesser demonic?' Holly said, her eyes were stinging like hell.

'Yes, unchanged, Baalic. I also speak Slavic, Latin, some Punic. No Dravidian. Good, yes? For scum from Pandemonium.'

'You're not scum.'

'Some think we are.'

'Not me. I think that's a misconception anyway.' Holly blinked. She was looking upwards; her head was tilted back; her eyes swam, and she could only see a distorted blur.

'That feels as good as new. Better in fact, will you hand me some of the cotton wool pads.'

'I will do it,' said Luca.

Holly nodded and smiled, acquiescent; she allowed Luca's continued ministration. It had been frantic at first. Holly had acted quickly; she had no idea how badly Luca had been burned by the caustic effect of the alchemical. She was used to occasional minor burns herself in her activities, and she kept a jar of the alchemist's salve, the golden balm, in her laboratory. It was highly effective, even the most terrible burns were treatable. She had made Luca sit upon a high elm stool, with a rectangular shaped top, while she examined her foot through stinging eyes. The lower instep had suffered blistering, but she had removed the boot in time before the *acrimonium* had seared away all the fabric. Anointing with the salve was quick and easy, she had applied it carefully and liberally with her fingers. By then her eyes were watering so badly she was barely able to see anything, and they were stinging like crazy; in a very little time it would feel like she had rubbed them with a raw Scorpion pepper. She had voiced a little murmur of distress; she had got down a liquid salve and a wash from the shelves, but she was unable to see them by then.

'Let me; sit,' Luca said. she had risen to her feet; she guided Holly onto the stool.

Holly breathed deeply in relief as the pain relented and the salve worked its cool magic. She quite enjoyed being tended. Luca's touch had been gentle, considered. She had carefully pushed back the lids; then dripped salve into Holly's eyes, then the wash. Now she drew the little pads of cotton wool over the closed lids. Luca studied the beautiful, upturned face; a wry smile tipped the corners of her mouth. A few hours ago, she had hated this pretty woman; now she no longer hated her; she would have struck at her, frustrated and angry at what she had done to her; now she was tending her and concerned that she was not hurt or in pain; she wanted to please her now; she was fascinated by what she did and who she was. Was this irony, she was unsure; she was from Pandemonium after all. Some of the wash had dripped, trickling down from Holly's eyelids to fall from her jawline; some had trickled onto her collar bone and her upper breast and beneath her camisole; some had splashed the fabric, spreading. One splash had fallen where a pointed nipple pressed through the smooth fabric, defining it more. Luca found it erotic. She wondered if she had used the wash too liberally.

Holly opened her eyes, they felt cool, restored, good. Luca's face came into focus. Holly smiled at her searching gaze.

'Thank you, Luca.'

Luca studied Holly's face; she appeared a little uncertain. 'Your eyes are beautiful,' she said after a few moments hesitation. Holly let the comment hang for a few more moments.

'Are they?' she said at last, uncertain herself. 'How is your burn?'

Luca peered down at her foot, she raised it a little off the floor and extended it. 'Like magic.'

'It is a kind of magic.'

'There's redness. But the blistering is gone so it will not spoil your photographs.'

'Why do you say that? They don't matter!' Holly frowned.

'I thought they were essential.'

'Luca, I'm sorry. I should never have begun this. I should never have imprisoned you!'

'It's not the first time I've been locked up. It was an improvement on the previous times.'

Holly half laughed. 'This was my fault!' she said. 'It was a stupid idea to place the bowl there. I wanted to tempt you.' She looked guilty. 'Maybe even taunt you.'

'A little honest cruelty?'

'Yes; maybe, probably! Do you still want to go through with this?' She gazed earnestly at Luca. Luca nodded firmly.

'I have already earned a flogging; it should be made worthwhile at least,' she remarked drily.

'Fuck!' Holly said, her voice had fallen low with dismay; she both looked and felt, ashamed.

'Don't,' Luca surprised her by cupping the side of her face in a slender hand. 'Take me and show me what you do.'

They heard a repeated clicking sound on the tiled floor, getting closer, and turned to look. A huge red spider emerged slowly from Luca's former prison; it had slender articulated legs with pointed tips, and eight empty now dimmed black eyes; it was the size of an Irish wolfhound. It swayed drunkenly as it walked.

'Your guardian?' Luca regarded the spider with interest. She exhibited no concern; she felt safe with Holly. 'It looks in a bad way.'

'Shit,' Holly breathed. 'I forgot about him in the panic. He'll have absorbed the fumes, and they're toxic even to him.' As she spoke the guardian reared up and collapsed sideways with a rattle of legs and lay still.

'Is it dead?' Luca asked.

'Dormant; I'm afraid he'll take quite a bit of putting right, shit!'

'There are no paintings,' Luca commented as she looked around Holly's neatly maintained studio. In racks against one wall there were stacked canvases on stretchers: portrait and landscape. One size for each; of the scale that Holly favoured. There was a single substantial shelf unit occupied by equipment and paints. An easel and a draughtsman's table,

'You are to be my work in progress. I don't know how I'll phrase you; but I've a few ideas. Perhaps with a ball of wool!' she suggested playfully.

'A ball of wool?' Luca repeated, puzzled.

'I'm joking. Probably in Claire's Garden with your net, but that can come later. I intend to paint you in several different scenarios. Crawling up a bed; bathing; maybe fighting for your life with a huge Fae-wolf,' her voice dropped as she followed the thought intently.

Luca frowned at her in concern, as Holly revealed her inner imagining with her last spoken idea.

'Have you one?' she said worriedly.

Holly smiled indulgently. 'No, it would come from my imagination.'

'You would create a form for me to fight?'

'No, it would stay in my imagination. Call it a fantasy then.'

'It gives you pleasure to fantasize me fighting for my life?' Luca's large yellow eyes widened.

'No. The joy is in the image, of how fierce you would be, how stunning!'

'Will I win?'

'Of course, you will.'

Luca was not finished. She engaged with the moment, and she smiled quite gleefully. 'My flesh ripped to pieces and covered in blood. Would I hold the beasts severed head up in victory?'

'God, what a wonderful image!' Holly laughed appreciatively. Luca continued to smile, as she grew pleased with herself. 'And that is exactly how I'll paint you. Brutal and raw.'

'I want to see your paintings,' Luca said thoughtfully.

'You can. There are some in the house. I'll show you, in a bit. Come on; I'm eager to photograph you. Come on into the studio.'

She led Luca through a door straight ahead of them, into a room where all the brick walls and ceiling and floor had been painted white. There were studio lights like umbrellas on stands and reflectors and an expensive digital camera on a tripod. And on a small folding table next to it an expensive SLR for Holly's black and white photography, which she favoured as an art form, and a hobby about which, in the last couple of years, she had become increasingly enthusiastic.

'I would have liked to photograph you in your chain mail. I found it quite erotic. In the nude will do.'

'You want me naked?' Luca said.

'Are you uncomfortable with that?'

Luca tilted her head to the side. 'Why should I be?'

'This is the camera. This will capture your image.' Holly indicated the digital camera, resting her fingertips on its upper casing. 'The other is a different type of camera which I use for Black and white photography. The finished photos take longer to acquire. The results are more nuanced, it produces more depth and shading. More character. It is more glamorous in my opinion. I'll use both cameras. But I might only be able to show you the images from the digital camera. Are you ready?'

'Now?'

'Yes.'

Unhesitant, Luca stooped, and raised her foot, with an easy, elegant balance. She drew off her remaining boot and tossed it aside. She stood in bare feet, staring down at them, as she loosened her tabard and allowed it to tumble about her nubile body, to the floor. Only then did she look up to meet Holly's gaze; she tilted her head to the side and smiled with just the right amount of hesitance. It was an invitation to look; that was not lost on Holly, but she did not feel inclined to decline it. Her eyes played over Luca's nudity for en entire minute, before they lifted to her beautiful, expectant face.

'You'll do,' she said, deliberately mean. 'Stand in the middle of the floor.' Luca's eyes flashed in disappointment, and she quickly turned her head away, then her body, casting her eyes down.

'There will be strong glare from these studio lights; you'll get used to it. Check the soles of your feet for debris Then I'll tell you what I need from you.' Holly's manner had become efficient and direct; she was suddenly purposeful and business-like; though she realised with a growing intensity just how much she wanted to capture this girl in her Lens.

Luca knew many modern English words and phrases; the meanings of more than a few were a total mystery to her, hence presently she avoided using them; others she understood and related to without any ambiguity whatsoever; one of them sprang to mind right then. She raised her brows and smiled a little private smile, out of Holly's sight, as she did as she was told. She turned round, and watched Holly move with precision adjusting her camera and lights. She blinked, narrowing her eyes against their sudden intensity. Bossy was the word, Luca decided.

Eight

'Good morning, Ayesha; good morning, Saskia,' said Hattie Dillinger, as they ran out of the sudden cloudburst over the city of York and into the shop. She paused as she encountered them, twisting her hands. They burst through the swing doors as she crossed the showroom floor. She regarded them anxiously, with intense grey eyes behind her vintage style, winged spectacles. She looked very cute, Saskia thought as she shook herself down like a terrier; Hattie was in Mary janes and black tights, a black mini skirt to mid-thigh, and a black cardigan over a white blouse, with a big, oval, grey lace Scottish agate brooch, fastened at her throat; nice touch.

'I'll take your jackets; they look wet through' Hattie said, concerned and helpful.

'Remember to smile Hattie!' Amber told her as she came up.

'Yes Amber,' Hattie broke into a nervous death grin.

'And relax Hattie. It's only Ayesha and Saskia.' Amber's eyes widened. 'Hello you two. God you're like drowned rats!'

'I feel like a drowned rat!' Ayesha growled, as she set her bag down at her feet. She peeled off her jacket.

The rain had soaked right through to her dark, blue silk blouse. Her jeans were wringing wet, and her hair was dripping. Hattie avoided her acrimonious eyes as she snatched the sodden garment from Ayesha's hand, receiving a darkly puzzled look in return. Hattie felt like backing away; she preferred as little contact with the Gorgon, her secret name for Ayesha, as possible. She smiled shyly into Saskia's large appraising eyes, as she accepted her dripping blazer.

'It came out of nowhere. Total whiteout!' said Saskia.

'Hattie, will you make Ayesha and Saskia usual black coffees please.'

'Yes Amber.' Hattie whisked gratefully away.

'How have things been?' Ayesha asked.

'Really well. A steady stream of customers both days and a good proportion of buyers. Thank you, by the way.'

'What for?' Ayesha frowned.

'For not phoning us every five minutes; it was appreciated.'

'We had every confidence in you.' Saskia told her.

'Never gave you a thought,' Ayesha lied, deadpan. She had kept the promise, Saskia had extracted from her, to not contact the twins at the shop or at home during their absence. It had not been easy. A cackle of laughter erupted from the right; they glanced in its direction and saw Pearl. She was in the process of polishing glass cabinets, but she paused when she saw their condition to mock. She waved, then got on with her task.

'There's no one in or she wouldn't do it,' Amber said reassuringly. 'It's odd, but yesterday before we closed, I could have sworn we were empty, in the gallery and down here. I'd looked, but Pearl insisted there was someone. Then five minutes later I looked up from cashing up and here was Felix Malek grinning at me from the other side of the counter. And the buzzer that tells you people have come through the door, had not gone off. So, she knew, didn't she?'

'Sounds like it. He has an ability, apparently,' Saskia remarked.

'Does he?' Amber replied, she narrowed her eyes; fascinated.

'What did he want?' Saskia inquired,

'You two.'

'Did he say why?'

'He wanted to buy another picture, but he would only do business with you; preferably together. He was very polite about it; he said it was simply because he wanted to renew your acquaintance.' Amber chuckled knowingly. 'He was quite sweet really. He's coming in again today; I told him that you'd be in by late morning.'

'We'd better go and change, we look a total mess!' Ayesha said looking uneasy. Saskia was not so sure; she thought the drowned look probably rather suited her, and Ayesha looked ravishing. They were nearly at the counter when the buzzer sounded from beneath it, indicating that someone had entered the showroom. Amber glanced back; she smiled.

'Too late,' she said. 'He's here now, maybe he was following you.'

The immaculately dressed mountain that was Felix Malek advanced towards them. He strutted like a Spanish bull, with an easy fluid power, imposing himself on the room. His golden eyes surveyed them as he approached, his expression filled with pleasure. Saskia felt her body stiffen as if for appraisal; she wondered if Ayesha and Amber had reacted in the same fashion.

'What an event!' he exclaimed, 'I have left my umbrella inside the door. Good heavens! Saskia! Ayesha! You were caught in it!'

Saskia was aware of the water pooling at her own and Saskia's stiletto shod feet; also, the trail of dripped and imprinted water across the polished floor, where they had walked. Some instinct made her look at Felix Malek's shoes, and she was not too surprised to see that there was barely a splash on their polished, handmade surfaces; no trail from their treads to the door and no hint of dampness on the legs of his expensive Dormeuil Mohair suit. She accepted the anomaly and lifted a smiling expression of pleasure and welcome to Felix's inquiring eyes.

'Felix! How lovely to see you,' she said, she moved towards him hesitantly because of the condition of her clothing, to greet him as a friend. He stooped to receive her kiss on his closely shaved cheek. She guessed the product of a straight razor and a skilled barber. His hand rested on her arm.

'You're soaked through Saskia.' He turned to accept a similar greeting from Ayesha.

'Hello Felix.'

'Ayesha. You cannot remain like this,' he told her.

'If you don't mind Felix, we'll go and change into some dry clothing.'

'Of course, I'm in no hurry!'

'If only we'd known,' Saskia remarked to Felix over her shoulder as she walked towards the stairs with Ayesha, 'we would have brought our umbrellas.'

'Who could have predicted a cloudburst!' Felix called after her and grinned.

Hattie arrived at that moment with two black coffees on a tray. Her eyes widened with anxiety as they fell on Felix Malek.

'Ah! Hattie how nice,' Felix said pleasantly, 'black coffee how did you know?'

'Go on ahead, I'll be five minutes,' Ayesha said pausing the hairdryer, she sat on the edge of the bed in just panties. Saskia was in jeans a white shirt and a black cashmere sleeveless top; her French bob was still wet; she had combed it back.

'Okay I'll see you out there. Fingers crossed it's the Duncan Grant or the Beardsley.' She peered at Ayesha, thinking she looked preoccupied.

'Are you okay?' she said.

'I'm alright little mantis. Just a bit strung out.'

'I know. I'm stressed too you know.'

'You must be, and I stress you, I know that' Ayesha admitted.

'We're stressing each other presently. It's solvable.'

Saskia closed the black door of the flat, her hand on the chrome handle behind her, shutting off the noise of the hairdryer. She looked out across the gallery. Sunlight shone between the long vertical blinds in the two tall windows, the freak rain only a memory. A young affluent looking couple were staring at a little sketch by Edna Clarke Hall, which hung on the gallery wall to the left. They were intent and probably only needed a nudge. She saw Felix and Amber on the other side of the gallery, at the far end; Amber was dwarfed by Felix's huge frame; she was stretching, her red mini skirt riding up as she reached, intending to take down the Duncan Grant. Saskia was not a fan of the artist. She saw them look in her direction as though suddenly aware of her eyes on them; Amber paused in her action, relaxing back into her stance; she gazed expectantly at Saskia. Saskia signed to Amber that she would take over by pointing to herself and then Amber, she smiled and then indicated the young couple. Amber nodded, comprehending; she smiled back, and excused herself to Felix and walked along the isle towards her. She rolled her eyes at her as they passed. 'Mister Malek would like the Duncan Grant, Saskia, he has selected two other pictures from the walls in the showroom; they are at the counter downstairs,' she announced. Saskia could tell she was bubbling and very pleased with herself.

'Felix, thank you for that, I'm so much more comfortable,' Saskia said. She squeezed her face into a friendly conspiratorial smile as she came up to him, she deliberately stood closer than her preferred distance, creating intimacy. 'You are spending a fortune with us.' She had to tilt her head back to look up at him.

'It's only money Saskia, look at what I'm getting in return.'

'You should let us discount.'

'No, I insist that you don't.' He said firmly, frowning and smiling simultaneously.

She shrugged. 'If you say so.'

'I don't need to be encouraged to buy.' Felix bowed his head slightly forwards, then tilted it from side to side; he looked around the studio, exhibiting interest.

'I had it from Holly that you inherited a large collection of art; is all of that on display here?'

'I've retained about twenty-five percent as a long-term investment. On advice from Holly and Ayesha. Also, the works I liked, and those Ayesha liked; we live with it after all.'

'You are together of course in life,' he said. 'As well as business partners.'

'We are a same sex couple, yes.'

'I sense a powerful bond between you; it runs very deep. I am not just saying that.'

'I know you aren't. Theo Bacchus said pretty much the same thing.'

'Ah yes, you know Theo. We are on friendly terms he and I. Holly said that he unfettered you.' Holly appeared to have told Felix Malek quite a bit about her. Not that she was bothered.

'I owe him. It was dreadful though.' She searched his face; she wondered if it represented his true appearance, or if it concealed a more diabolical image, which was less acceptable to the ordinary world. 'I know what you are Felix!' It just came out. She surprised herself when she said it. She went silent; he eyed her with curiosity, amused.

'Does that knowledge disturb you?'

She shook her head. 'Nothing disturbs me. I don't think anything can. I see you as a friend Felix, as well as a client.'

'In that case, I expect first refusal when you do eventually decide to sell any of your other paintings,' he said.

'Done! Will you let us take you out to dinner, as a friend and a client?' It was spur of the moment.

'No. I dine at my apartment or at Bezants restaurant which I own, in Knightsbridge; but I rarely eat outside my main home, unless I get invited to a party of course.'

Saskia felt disappointed; she had been convinced that Felix would accept her invitation.

'I want to get to know you better,' she explained, 'I think I speak for Ayesha too.'

Felix considered her intently; he found her eyes and searched their green depths. He was cautious, but the wolves were lazily watchful.

'Come to dinner with me then,' he suggested, 'I have an excellent chef. Come to Baal House.'

Saskia grinned, thinking it could not have worked out any better. 'I like the sound of that. Baal House!'

'Is Friday evening too soon?'

'No, yes! After the weekend, it's Ayesha's birthday on Monday, can it be then?'

'Will Ayesha agree to that?' he asked.

'She must...I mean I think she will.'

'And if she doesn't?'

'I'll cross that bridge if I come to it.'

'Here comes Ayesha, you could ask if she is agreeable now.'

Saskia shook her head. 'I'll speak with her later.'

'As you wish.'

Saskia turned about and saw Ayesha coming towards them from the direction of the flat; she paused to allow the young, affluent looking couple to pass in front of her, and descend the stairs with Amber, who was carrying the Edna Clarke Hall sketch.

'Is it hard to find?'

'It's near Blackfleet, by the Humber,' Felix told her.

'I don't know where that is.'

'I'll email you directions and a map. I have your email address, curtesy of Pearl. A clever young woman, she told me that she is currently designing you a website.'

'Is she? I didn't know.' Saskia sounded distracted. Felix peered at her thoughtfully; again amused.

Ayesha was wearing tight grey jeans and a roped, vee neck, burgundy jumper, which showed an occasional hint of toned navel. She put her head engagingly on one side and gave Felix her most enchanting smile. As she came up to them Saskia turned away to take down the Duncan Grant. She smiled to herself; she had seized the day; she was pleased with herself. The rest would be cold reason, and maybe a few fireworks.

Nine

'Alright, what have I done? You've simmered all the way home! Is it because I wore this top?' Ayesha's outburst came as she drove them down Culverin Road on their way back to the Leeds apartment. It jolted Saskia out of her stream of thought and made her twist in her seat and stare at Ayesha with a startled expression; she had thought she was letting her get on with it as she often did; enjoying a conversation free zone for a while. Ayesha glanced at her, then back to the road, then back again; four glances in all; that was a lot; her expression was anxious and resentful, quite intense; her mouth was set, and her dark eyes burned.

'I haven't simmered at all!' Saskia protested. 'I've been thinking.'

'I've picked up a vibe from you the entire journey! Don't deny it!'

'You misread it! I'm just distracted!'

'I don't know if I believe you, Saskia, you can be very secretive!'

'I'm not vibing you. I'm not simmering at you. I chose that top for you anyway. It's casual and cute. It's nice to see your taut midriff on display!'

Ayesha sighed. 'You're right! It is inappropriate wear for the shop, I should never have worn it in front of Felix! But you don't have to give me a hard time about it.'

'You have got other things you could have worn I suppose,' Saskia mused. 'But I don't blame you; he turns you on. He rattled you again. It's what he does.'

'You seemed resistant; you were quite chilled in fact.'

'I suppose I was. I could feel him moving around me, but I was busy thinking about other stuff! he just turned into background. I didn't think he'd stay most of the afternoon.'

'Well, if I haven't pissed you off, why are you distracted. What's on your mind?' Ayesha demanded.

'Usual stuff.' It was a throwaway response. Ninety-nine times out of a hundred, Ayesha would have regarded it with indifference. This time it sounded different; it resonated with implication. It gained her attention.

Ayesha switched off the engine. They had stopped in the underground carpark beneath their building, next to Saskia's jeep. Ayesha turned to Saskia, but she had already swung her legs out of the vehicle. Ayesha clicked her tongue softly and got out too. The sound of their doors closing reverberated, emphasized. It was a clinical space with a resin floor; as carparks went, it was upmarket. The car flashed and sounded loudly in the under space as Ayesha engaged the lock. Saskia was already walking to toward the lift. Ayesha caught her and fell into step.

'That's no answer.'

'No, it isn't.'

'You're ever so slightly worrying me. I want to know what's on your mind.'

'Can we eat first,' Saskia begged.

'It's obviously important to you.'

The lift ended its ascent, and the door opened into the lobby of Ayesha's penthouse apartment. Ayesha key carded the door, and they went inside. She rounded on Saskia looking fierce and pale. Saskia eyed her worriedly.

'Am I at fault?' Ayesha demanded.

'No. It's on me Ayesha. Eat, then talk; please.'

'Not until you explain,' she said determinedly. 'I want to know what's going on in that head. We're not moving from this spot until you do.'

Saskia gave an exasperated look. It was not how she had planned this moment. She had wanted them to work their way through a bottle of wine before she revealed what she had to say. Trust Ayesha to home in like hawk. Sod it! She folded her arms and looked Ayesha in the eyes.

'Very well!' she said with a touch of challenge in her voice. 'If you insist! I want us to have sex with Felix Malek.'

There, it was said! it was out of the box; at large on their personal stage; it could not be put away again. Saskia felt her heartrate elevate, but she was determined to keep her cool. She looked at Ayesha with a promise of defiance; her pupils expanded. She swallowed and moistened her lips. Ayesha had not responded; she regarded her, presently, without expression.

'I mean that I want us to undertake Radical Aphrodisia. Demonic sex magic! Bad timing, I know,' She followed up; she scanned Ayesha's face. Aware of her dark eyes as they undertook a search of her face. Saskia could see the thoughts processing behind them. She expected them to harden into hostility at any moment, but she was prepared to fight her corner all night if she had to; and ultimately accept the consequences; because she had decided to go it alone if she had to. She prepared for the hammer to fall, anticipating coolly sardonic, or dependant on mood, angrily scathing.

'Okay. I think that we should too,' Ayesha replied.

Night fell over Leeds; watched by Saskia and Ayesha as they ate Pizza and drank Chardonnay. They sat in front of the vast living room window. The Leeds lights limned the canal and river and sprawled out over the city's infrastructure, compensation for the lack of visible stars in the night sky. A partial moon exposed striated broken cloud. it would be full in time for Ayesha's birthday, Saskia realized, with satisfaction.

'One of the benefits of Mocking beck is the number of stars you can see,' She remarked, 'They're up there somewhere.'

'Cities and starry skies aren't compatible,' Ayesha responded. She was perched on the Barcelona, knees drawn up in front of her, her bare toes peeping over the edge. She nibbled on a crust of pizza held delicately between the fingers of both hands. The room was in virtual darkness, a couple of LED displays glowed, the phone and the DVD player, and the concealed lighting in the kitchen softly illuminated the inner doorway. Light pollution and a hint of moonlight filtered in through the window glass, diluting the dark.

Ayesha's eyes looked as if they were set in large dark hollows in the shadow paleness of her face. She looked wraith like, grave, like a little mouse nibbling on a stale crust, Saskia thought. Her dark hair spilled over her hunched shoulders; Saskia recalled how wet it had got in the downpour in the morning; she had looked like something dredged up from a lake, and here was its ghost sitting opposite her. She felt sorry for her; she had done this to her, Saskia destroyer of worlds, kicker of castles built on sand. She felt a bit guilty, but it was only a bit.

Ayesha gave a little huddled shiver. It was cool in the room but hardly cold; there were occasions when it had need to be though. Saskia got to her feet from her cushion on the floor and fetched a knitted throw from where it was folded on the couch. She draped it around Ayesha's shoulders; Ayesha lifted her face giving a little grateful smile; she looked forlorn in the almost darkness, her features jutting up at her. Instinctively Saskia kissed her on the tip of her nose, it proved to be quite cold.

'Are you okay?' she inquired.

'Yes. I'm fine, I was simply thinking about what I'm letting myself in for. Don't worry, I'm not thinking of backing out. Will you pass me my wine little mantis?' she peered at the Pizza crust, suddenly not knowing what to do with it. Saskia took it from between her fingers; she discarded it with their other crusts on a plate on the low glass table a little way from the chair. Ayesha's wine glass had been placed there, next to a part empty bottle of wine. Saskia topped up Ayesha's glass and passed it to her. She was in her white shirt and her jeans, barefoot like Ayesha; the shirt was loose, fastened by a couple of lower buttons; it revealed her firm neat breasts as she leaned over; Ayesha's eyes followed them, watching them almost curiously, though she wanted very much to reach out and caress a nipple with her fingertips. Saskia went to curl in the womb chair, she scooped up her wine glass from the floor by the window as she passed it; she stared at Ayesha; her lips curled in a sensual, half sardonic smile, that told Ayesha that she had been aware of her interest; she had done the same to her that first day they had met in Claire's office. Her shirt had fallen away from one shoulder almost revealing one of her breasts. She studied Ayesha's face, but she had hooded her eyes, and she was being hard to read.

'I thought you would just blow me out of the water!' Saskia said.

'And we would fight all night, and you would threaten to go it alone. And you would, despite anything I said,' Ayesha replied with certainty. 'I knew at Holly's, when she told us about Felix. I saw your thoughts.'

'So, you can read minds,' Saskia grinned.

'Saskia it was fucking obvious. They were my thoughts too!'

'And all those things she said about magic, they resonate with you too? Saskia asked. 'I just need to know that I'm not forcing you into this.'

'Saskia! look at me, I've got silver thorns inside me that are state of the art! I simply lost my way and got too cosy! If it hadn't been you, it would have been someone or something else that kick started me. When I spoke with Claire, I told her how much you wanted to advance. And she asked me how I felt about that and what I would do. I said that I'd do whatever it takes. She's perceptive and she knows me well, I just didn't think quite that well.' Ayesha's tone became derisive, contempt flashed in her eyes. 'She saw through me straight away. She made me confront my darker, selfish side!'

'I don't know what you mean.' Saskia gave a bewildered frown.

'I'm not scared of being left behind by you or that I would lose you, if that's what you think. There's a different dynamic at play; and I didn't want to admit it; God knows why, me being me. It was Claire that made me admit the truth. And it freaked me out for a bit, and it still does. You see, I'm not being dragged kicking and screaming to some place I don't want to go. It's plain old rivalry I'm feeling. The simple truth that I really need you to know, is that I do not intend to be outshone by you Saskia.'

'Bloody hell Ayesha!' Saskia's eyes became lambent as understanding dawned, Ayesha could see them glowing in the semi-darkness, with that wolf eye glow. Saskia sat forward in the womb chair and laughed with pure delight.

'Please don't make fun of me Saskia,' Ayesha said coldly.

'You can't tolerate me being more powerful than you! You're jealous! Brilliant! God, I love you to bits! That is so cool!'

'So, I'm cool, am I? envious resentful Ayesha, determined not to allow the love of her life to become more powerful than she is.' She raised her voice and too sat forward in her chair. 'If you want the thunderbolt Saskia, then so do I!' she exclaimed, her voice pitched angrily.

'I don't think you know how cool you are. And how much in awe of you I am. You are magic Ayesha! When Holly Penn described magic to us, what she described was you, word for word!' she paused, tears filled her eyes. 'You just said that I am the love of your life.'

'You are, I thought you knew. There'll never be another!'

Saskia felt overjoyed. She knuckled tears.

'And anyway, what if he rejects us?' Ayesha said.

'How likely is that?'

'He might.'

'Ayesha, I know this sounds vain, but I do know that I'm seriously hot. You my darling are even more seriously hot. He's a sex demon; he's not going to turn us down! Anyway, we'll know for sure on your birthday!'

'Why on my birthday?' Ayesha looked puzzled.

'Because that's when we've been invited to dine with him at Baal House,' Saskia announced.

'Baal House. On my birthday. You have been busy, haven't you?'

'He invited us,' Saskia responded blankly.

Ayesha narrowed her eyes suspiciously. 'I dunno so much, you're conniving.'

'Does it matter. You said you'd fuck a demon if you wanted to. Now you can, on your birthday, with serious benefits, and I get to watch.' She drew a sharp breath of surprise as she voiced the thought. Her next words were spoken with dark glee. 'I never thought I would hear myself say that.'

'Saskia,' Ayesha responded, 'you really are fucking odd.'

Ten

'Do you approve?'

Holly eased her shoulders, lifting them and rotating them; she heard a joint click in her neck. She asked the question as she laid aside her sketch pad. Luca was absorbed, but she heard and responded without looking up.

'You don't need my approval.'

She was looking at the digital images that Holly had taken of her. Holly had loaded them onto her laptop; Luca had quickly picked up the basics of scrolling through them. Holly had taken Luca into the house; she sat on the couch with Holly's laptop perched on her knees. They had spent most of the afternoon in the studio. Holly had been demanding of Luca, but she was feeling strain herself; she had quickly abandoned the tripod and wielded both cameras free hand. She was feeling back niggles and tightness through her shoulders. Luca's lithe small body was athletic and supple, like a gymnast and she had shown off. It had amounted to theatre; it had only lacked music; though maybe the silence proved more effective, more sensational even. It had become mesmeric, a silent drama that she was sure Luca was enacting for her. They had talked and laughed at first, but the conversation had gradually become visual, the language Luca's body, her words its elegant shaping, Holly's responses the click and shutter sound as she took the shot.

'I think that we should eat and then you need to decide.'

'Decide what?' Luca said.

'If you want to return to Pandemonium tonight or in the morning.'

'I thought you needed to capture the essence of Luca.' Luca raised her head, her attention forced from the images on the laptop. Her brows indented. She looked surprised, disappointed, then she seemed to look put out, but only briefly.

Holly leaned forward in her chair. 'I think I've done that,' she said. 'I've got under your skin so to speak. The sketches I've made of you are enough. The couple I've made of you while you looked at the images were indulgence on my part.'

'Indulgence?'

'Don't worry about it. Let's eat and then I'll go and reclaim your knife and clean off any residue; it seems pretty resilient.'

Luca shrugged. 'If that's what you want,' she said quietly and maybe a little offhand, Holly thought. 'Can I look at your drawings?'

Holly regarded her thoughtfully and handed her the sketch pad. Luca put aside the laptop and accepted them from her. Holly watched as Luca's head bent over them, and her slim fingers turned the pages with unconscious elegance.

'They are beautiful.' Luca raised her large yellow eyes to regard her solemnly. 'I'll go now if you want me to.'

'It's not what I want. It's your decision,' Holly told her. 'I don't want you punished on my account.'

'I can't avoid that now.'

'Now I feel guilty,' Holly said with remorse.

'I should go. I think you'd prefer that?'

'What do you mean I'd prefer?' Holly responded a little irritably. She became intense. 'What I'd prefer is to eat with you and talk and laugh and drink wine with you, for fucks sake.'

Luca regarded her impassively. 'Now you're angry with me?' she said, laying the sketch pad aside.

'Angry with you, of course not. I'm angry with myself for doing this to you.'

'Don't be. You're going to paint me; and you've taken my images, like in the magazines. There'll always be something for me to be remembered by,'

Holly stared at Luca long and hard. She could not decide if she was being perfectly genuine; she was not sure that she actually cared one way or the other. She stood and reached out a hand for Luca's. 'Come with me and I'll put us a meal together while we talk. There, I've decided; you're not going anywhere tonight, Luca.'

'Your Manor is big for just you; you don't have any retainers, or servants,' Luca commented curiously. She raised her wine glass cautiously; she was more familiar with a rummer or a chalice. She had never tasted chardonnay.

'No. I've no need of any. I'm content pottering around it on my own. I like company though. I have a cleaner, Saskia and Ayesha visit. Is that what you were, a retainer?'

Luca drank; tasted and swallowed. She gave a little frown a little thoughtful sideways tilt of her head.

'Good?'

'Yes good. I like spirit too. To reply to your question, I am a henchman.' Luca chuckled softly.

'What does that entail?' Holly said, intrigued.

'I do what needs to be done. What Satran Saradina requires of me. Pretty much anything.'

'So have you killed for her?' Holly was intrigued.

'Often. Robbed for her; beaten for her; warmed her bed occasionally. She's a cruel mistress.'

'Is everyone cruel, in Pandemonium? You don't seem to be cruel by nature Luca, so there must be others.'

'I am sometimes,' Luca replied thoughtfully. 'We do what we must to survive. Most people in Pandemonium are capable of cruelty. Some are addicted to it; others are cruel out of necessity. Isn't it the same here in Kadman?'

'Yes, it is but here we punish cruelty if we can,' Holly said. 'You mentioned that you have a cat. Do you love it?'

'We get along.'

'Aren't you worried about it?'

'No, it has other homes,' Luca shrugged, amused.

'Do many people keep other pets, besides cats?'

'Hounds, Rats, other things.' Luca chuckled. 'People.'

Holly wondered if she was joking and decided that she probably was not. 'If you're a henchman, why do you serve on the watch?'

'We all serve on Saradina's watch, there are no exceptions. Saradina lives in a fortified palace.'

'So, it's obviously taken very seriously.'

'Saradina has enemies. Taking watch is a serious business. So, when someone doesn't turn up for duty...'

'I'm sorry about that.' Holly said glumly.

'I'll live.'

'You're indentured to Saradina. For how long?'

'Questions!' Luca said in mock irritability. She smiled and shook her head.

'I'm sure you have enough of your own,' Holly countered. 'For how long?'

'Probably life! I'll never be able to afford to buy my independence. So, I take my wage, meagre though it is.'

'How much would it cost?' Holly inquired.

'For me, my weight in pure gold. To purchase me from her much more. I'm valuable, though I lost value when I failed to acquire Saskia and lost the net, which I'm still in debt for.' She shrugged and pulled a face.

'That wasn't your fault surely,' Holly protested.

'What does that matter?'

'Do you have anyone in Pandemonium. Anyone close? Parents?' Holly asked.

'I'm halfling; demonic; My mother gave me up to Saradina. I have two sisters. The knife came down my father's line, to me; I'm the eldest. He died in a street fight.'

'Are you close to them, your sisters? do you see much of them?'

'I see them, as much as I need to. We aren't close. They are indentured to Saradina too.'

'Do you have a friend? A lover?'

'I've had many sex partners. Some I wanted, others I didn't want,' Her face hardened. 'Never anyone special. I don't want to talk about Pandemonium anymore,'

'That's okay I understand. It's nearly time to eat.' Holly finished chopping and bowled up the Kachumber salad. She began to dish up reheated lamb Dansak from the previous evening. Luca eyed it fondly; she could hear her stomach giving little growls.

'I don't expect you to eat the salad; you never ate the fresh salad I prepared for your meals.'

Luca shrugged. 'You never gave me fresh meat,' she remarked.

'I never thought!' Holly registered dismay. Luca narrowed her eyes; she peered hard and searchingly at Holly, unconvinced. A slow smile spread over Holly's face.

'You're not a cat,' she said. 'I'll carry these; you bring the glasses and wine.'

They sat together on the couch in front of a moody fire. They consumed their meal and wine, and Holly fetched another bottle. They talked until late, and Luca relented and told Holly some dark little humorous tales of Pandemonium. But she became more muted eventually and subdued. Eventually she lapsed into silence, her hands clasped between her knees and smiled forlornly at Holly. On impulse Holly bent toward her and kissed her on the mouth, surprising them both. It was quite a sustained kiss, and it worked for them. When they eventually ended it by an unexpressed mutual consent, it was Luca who spoke.

'If you put your tongue in my mouth, be careful, my upper canines are very sharp,' she cautioned.

'I've seen,' Holly grinned 'It was wrong of me to kiss you, I took advantage,' Holly said, suddenly shamefaced. 'I want sex, but we can't.'

Luca pulled a wry face. 'Then we won't.' She held Holly's gaze; it was difficult to decide if she was disappointed that she had not been more insistent.

'I should go to my bed,' Luca said.

'You're not sleeping out there tonight. I'm ashamed of myself for keeping you out there. It's not safe to anyway, the atmosphere will still be toxic.' Though she was not certain about that. 'You're sleeping in the house tonight in a comfortable bed.'

'I was comfortable,' Luca assured her. 'You made up a nice little cot for me. It's like my own in my flat.'

'How come you have a flat, why don't you lodge at Saradina's fortress?'

'Independence. Less chance of being raped,' Luca was matter of fact. Holly's eyes widened in dismay. 'My status gives me the right,' Luca continued. 'I told you I take a meagre wage. It all adds to my debt.'

'That is grossly unfair.'

'I received an education. Training,' Luca reasoned. 'And there's always hope of possibilities.'

'What sort of possibilities?'

'War foremost. We get to keep our plunder. I could buy myself out of service if I got lucky. Others have.'

'How old are you Luca?'

'I am twenty-six. The years of Pandemonium and Kadman are not dissimilar. How old are you?'

'I'm twenty-eight.' Holly smiled somewhat despondently. 'I know that we'll probably never meet again after tomorrow morning, but you must know that you have a friend in Kadman, in me. I hope that I have a friend in Pandemonium.'

Holly awoke and became instantly alert. She sensed another presence in the room. It could only be Luca; nothing else could have entered the house or grounds. It would have resulted in an encounter with her guardian. Then she recalled her guardian was presently out of commission. She readied elemental intent; Luca was physically strong; she was resistant to energised intent; she had witnessed that; against elemental intent though, she would have no chance. Holly did not sense menace, but it was possible to conceal it. She listened to the barely audible tread; it was Luca's normal footfall. She was not trying to creep. Had she been, the realist in Holly realised that she would not have heard her, but it was not sound that had wakened her anyway. She listened to the movement, then it stopped. She could hear Luca's breathing. She followed its slightly quickened rate, knowing it indicated stress.

'I know you're awake Holly,' Luca said softly from close by. 'I promise I'm not here to attempt to murder you. I couldn't sleep.'

'What do you want Luca?' Holly reached and turned on the bed side lamp. Luca had knelt on the floor next to the bed, she was nude; she had not bothered with her tabard; Holly peered at her intently; she focused on her large eyes, they were worried and as always sad; filled with thoughts.

'I was angry with you at first you know, and I hated you,' Luca began. 'Saskia told me that you were nice, but I didn't believe her. Today was to be a torment, not a delight. I am distraught because I don't want to leave you.' Two tears spilled from her eyes and coursed down her cheeks; she looked utterly forlorn. She continued bitterly. 'But I know that you will tell me that I must go back to Pandemonium. And I know that I must. I have come to say goodbye. I wanted to thank you for showing me myself in the photographs before I left.'

'You want to go now you mean? Why?'

'I know that I'll never see you again. Better if I go now. Please let me go.'

'What about your knife? It needs to be cleaned.' Holly said, she thought it sounded lame. She sat upright; she turned towards Luca, scrambling with her pillows.

'I don't care about my knife!'

'That doesn't make sense, its valuable to you. Stay until morning Luca; we'll talk for the rest of the night if you want to.'

'I must go, or I'll break.'

'Are you saying that you want to be with me?' Holly frowned. She peered intensely into the face of this strange girl. There seemed to be no guile, no deviousness, just twisting emotion, which was unable to find solace. She had laid Luca bare she knew that; the day had been intense, searching, for them both, and if she was hiding anything, Holly was uncertain if she cared.

'You know I wouldn't care if I never saw Pandemonium again, but I must go back. I can't be with you, because eventually I'm sure they'd come for me; they would take me, and they would hurt you.' Luca looked down, tears dripping. Her shoulders began to shake. Holly scrambled out of the bed and knelt next to her; she put her arms around her and shushed her. Luca returned her embrace and clung to her.

'That would be the day!' Holly said.

'What do you mean,' Luca mumbled, her face buried in Holly's bed-tee.

'I mean that they are welcome to try.'

'Life is strange,' Luca said. 'Who could have guessed that I would become enamoured of my jailer?'

They had got into Holly's bed, they lay talking. Holly enjoyed the pressure of Luca's warm slender body pressed against her; she stroked the fur of Luca's arms and shoulders with her fingertips. More cautious on the smooth, toned, naked skin of her abdomen and firm breasts, though she was uncertain why. The tips of Luca's small breasts had hardened. She was warm, her scent musky. She was on her side, her hand and elbow supporting her head, looking down at Holly.

'When did you know?' Holly asked curiously.

'When you were blinded.'

'You felt protective,' Holly smiled sardonically.

'You don't believe me do you,' Luca laughed. 'I wanted your mouth then. It surprised me. Will you beat me if I am disobedient?'

'That's a strange question. Are you likely to be disobedient?'

'Occasionally. Or I might get drunk.'

'I hope not. I don't own you though.'

'Yes, you do.' Luca smiled coyly; a little shyly. She pressed her fingers to her heart. 'Maybe in here. I'll find a suitable strap.'

Holly shook her head; it was pointless arguing. Besides she might enjoy it. Luca bent forward and kissed her tenderly on her eyebrows and then her nose. She cradled the side of her face with her right hand and kissed Holly on the mouth, a warm, dry, pliant kiss. Holly shifted sensually as sexual need acquired her. Luca sensed her desire and moved her mouth down over her throat and breasts. She smiled as Holly's breath quickened and she could hear the beating of her heart. She lifted Holly, easily with her strength, knowing she had to be careful of it; she eased her garment upwards, hands on her sides. Holly raised her arms above her head wanting nakedness. She chuckled as the garment was taken from her. She whispered soft obscenities to Luca as she experienced the unguardedness of desire. Luca pushed her down against the bed again; she eased her lithe body between her legs.

'Pretty rune bees!' She glided her tongue across Holly's tattooed skin; she pressed its moist tip into her navel. 'Do they make sweet honey?'

'You'd raid their hive.'

'I intend to raid your hive! Hand me a pillow.'

Holly gurgled with laughter, she seized a pillow from behind her and passed it to Luca, striking her playfully with it.

'Play rough?' Luca responded.

'Not this time.' She raised her hips to accommodate the pillow. 'Get on with it! fuck that's good! Thank God it isn't raspy.'

'It's because I'm not a cat.'

In the morning Luca woke to find Holly absent from the bed. Frowning she sat up and draped her slim arms around her slim knees. She sniffed the air, scenting bacon wafting up from below. She smiled, looking pleased with herself and slipped out of bed; padding on bare feet, she went down to the kitchen. Holly was making bacon, eggs, and beans, dressed in just a denim shirt; her hair was wet. She turned as her sharp ears caught Luca's almost silent tread. She smiled charmingly, her eyes enjoying her lovers nakedness. 'Look on the table,' she said.

'My knife!' Luca grabbed the weapon from the centre of the table. She examined it eagerly.

'I was up at six, cleaning the alchemical residue from it; the incendiary didn't harm it at all. I made the portal room safe to go into again,' Holly told her. 'You were still asleep, so I showered in the bathroom afterwards.'

'Did you destroy the portal?' Luca inquired.

'Not yet. It's not a quick fix,' Holly replied. 'I'll get round to it. It's locked I promise, and its dormant. It needs intent to restart it. I suggest you put that knife away in a drawer and we'll find you something to cover the blade, after breakfast. There're a couple of old knives in the greenhouse with leather sheaths; one of those might fit. Are you putting some clothes on, or eating like that?'

Book Two

One

Ariadne Leech glanced at the time. It was seventeen minutes past seven and her visitor was late; by over an hour, though time in this instance was not exactly a reliable factor. She continued to do what she had been engaged in for the last couple of hours; to some it might have seemed a boring, unrewarding activity; to Ariadne it was enthralling. She was looking at a map through a large domed magnifying glass which she slid around on its surface with thick, stubby, badly cared for fingers. It was an old map, on pressed paper, the kind old documents like wills and mortgages and deeds were handwritten on. The map had been hand drawn in brown iron gall ink. It had brown patches on its surface, foxing they called it.

The map was not in one piece; it was in several numbered, folded sections. Number one was from the top left corner of the map. It was dated too: 1803, and signed Philip Challoner, lieutenant. R.N. in a beautifully scripted hand. She had researched lieutenant Challoner; he had not survived Trafalgar. She had laid the map out on a large antique mahogany dining table, which stood on eight legs, on brass castors. She had bought it at a Cardray Adams auction for the specific purpose of looking at the map, which she regularly did, to the point of obsession. She knew every inch of the map, every detail, though there were four missing sections, and these were a source of incredible frustration. Ariadne was not a fan of antique maps; only this one interested her. She had paid a high sum for it; she considered it worth every penny. She had not even originally been looking for a map per se; her requirements had been non-specific. It was location that inspired her. She had commissioned several finders to hunt down anything they could about the locality; requesting that they draw as little attention as possible. Eventually Rachel Zimpara had found the map, in the possession of an elderly male magician, who farmed hardy sheep breeds as a life interest, deep in the Yorkshire dales. The map had a title under the date and signature; again, in a beautifully scripted hand, and it was underlined. Its title was the nAill, and in brackets: The Wild.

'Ariadne.' Someone tapped on her study door and spoke her name in a subdued male voice. 'Our visitor's arrived.'

'About time,' Ariadne yapped. Ariadne drank some cold black coffee from a porcelain mug; she had stood on her desk. She had stopped having coffee on the table when she had almost knocked a mug over, splashing a section of map. The resulting stain was a permanent irritant. She clutched a gnarled stick from the desktop; her very special stick; she could smell the strong coffee on her protruding lips, as she planted a kiss on the grinning half beast half man head that crowned it; a habitual act she performed before picking it up or setting it down. She pushed her bare, red skinned feet, into single strap flat, slip on shoes; she was wearing a dress, in a dusty pink; it was knee length and too tight; she was full figured, but her shape was solid rather than voluptuous. She pushed back her straight white hair and left her study heading downstairs, to greet their visitor, in the circle.

The Cult of the Wild Hunt as Ariadne preferred to call her Order, occupied an old, brick-built church boarding school, standing amidst half a dozen trees on the edge of the town; it had subsequently become an approved school; it had been built in the late eighteen hundreds, and was considered spooky by any resident of the town with an opinion. Ariadne had bought it as an almost derelict, boarded up building from the local authority at auction, in competition with builders who wanted to convert it into flats, and had restored it to its original state.

She had crafted her witch's door in the old meal hall where it was said that men of the church practised corporal punishment on their juvenile charges for various misdemeanours. She had protected the door with a two-fold elemental circle. This was presently occupied; by a tall, outlandish figure, which looked very eldritch in the light of a dozen candles, the big room's only source of illumination; the big, panelled shutters at the tall windows were closed and bolted, and no hint of light pierced them. The figure was dressed in a long leather coat or habit with a pointed hood, and splits down the sides for its arms. It's face looked like a particularly hideous plague mask. The figure was standing next to a metal cage, about two feet square, with a ring handle; it was covered in a grey blanket; the carrying ring had been pushed through a hole, made in it. Distressed mewling noises came from under the blanket. Large, round, black eyes observed Ariadne as she entered the room.

'Good evening Panqual. You're late,' Ariadne said, displeased.

'I had to catch this creature. It took longer than I thought,' Panqual replied, in a feminine voice that should have belonged to a beautiful seductress. A clawed hand emerged from her coat and indicated the cage.

'Her cat? Not trying to win friends, are we?' said Ariadne. She had bizarrely mad eyes, but even they were capable of contempt.

'She needs to be taught respect,' Panqual stated.

'Have you brought a message for me?'

'Indeed, I have,' Panqual said, enthusiastically. 'The Satran, Saradina, sends her greetings and her friendship. She is delighted to have found a new, powerful ally, and possibly a friend in the world of Kadman. One with a more realistic attitude than most and with fewer scruples. I think she is very pleased.' Panqual nodded ponderously and folded her hands in front of her, to emphasise the point.

Ariadne narrowed her eyes; she was rarely duped; she could read a lie and a liar, at a hundred paces, though she was capable of allowing personal jealousy to corrupt her perceptions; then she would defend her own mistruth, tooth and nail. She nodded in satisfaction, there was no point in Panqual being insincere, what was to be gained from it. 'When will I get to meet her?'

'Perhaps we can arrange for a moot, in just a few days; after this has played out,' said Panqual, full of hope.

'Okay. I like the sound of that. Fate certainly lent a hand when our paths crossed.' Ariadne nodded, decisively. Then her big cow eyes became black with meaning. 'Remember this; cross me at your fucking peril,' she said. She pointed her stick at Panqual and extended it beyond the two concentric circles, which denied the demonic access beyond them. 'Touch the stick. No need to grip. Cross over the circle, but do not lose contact with the stick.' Panqual hesitated, still considering Ariadne's warning. Cautiously she extended her clawed, incredibly long fingered left hand; she rested it on the levelled stick and stepped over the boundary. She towered over Ariadne's squat figure, peering down, perhaps expecting to see some trace of intimidation in her big, mad, mocking eyes. If she did, she was disappointed. Grudgingly, Panqual stepped away, creating space.

'Goat,' Ariadne spoke over her shoulder.

'I'm here,' a nasal voice replied. A small wiry man stepped forward; he was carrying a small black leather case; he had maintained a cautious distance; remaining silently in the shadows, where the candlelight did not stray; waiting for his cue. He eyed Panqual guardedly with small calculating eyes. He was dressed all in black and he had on a plastic kitchen apron, which looked oddly out of place, even bizarre, though it was essential, given what he was going to set about. he had thick greasy black hair, shaved at the sides; he was small, with a high forehead; he looked like a little goat. It was not for that reason that he called himself Goat; though many believed it was. He had never revealed the reason; he was happy for it to remain a mystery. Goat possessed a talent, and he had chosen to pervert it. Like anywhere, the subtle plane, the etheric, owned its scum, and Goat was familiar with them; he had the ability to connect with them and channel them and act as a conduit for them; he knew what made them tick. Because the same twisted, perverted needs made him tick, too. Ariadne felt the sudden clawing of shame, but she was disciplined, and she drove it out as she had many times before, for many reasons.

'Do not extend it beyond necessity, do you understand me?'

'Yes Ariadne.'

'Do you understand me!' she repeated, in an angry squawk. 'I will know.'

'Okay Ariadne, I promise.' Goat blinked, he knew better than to disobey Ariadne Leech. He addressed Panqual: 'Have you brought a personal item like I asked for?'

'A rag from her last bleed I believe,' Panqual replied. 'I have it in my pocket.'

'Fuck, yeah! That will do nicely,' Goat said enthusiastically. Ariadne wondered how Panqual had obtained that.

'I suppose you're staying to watch,' she said to Panqual.

Panqual inclined her head confirming it. 'I will. I'm also interested to see what enters the circle.' Ariadne's mad eyes fixed on her for a moment and then discarded her like trash. 'Don't interrupt him. We do not want to have to repeat this,' she cautioned her. Angrily chewing her under lip Ariadne left. She wanted coffee and strong vodka. There was a special place in Hell for Goat; one day she intended to send him there. Sometimes, the way he looked at her, she wondered if he knew.

Two

Saskia brought Ayesha's car to a halt under a vast concrete awning, at the side of the brutalist beast of a building, which was called Baal house. This was spectacularly massive, part of it obviously buried in the hillside. The last half mile of the journey had been through woodland and the Humber lay somewhere behind them beyond the trees. A couple of hours daylight remained yet, and the evening sky was mostly blue, but the sun was shining on the other side of the house and hillside, and it was dark under the awning and strong sensor lighting spilled over them, exposing the gleaming symmetry of the vehicle, striking from several angles beneath the awning. Saskia stopped the engine, and she and Ayesha climbed out; they made slight adjustments to their dresses; Saskia changed from the slip-on sandals she had driven in. It was chilly under the awning, their stiletto heels ground at the brushed concrete under them, eliciting echoes.

'Holly was right, a great brutalist thing. It's huge!'

Ayesha had become attentive as soon as Baal house appeared through the trees. She had frowned and focused curiously on its grey expanses and towering curves.

'I think it's magnificent,' Saskia remarked. 'Who would have thought it was here?'

'Let's get inside because its cold under here.' Ayesha gave a little shudder; she was not sure if it was the chill, after the warmth of the car that caused it, or a cocktail of deviant anticipation and very real trepidation, which had been stirred together when they arrived at their destination. Saskia did not seem in the least bit apprehensive; in fact, she looked exhilarated. She reached to take Ayesha's hand and squeezed it protectively. She smiled warmly; her green eyes had softened as they moved admiringly over Ayesha. A visit to the hairdressers that morning had made her gorgeous hair even more breath-taking, and a mass of dark auburn ringlets cascaded to her shoulders. From the top of her head to the tips of her exquisitely painted toenails she was utterly delightful. She was wearing a close fitted dress, a new purchase, which Saskia coveted. It was in dark red silk, with a shirt style collar and full-length cuffed sleeves. the mid-section resembled an embroidered corset from her waist to the level of her breasts. The pencil skirt was knee length and split up the back to mid-thigh; it adjusted beautifully as she moved. She had hoops in her ears and a dozen bangles stacked on her left wrist, flashing rings on the fingers of both hands and a slave chain around her right ankle; all of them made of red gold. She was carrying a stylish red leather designer clutch bag, which together with the slave chain, comprised two of the presents for her birthday from Saskia.

Saskia had opted to wear an incredibly short black dress; it was sleeveless and had a square neckline. Her black suede pumps had chrome plated stiletto heels. As on the night of their shop launch, she affected a single black pirate pearl drop earring. Her fingernails were varnished black, as were her unseen toenails. She carried a simple black clutch bag and a delicate looking shawl in crocheted black lace draped over her wrist.

'That's a hell of a door!' Saskia commented. Ayesha followed her gaze; she nodded, finding herself in accord with Saskia's description.

'I don't see a knocker or a bell,' she remarked.

'Neither do I. It might be part of the handle.'

They made for a massive door of textured green bronze; it towered several feet above their heads, and it had an equivalent width; it possessed a vertical bronze cylindrical handle set at upper body level. They continued to look for a knocker or a bell as they approached it, but neither became apparent. They had almost reached the door when it slid from its recess in the wall, it moved easily along metal channels in the lintel and the floor, and as it moved it made a sonorous tone like the reverberation of some large temple gong. It came to a stop and a young woman appeared in the partial opening; she was still holding onto the handle on the inside with just the one hand which she had used to draw the beautifully balanced door along its tramways. She inclined her head in a polite greeting. She was elegant and about Saskia's height and exquisitely dressed, in ruched trousers and a matching, waist length, sleeved jacket; these were in ivory coloured silk and fitted closely to her slender legs and lithe body. Her pretty feet were nude. Her large, dark eyes flickered over them, quickly taking in detail for immediate processing. They were unable to see if she was smiling. She was wearing a rainbow silk fashion hijab that covered the top and sides of her head and the lower part of her face. She moved this aside, to reveal that she was stunningly pretty, with exquisite makeup, and a beautiful red mouth that only just curved in a very faint almost cabin staff smile.

'Ms Shah, Ms Challoner, please enter. My name is Sofia.' She said in a rather beautiful, musical voice. 'Please come in. Ms Shah, may I take this opportunity to wish you happy birthday.'

'Thank you, Sofia,' Ayesha's smile was low key but appreciative. Sofia stood aside to let them pass. They entered and found themselves in a vast entrance hall. Its floor was made of jet-black obsidian, and the walls were constructed of huge blocks of uneven sandstone. Occasional light washed from concealed sources at the edges of the floor and the ceiling. Sofia slid the door back into place behind them with the lightest of touches, it closed with a cadence, like a huge mantric Om voiced in the stone. The room was dominated by a massive brutalist reclining nude by Henry Moore; it rested on a massive elbow and seemed to regard them obscurely.

'Please will you follow me, I'll take you to Felix,' Sofia said. She led them through a large circular portal, its symmetry broken where it connected to the floor. Saskia gauged that it was easily two and a half metres across. A succession of spacious chambers was similarly illuminated in softly toned light; passageways appeared non-existent. They possessed sometimes more than two portals and linked to other chambers. Some were constructed of Sandstone blocks like the entrance chamber; others were faced with beaten bronze or beautifully aged copper; others were resinous concrete with abstract, occasionally eldritch designs pressed into or embossed on them. The vast obsidian floors shifted through mottled red, yellow, and green. There were no doors on the portals or concealed in the walls; these were about a metre deep, and the interior surfaces were lined in the beaten bronze or the aged copper that dressed the walls of the chambers. The atmosphere was pleasing, a vast weighty comforting silence. Saskia could smell stone and taste and smell the metal of construction, but that was her; she wondered if Ayesha was at all conscious of it. She touched the differently constructed and faced walls with trailing fingertips as she passed them; they were ambient.

A beautiful female voice began to sing unaccompanied, the sound reaching to them from somewhere ahead in the maze of chambers; its tone was lilting and clear; it sang in a language that they did not recognise; a vital chanting lay. It contained an element of Indian song craft, which Saskia found beautiful; it possessed the potential to be mesmeric.

Sofia did not hurry, she went at an easy walking pace, her nude feet padding on the hard smooth floors, her tread overshadowed by the tapping of their heels. She did not show any inclination to hold a conversation more than she had already done, and Saskia and Ayesha were absorbed in their surroundings; their own conversation limited to hushed: 'ooh look' or 'look at that' as in every chamber they encountered rare and magnificent stand-alone pieces and screens hung with fine art.

Eventually they arrived in a massive double height room; where the walls alternated between expanses of sandstone and bronze, and in front of them across a stunning floor of gold sheen obsidian, a window that appeared to be around the size of a tennis court looked out across hillsides and woods. Saskia looked at Ayesha, who lifted her long brows as she reached the same conclusion as Saskia; they had walked right through to the other side of the hill.

'Your guests, Felix,' Sofia announced.

'Saskia, Ayesha, it's good to see you! Welcome to Baal House.'

Felix Malek rose to greet them from where he had been sitting on a massive leather and fabric modular corner sofa probably of some exclusive Italian design. He had been looking through a glossy, New York auction house catalogue, which he tossed onto a sculptural Silas Seandel bronze and glass coffee table. He was immaculate in a silver grey Dormeuil mohair suit and white silk shirt. He crossed the golden sheen floor to meet them, bending to receive kisses, smiling in pleasure.

'Ayesha happy birthday. You look stunning! I am a very lucky fellow to have two such beautiful young women to myself for the evening. Sofia, will you bring drinks for our guests. Martinis? G&Ts? G&Ts Sofia!'

'What do you think of my domain under the hill?

'It's amazing! I envy you it!' Saskia turned about; she sipped champagne; she had to raise her voice to make herself heard across the room. She had undertaken exploration; she had gazed out over the view from the vast expanse of windows, at the reddening sun falling behind trees on the opposite hillside. There was a long terrace beyond the windows accessed by sliding glass doors on mechanisms, but no garden to be seen. Saskia was enthralled by the room and its contents, and she wandered away from Felix and Ayesha after a few minutes. There were several stand-alone pieces in the room which fascinated her; including a Babylonian wall frieze in bricks, of a bull; a statue of a seated Egyptian queen made during the middle kingdom period, it was carved in stone and was a little more than life size; dominating the room was a superb striding Hittite

Chimera carved in Basalt, almost perfectly preserved. There were more contemporary pieces too, a modernist bronze plaque by Roger Tallon occupied part of one wall, and the three huge, contemporary blown glass chandeliers suspended from the high ceiling, unlit at present, were visually stunning. Saskia peered through the portal into the adjacent room; this was single height, there were no antiquities on show, but a huge Spanish-revival, baroque dining table, stood a little to the side, almost level with another portal on the right; it was massively thick; it probably consisted of the mid-section of a tree Saskia mused. It was set at one end for dining, and three massive matching dining chairs in the same darkly polished wood awaited their occupants. The near half of the room was dominated by a portal set into the middle of the floor which had transited to jet black obsidian; the portal drew Saskia's gaze and piqued her curiosity; the figural gallery of a bronze staircase descended to a subterranean level; she was about to step into the room to take a closer look when Felix called out to her. She headed back to them, she had been aware of the beautiful voice continuing to sing as she explored, now she paid attention as it transited to a new lay; it did not matter that she did not understand the words being sung; because they reached inside her and resonated at an instinctive level.

'The songs are beautiful,' she said to Felix as she halted beside Ayesha. 'Quite magical in fact. Is the singer close by?'

'A couple of rooms distant; the acoustics are excellent are they not?' he said.

'How long will she sing for?'

'A while yet; others will take their turn; you'll notice differences in technique and speciality, with the change in voices.'

'We've been talking about them while you were nosing,' said Ayesha, she turned her head and smiled at Saskia, flashing her brows meaningfully.

'They are Felix's wives!'

Saskia's eyes widened in surprise. 'Really!'

'Concubines, not wives; I am unmarried,' Felix corrected.

'How many 'concubines' live here? How many do you have?' Saskia asked, she was intrigued. She wondered if she was being impolite or indiscreet. This was fascinating stuff, and she wanted to know. She was aware of Ayesha's amusement at her reaction.

'I have eleven concubines in Baal House,' Felix replied indulgently, he too seemed amused.

'Is Sofia one of them?'

'Sofia is mistress of the house, my housekeeper, I don't know how I would manage without her!'

'Do you employ staff too? It's a huge place.'

'Several are here during the day.'

'What about cooking, you said you employed a chef?'

'One of my concubines is an accredited chef, a couple of others are excellent amateur chefs.'

'Do you pay them?'

Felix laughed aloud. Ayesha rested a restraining hand on Saskia's forearm. 'Saskia, too much.'

'It's alright Ayesha. Why should I mind? Aren't you curious too?' Felix said. He smiled. Ayesha set her head on one side, indicating that she was.

'We have a perfect arrangement,' Felix began. 'They are paid a formidable salary for ten years; though they can opt out of the arrangement whenever they wish. I was fortunate to encounter Niamh my chef, at my restaurant; she was the sous chef there until a year ago; we hit it off so to speak; she's a deviant little soul; most of them are. They all have their own stories, some more arcane than others. Four of them are Demonics, including Sofia, but they all muddle along quite well together; most of the time.'

'How many of them have such lovely voices?' Saskia asked.

'All four Demonics, and Jyothi who is Indian.'

'Felix.' It was the voice of Sofia. They turned to find her standing in the portal to the dining room. She regarded them solemnly and executed a formal little bow.

'It is almost time to serve.'

'Thankyou Sofia,' Felix said, he looked inquiringly at Saskia and Ayesha. 'Shall we take our seats at the table?'

Three

Bang! Bang!

Rachel Zimpara rolled her eyes and paused the delicious Belgian chocolate truffle that resided between her long red fingernails halfway to her mouth. She had already consumed six and was about to experience the delights of a seventh. She placed it back in the box, refusing to consume it hurriedly. Truffles and a good cabernet Sauvignon red had been her plan, together with a selection from her DVD film collection, in this case 'So long at the Fair'. It was almost midnight, but she never went to bed before two, unless it was with someone. Her wide mouth and beautiful sly looking eyes framed annoyance as she paused the film; just when they had begun to search for Jean Simmon's brothers room, too. She swung her legs off her stylish Italian sofa and stood; she was wearing a tiny white silk kimono decorated with red dragonflies, it was open, its flimsy belt swinging on one loop, revealing her svelte nakedness; she pushed back her shoulder length brown hair and went barefoot, to answer the door. She passed the ghost, John Pickering, on the way; smirking as usual; he was half materialised in the semi-darkness by the door of her lounge, watching her by the light from her Tv. He often watched her, when she was alone or with lovers, and she allowed it. At present he was in residence at her house; he had proved useful a few times over recent months, since she had acquired him; after the Saskia business that Nathan Xavier had got her into. He would have to go soon though; he was well on his way to becoming entity; then he would be very hard to control. He was strong already. She had decided to bottle him in the next few days and sell him to Theodor Bacchus, who collected that sort of thing.

Bang! Bang!

'Okay! Alright!' Zimpara yelled. She wrenched open the heavy front door, with its beautiful bronze sarcophagus door knocker, which had been applied so robustly. She glared unambiguously, up at her visitor.

'Where's the fire and brimstone?' She demanded. The shifting night air felt cool on her nakedness.

Two large, round, pitch-black eyes, regarded her emptily; a soft feminine voice, responded. 'What fire and brimstone?'

'The fire and brimstone that my mind imagines accompany you, Panqual, every time you arrive at my door. Ordinarily I stay silent. This time I couldn't help it!'

'How droll.'

Zimpara narrowed her eyes and peered into the night behind Panqual, towards the shape of an SUV parked in the darkness on the other side of her forecourt. She heard the sound of its engine start up; its lights flooded the space in front of it.

'I have a commission for you' said Panqual.

'I thought you might somehow. How quickly do you need them finding?' It was usually that. Panqual, or more exactly Panqual in the name of her mistress, Satran

Saradina, required some poor bastard to be hunted down.

'They are already located.' The SUV pulled round in a circle; there were a couple of occupants; Zimpara tried to make them out, but it drove away, accelerating along her drive, towards the road. Zimpara made no comment; it was none of her business if Panqual had dealings elsewhere and cadged a lift.

'That was fast!' Zimpara's eyes narrowed suspiciously. 'How did you manage that. No don't tell me.' Her face registered disgust. 'So, you want me to serve notice?'

'A warrant, yes, then, if they won't comply with it, I want you to procure them, so that they can be returned to Pandemonium.'

'Fair enough,' Zimpara shrugged. 'I take it you intend to stay.' This in itself was not unusual. 'From that I assume you want me to serve this warrant imminently.'

'In the morning. Early.' Panqual dipped her head keenly and extracted a leather draw purse, from a side pocket; it was very Elizabethan in style and looked quite full as she offered it to Zimpara, held between the cruel talons of her triple jointed fingers and thumb.

'Fifty Venetian gold ducats,' she said. 'For the warrant. Fifty more on completion.'

It was a healthy sum. Uncirculated renaissance coinage was the chosen currency used by Pandemonium for trade with the human world; Zimpara preferred it, because of its appreciating value as a collectable; she had acquired quite a hoard of it over years of transactions. For that sum to be offered the subject had to be highly prized. She considered the question of their status.

'Why are they wanted back in Pandemonium?' It might be for any number of legitimate reasons, from murder to theft; mostly it was indebtedness.

'Your perennial question,' Panqual said, unable to keep a sneering note from her voice.

'As always, I reserve the right to ask. There must be justification,' Zimpara said.

'Yes, alright,' Panqual jigged her monstrous head, testily. 'The subject is Luca Rajal; she has been absent from duty for almost a week and thus has broken the terms of her indenture to the house of the Satran.'

Zimpara knew that there had to be more to it than that; she was being offered way above her going rate, but there was something else, something deeply personal in the mix, her spidey senses could feel it crawling around in the dark, and they were seldom wrong. She told herself it was none of her business. This Luca had broken the terms of her indenture, and that was sufficient to justify intervention by Zimpara. She accepted the purse of gold coins from Panqual. She stood aside, and with a little jerk of her head indicated that Panqual should enter.

Four

'Enacting magic, like any action is an extension of the will, a desiring. Raise your index finger from the table Saskia. That itself is an act of magic, though the ordinaries can't comprehend that it is.'

They had consumed a series of quite delightful courses, served by two beautiful women, a pretty ash blonde in a knee length red dress and a black skinned girl, her head shaved, dressed in a grey sari. It was Sofia herself who had served them drinks.

'Felix has suggested Dom Perignon, but of course you can choose whatever you desire, from the cellar,' she told them.

'Then we shall have Dom Perignon,' Saskia announced before Ayesha could respond. She flashed her eyes at Ayesha who was sitting opposite her. They had turned the full intensity of their personalities on their host and Felix had wallowed in it unashamedly. Pretty animated faces, enchanting bodies and flashing bewitching eyes were his chosen candy. He was seated at the head of the table, a massive presence, fully occupying his baroque chair; Saskia and Ayesha merely perched in theirs. They had discussed art to begin with and then antiquities, passions all three shared; though Saskia was more than aware of her inadequate expertise in either field, compared to the excellence both her companions exhibited; she was in the process of voraciously devouring knowledge though, and she fed from the exchange. Then the conversation switched to magic, and Saskia found herself wondering when it had done so. She realised she had drifted, and she could feel the threads of another curious presence inside her that was gradually gaining in strength. She had experienced it before on the night of their opening, except then, it had been focused on her sex centre, and on Ayeshas. She directed a slightly challenging stare at Felix, which he met with amused golden eyes.

'Lower your finger,' he instructed her. Saskia realised that the index finger on her right hand, which rested flat on the polished tabletop, was angled at sixty-degrees pointed towards Felix. As instructed, she allowed it to return to rest alongside her others. The golden eyes of the Lalyt narrowed almost imperceptibly; he had expected more defiance, more objection, surprisingly in their place he saw default to acquiescence. Mentally he shrugged.

'Try to raise the same finger again but use thought only,' he said.

'It doesn't happen. I know that.'

'Try anyway Saskia.'

'See.' Saskia set her head coquettishly on one side,

'What does that tell us?'

'That our actions are controlled via motor neurones from the cerebral cortex?' Ayesha intervened, she had leaned back in her chair; she was smiling and looked relaxed, her elbow rested on the arm of her chair as she ran the painted nail of her own index finger across the edges of her fine white upper teeth. Saskia glanced admiringly at her, and gave a little nod of approval, this much at least she knew, though how the blob of fat located between her ears was capable of this she had no idea.

'It tells us that our will is essentially a weak instrument, our thoughts alone have no power,' Felix observed. 'Something else is at play.'

'The same thing that makes me want to fuck Ayesha?'

'Probably the same thing,' Felix replied, unfazed by Saskia's deliberately provocative words. 'Also, the same mechanism that enables you to fuck her and for the length of time you fuck her.'

Deliberately casual, Saskia allowed her index finger to rise until it was pointing again at Felix, at a sixty-degree angle. He chuckled appreciatively at the gesture. Saskia smiled amiably and lowered her finger to rest, then frowned as she realised it had failed to perform the action.

'A type of beguiling,' Felix explained. 'Similar, but by no means as subtle, as the CaolShee practised on you, when they drowned you like a dog.'

'Felix, I've felt you probing around inside me and I'm sure you are at work in Ayesha too. May I please have control of my finger again?'

'Of course. There it's done,'

Cautiously Saskia lowered her finger to the table again.

'All magic is a form of desire, of desiring,' he said. 'Thought, the will, merely creates the desired objective, after that it gets in the way. No matter how intensely you exert your will to possess something or perform some action, you will never achieve it without involving some other mechanism. Intent is the evolved instrument of that mechanism.'

'With so many variations too,' Saskia observed.

'Several that you won't have experienced or even heard of,' he replied enigmatically. He regarded her with eyes that contained his customary humour and assured assertiveness; as she searched them, she encountered something she had not picked up on before; they were uncompromising. She was aware that he was deliberately holding her gaze, he had no intention of allowing her victory by breaking contact.

'We possess, potentially, an incredible box of tricks Saskia,' she heard Ayesha say. 'Remember Holly said that we are magicians for a modern era. Magic has evolved.'

'Imagination is the key. It's the key to everything.' Felix observed. He watched her pretty face. She was fascinating, he thought. They both were, and they intrigued him. He watched in anticipation for the wolves in her eyes to emerge, and challenge in response to his sustained scrutiny, but they remained slumbering.

'I understand that. But without energy, the kundalini or whatever you want to call it, it's as useless as thought,' Saskia stated.

'That's a given,' he agreed. 'You mention the kundalini, the serpent; it's as near as we come to recognising that the energy we use is the same energy that manifests in sex, and the same energy that emerges sometimes in girls during puberty. It's worth noting that the patriarchy of many tribal societies feared it so much that they virtually imprisoned young women until puberty was passed, an interesting anthropological fact. I wonder if it manifested through tribal cosmology or in other ways.'

'I've seen it first hand,' Saskia said. 'Nothing special, just a couple of girls at school with low level entities hanging around them.'

'You are able see the supernatural world, of course,'

'Some of it.'

'Did that start when you began to bleed?' he asked.

'Earlier. It intensified about then.' Her voice fell, softened, slightly defensive. It became smaller. Ayesha saw her lover become vulnerable in that moment; it surprised her. For her part Saskia deemed it an appropriate moment to drop her gaze deferentially and look down at the little that remained of her caramel pudding and hazelnut ice cream; if Felix required vulnerability, she would give him the win.

'You were visited?' He asked.

'Often.' Saskia gazed to the side, not looking up.

'Were you afraid?' He leaned on the table with an elbow. She was piquing his curiosity.

'Not really. My first lover was a ghost, if you want to call it that.'

'An identity then.'

'Entity.'

'Are you willing to speak about it?' he said.

'Saskia you don't have to,' Ayesha intervened. She leaned forward, concerned for her lover. She willed Saskia to meet her gaze, but Saskia continued not to look at her.

'It's okay, I don't mind.'

'How old were you?' Felix asked.

'I was twelve. He started to visit after I was fettered. He came to me in dreams. I remember the first time he made himself known. I recall the dream clearly. I was walking in the street some distance from where I lived. It was very late at night, maybe even the same time at which I was having my dream come to think of it. The street was empty of people but filled with fog. I was in bare feet but dressed for bed. Suddenly he was just walking beside me. A tall thin man: he was dressed all in black, but I think they were clothes of a different age; he was pale with white hair down to his shoulders, he had a gaunt face and a thin red mouth; he was old, but age didn't seem to matter; I can't explain that thought. He said my name and then he said I should go with him. I said that I didn't want to. He held out his hand. It was long, his fingers were bony, and he had no fingernails. I reached to take it, then I'd woken up and I was sweating. I thought nothing of it at the time. But then a few nights later I had the same dream. This time when he offered me his hand, I accepted it, I recall it was very cold; it seemed I had no other choice, but I said to him you must take me home. I entered another part of the dream, and he was in my bed with me. I woke up, I was sweating, but he was still there. I was allowing him, and I continued to allow him. And when he was finished with me, he simply wasn't there. I went back to sleep. I didn't tell my mum or auntie Ben. It was my secret. It continued for six months. But as time went on, in my dreams he became more insistent that I go with him. It became less easy to resist, as I became more accustomed to him. Then one night I couldn't resist anymore. And when I gave him my hand, he began to lead me away through the fog, and I knew that I couldn't let that happen. If I had I don't know what the consequences might have been. It was the first time I felt real fear, desperation in fact. But I couldn't do anything, I had no will of my own. I remember I weed myself. I remember it running down my leg and splashing on the ground. The dream had become almost lucid. Then I saw a shape coming through the fog towards us. My companion halted and the shape stopped in front of us. It was the first time I encountered my monster. The Frankenstein monster, the Boris Karloff version,' she explained to Felix. She realised she was looking at him, searching his face for reaction. He was frowning slightly, puzzled. 'I watched the film with auntie Ben, I felt sorry for him. I've discovered since he represents my intent, my power all bundled up into a kind of gestalt. What better than a creature of many parts. He stood in the street barring my companions way, he wouldn't let him pass. My companion released my hand and fell on him like a wolf. They fought with unbelievable ferocity, they melded, and they spun like a wheel, faster and faster, like a Catherine wheel. I ran away, I ran, and I ran, and I woke up. I'd wet the bed. I'd never done that before, or since. I never saw him again, my lover. I am happy to say.' Saskia's voice trailed away.

'Are you okay?' Saskia became aware of Ayesha on one knee beside her chair, the fingers of one hand laid over her wrist; she felt its warm pressure and admired the perfect red varnished nails. Ayesha smiled up at her, but there was concern in the smile; Ayesha had her own psychological pain to deal with and she recognised the power it possessed.

'I'm fine. Because I have you.' Saskia flowed to her feet unexpectedly, breaking the mood. She flashed a smile at Ayesha, took hold of her hand and drew her to her feet. She led a slightly puzzled Ayesha to the bronze gallery around the stairwell and rested her free hand on the head of one of the fierce looking figures that composed it, that of an Achaean warrior.

'I find this very intriguing Felix,' she observed staring down into the portal.

'It leads to an intriguing part of this house Saskia,' he replied.

'You are more than piquing my interest!'

'As well as being a very personal place,' Felix continued, he rose from his chair and joined them. He rested his hand on Saskias, easily covering it with his own; she felt its heat and weight.

'Agammemnon,' he said. As he spoke, he acquired her gaze again and retained it. His hand rested on Saskias only briefly before he slid it along the heavy rail, passing it over the top of the heads of two more figures, pausing briefly on each. 'Menelaus his brother, and Achilles,' he said as he came to the next. 'The rest also represent Achaeans who participated in the siege of Troy and its ultimate destruction.'

'Rather suitable guardians for an inner sanctum! Are we not allowed?' Saskia took the opportunity of lowering her stare with what she hoped was a look of charming almost compliant disappointment; though the sense of disappointment was real enough, and to her surprise she realised that her sense of compliancy was not totally feigned either, as it had previously been.

'Did I infer that' replied Felix, obviously amused. 'I'll take you down there, if that's what you'd like.'

'Fascinating,' remarked Ayesha, though she was observing Saskia, when she spoke. 'I believe that we'd like that very much.'

'I think these bronze treads would prove lethal to stilettos,' Ayesha said as she slipped off her Louboutin's, and carrying them by their inside heels, began her descent. Saskia followed her lead; she felt the cold hard bronze beneath her toes and gave a little shiver. Felix was immediately behind her, and she recollected descending the staircase at Challoner-Shah, during the night of their launch, with Felix making it groan with his weight; this was a far more substantial structure. Both Saskia and Ayesha felt a growing sense of excitement as they descended into an expansive double height chamber. It was lit from below with concealed lighting along the edge of the wall, and by a dozen beautiful clear globes suspended from the ceiling. The curved walls were decorated with a full scale, continuous mural, depicting Achaean hoplite soldiers in the act of slaughter and rape, in the plazas and streets of a city. The death of Troy, it had to be that; Saskia drew a long breath as she took in the vast scale of the work. Also, the scale of the floor which she realised as she descended towards it, was a vast and beautiful mosaic. She watched as Ayesha's body shaping altered and she became animated, her gaze casting about at the scenes depicted in the floor.

'This is a fabulous mosaic, Felix!' she exclaimed. 'It's not ancient, but the traditional craftsmanship is masterful.'

'You approve that I chose the Roman type, to depict Trojans and Achaeans?' He asked.

'God yes! Who wouldn't?'

'Then I am most gratified!' Felix laughed appreciatively. 'This is my subject of preference, my fascination. Hence my desire for your Rhyton.'

'Why Troy?'

'My obsession. The mystique.'

'Look Saskia!' Ayesha stalked about the mosaic in her bare feet; she pointed and turned her animated face towards Saskia, her eyes flashing. 'Kassandra attempting to burn the wooden horse. She knew they were in there! She is a seer, the priestess of apollo, a princess of Troy. They didn't believe her. Then here, later, she is raped by Ajax the lesser, the Locrian. He found her clinging to the statue of Pallas Athena, the Palladium, but not the original. That had been stolen by Odysseus. And here in the centre, this vast storm raised by Athena, in a rage, destroying the Achaean armada on its return from Troy. Ajax swore on her statue that he had not raped

Kassandra in her Temple, otherwise he would have been stoned to death; this was Athena's reckoning. Here is Triton smashing the rock with Ajax clinging to it, after his ship had been wrecked! This is magnificent.'

Saskia followed Ayesha's movements as she listened to her; she took in other details too, set around the walls at intervals were chairs of oxblood leather and chrome, and to the left of the staircase a group of chairs and couches, situated around a table made out of dark red onyx; there were exits too, one of the familiar circular portals was located in the wall behind the staircase, another to the right of the wooden horse; another through the floor in the centre of the right hemisphere of the room, girdled by another bronze gallery. Casually Saskia wandered towards this. The gallery depicted an Achaean Trireme, a warrior blinding a cyclops with fire, a beautiful woman with pigs. Whirling water, cast in bronze, dragged wrecked triremes into the spiral descent of the staircase. Saskia leaned with her back against the heavy bronze rail and gazed down at the scene created in the floor next to it. At which point she spoke, pleased with the tone of her slightly raised voice in the precincts of the room. 'I believe this panel shows that Kassandra has become the concubine of Agamemnon; his slave mistress, a suitable humiliation in his mind, for the single survivor of the royal house of Troy, and a less than clever kick in the teeth for Athena, goddess of war.'

'You're learning fast!' Ayesha laughed.

'It makes for easy learning!' Saskia responded, grinning in pleasure.

'Impressive!' Felix remarked, with no indication of condescension; he looked at Ayesha with renewed interest. 'Perhaps now I understand a little better, why selling me the Rhyton is no simple decision.' He placed his large hand in the middle of Ayesha's back and guided her to where Saskia leaned casually on the bronze handrail of the second staircase. Her expression was quite artful as she watched them approach.

'Charybdis, I would guess,' she tilted her head sideways indicating the stairwell, 'descends to another intriguing place. Are we permitted our own Odessey Felix?'

Felix chuckled appreciatively. 'Lead on Saskia, I won't deny you.' His golden eyes watched admiringly as she began to descend the staircase followed by Ayesha. It crossed his mind that only a select few had seen what lay beneath them; Saskia and Ayesha were about to join an exclusive circle. He followed them, indulging in their beauty; these were young women of a modern age, intelligent, chic, cool, independent, achingly beautiful; it would feel good to own them, if only intermittently. The recent conversation Holly had initiated with him about them had not been to pre-warn him of their intention, he had already sensed that need in them; it had been to make it understood to him that they were special to her; both were flawed, both were unique, and they were damaged. That was probably why he liked them, he decided.

He did not immediately follow them, but paused briefly and turned to find as expected, Sofia standing twenty feet away, politely waiting.

'Bring Mandragora Serpens Sofia will you please, and more Dom Pérignon,' he instructed her.

'Yes Felix,' she replied, she inclined her head in a little bow. Impassively she watched him turn and follow Saskia and Ayesha down the staircase.

A succession of ships cast in bronze, each broken differently by Charybdis, lined their way. The imagery continuing the style of brutal modernism. Saskia's interest shifted from them to another mosaic floor, as it appeared below. It depicted octopi and eels and dolphins, they threshed in swirling water, and pretty sea nymph faces emerged from between coiling tentacles; wrecked ships timbers and drowned seamen floated forlornly here and there. The chamber was smaller than the Trojan room, but still probably fifteen metres in diameter. The air became chilled and the bronze treads no longer cool but cold under their bare feet. Saskia gave a little shiver as she stepped from the stair and gazed about; she felt Ayesha's hand slip into hers and she closed her fingers around it. She no longer stared in fascination at the mosaic floor, she was barely aware of the faces of the twelve Olympian gods who stared from the walls in the form of huge bronze masks; they circuited the room, each one, maybe two metres across. Her entire attention was drawn to the massive vertical disc, located without apparent means of support at the centre of the room. It faced towards the stairs. Ayesha guessed it too to be a couple of metres across, constructed of patinated green bronze, un-decorated, apart from a single massive eye, a metre wide. Curiosity filled Saskia's eyes; this was no fabulous art installation; she felt a powerful sense, similar to Place, but whereas Place felt fixed and permanent the sense she had was one of variation without context; she decided that she was gazing upon a very powerful, magical instrument.

'What is it?' she asked. 'It looks what it probably is a portal! A doorway, like an elaborate safe!'

'It's a porta magica, a true wonder, and no, I've never seen one either, but I know what I'm looking at.' Ayesha's expression displayed a fascination equal to Saskias. Almost synchronised, they lowered their stilettos to the floor and leaving them side by side, they approached the door together. Their breath plumed like on an icy day and the floor under their bare feet was freezing cold.

'A magic door,' said Saskia, she shivered, she saw Ayesha shiver too. 'Where does it go?'

'Almost anywhere' Felix said. 'If you know where you want to go.' He watched them indulgently, two enthralled little creatures; inquisitive, in spite of the cold. They disappeared behind the porta magica and emerged again on the opposite side of the device; intrigued; fascinated.

'It's just hanging there,' Saskia remarked. She shivered again and folded her arms across herself. 'You keep this room so cold.'

'There's no handle, I can't see any hinges.' Ayesha observed.

'Will you open it for us?' Saskia said.

'Another time.' Felix looked adamant. 'Yes, I know, disappointing, isn't it? and you're far too cold. I don't deliberately keep the room cold Saskia.' He felt slightly mean, almost guilty; he was capable of such things, as they looked disappointed at his reply; they accepted his decision, however. Saskia touched the lower lid of the great bronze eye with her fingertips.

'It's icy cold. It doesn't absorb the ambience of the room. No! it's causing the room to be cold!' she said, her teeth had begun to chatter.

'It exhibits variation. Sometimes it is ambient, other times warm, occasionally hot even. The door is not itself the portal; it merely contains it in this reality. The portal exists between, in sub space, but it also penetrates it. It's anchor lies somewhere in the boundless edge, I think that location determines its temperature at any given time and is, I believe, peculiar to this gate.'

Saskia splayed her fingers on the bronze eyeball, the cold leached up into them, she frowned and tilted her head as if she was listening. She was freezing, but she was not ready to go just yet.

'I can feel its beating heart,' she announced.

Ayesha rested her hand next to Saskia's. After a moment she shook her head. 'I can't feel anything.'

'Boom! Boom! Ever so slow and so distant,' Saskia insisted.

'I can't feel it.'

'I sense presence. Entity?' Saskia flashed a frown at Felix. He responded with the most infinitesimal of shrugs. Whatever she was sensing or feeling, he had never experienced it.

'I'm getting really cold Saskia.'

'Then heat up. I'm enjoying it!'

'You're strange. We shouldn't deploy any intent near it,' Ayesha pitched her voice low.

'You wouldn't have me any other way.' Saskia relented. 'Oh, come on then!' She took hold of Ayesha's cold hand. 'Felix we'd like something warm inside us!' she announced playfully; she led Ayesha away from the portal. They scooped up their stilettos on the way.

'How delightful!' Saskia's eyes shone with appreciation. She and Ayesha had warmed themselves through. She referred to an antique, parcel gilt, silver bowl; it occupied the space between them, on the shiny, red onyx tabletop, where Sofia had set it down. It was about six inches across, with beautiful opposing handles in the manner of a quaichs; each handle was composed of two snakes curving from beneath the rim with heads pointed over the inner bowl, flanking two miniature crouching lions. It stood on little claw feet; Saskia could see a hallmark impressed below the outer rim. Sofia lifted a small jug from a tray, she had placed on the table, both of which matched the bowls design. She poured some of the contents into the bowl; it was clear; colourless. It bubbled as it filled the bowl to the halfway point; a thin vapour rose above the surface but quickly dissipated, like fragile smoke. Sofia replaced the jug upon the tray, gave a little bow and left them. Saskia sniffed delicately like a cat at a stalk of grass, as the scent of the elixir drifted to her nose; it was a fragment of smell, barely possessing any substance; what hint of it existed, reminded her of surgical spirit.

'Mandragora Serpens. Known as alchemical lust, though this version has added properties,' Felix announced.

Ayesha chuckled softly; Saskia decided her tone contained a hint of sensuality. She leaned back into her seat, which was a low couch covered in smooth red leather, framed in chrome, Saskia occupied its twin, positioned on the other side of the red onyx table, Felix was seated in a chair of identical design. Ayesha folded her fingers in and rested their backs against her mouth. She gave her head a little shake and lowered her hand, smiling; amused at her thoughts. 'Known in some circles as 'demonic fuck juice,' she said. 'Our covers blown. He knows.'

'Does he? He knows what we came for, why we are here?' Saskia realised that she felt quite aggrieved at the revelation, and moderately embarrassed. 'Are you sure?'.

'Yes, little Mantis. Didn't you have some suspicion that he might?'

'No, did you? Do you, Felix? For how long?' Saskia pouted.

'I might simply be attempting to drug you,' he replied, amused. He relented at once. 'When Holly Penn first told me about you, with great enthusiasm; she inspired my curiosity. When I met you, I wanted you sexually; I am what I am, after all. I explored you, I know you were aware of me; yes, I toyed with you, and you allowed. At first, I thought it was because you wanted me to buy paintings. Don't look so horrified; I discarded that idea quickly when I realised you knew what I am. So, I looked deeper inside you both and you glowed; when you are apart you know your centres just burn, but when you are together, you become incandescent. That is when I decided that I wanted to own your Desiderata.'

'What is, Desiderata?' Saskia asked. 'I know it means desire.'

'It's ambition; the path to power. Mine is the path called Radical Aphrodisia.'

'You said you would own our Desiderata,' Ayesha said suspiciously. 'Own, can be a provocative word.'

'I've no wish to own you, Ayesha. The meaning is subtle.'

'So, you own Holly's Desiderata?'

'Not any longer; Holly's chosen her path,' Felix said. 'She's no need for Radical Aphrodisia; she achieved what she wanted. We remain good friends and occasional lovers. The rewards can be great. You're limited only by your own desire. I can't explain them to you, because I don't know them; they're yours to know. When we seal this deal tonight it is with both of you though; you come as a pair always, or not at all.'

'We wouldn't have it any other way,' Ayesha said. She looked at Saskia, nervous excitement in her dark eyes, and smiled her Ayesha smile. Not for the first time, Saskia felt a sense of wonder, that this beautiful young woman seated opposite her, was deeply in love with her, and felt a fear that at any moment she would wake up and discover that it had all been an amazing dream. Sometimes the idea brought her close to tears, but not this time, she felt inspired by it, and in love, and that felt so cool.

'No, we wouldn't have it any other way.' She directed a tight significant smile at Ayesha and wrinkled her nose. 'What do we do now?' she inquired, not breaking her gaze.

'You're determined to go through with it?' Felix said.

'Oh! Get on with it Felix!' Saskia laughed, 'I've never been as unsure and yet more sure about anything, and neither has Ayesha.'

'In that case, say your chosen words Saskia and drink from the bowl.'

Without hesitation, Saskia reached out with both hands and took up the vessel by its handles between thumbs and index fingers, she rested her elbows on the onyx, still maintaining her visual connection with Ayesha. She had begun to feel amused that Felix had understood their intentions from the outset, and she experienced a momentary feeling of anticlimax, but a renewed surge of excitement brushed it aside. She spoke quietly, without emphasis. It seemed appropriate that way.

'Saskia Challoner!' She announced. 'It's all my fault, yes, it's all my fault and I don't give a damn cos I am what I am.' Without lifting her elbows from the table, she moved the quaich to her mouth and drank some of the Mandragora Serpens. Her eyes widened, almost rounded, and she gasped like she was coming up for much needed air. 'Fuck! That's like the coolest strongest vodka I've ever tasted! Is it alcoholic?'

'It's an elixir, with the properties of a stimulant.'

'It's used recreationally' Ayesha said, 'though probably not at this strength.'

'It is the poison of choice to some magicians,' Felix confirmed.

Saskia nodded she could already feel the stuff turning her blood to cool fire, and she was certain it was not her imagination. She placed the Quaich back on the table then pushed it towards Ayesha. 'Your turn I presume.' Ayesha leaned forward in her chair, to take up the quaich as Saskia had done, but did not lean her elbows on the table, she played a brief sideways glance over Felix; he was studying her, his expression obscure. Her eyes found Saskia's again, and she raised her brows and gave a little roll of her eyes; she shrugged.

'Ayesha Shah. I stare at the sun, and I dance in the hail, I know myself; I am tooth and nail.' Not hesitating, she too drank some of the elixir, then placed the quaich back on the table. She compressed her lips drawing them inside her mouth as though tasting a wine, other than that she did not display a reaction. Saskia who was waiting in anticipation for her response, found herself in awe of her lovers sang-froid and gave her a little round of silent applause. She watched, her green eyes animated, as Felix extended his big hand and scooped up the bowl; she caught the malevolent flash of the huge carnelian stone in his gold ring.

'Felix Malek. I bellow in the mist, I am horn, I am clay, I'm master of the moon sure as night follows day.' He raised the cup first to Ayesha then to Saskia, he drank from one side and then the other, where both their mouths had touched it, until it was empty. He licked his full lips and placed it back down; then reaching for the jug he filled it again. His broad face wore an expression of satisfaction.

'We have sealed the deal,' he said. 'Drink more Mandragora Serpens, the rest is yours, and drink Dom Pérignon too. I will enjoy more of your company and then I will fuck you both.'

'Have you had this before?' Saskia asked Ayesha. 'You seem familiar with it. 'Demonic fuck juice' you called it.' She held the bowl of Mandragora Serpens cupped in both hands, the metal felt cold, as cold as the elixir it contained. She had drunk several mouthfuls, and her mouth and throat felt numb and tingly. Her heart rate had increased; it was definitely pounding; little ribbons of cool fire played under her skin; the stuff now coursing through her veins possessed a strange sense of purpose.

'Yes, I've had it before when I was younger, when I was being passed around at my uncles gatherings. But this is in a different league to the stuff I was used to.' Ayesha knew she had already drunk more of the Mandragora Serpens than she should have, now she was sipping Dom Pérignon and studying Saskia. Sensation in her body had heightened, intensifying her awareness, Saskia would be experiencing similar. A woman's voice began to sing somewhere beyond the portal to the left, the lays had ceased as they descended to the lower level, but now they were taken up again, perhaps by the most beautiful voice she had yet heard; Ayesha felt her skin lift into goosebumps, horripilation was the medical term for the response, she preferred the alternative, piloerection and felt her mouth form a tight smile at the thought.

'Is that Sofia singing now?' She heard herself ask.

'You recognise it? In song.'

'An inspired guess.'

'She has the most amazing voice don't you think?' Felix said, his golden eyes appeared to consume her, they seemed larger, more intense, they were no longer avuncular but arrogant and lascivious.

'That song feels very erotic,' she said. 'Though I don't understand it.'

'As it should be on an occasion such as this,' Felix replied. She could feel his mind inside her clambering around, delving, and drawing up her dark thoughts and hidden memories like mud from a well. It made her feel dirty, but it wasn't such a bad feeling.

'So, is this the alchemical equivalent of a thirty-year-old malt? Compared to your flute full of Lambrini.' Saskia's expression broke into silent laughter, and she bit her lower lip. For some reason she felt inordinately pleased with her analogy. 'What's in it that sets it apart Felix?'

'Besides Mandrake and assorted venoms? My semen.'

Saskia's eyes danced. 'So, we are drinking your distilled spunk.'

'Perhaps the most essential ingredient in our transaction,' he replied enigmatically, causing Saskias eyes to narrow inquisitively; she responded.

'I believe that I can feel its masculinity inside me, I don't think its self-deception on my part. Its uncompromising. Are you that uncompromising Felix? I watched your face so full of humour and benevolence. So pleased to see us whenever we encountered you. But there was always something else held back, and it touched your expression very occasionally, and now and again, it passed across your eyes. You don't compromise, do you?'

'I always get what I want Saskia. Or we wouldn't be having this conversation. None of us lose in this, take the win.'

'I get it Felix; I really do and I'm cool.' As if to prove her assertion she raised the quaich to her lips and drank more of the elixir in long swallows, her eyes gleamed above the rim at Ayesha, it was the second quaich the two of them had shared.

'Semen is not a typ...typical ingredient though is it Felix,' Ayesha inquired, she frowned, her thoughts had become very swimmy.

'The impulse is usually the blood of a beast; sometimes human blood is added, male or female from a willing donor, though more often that of a powerful male,' he replied, his tone was matter of fact. 'Tonight, the sex will be of a different order, its purpose beyond the satisfaction of physical desire. Simply put we will engage in a form of astral sex enabled by physical sex. The Elixir will stimulate your sex centres, it will be the instrument that unlocks the flow of the so-called Kundalini force, into your pillars, it can only do this with the addition of my semen, and my energised intent will be the key. After that your centres will begin to hold more energy, your aura will rotate and increase its layers. Your powers will increase;

how quickly will depend on how quickly you evolve. This is the gift of the Lalyt. In return I draw away some of the energy that we induce, that is my commission.' Felix fell silent, he gazed at each of them in turn.

Saskia decided that his expression contained a hint of smugness. 'Now I feel underappreciated,' she said after a short pause for effect.

'Why so?'

'In fact, I feel a little insulted. On behalf of both of us.' Saskia got to her feet. She fixed Felix with her gaze and circled the table smiling archly and went to stand over Ayesha. She reached down and trailed her nails delicately over Ayesha's slim bare knees; she looked searchingly into Ayesha's bemused eyes and decided that she looked almost totally out of it. She took Ayesha's hand in hers and drew her, swaying, to her bare feet.

'You've omitted the best of the deal Mr Demon, you get us!' She stood behind Ayesha and placed her hands on her smooth toned upper arms. 'You get this!'

'I am aware that I have added two more, extremely beautiful women, to my collection, Saskia.'

'As beautiful as this?' Saskias hands disappeared behind Ayesha's back. Ayesha felt her dress loosen around her body as she heard the unmistakable sound of her zip. An instant later she was aware of it slipping from her body to the floor; she was aware that her skin was becoming hypersensitive, and it leapt in tiny movements where her dress touched as it fell. Exposed, the surface of her skin felt febrile, it tingled, and she shivered,

'Saskia!' she breathed; it was barely a protest though. She tried to glimpse Saskia over her shoulder, turning her head.

'You didn't prevent it,' Saskia chided. Her words came softly spoken, almost huskily into Ayesha's hair; they tingled in her nape hairs and fluttered like moth wings along her compliance of thorns. She gasped.

'I didn't want to,' she replied. Her dark eyes became misty, she turned their gaze on Felix; he regarded her nudity almost dispassionately she thought vaguely; memories flooded her, the well of shame giving them up, she felt humiliation, and tears welled and trickled down her cheeks. Her thorns ached and she could feel her body responding with the need for pleasure.

'Oh Saskia!' Her words were barely audible. She swayed unsteadily and Saskias arms slipped around her waist to support her. Ayesha leaned into her body, her fingers rested on Saskias, spreading, they were warm, and Saskia felt a tremor in them. Ayesha's body made little sensual movements; she was in a state of intense arousal, Saskia realised, and she felt her own body begin to respond; the mandragora serpens was affecting Ayesha much more intensely than herself, yet she had consumed less; she considered the nature of an alchemical elixir, surprised by her own detachment of thought, unlike a drug to which the body produced a tolerance, perhaps the reverse was true of alchemy, its effects growing more tangible with use instead of less so; interesting; she would ask Holly. She became aware of Felix who had risen from his chair and now towered massively in front of them, she smiled tightly up at him, her expression unfathomable.

'Take her from me, she's yours after all for now. She's my gift to you. Go on!' Saskia withdrew her arms and gave Ayesha a little push behind her shoulder blades; Ayesha stumbled forwards, her legs almost gave way beneath her; Felix reacted quickly, and steadied her; she clung to him, her fists clenched in the fabric of his shirt. Felix regarded Saskia searchingly.

'I'll follow soon. I'm not ready yet,' Saskia responded with a touch of defiance. 'I just need a little time.' She rocked a little where she stood. 'Fuck! that stuff screws with you Felix! I'm not complaining mind.' She was breathing rapidly, shallow breaths; she had begun to experience hallucinations, little shifts of movement in the mosaic floor and among the figures around the wall.

'Go on take her,' she said, her voice suddenly sounding very loud. She rested her fingers in the crook of his elbow where he supported Ayesha's upper body. 'I'll be along soon, I promise!'

Briefly, his features underwent change, and she was looking at the features of a bull. A bull man. A minotaur? The analogy seemed inadequate: she would have smiled but there were wolves in her eyes; she was unable to make her lips move. Was she seeing him as he was or was it hallucination. He was inside her; she could feel him exploring her; she wondered if he could sense her steadily building sexual desire, or the little black patches of interrupted consciousness from which she kept emerging. Felix nodded to her; she felt him leave her; taking Ayesha away from her; she felt a strange, yearning loss, which became almost panic; then darkness consumed her, and by the time it relented, Felix and Ayesha had disappeared.

Five

Drunk? Not drunk! God, she felt odd! Saskia was aware of her appetites being enhanced by the Mandragora Serpens, and by Felix's own fascinating abilities; she was aware of them, still active inside her; they would be active inside Ayesha too, in her sex centre, God knows, what they were doing to her compliance thorns. She stumbled, a little dizzily, and she turned to the onyx table to lean on it for support.

Saskia felt watched! the snake head handles of her silver gilt bowl watched her; the snake heads on the handle and mouth of the silver gilt ewer watched her; something stood behind her and watched her. She resisted the urge to look. She felt watched from every side, every angle. She stared at the last swallow of Mandragora Serpens in her cup. She reached out, though it seemed a long way off. She swallowed the bitter fire, though she could not recall raising the cup to her lips; she considered pouring more from the ewer, but she decided that the action might be beyond her, even inadvisable. She straightened her body again. She clung to the table in sudden intense vertigo. She waited for the vertigo to pass, and it did, mostly, it drained away like rain through a grate, taking with it any sense of panic or fear. She turned around because she really did feel as if there was something behind her. And there was and she smiled in recognition.

'Hello you.' He regarded her impassively with his heavily lidded eyes from seven feet of height. His forward leaning stance seemed somehow reassuring.

'I'm pleased you're still around!' Saskia narrowed her eyes, and she pursed her lips; they felt big, like they had been stung by bees; she peered intently at her creatures sinister face.

'Are you pleased to see me? Are you going to smile?' Her voice sounded odd to her; muffled. The words felt huge in her mouth, and they sounded like she was talking through water. Her creatures trap of a mouth proceeded to form the very thinnest of smiles in response.

'I feel very strange you know,' she told it. 'And exceptionally fucking horny. Don't worry you're safe. I'm keeping that for something else. But before I get boned, I'm going to get up to no good because that's what I'm like. I'm going to confide in you. I want to look behind a door and you're coming with me.'

She turned her back on her monster, moving as if she was in training for deportment, sensing disequilibrium no more than an incautious movement away. She did not pause to see if he was following, she anticipated that he would. She hallucinated immediately; pitch-black engulfed her in temporary oblivion; relented, and fell on her again, passing through her in a succession of waves; her mind felt like chunks of time were eluding her; she could not hear the padding of her feet on the floor; she could not remember beginning to walk even. She looked down at her feet, the touch of the floor felt sensual, the tesserae of the mosaic appeared to be liquid; her feet passed through its surface, and it behaved like multi coloured mercury; it poured over her toes and insteps in globules that left no trail or residue. Blackout. Saskia gasped, the taste of bronze filled her mouth and nose, unbearably strong, Verdigris bitterness; it was on her breath, and it was everywhere in her skin, the cold metal closing around her bones, and moving inside her veins. She was not aware of passing through the portal in the floor or beginning to descend the bronze staircase. She came out of pitch-black half-way through her descent; holding onto the railing two handed for support; the liquid bronze of the stairs and rail trailed from her feet and fingers like strands of treacle. She had always possessed the ability to taste through touch but never like this, the Mandragora Serpens had magnified the sense to a whole new level. Blackout. Please stop. God, she decided that she hated tripping! She gasped. The mosaic floor was alive, five treads below. A pool of sinuous tentacles and giant undulating bodies, and every black cephalopod eye was fixed on her. She was tempted to turn back. To simply go, to find Ayesha and Felix. The need for sex was becoming quite intense. Blackout. The tentacle slipped from around her thigh; fascinated she watched it unwind down her knee and calf, it paused at her ankle and tightened like a restraint; it relented disengaging entirely and arched elegantly back into the pool. Somewhere underneath her hallucination was the surface of the mosaic; but it did not feel like it; it really did feel like she was walking on squid. Blackout. The impassive eye on the Porta Magica regarded her. She expected it to blink, to come alive and look her up and down, to participate in hallucination, but it did not do so.

'Delusions and phantasms verboten then?' she asked it. Tentatively she extended a hand; she could see the sweat standing out on her skin, a gleaming film; she stroked the cold surface of the eyelid with her fingertips, not bitterly cold as before, simply cool; the temperature of the room was not freezing cold either; it had become ambient. It might be the Mandragora Serpens at work, but she decided not. She tensed, sensing entity inside the patinated metal again. It was aloof, austere; if intellect existed it concealed it. She tasted nothing through her touch, or she tasted silence; the metal might not even be metal. She shuddered; the door possessed the potential to be inimical, but it regarded her with indifference, which in a way was a win. As before she could see no handle, no recess, no finger holds in which to gain a purchase; so, it opened outwards! But how could you close it again? So, it did not open outwards then. She pushed hard with both hands just to test it. The door remained fixed. She wondered if it was locked somehow. She was aware that her nausea had intensified; her vertigo returned spinning the world around her. She felt very sick. Inspired, she went with instinct. In the world of magic *'open sesame'* seemed like an option.

'Will you open for me,' she said, politely. 'Please.' In her mind, and there did not seem to be much of that beyond a sense of identity, and that kept floating off, she imagined that the door opened. Nothing happened. She swallowed, with difficulty, her mouth dry. She recalled something Ayesha had told her when she was teaching her to access Place; in magic of any variety, and there were many forms, they were all actions of the will; but you never imagined the action, you assumed it had already taken place. You imagined it done, with an almost casual acceptance that it was so. Just like throwing intent, echoing what Felix had said about another mechanism in play.

'And I'm pretty damned good at that now,' she told her creature, who she was damned sure was still behind her. With difficulty, because her memories were fudge, she recalled the quote even though it was not peculiar to this action, it focused her; she saw the door opening; knowing that it was.

'*It is not down on any map*,' she quoted from Moby Dick, '*true places never are.*'

The door swung; she felt conceit as it opened; its edge missed her by inches. Like a great big circular vault door in the movies. She expected to see a bevelled edge, satisfyingly immense, swing before her eyes. Instead of which it appeared to be so thin that she could not see it, or maybe it was invisible, or there was no edge at all; some property of the door at work, or maybe the door was imagination, just like everything else in the universe; don't go there! not just now Saskia! The reverse side of the door appeared as it had when she and Ayesha had examined it.

She gazed through the hole in reality. Blackout. She stood in the hole. A girl in a circle. She gasped in fear. The great white whale rushed at her, vast; she could see the harpoons in it, the scars, and the barnacles on its skin; it turned at the last opportunity and she looked into its great knowing eye as it passed by her, the things gigantic body going on and on. It turned away and soared down into unimaginable emptiness, receding to a distant smudge which then became nothing at all. She gazed over the edge of what appeared to be infinity. She felt a rush of vertigo again and swayed. Then she bent forward and vomited. Then she vomited again; through tear blurred eyes she watched her vomit trail out of sight into the cavernousness below. Blackness.

Saskia swayed, unstable, her world spinning. Her eyes rounded in alarm, and she reached out to steady herself against the edge of the portal. She expected to encounter something, whatever that something might be under her fingers. She encountered nothing. Alarm escalated to panic; she was about to pitch into whatever this was. She felt the pressure of hands on her waist; they steadied her; they were too small to be her monster's hands; had Ayesha come to find her?

'Do you want to fall forever?' It was Sofia's voice, its tone sardonic. Saskia shook her head, then wished she had not. When the spinning stopped Sofia spoke again.

'Go on, take a good look.'

'Would I fall forever?'

'Yes, you would fall for eternity, or until something found you.'

'That doesn't sound very nice. Surely, I would die? There can't be air! Am I looking at space? Why would I fall, why did my vomit fall? There's no gravity!'

'You aren't looking into the cold expanse. You're looking into the Abyss, and the only way is down! It has its own rules. It's compelling, isn't it?'

'The Abyss?'

'Yes. The Abyss.'

Saskia straightened unsteadily, confident that Sofia would not let her fall. She did not want to gaze into that profound emptiness anymore. She turned and felt Sofia's hands relax to allow it. She came about too abruptly, and she began to spin again; she looked down and shut her eyes but that made things worse, and she panicked and clutched at Sofia. Something pulled loose and slipped from her hand, she clutched again and opened her eyes in time to glimpse Sofia's rainbow silk Hijab undulate through the portal into the Abyss. She waited for her vision to stop its rapid rotation, and she looked at Sofia apologetically. Her eyes widened in surprise. Sofia closed her eyes and compressed her lips in exasperation. It looked as if she was counting to ten, Saskia thought. She opened her eyes again and levelled a look of displeasure at Saskia.

'That was expensive!' she said.

'I'm sorry! Are those real or am I hallucinating them?' She was referring to the eight little red snake heads that protruded from Sofia's crown in place of hair;

they had shot erect as she had pulled away her Hijab. The heads were on slender scaley necks, each around thirty centimetres long, and they stared at her with little, black, uncompromising eyes.

'They're real. And you owe me three hundred and fifty quid for that Hijab. It was designer.'

'That's not a problem,' Saskia whispered; she continued to be fascinated by the snakes; she could see tiny, forked tongues flickering from their mouths; they did not appear to be aggressive though, at present.

'You have vomit on your chin,' Sofia told her disgustedly. 'You might be the first person to throw up into the Abyss!'

'Do you think so?' Saskia resisted the temptation to wipe her chin with the back of her hand.

Sofia gave her an enigmatic look. 'Felix told me to keep an eye on you! He knew you would be trouble!'

'Is that why you stopped singing? To keep an eye on me!'

Sofia tilted her head to the side retaining her smile.

'Your skin is flushed; you're sweating like a pig. You need to clean up before you go to Felix. Come with me. hold my hand.'

*

Lucidity was intermittent, it did not fluctuate, but switched on like a lightbulb, and as suddenly, switched off. Between was a mixture of blurred event and abstract image, the intermittent sound of Ayesha's own voice as it vocalised pleasure and laughter and spasmodic strings of obscenities. Felix had brought her to a Place, she could barely remember getting there. She remembered darkness and dim astral light. she could feel thick furs beneath her feet. She swayed, but Felix steadied her with a finger beneath her chin; he traced the contours of her body with his fingertips, their touch intimate and beguiling. The waves of sensation induced by the mandragora serpens followed his fingers; Ayesha moved sensually with their journey, voicing little cries of pleasure. She heard a beautiful voice begin to sing close by, charmingly and lasciviously, as Felix discovered the location of her compliance thorns and turned each one to aching fire under his fingertips. She arched to the sensation, kissing his hot naked skin; her fingers reached for him, until his hardness filled her hands. She began to lower her body so she could take him in her mouth, but she felt herself prevented and lifted up by strong hands; her fingers clasped his powerful neck, and she drew up and parted her knees, against his sides; she arched at the erotic pain of penetration. She felt his fingers at the back of her neck under her hair, her own fingers dug into his shoulders as she pushed herself up and lowered herself in rhythm with the erotic song; its words entwined with each rush of sensation compelled in her by the mandragora serpens. Some lucid part of her mind was aware of Felix's fingers as they brushed her lips, and of a red glow that bled over them, from the massive ring on his middle finger. She saw his face in the malign radiance, broad and bull like. His eyes gleamed like hot gold in his dark skin, they burned into her, but there was no look of passion or lust, they did not devour, if anything they were impassive. A red orb emerged from the glowing ring; it was about the size of a golf ball; it resembled a brooding, miniature red sun. It rose vertically, stopping just above their heads, shedding a red aura. Another orb emerged from the ring, followed by another, until five orbs had emerged and risen up to form a colony of little malevolent red suns. A sixth emerged and entered her brow, she felt its progress inside her; descending through her pillar, through each of her centres; throat, heart, plexus; it felt cold, like she had swallowed the coldest of ice creams. When it reached her sex centre it stopped. It seemed to burst, and bliss followed. Ayesha orgasmed; pleasure became her world, never breaking, filling her. As it extended to her silver compliance thorns it transformed to bittersweet agony, each one became like a briar of hurt, winding inside her, amidst the consuming pleasure. She was oddly conscious of sweating, the trickle of it on her febrile skin felt like tiny rivulets of fire. The Lalyt's skin felt pliant and hot under the rake of her nails and fingertips, but there was no indication of sweating. A red ambience bled from his skin; it prickled her skin in little waves of tingling bliss that became one with her orgasm. Her mind blurred into abstract, the colour black, speared with red. Her orgasm filled her, and consumed her, and there was only sensation and the distant sound of her own calls. Her imagination flooded with images, Saskia, Khalid, Nathan, and familiar faces of her abusers. She saw Saskia and Khalid on his bed, locked in the act of sex; Saskia's face contorted in bliss as Khalid took her. Jealousy swarmed through Ayesha like a thousand stinging bees in waves of delicious agony. She emerged into semi lucidity her mind struggling to focus, aware of furs against her back heated by her skin, and Felix's mass on top of her and inside her. The image of Saskia clung to her mind. A rush of resentment entered her; where was the little bitch, her little bitch; she'd left her alone to Felix; up to no fucking good. 'Fuck oh fuck!' she heard her own voice yelping. She felt her sense of self slipping away again, but then something happened that brought it back and caused her to focus. The pressure of familiar lips on hers, a familiar kiss. A familiar scent intensified by her senses. Saskias.

*

Blackness relented as Saskia raised her dripping face from the granite washbowl. The blackouts were no more frequent, they were simply too arbitrary. She glared at her reflection through her spinning world. Her makeup was a total fucking mess, she decided; she did wonder if she actually gave a damn and decided not. She had washed the vomit from her chin, then swished her mouth and gargled with several of mouthfuls from a bottle of Dom Pérignon she had scooped off the table, on her way to the bathroom. Sofia had pulled a disapproving face, and Saskia had returned her a look which said: Don't you dare condemn me. Sofia had left her in the bathroom stating that she would return shortly and to stay exactly where she was. The image of her creature appeared in the mirror forming behind her right shoulder. It regarded her solemnly.

'Don't look at me like that. I know I need to attend to business, but I just need a few minutes. Anyway, where were you when I needed you? I nearly fell into the Abyss! I had to be saved by a Gorgon!'

'Who or what are you talking to?' Sofia asked suspiciously as she came back into the bathroom. 'And I'm not Gorgon.'

'I'm talking to myself,' Saskia replied sulkily. Her hallucinations had diminished, which was a relief; she now only experienced little flickering movements around the edges of her vision; now if only the blackouts and the dizziness would stop. She did not turn round to face Sofia; she did not want to wait two minutes for her to stop oscillating. She gave Sofia a brief once over through the mirror, whilst trying not to move her eyes. The demonic was eying her with calculating interest. All her snakes were coiled and asleep, they looked like beautiful little scaley braids. Pitch black, nothing.

'What?' she was aware of Sofia's voice as her stream of consciousness returned.

Sofia clicked her tongue, frowning. 'I said I know about you! You see ghosts and entities.' Sofia held a glass tumbler. It was half full of liquid; it fizzed, and it resembled Alka seltzer. 'You drank far too much mandragora serpens. You were greedy. Now drink this,' she said.

'What is it?'

'It will help you to hydrate. More significantly it will stop your vertigo. Among my skill set I've medicinal alchemy. Drink it! It does taste disgusting though.'

'Did you create the Mandragora serpens?'

'No. Felix has that specially prepared.'

She set the glass down in front of Saskia. 'It's for you to decide. It makes no difference to me.'

Saskia doubted that; Sofia had gone to the trouble of mixing it after all; she picked up the glass and faced Sofia's reflection. She drank without hesitation. Sofia allowed her lip to curl into a slight smile as she saw Saskia's grimace in the mirror.

'You haven't covered up again,' Saskia remarked.

'I didn't see the need,' Sofia responded.

Saskia gasped as her world suddenly became still. 'I could kiss you,' she told Sofia.

Sofia frowned. 'Please don't.'

Saskia wondered if the solution Sofia had given her would counter the blackouts; she was about to tell her about them, but blackness tried to suck her in and failed, possibly providing her answer. She was left standing with her mouth open like a goldfish, staring at Sofia in the mirror.

Sofia eyed her dubiously. 'I'll leave you to your privacy,' she said. 'When you're done in here, the corridor behind the staircase will take you to Felix and Ms Shah.' She nodded, turned about and left.

'So bloody uptight,' Saskia told to her reflection in the mirror. She looked for her creature, but he had left too, along with her hallucinations. Only Saskia remained. Slim and barefoot and beautiful. Need clamoured inside her; it had never gone away, simply stepped into the background; now it made itself known again, like an actor returning to centre stage. Her need for sex became consuming.

'Time to fuck.' She told her reflection.

She returned to the Trojan room and made straight for the onyx table where they had been seated. She took up the parcel gilt jug and emptied the last of the mandragora serpens into the quaich; it didn't amount to much, no more than a couple of swallows. Saskia was certain it was not sensible to drink any more of the elixir, even a small amount was potent. She imagined Sofia's disapproval as she drank. Deliciously heightened sensations scurried through her body; her demon walked free, leading her thoughts down disturbing ways and opening doors to dark places in her mind. She felt an almost instant hit, a surge of sensation; a sense of euphoria that left no place inside her untouched. She heard herself gasp and pant in shock as the elixir penetrated. She set down the quaich, her hand trembled slightly; she straightened and stalked through the portal, where Felix had taken Ayesha. Beyond stretched a corridor of polished concrete. It felt cold under Saskia's bare feet but not unpleasant; her body felt hot and stretched; pulled threads; all elements laid bare; the ache for sex penetrated to her very core, a fluid hungry fire. She concentrated on the soft pad of her feet, and their softly tantalizing echo. No blackouts since the bathroom, she thought, so the potion had countered those, too. Yay, for Sofia and her medicinal alchemy. Low lights burned in the concrete ceiling, puddling her shadow around her feet.

She felt a deviant excitement and anticipation; it was exquisitely wanton. 'Ayesha! Felix!' Saskia's words sounded hollow, echoing. She reached behind her; she heard the sound of her zip and felt the sensual tumble of her dress; she walked from it without pausing her step; the air transited over denuded skin, feeling so intense that it almost took her breath away. The end of the passage was close, a few more steps away. She halted, at the edge of another hole in the floor. A portal and a circular concrete stair, which plunged away into darkness; the 'rabbit hole'. Saskia smiled at the thought. She began her descent without hesitating; the darkness quickly swallowed her. She sensed alternative a few steps down and immediately recognised Place; doorway, undenied. She had the mildly bizarre experience of leaving above her, the darkness that belonged to another space, as the low-key astral light that always occupied Place, appeared around her, and the stairwell ended abruptly. The atmosphere changed the instant she entered Place; it appeared to vibrate and shift; it felt as if a hundred moth wings were beating on her skin; her sexual need intensified even more, she had not thought it could; desire clawed at her vulva. She could hear a beautiful song, produced by an equally beautiful voice; it possessed an Indian character; so, probably Jyothi, who Felix had mentioned. She sang softly and her tone had a lascivious quality. Saskia heard an exclamation, followed by another. Ayesha's voice: it sounded almost distressed, but she quickly recognised that she was expressing pleasure. She found she was in a circular room, about ten metres in diameter. The walls and floor were mosaiced, with erotic panels, in the manner of Athenian black figure earthenware; they depicted naked nymphs copulating with various male figures, including fauns and minotaur's. A cluster of red lights swarmed about two metres above the floor at the centre of the chamber. Beneath, on the floor, on a giant bed of furs, Felix and Ayesha were engaged in sex. Saskia could hear Jyothi's voice close by, but there was no sight of her; she presumed she was in an adjacent room, or a space hidden in the wall.

    Ayesha made small lascivious movements, she encouraged Felix on with a succession of obscenities and clawing fingers. Fascinated Saskia knelt in the furs to observe more closely; tentatively she extended her fingers and ran their tips through a red nimbus that lay across the surface of their skin; it was less than a centimetre and it prickled pleasantly to the touch. She extended her fingers further and touched Felix's shoulder; the skin felt hot. Out of an expensive Savile row suit, Felix appeared even more enormous; quite intimidating, in fact. She stared into his face; his expression was darkly sensual. She realised he was watching her; his golden eyes had a reddish tint; they looked quite malevolent. His lips parted revealing his white teeth. Saskia laughed, her voice sounding strangely distorted; her breathing and heartbeat elevated; her eyes widened as Felix's teeth parted and his tongue emerged; it was pointed and thick; it glistened as it extended, becoming abnormally long; its tip brushed her mouth; it felt warm and wet on her lips; tentatively, feeling very kinky indeed, Saskia opened her mouth to allow it access; sensually it slid inside, searching her mouth and tongue.

She shivered with pleasure as the deviant aspect in her own nature acquired dominance. She was aware that one of the red orbs had descended, reducing the interweaving system of four. It hovered, level with her brow, bobbing ever so slightly, like an annoying, exotic insect. She resisted the urge to swat it. It brushed against her brow, making it tingle, then to her surprise it entered her; she almost panicked as it began its journey through her centres, until it stopped in her sex centre; for the present inactive. She felt Felix's tongue leave her mouth and experienced resentment. She heard Ayesha say something, but she could not make it out. She peered closely at her face; it was covered in beads of sweat. Saskia leaned into her and placed a kiss on Ayesha's mouth, her lips were hot, salty with sweat. They responded needily and Ayesha's eyes tried to focus on her; her body made small lascivious movements, in response to Felix's movements. As Saskia withdrew her kiss, Ayesha focused and spoke, barely audibly through her fast, shallow breathing. She tried to smile. 'Saskia! I thought you'd backed out!' Her black eyes glistened; they searched for Saskia, but they did not seem to see her; he gaze was inward looking, focused on a universe of pleasure.

'I wouldn't do that darling!' Saskia said. She saw anxiety pass over Ayesha's face. 'My orgasm, it won't fucking stop.' Ayesha gasped; she tried to arch her body; her eyes closed. Felix withdrew from Ayesha, though she tried to cling to him; he reached for Saskia, drawing her to him; she reacted with fingers and mouth and tongue, responding to his intimate fingers. His mouth devoured her body, his prehensile tongue explored. She heard her own words urging him. When he entered her, she was first aware of the pain of distension, this gave way to pleasure; she climaxed almost instantly; the feel of orgasm penetrating every part of her. She could hear her voice telling of her bodies pleasure. Then the orb in her sex centre appeared to burst and blew her away. She experienced the sensation of being held by something supple and powerful; something with purpose and volition. She felt penetration of her vulva and her anus. She gasped in surprise; allowed. She saw the red ambience bleed from Felix's skin and felt its heat on her skin, and then its barbs, and intimately inside her too; the penetration of a thousand tiny needles. She gave an exclamation of surprised pain; followed by a silent scream as each needle began to sting like a hornet. The agony lasted for only seconds; she had known more intense pain, she decided, more brutally traumatic. She sobbed as the pain ended and the pleasure renewed; each sting became a little probe of bliss. She clutched at Felix's head with her fingertips, her nails digging in his short hair; she searched his gold eyes and his big impassive face; he almost did not seem to be present, but she could feel him moving through every tiny piece of her. She was aware of Ayesha close to her, their bodies almost touching. Ayesha convulsed and apart from her rapid breathing, she went still. Saskia followed the Lalyt's progress within; it was relentless. She felt a surge of panic as it threaded up through her core, and climbed through her pillar, winding like a serpent, flooding her centres with bliss. She lost sensation of her body. She felt her mind detach, more than her mind. She felt that she was losing identity, but something in her denied that. She felt her personality being stripped naked, piece by piece, until nothing was hidden; the amount of darkness in her surprised some detached part of her; it loitered like a spectre in a cloister. Could Felix see everything that she was, she wondered. She was surrounded by a fine luminous mist that extended for several feet all around her and above her; beyond that she could perceive nothing; there were no movements or substance. She existed at its core and felt that she might be its core. Remotely she was aware of continuing sexual pleasure, but it did not reach to the plane of existence she was occupying. A figure approached her through the mist, slim and straight. It was Ayesha, naked, as was she. Her hair flowed behind her like black fire. She smiled with calm assurance; a ribbon of dark fire trickled through her eyes. She framed the word 'Saskia' with her lips, though Saskia did not hear her speak it. Equivalent to the location of her compliance thorns in her physical body, a sequence of black forms, each a tiny vortex twisted down into her ethereal body. Ayesha was gazing at something on Saskia's own body; she looked down and saw threads of black light, extending around her from her back; they moved like the tentacles on a sea anemone, and for all the world looked like thin fibre optic cables. They merged closer together the further they passed behind her, and with a sudden certainty, Saskia realised that their source had to be the location of her removed fetter. How curious. As she thought this, she observed Ayesha's five centres, the chakras from heel to throat excluding the delusional third eye and the spiritual crown, they lit up and become visible within her; they burned white, with the intensity of tiny suns. She felt her own chakras become cool, and they lit up too. They began to pulse and release charges of energy like tiny burning darts, which pierced the mist at speed. She saw that Ayesha's centres had begun to do the same. They exchanged looks, and with unspoken agreement they each reached out a hand for the other to hold. Their touch felt like burning ice. They willed their astral bodies to follow, and they did with the instancy of thought. They halted abruptly and without the effects of inertia. Through the mist they saw Felix or some astral version of Felix; naked, seated cross legged; he appeared immense, almost a giant; his features were saturnine, demonic; a large red chakra burned at the lower middle of his body, visible through his astral form, another behind his brow; a third was located in the region of his throat. Only three chakras to a demon, Saskia thought, as they flared like they were in a solar wind as the energy from herself and Ayesha rained through the astral mist onto them and merged with them. The Lalyt's commission. She saw Felix's eyes open and rest on them, aware of them. His mouth split in a wide grin; its glee spread into his gold eyes; it was certainly not an indulgent expression; it contained cruelty and arrogance; entitlement. He raised a hand in a gesture that she should go to him; Saskia turned her head to look at Ayesha, she could no longer feel her hand in hers; she saw that Ayesha had disappeared. Saskia decided to make a fast exit too, which she did.

    Saskia awoke in the physical, her body a furnace, shaking and covered in cooling sweat; residual pleasure continued to claw inside her. Felix had withdrawn physically from her and returned to Ayesha who was astride him, enclosed in the fragile red nimbus. She rode him frenetically as she raked his gleaming torso; her face was intense; white and drained, her eyes burned black out of hollows. Saskia pushed herself up on one elbow, her hand in sable; it slid, and she readjusted. She glanced up and saw that only a single red orb remained above them. Her heart pounded as it descended; her mouth curved in a smile and she closed her eyes and lifted her face, as the orb penetrated her brow.

'Ow!' Saskia exclaimed, suddenly awake. 'Why did you pinch my tit?' She glared up into Ayesha's smiling face. Dissatisfied with the dim astral light, Ayesha had formed a tiny ball of static; whereas it was unwise to use intent in a Place, static could be. It hovered and crackled softly, close to their faces. Ayesha's face possessed a hint of the diabolical in its stark light, as she peered down into Saskia's own.

'I wonder, you know,' Ayesha smiled sinisterly. 'If I've been fucking a little demon all along. Yes, you little mantis, you'd make a fine demonic.' Ayesha leaned down and kissed Saskia lightly on the tip of her nose. They were alone on the tangled furs, the glow from Ayesha's static, illuminating only their immediate space.

Saskia became fully awake, she was surprised how clear headed she felt, she had expected to be hung over or something similar; it appeared, she assumed, that alchemical stimulants worked very differently to alcohol.

'Your nails are sharp,' she said accusingly, between clenched teeth; she massaged her left breast close to the nipple. 'How long have you been awake?' she asked.

'Ten minutes, perhaps,' Ayesha shaped a tiny shrug. 'I woke and Felix wasn't here; I hate men in the morning though; I simply won't have them around.'

'I'm with you there.'

'I did prod you at first; eventually I resorted to pain; I thought you'd like that little Mantis.' Her voice softened, becoming sensual, her eyes had not left Saskia's.

'I prefer to be ready for it,' Saskia protested, though not wholeheartedly. Unexpectedly Ayesha pressed her mouth down onto Saskia's, surprising her; she responded automatically. It was a moist, elegant, pleasing, open mouthed kiss. Right then it seemed one of the sexiest they had ever shared. She gasped as Ayesha's teeth bit into the soft middle of her under lip; she tasted her own blood. It was not deep, barely surface, just a stinging little bite. She followed the tiny micro movements in Ayesha's beautiful, presently slightly cruel eyes, as Ayesha studied the same in her own. Watching for resentful wolves perhaps. Ayesha's teeth relented their bite in her lip. Saskia examined the tiny wound with her tongue.

'Do you feel any different?' she asked.

'I should ache, but I don't. I should feel exhausted, but I feel alive.'

'Me too.'

'We should talk about it, but on the way home. I do need a shower,' Ayesha told her, her voice remaining softened. 'Badly!'

'Me too.' Saskia repeated. Their lips brushed almost imperceptibly as they spoke.

'But do you know something little mantis?' Ayesha said darkly.

'What Ayesha?'

'Not before I fuck you.' She opened her moist little mouth to Saskia's again, stifling any reply.

Six

Bang! Bang! Bang! Bang!

'Who the hell is that?' Holly flung herself on her back on the mattress. Temper flashed in her copper-coloured eyes. She had been on the edge of orgasm; she was flushed and covered in sweat. Now it was ruined, and her resentment was directed at whoever it was that felt the need to beat on her door so insistently at seven in the morning. Luca regarded her with amused indulgence, her own orgasm was twitching on the point of release; she suspected Holly had abandoned the sex out of pure pique, not because the pounding on the door had ruined her enthusiasm or disrupted her tempo, but out of petulance. It was a spoiled moment; there would be many more moments.

Bang! Bang! Bang! Bang!

'Fuck!' Holly switched from angry to incandescent. She exited the bed in a single fluid motion; she stooped to snatch her grey cotton bed-tee from the floor and pulled it on as she stalked from the bedroom. Luca thought she could almost hear the angry buzzing of the bees in her tattoos. Her approach significantly more casual than Holly's, she got out of their trashed bed and located her own white cotton tee; it was an identical one to Holly's with an asymmetrical hem, one that Holly had given her, among others. She thought it suited Holly better, particularly how the higher edge hung across the curve of her pretty hip. Luca drew it on and followed Holly out of the room; she was interested in how the encounter at the door would pan out, though she would hang back, her appearance being an issue.

Holly wrenched open her big, old, iron strapped front door in bare feet and a rucked-up bed-tee. She had prepared angry words and was looking forward to using them. 'What the fuck do you mean by pounding on...' She stopped abruptly; her face took on grim purpose, a look of almost ferocious intensity; her eyes narrowed, and she summoned elemental intent, aware of the rapid drumbeat of her heart.

The conditions outside were dank and overcast, the morning was struggling to break through. There were two callers. One stood three to four metres back from the door, next to an almost blood red Audi Spyder. The other morning caller occupied Holly's broad, two-tiered, dressed stone doorstep; its clawed hand was still raised in the act of applying Holly's large Medusa head door knocker, until Holly wrenched open her door and dragged it from its fingers. Holly decided the diabolical stood maybe two and a half metres in height; It wore a hooded garment of well-worn brown leather; a sort of riding cloak or habit, which reached almost to the ground; this was fastened down the front, with buckled straps. Its arms poked through slits in the sides. Its hands were bone white, with cruel looking yellow talons, on the ends of long fingers, each with three joints. It had a raised hood and initially Holly thought that it was wearing a sort of plague mask; she quickly discarded that idea, as it was apparent that the long-pointed features constituted its real face. It gazed down at her, and large, round, soulless eyes regarded her emptily.

'Get the hell off my doorstep, and back off!' Holly growled.

'I did advise her that beating on your door like that was not the most diplomatic way of getting your attention; particularly at seven in the morning, when we could easily have waited until nine.' The other caller spoke in a confident tone; she possessed a slightly sharp, reasonably educated Mancunian accent.

She was small, attractive; very human in appearance, though Holly's spidey senses indicated demonic. She was dressed entirely in designer black; a short tight skirt, and waisted, fitted jacket; a Chanel bag, hung from her shoulder, rested on her right hip; she wore Louboutin's, without them she would have been a mere couple of centimetres taller than Holly. She had shoulder length brunette hair; she was beautiful in an unorthodox way, with a wide mouth that hinted it could smile, which was presently set in an uncompromising line. She had sly grey-blue eyes, and they regarded Holly with calm assurance. Holly decided she looked about forty, but that counted for nothing; she was as much a demonic as the creature she accompanied. She watched Holly cautiously; her work rarely brought her into direct contact with many adepts.

'Fuck!' Holly heard Luca's muttered expletive as she arrived in the hall behind her and took in the situation.

So did the diabolical. 'Luca, come closer, I want to speak with you. This is serious, but it can be handled.' She spoke persuasively, in a soft, almost melodious voice, which was distinctively feminine and was made all the more sinister because of what produced it. The creature peered beyond Holly, fixing Luca with black eyes that resembled circular pits; they did not move, and they did not blink.

'I'm not coming anywhere near you; I know how you want to handle this.' Luca said cryptically. 'Holly, she's called Panqual; she's from Asmodeum and she's Saradina's captain. I mean truly dangerous.'

Holly knew about Asmodeum, another of the demonic realms; she had once heard it referred to as Pandemonium on steroids. It's inhabitants had a cruel and sinister reputation and possessed few of the more human traits that existed in the denizens of Pandemonium.

'Back off from my door, before I make you,' Holly warned her.

Panqual fixed her empty gaze on Holly. 'You think you can?' she said, curiously.

'Try me.'

Designer demonic, regarded her companion dubiously. 'I think she can Panqual,' she said, matter of fact. 'Please stand back and let me do my job.' Her voice became stiletto sharp. 'Like now!'

Panqual emitted what sounded like a low growl; for a moment it looked as if she did not intend to comply; then she shrugged and stepped back from the porch, taking four long backward paces. She withdrew her hands inside her garment; Holly thought she resembled a huge demonic Wally bird, and despite her mood she experienced the desire to paint her. As Panqual withdrew, Luca moved into view and took up a defiant stance next to Holly.

Panqual regarded her. 'Luca, by being here you're betraying the trust of your benefactor; end this nonsense now and return with me to Pandemonium, before the consequences become any more dire than they already are.' Her tone sounded reasonable, almost placatory; yet it was loaded with subliminal menace. Holly could feel the tension between them; it could have been cut with a knife.

'Luca isn't returning to Pandemonium,' she stated. She took Luca's hand in hers. 'She's staying here with me.'

'My business concerns Luca Rajal. It has nothing to do with you.' Panqual did not look at Holly as she made her reply, her empty gaze remained fixed on Luca. 'You know how to make this right.'

'Fuck!' Holly heard the other demonic say under her breath.

'It's everything to do with me!' Holly stated indignantly, her eyes hot with anger. 'You're on my property, at my door and I suggest you leave, now.'

'I know you're powerful,' Panqual said, now looking at Holly. 'But that does not give you the right to keep Luca here.'

'Your point?' Holly replied.

'I am concerned you are keeping Luca against her will.'

'That doesn't really merit a serious answer.' Holly said contemptuously. She stared at the other demonic. She stared back; she was in the act of screwing the four-inch heel of one of her Louboutin's thoughtfully into the pea gravel. 'Who are you?' Holly demanded. 'And what is "your job"?'

'My name is Rachel Zimpara. Good morning,' she said politely.

'I've heard of you.' Holly frowned.

'I've a reputation.'

'Not one to be proud of. You appropriate.'

'I prefer the word facilitate,' Zimpara replied. 'It's what I do.'

'Is there a chance of you facilitating your departure?'

'Is there any chance of Luca returning to pandemonium this morning, with Panqual?' Zimpara responded.

'Simply, not happening,' Holly stated.

'She is indentured to Satran Saradina...'

'She has duties! She's shirked them!' Panqual interrupted, her voice rising. 'She owes our mistress her loyalty. Luca must go back to Pandemonium with me! She knows we can resolve th...'

'That's enough!' Rachel Zimpara's voice cracked like a whip. 'I would remind you that this is my transaction.' Panqual fell silent; she acknowledged Zimpara's words with a small, begrudged inclination of her head.

'How did she even fit in your car?' Holly asked.

'Uncomfortably.'

Anyone glimpsing her must have thought her an incredibly odd sight scrunched into the passenger seat of the Spyder, Holly decided.

Zimpara threw Panqual a look of pure displeasure, then turned her attention to Holly and Luca again. 'In Pandemonium, the practise of indenture is regarded with unparalleled importance,' she said. 'It's pledges can't be shirked. What's preventing Luca from returning there to resume her obligations to the house of Saradina?' She looked pointedly at Holly and Luca's linked hands.

'Luca isn't a citizen of Pandemonium anymore,' Holly stated.

'Even if that's the case, her indenture is still binding.'

'Not here, in my world,' Holly said grimly.

'Pandemonium reserves the right to reclaim its denizens. That's where I come in.'

'What do you get out of this?' Holly shook her head in disbelief.

Zimpara gave a little harsh bark of laughter, returning holly's disbelieving smile. 'Dirty, filthy, money what else?'

'If Luca goes back to Pandemonium, she faces horrible punishment. Haven't you any qualms about that?'

Zimpara's eyes became hooded and she fixed Holly with a sardonic stare. 'Not my problem,' she said.

'Equally it's not our problem what Saradina wants. Luca and I have discussed her situation, and I've assured her of my protection. I've powerful friends; Saradina has already encountered them, and it didn't end well for her!'

'Maybe we should ask Luca.' Zimpara moved her gaze away from Holly, to meet Luca's cool, yellow gaze.

'Love can be shit, can't it?' she said. 'It shouldn't cause all this strife for people who don't deserve it. Do you trust this woman Luca?'

'Totally,' Luca responded, with certainty 'We've asked ourselves every question too. Gone over every doubt. I'm staying with Holly.'

'You have your answer,' Holly said, squeezing Luca's hand.

Zimpara narrowed her eyes, continuing to study Luca's expression for several moments. 'I guess I have,' she said.

'Totally fucking unacceptable!' Panqual snarled.

'Oh, shut up!' Zimpara snapped. She shrugged. 'I guess we're done here, except for this.' She opened her shoulder bag and drew out a folded document. It looked like parchment with a black wax seal along its fold.

'You have three days.' Zimpara presented the document to Holly, who regarded it suspiciously.

'It's safe,' Zimpara said, sensing her hesitation. Holly took the parchment from her, accepting her assurance. 'Take time to consider the consequences. Try to think about this with a cool head. I've written my number on the back of the document. Unless I hear from you before, I'll return in three days. You've been served,' She closed her bag with attitude. 'Get in the car Panqual, before I insist you catch a train.' She began to walk away, but on impulse she paused, half turning, to regard Holly and Luca not unsympathetically. 'I do get it, you know,' she told them. 'I know it isn't fair, but it's how it is. You've chosen a hazardous path. I'm sure you believe that you're reconciled to it.' She shrugged and continued to her car. Panqual followed reluctantly. She paused next to the open passenger door to look back, her empty eyes fixed on Luca, in a long look. Luca returned her stare, there was hatred in her eyes, and contempt and fear. Holly saw her shudder. Panqual folded her rangy body awkwardly into the passenger seat; moments later the Audi disappeared around the curve of the drive, passing between shrubbery and trees.

Holly and Luca exchanged looks. Holly closed the door and stood with her back to it, her face was dark with her thoughts, and her feet had chilled in the cool air.

'What now?' Luca asked; she studied Holly worriedly. She realised that this would be a personal test for them both, almost a trial by fire. She wondered if Holly was regretting her decision in the dull morning light.

'Time, I showed you off, I suppose,' Holly said. 'I need coffee, then a shower; I need to think; then I'll phone Saskia and Ayesha.'

*

'Stop here! Where the other vehicle is.'

'The one that's half blinding me with its headlights! Why?'

'Don't question me, do it!' Panqual snapped.

Zimpara huffed, hard and long. Since she had insisted on accompanying her, Panqual had managed to push every wrong button she could. She had not bothered to conceal her obvious contempt for her, and an attitude of superiority. A couple of times like now, she had acted like her boss; the diabolical might have clout in Pandemonium, Zimpara thought. Here in Kadman, she was just another outlandish body they would find in a ditch, for the police to cover up. She dispelled her fantasy; the creature next to her was a beast. 'You're getting on my tits,' she said.

Panqual shrugged. 'You only need to follow orders.'

'I'm not here to follow orders. I'm here to do my job. Which you have made difficult.'

The rain had begun as they turned out of the drive from Larkspur onto the adjacent lane. It was heavy and persistent, and the Audi's windscreen wipers worked hard to maintain visibility. The stationary vehicle was in a layby on the left among the trees, almost a mile from Larkspur; its headlights glared, on main beam, refracting through the rain into Zimpara's eyes. Panqual seemed unconcerned. Zimpara slowed the Audi but carried on past the other vehicle.

'I said stop!' Panqual hissed.

'I am!' Zimpara snapped. 'I'll stop beyond it. I'm not going to be blinded.' She pulled in and stopped her car a few metres past the other one. Panqual opened the passenger door and climbed out, unfolding herself into the pouring rain. She drew up the deep leather hood of her riding cloak. About a hundred metres along the lane, Zimpara could see a black, Land Rover Freelander pulled up, half on the verge, facing towards them. Her mouth set grimly. She was getting a very bad feeling about this business.

'What the fuck are you up to!' She demanded, turning in her seat to peer at Panqual through the open door.

'Come and find out. Do your duty,' Panqual replied haughtily.

'My duty's to myself. This is a commission. If you're doing what I think you're doing, I want no part of it. I've a reputation to maintain.' Despite her words she opened her door and climbed out into the rain, plucking her collapsible umbrella from the door pocket. The layby was more of a passing point for heavy farm vehicles to pull into, to let other vehicles by; its muddy surface was pocked with holes filled with water from the rain. Zimpara picked her way between them, three or four steps behind Panqual, who did not seem to care about splattering through the puddles. Zimpara was aware of the slanting rain pounding onto her umbrella and soaking into her skirt, and trickling down the backs of her legs, but she was more concerned about the mud on her Louboutin's and her sharp heels sinking into it. The other vehicle had looked familiar; she felt sudden apprehension as she recognised the red shogun sport. Her gaze travelled along it, observing the rivulets of rainwater flowing down its waxed sheen. The rear driver's side window had been wound down and Panqual halted and peered inside at the occupant. She was not to be invited to sit inside then, Zimpara thought. She positioned herself behind Panqual and to her right, visible from the interior of the shogun. Two occupants sat in the back; one, a woman, had her mass turned towards the window. She peered at them through black, bulbous, cow eyes; these were set in a broad face, that to Zimpara was irksomely familiar, along with its equally irksome expression of perpetual gloating. Her head snapped round, turning the big face to Zimpara; the black eyes observed her with critical malice, whilst creating a pretence of friendly joy.

'Rachel, what a pleasure it is to see you. It's been months!'

'Has it?' Zimpara looked suitably surprised.

'I left messages for you. I had commissions for you, but you haven't returned any of my calls. You're missing out; unless you're avoiding me; you wouldn't do that now, would you?' The cow eyes roved searchingly over her face.

Zimpara hated the sight of her; carefully she protected her thinking; Ariadne Leech had a knack of acquiring thoughts that were not her own.

'I would never do that,' she lied. 'There must be a fault on my phone.'

'A fault on your landline and mobile phone, how mysterious. Work must have suffered as a result,'

'I've never been busier,' Zimpara replied. 'I almost refused this commission from Saradina.' At this reveal, Panqual regarded her very deliberately with her large empty eyes, from beneath her hood. 'I only accepted it as a favour,' Zimpara shrugged, glancing at her. 'I have a new patron. Well not exactly new, but one I've developed a personal friendship with recently.'

'Forgetting old friends as a result.' Ariadne pursed her displeasing mouth rather sullenly, and shook her head admonishingly, swooshing shoulder length, white hair. 'My! Just who can this new patron be? Outshining Ariadne and Saradina. Are we to be told? Come on Rachel, don't be coy.'

Zimpara shrugged again; she resisted curling her lip in contempt. 'It's no secret. It's Bernadette O'Hare.'

The slightly maniac gleam in the cow eyes intensified. Ariadne paused, considering what Zimpara had just told them. Panqual tilted her head in interest, her long beak swishing in the rain. She recalled an incident a few months previously, involving Bernadette O'Hare and the denizens of Pandemonium; two in fact; one of them to execute a commission on her behalf, the other to obtain restitution from her. Neither had ended well for Pandemonium.

'My, you are flying high, Rachel,' Ariadne remarked softly. 'O'Hare likes familiarity with her intimates. What are you allowed to call her mightiness?'

'Testing me Ariadne? Ben of course, though I could just be saying it.' Zimpara replied, an element of conceit in her voice. She narrowed her eyes and peered into the interior of the shogun. The figure of a man shared the rear seat with Ariadne; he was perched on its edge; he was dressed all in black, in a leather bomber jacket; he had it zipped up to his collar. He had one of those bald heads with a little point on the crown; his skin was very pale; paper white almost; and he had long fingers like bones, interlocked in his lap. He peered impassively back at Zimpara with the pinkish, vaguely sore looking eye rims of an albino. They had crossed paths in the past, but there was no kind of friendship between them, or ever likely to be. He was called Josh Devlin, but he insisted on being called Baldur, after the Norse God. He was Ariadne's deputy, the major domo of her cult. Ariadne styled herself as a witch, a high priestess, but not of a coven; hers was a cult, she claimed. The cult of Herne the Hunter, and she named her followers, the Wild Hunt; God knows why! Zimpara recognised the driver too, though she did not look directly at her, merely glimpsing the long black hair and pretty tapering face. She was another high ranker in Ariadne's entourage. She had climbed into Zimpara's bed a few times, a dozen or so years ago, when she first crawled into Ariadne's dark world, straight out of sixth form college. She was called Cassandra, though she only used Cassie; she had an older sister called Calliope, who had started to make a name for herself, writing and making documentaries about the supernatural, under the name Callie Crow. She came with a dark history; she had been accused, unsuccessfully, of killing her stepbrother, still an unsolved crime as far as Zimpara knew; not that she cared. She entered the darkly immersive experience of Ariadne's witch cult with eyes wide open and an exceedingly dark vibe. She was, it had turned out, a siren, and she could bewitch almost anything that walked or crawled. It had shocked her to find there were individuals beyond her reach. That, to Zimpara, she was just sex. which of course made her desperately want more than just sex. Zimpara had quickly backed off from her intensity; nowadays if they encountered each other, they only spoke if they had to. Zimpara sensed her gaze drilling out of the wing mirror at her, her blue eyes cold, just like glacial ice.

'What's going on here Ariadne?' Zimpara demanded. She scowled darkly at Ariadne and transited it to Panqual. 'What the fuck!' she said to the diabolical.

'Hasn't Panqual told you?' Ariadne seemed amused, the mad eyes burned into her, but no more than they usually did.

'Told me what?' she was certain she knew, but she wanted it said aloud.

'We're here on the same business, dear.' The eyes burned through her, clutching at her thoughts. She protected them; don't dear me, you evil bitch.

'Not the same!' Zimpara scoffed. 'I've served a warrant.'

'that's good, because it reassures them, and makes our task much simpler,' Ariadne said enthusiastically. 'You didn't even have to find our little AWOL with your exceptional skills; and you've been well paid. She's indentured Rachel, to the Satran, Saradina, of all creatures. And I think it's hilarious that she's shagging that stuck up little bitch of a shadow binder.'

Zimpara continued to stare at Panqual, her look had become scathing. She looked on the point of incandescence, but she quelled it; she knew she was seriously out gunned. 'You used me.' Her tone was ominous.

'Shit happens,' Panqual replied, she performed a dismissive shrug under her riding cloak. 'You're in on this; you're earning your pay, Rachel. You're in this up to your neck.'

'Fuck off! you exploited my reputation. The warrant I served had the seal of Saradina for fucks sake. This is dishonourable, you smug bitch.'

'I am told that principles are going out of fashion in the world of men,' Panqual mocked.

'That's your defence, is it?'

'There's nothing to defend.'

'Has Saradina sanctioned this?'

'You think Saradina even cares?' Panqual asked sarcastically.

'We're on the same side Rachel,' Ariadne said, reasonably. 'Think of future commissions.'

Zimpara shook her head definitively. 'You should know Ariadne, that this is way over the top; we've both been lured into something personal. This is so much beneath Saradina's attention. Count me out.' She turned abruptly and walked away, clutching the handle of her umbrella in both hands.

'Think about this Rachel,' she called after her. Ariadne watched her walk away. She frowned, there was something about Zimpara's words that clawed up uncomfortable feelings in her mind.

Zimpara felt suddenly exposed, walking in the crosshairs of four pairs of eyes, that she now had to assume were hostile. It was a long ten strides back to her car. It took all her nerve to stand and shake the rainwater from her umbrella, then collapse it. Does seventy-two hours matter that much? Her own personal demon asked her. She hissed a silent yes under her breath. She climbed into the Audi, tossing the umbrella onto the floor of the passenger side. Are principles that important? 'Yes!' she hissed out loud as she started the engine. She glanced in her wing mirror and pulled out of the layby, she wanted to send mud and water flying, in the hope of getting Panqual, but she resisted the temptation. Along the road the headlights of the range rover came on as it started up; her heart beat quickened, as she thought for a moment the driver intended to pull out and bar her way; but they allowed her to pass. She stared straight ahead as she drove by, but she had made out two figures in the vehicle as she approached it; she accelerated past, having no intention of trying to see who they were. At her speeds, she was an hour and thirty minutes of white knuckled, angry music from her home. She was less than thirty minutes from home, when, totally furious with herself, she drove the Spyder into a service station and back out again, beginning the drive back the way she had come.

Seven

Sofia was waiting for Saskia and Ayesha when they emerged after their showers. She was dressed in coral-coloured garments similar to her costume of the previous evening, including her Hijab; her eight little snakes hidden from sight once again. She was standing in the portal between the dining room and the viewing lounge, waiting for them; she inclined her head politely as they ascended the stairs from the Trojan room, and approached her.

'Good morning,' she said, 'Felix sends his apologies, but he had to leave early on business. Can I get you breakfast?'

Ayesha glanced at Saskia who was always the hungriest. She received an enigmatic stare in reply.

'No, we're fine thank you.' She ignored Saskia's non look.

'Tea or coffee then?'

'Thank you, no. I think it's time we were on our way.'

'Of course. I'll show you out.'

'Has Felix's business taken him out of the country?' Saskia inquired as they walked with her. 'I'm not being bad mannered by asking, am I?'

Sofia glanced sideways at her; strangely, the look was almost indulgent. 'He had to go to London. He'll be back this afternoon. Shall I tell him you want to speak with him.'

'No, it's okay. It's nothing. I was being nosey.'

Sofia led them back the way she had brought them in; she remained silent after her exchange with Saskia, and Saskia and Ayesha were introspective. She opened the bronze door for them. The day had an early cast; It felt cool too. To Sofia's surprise Saskia embraced her; in reflex her hand shot to her Hijab, ensuring it stayed in place; this action drew a puzzled look from Ayesha.

'Thank you for looking after me last night,' Saskia told her, before releasing her from the embrace.

'You're welcome,' Sofia replied. If she was surprised or thrown by Saskia's gesture, she did not reveal it; she maintained a poker face.

'I enjoyed meeting them, by the way.'

'Did you?' Sofia looked unsettled, without actually appearing to be.

'I think that they are quite lovely. Goodbye Sofia.'

'Goodbye.' Sofia inclined her head and turned away; when she had gone inside and closed the door, a little frown delved her brow. She shook her head, allowing herself a small smile.

'I can't wait!' Ayesha remarked as she climbed into the passenger seat.

Saskia started the engine; she glanced at the display; it was a couple of minutes after 7 a.m. She drove the car out from under the shadow of the concrete awning. She assumed correctly that the drive circled back on itself.

'Tell,' Ayesha said, as she inspected her face in the vanity mirror. She fished about in her bag and extracted lip balm. 'I know you got up to no good last night. Don't look innocent it doesn't suit you.'

Saskia threw her a look of mock disdain. Ayesha was revealing pale beauty, a drained loveliness that few women possessed, Saskia thought admiringly; she knew that she too possessed it, but that would remain a secret vanity.

'Sofia is a Gorgon of some kind.'

'Really! Of some kind,' Ayesha responded, applying the balm.

'She claims that she isn't. But she has eight little red snakes growing out of her head. They are so cute.'

'If you say so.'

'I do. Sofia said they weren't bothered by me, which she implied was unusual when they meet someone.' Saskia put her head on one side and smiled.

'That say's a lot.'

'She reckoned it was in my favour,' Saskia said, smugly. 'Which is probably the nicest thing she has ever said to anyone.'

'Possibly,' Ayesha agreed. 'How did you find out she was a Gorgon? or Gorgonesque anyway!'

'I accidentally pulled off her Hijab and it fell into the Abyss.'

Ayesha moved her reflection around in the mirror, studying her beauty. Satisfied she relaxed into the passenger seat; she had no intention right then of replacing her makeup. She dropped her balm back into her Gucci bag, zipped it up and tossed it into the back.

'Were you hallucinating at the time?'

'I was.' Saskia admitted. 'But I know the difference. I'm me, remember.'

'True,' Ayesha widened her eyes expressively.

'While you were having sex, I went down to take another look at the Porta Magica,' Saskia told her.

'That simply exhibits such bad manners on your part Saskia. You really are a nosey little cow!'

'Yeah, I know,' Saskia admitted. 'Anyway, I took a look through the door.'

'So, you opened the door? How come you knew how?' Ayesha frowned, thrusting out her under lip.

'I didn't. I just expected it and used the principle of entering Place,' Saskia explained.

'Well thought out.'

'Thankyou.'

'Go on.'

'I'd been blacking out,' Saskia continued. 'I had one then, and I found myself standing right on the edge of the portal after the door opened, and I was dizzy, spinning dizzy. It was black, endless black.'

'Shit Saskia, you were being an idiot.'

'I do know!' Saskia's eyes widened. 'I saw Moby Dick; I thought I was going to be eaten at first, but I think it was an hallucination, you know, subconscious association with the Melville quote.'

'Sounds reasonable, I suppose.'

'Then I threw up. Sofia got hold of me from behind, before I had chance to fall through; She told me I was looking into the Abyss; it was very disturbing. Felix had got her to keep an eye on me.'

'He's obviously got your measure.'

Saskia gave a little shrug. 'I grabbed hold of Sofia because I was so unsteady, and I accidentally pulled off her Hijab and it floated down into the Abyss. You should have seen her face.'

'I wish I had!' Ayesha became amused.

'She was so peeved! She told me it was designer and that I owed her three-hundred and fifty quid; she actually used the word quid! Then she told me I had vomit on my chin, and, that I was probably the first person to throw up into the Abyss. All her little snakes had shot up and were staring at me!'

Ayesha laughed out loud. 'Did you think you were hallucinating?'

'I did, I asked her straight out if her snakes were real. She looked after me Ayesha. I think she likes to look mean, in that respect you're alike.' Saskia smiled and glanced at her; she recognised a hint of the malign in Ayesha's expression; it surfaced now and again; it possessed an element of the dark fay.

Ayesha closed her eyes resting her head back into the seat. She allowed her humour to subside, until only a sardonic smile played on her lips. 'I might get very mean, if I don't get fed pretty soon!' she remarked.

'We could have stayed at Baal House and had breakfast.'

'I didn't want to. I just wanted you to myself,' Ayesha said. 'How about a McDonald's? there's one just coming up on the right.'

'Okay, if that's what you want.' Saskia slowed the car, she indicated a right turn, glancing in the rear view. 'Drive by is closed.'

'So, it is! I've decided to extend my birthday to include today. So, you're going in and you're buying.'

'Aren't we going to eat inside?' Saskia said.

'Dressed like this? We'll have it in the car.'

'So, I go in, in a dress with the shortest skirt I've ever worn and five-inch heels!' Saskia brought the car to a halt.

'You don't have to wear your heels!'

Saskia turned off the engine and released her seat belt. She huffed and turned to Ayesha. 'Yes, I do.'

Ayesha shrugged. Saskia gave her a little nonsmile smile and reached into the back of the car for her bag and shoes. She slipped her stilettos onto her bare feet. 'What would you like?'

'Bacon roll with brown sauce, a hash brown, a strawberry jam muffin and coffee,' Ayesha reeled off.

Saskia got out of the car and closed the door. Ayesha's eyes followed her as she stalked towards the doorway of the outlet, watched meaningfully by half a dozen middle aged anglers on a fishing trip, who had just disgorged from a minibus. An empty tour coach was parked close by; Ayesha blandly regarded supporters scarves on the seat backs and a rugby team banner across the back window.

'Dicks!' Saskia growled fifteen minutes later. 'I couldn't breathe for testosterone and body spray,' she added petulantly.

Ayesha suppressed a smile and secured their breakfast tray whilst Saskia climbed back into the car. She settled into the driver's seat and glared in the direction of several of the Rugby supporters as they milled by the raised carpark flower beds and near the door of the coach. Ayesha had watched them emerge in a gradual trickle; mostly young men in their twenties; several of them grinned; the odd one cast a mocking look back over his shoulder. Most of them ogled as Saskia emerged to return to the car; someone whistled, fingers in mouth, unpleasantly loud; there were a few unimaginative suggestions.

'Ignore them, they are only ordinaries,' Ayesha told her, feeling guilty and amused at the same time. Saskia was red faced, she looked embarrassed and furious.

'It's my birthday and I forbid you to be incandescent. Drive to the other side of the carpark. We'll eat there.'

Saskia huffed and nodded, acquiescent. She started the engine.

'Look on it as character building,' Ayesha advised; they had relocated to the other end of the carpark, she retained the breakfast tray and slid the accompanying tray from underneath it. She passed it to Saskia and proceeded to put her packeted food on it, consisting of two bacon rolls and tea.

'Did you know who they were, in the coach?' Saskia said.

'Yes, I saw the banner. You didn't look, which surprised me having grubbed around in the street.'

'I saw the banner!' Saskia admitted. 'You exposed me to my worst nightmare; quite mercilessly.'

'You can't make me feel ashamed,' Ayesha insisted.

'I don't want you to,' Saskia responded, she shrugged. 'Shall we talk?'

'Yes, we should. Are you okay with what happened to us at Baal House?' Ayesha fixed Saskia with a penetrating look.

'Are you?'

'No, Saskia I want a straight answer from you!'

'Okay then, yes, I am.'

'No going back on our decision!'

'No going back. Was there ever any doubt about that?' Saskia said surprised.

'I suppose there wasn't. You must be more careful. A Porta Magica is not a toy!' Ayesha regarded her sternly.

'I know that!'

'And you drank too much Mandragora Serpens! You were out of it.'

'I wasn't out of it; it's you that was out of it girlie!' Saskia protested. 'In between the blackouts, my thinking was clear!'

'In between the blackouts!' Ayesha scoffed.

'I coped with the hallucinations. The vertigo was a side effect.'

'A side effect that nearly sent you into the Abyss.'

'I'll be more careful in future Ayesha.'

'You take risks mantis!'

'I know! I'm sorry!'

'Don't take them without me!' Ayesha said quietly.

'I beg your pardon?' Saskia was about to bite into her bacon roll; she paused.

'I'm curious too you know. Another half inch and you'll get the whole thing in!' Ayesha observed; she took a ladylike bite from her own roll and chewed demurely. Saskia grinned and bit, deliberately filling her mouth.

'I was so out of it,' Ayesha said. 'It was so intense. I recall the orbs appearing. I remember Felix's face, it looked so different, yet it was his face.'

'Where did he get the orbs?' Saskia asked.

'They came out of that massive ring he wears.'

'Sofia Snakehead had my attention!'

'And doesn't Felix look even bigger naked?' Ayesha said.

'I'm putting her...on the Christmas card list.' Saskia paused in mid chew and thought briefly about Ayesha's question; a small frown delved between her brows; she swallowed. 'That's quite an understatement,' she responded. 'We're you scared?'

'I wouldn't admit it if I was. You weren't scared were you!' Ayesha said.

'I was afraid at first,' Saskia admitted, 'but once I got used to the idea that I wasn't going to die or lose my mind from the effects of the elixir, I just went with it.'

Ayesha nodded. She described her own recall of the events in as much detail as she could. She was not coy; it was not in her nature, and she knew Saskia would not be. She left the action of radical aphrodisia on her compliance thorns until last. 'It was aching bliss mantis. Extreme pleasure pain. I so needed that.' She looked at Saskia; she smiled wryly, there was a tinge of disappointment in her expression. The thorns and their goad were still an issue between them. Saskia chose to open her door and scatter crumbs to the carpark birdlife. Ayesha followed suit.

'I had intense pain too,' Saskia said, as she closed her door. 'Like a thousand stings from those big hornet things; over every part of me, and I mean every part; inside too. Then each sting turned to pleasure, which blew me away. Our experiences seem to have been similar, but maybe peculiar to us?' She described what she remembered of her own experience, though there were many blanks in here memory, as there had been for Ayesha. She fell silent for a couple of minutes,

'Do you recall us projecting,' she said hesitantly. She was cautious, she was not sure if the experience had been authentic or was simply an unconscious vision. If it was an astral event, it was not guaranteed that Ayesha would recall it.

'You experienced it too?' Ayesha said, guardedly.

Saskia shifted her grip on the steering wheel. She felt quite anxious; it was no easy reveal; confirming the reality of a shared astral event. 'How did you perceive me?' she said hesitantly.

'Apart from sprouting a loose bundle of fibre optic cables, you looked pretty hot. Your eyes are much greener on the subtle level. But my, you have cold hands.'

Saskia chuckled, suddenly relieved. 'It was real, then.'

'Mantis, I never doubted it,' Ayesha assured her. 'I simply wasn't sure you'd recall it.'

'No shop today!' Saskia announced decisively. 'We're taking the day off!'

'Are we?'

Saskia nodded firmly; she was expecting resistance. 'Today we chill. Tonight, I'm taking you out to dinner.'

'Sounds good,' Ayesha said, unexpectedly compliant. She smiled and snuggled down in her seat.

'We're okay, aren't we?' she said, studying Saskia's profile intently, still smiling.

'We're more than okay.' Saskia told her.

'Your phone.'

'Hmm?' Ayesha replied drowsily.

'It's buzzing.' They were almost home; they had driven halfway along Quayside Walk, less than a couple of hundred metres from the apartment block, when Saskia heard the dull vibration of Ayesha's phone. She knew it was not hers; she had switched it off the previous evening and not yet switched it back on. Ayesha had dozed for most of the return journey; turning languorous eyes now and again to gaze at Saskia with a look of contentment that led occasionally to a self-satisfied little smile. This delicious creature is all mine, it said, down to the last cool inch.

'So, it is.' Reluctantly Ayesha made circles of her eyes and blinked herself awake; she delved into her bag, retrieved her phone and peered at the screen. 'It's Holly,' she screwed her brows into a frown. 'I wonder what she wants.' She tapped the accept button with the edge of her thumb nail. Eight-forty-eight, she mused; It was unusual for Holly to phone before midday. The last contact they had from her had been a text, to say everything was okay, on the evening of the day they had left her with the cat girl thing, Luca.

'Hi Holly,' she drawled, her voice conveying pleasure and a hint of surprise.

'Hi Ayesha, I left a message on your house phone just now, and there was no reply on the York number; is Saskia with you?' She thought Holly's voice sounded anxious.

'Yes, she is, we've literally just got back from Felix's. Is everything okay?' Ayesha said, she glanced at Saskia who had stopped the car in front of the apartment block, electing not to drive down into the car park and probably lose signal. 'I'll put you on speaker.' She wondered what could be so urgent to cause Holly to be so determined to get in touch with them. She pressed speaker, as Holly replied.

'No, I'm afraid it isn't. I've phoned to tell you I need to fess up about something, and to ask for your help. Can you come to Larkspur, I'll come to you if you like; it's simpler if you come to me though.' She paused expectantly.

Saskia and Ayesha exchanged puzzled looks. Saskia shrugged and nodded; Ayesha nodded back in agreement. 'Yes, okay,' she said, 'we'll come to larkspur. When do you want us?'

'Is midday too soon?'

'No, midday it is.'

'Perfect. I'm sorry to spring this on you; I'll explain everything when you get here. I am grateful, really.' Holly ended the phone call abruptly.

'That was odd,' Saskia said. Perplexed.

'She sounded stressed.'

'I think she was more than stressed,' Saskia said. 'Somethings really got to her.'

Eight

Deep in thought, Holly replaced the phone on its hub. They were dressed. Holly in black leggings and a fine knit black jumper, Luca in jeans and fine knit taupe cardigan, with a crew neck, both Holly's, and a good fit. Holly's hair was still wet; she had intended a quick shower, but her thoughts consumed her, and she made herself take more time; thinking hard under the powerful spray of the showerhead. Dressed, she went down and found Luca. She had made coffee when she heard Holly turn off her shower; she had taken it to the dining room at the front of the house, turning on lamps to offset the dimness of the morning, and was waiting for her. She watched as Holly went straight to the phone and rang Ayesha and Saskia, leaving messages at first; then reaching them on Ayesha's mobile. She listened to Holly's tense words. She could see the tension in her; feel it too, it was palpable. Since the visit by Panqual and Rachel Zimpara, Holly had barely spoken to her, and then only tersely. Luca remained silent, she watched Holly from where she sat at the dining table, a worried frown emphasised her piquant nose and the intensity of her yellow eyes. When she had finished on the phone Holly stood in thought; Luca was familiar with the stance; Holly had one arm across the front of her body, her hand beneath the elbow of the other, which was angled up, so that she could prise her thumb nail vertically between her upper and lower canines; she did not usually look on the point of anger though. Holly sniffed the air, turned and glanced at Luca. She walked to the table and looked down at the coffee things.

'You made coffee,' she said, it was almost an accusation.

'We usually have coffee about now,' Luca said, puzzled.

'I didn't want coffee. You could have asked.'

'I assumed you would have coffee, I thought...'

'Because we always do,' Holly finished for her.

'I'll make you some tea.'

'Don't bother. I can make do with the coffee,' Holly said dismissively.

'I'll pour you a cup.' Luca rose from her chair.

'Don't bother, I can do it myself.'

'Why are you angry with me? You knew this would happen.'

Holly frowned; it deepened into a scowl. 'I'm not angry with you because of this situation.'

'Then why? What have I done?' Luca said resentfully; she folded her arms and revealed the beginnings of a glare.

'How and why did they find you so quickly?'

'I don't know.'

'There's no way they could locate you without using extreme measures, quite unthinkable measures. Otherwise, it would take weeks or months to locate you, or never.'

'I don't understand.'

'It's probably best that you don't. Are you really that important Luca? Why are you so important that it was necessary to find you so quickly?'

'The Zimpara woman told you, indenture in Pandemonium is taken incredibly seriously.'

'Really, so seriously as to take those measures, on magician central, of all places? Where most magicians would see them as perversions!' Holly dismissed the notion with contempt. 'No Luca, it was a very personal vibe I picked up on between you and that thing, so personal it made me feel like you'd put your knife in me.' She saw Luca wince.

'She scares me; we're all scared of her. She's supposed to scare us,' Luca said defensively; her eyes darted over Holly's face. It seemed implacable.

'It was more than that,' Holly said coldly. 'I sensed there was something personal between you. I got a sense of intimacy from Panqual, from you I got the sense you were ashamed.'

'Is this why you've been cold with me?' Luca demanded. 'Why you're angry with me now.'

'Is there something intimate between you and her?'

'How can you think that. I have never…'

'Tell me the fucking truth!'

'Alright! Fuck it!' tears blinked out of Luca's eyes. 'She wants me. She's obsessed with me! She's arranged with Satran Saradina to buy out my indenture; I would owe her a debt I can't pay back, so I will be in servitude to her, and in Pandemonium servitude means sex, Holly. But it's worse than that, she wants marriage. I'd rather be dead.'

Holly's eyes brightened with laughter. 'She wants arm candy,' she jeered cruelly.

'It's not funny!'

'So, I came along at just the right time then. I must admit you played me to perfection,' Holly applauded her silently.

'I did not play you!' Luca closed her eyes; she took a deep breath before opening them again. 'Alright, I played you! I'm not playing you now!'

Holly struck her hard across the face. Luca's head jerked to the side. Holly was stronger than she looked, she thought. Luca's eyes narrowed and she suppressed the instinct to strike back. 'I can take that all day,' she said.

Holly's eyes flared with anger, and she tried to strike her again, but Luca caught her hand by the wrist; she caught the other one by the wrist too when Holly took a swing with that, this time with her clenched fist. She was much stronger than Holly, easily as strong as a powerful man; she laughed, trying to make Holly laugh too, but Holly took it as mockery, and she writhed and twisted furiously and succeeded in throwing Luca a bit off balance. Luca regained it instantly, turning Holly and pushing her back towards the window. Holly looked daggers at Luca and prepared elemental intent; she had no intention of hurting her, but it would confirm who was actually in charge.

'Holly, listen. We don't love that much in Pandemonium. Mostly we lust! Or we obsess like Panqual is obsessed with me. I admit I didn't love you at first. I desired you. I was awed by you. I envied you. I used you. I manipulated you. I don't know at which point over these last few days it was, that I came to love you.'

'You expect me to believe you!' Holly said in a voice hoarse with emotion. 'I loved you with all my heart.' She could not hold back her tears anymore and they trailed down her cheeks. She saw Luca's eyes answer with tears of her own as they filled with emotion. Then the emotion left them, and she felt Luca stiffen. She watched the pretty face move to the side to look past her; Luca was only tiny herself. The yellow tear-filled eyes looked beyond her, to the outside, through the window.

'Holly,' Luca said, her voice hushed. 'There are people outside; Panqual is among them.'

Holly's eyes widened in disbelief as bad thoughts tumbled into existence; Luca released her wrists. Holly pivoted, wiping away her tears as she peered through the windowpanes.

'What the Hell happened to our three days,' she said.

'You trusted her,' Luca said. It was not a question.

'Of course! these things are supposed to be honoured; Fuck! Fuck! Fuck!'

'This is all on me.' Luca said.

'No, it's on me actually. I got into you and let things slide. I behaved like a sex struck adolescent.'

'Then it is on me.'

'Okay, please yourself; it's on you. Stop revelling in it and go get your knife and fetch my bow. I'll buy us a few moments.' She sensed Luca was no longer behind her; gone like a little ghost.

Holly fought down rising panic; her heart rate had soared; it was beating out of her chest; pounding in her ears as she raced to her front door; her thoughts were everywhere. She forced herself to focus, finding it incredibly difficult; Luca's reveal had made her feel like there were arrows passing through her body; now she felt numb inside; she felt she had allowed chaos into her previously calm world. She had given desire and infatuation a free hand in it. She knew where the fault really lay though, she thought, as she forced herself to walk the last few steps to the front door. The secret narcissistic self-view she hid so well, and quietly revelled in, the perfect Holly Penn. The invincible Holly Penn. The angry, adolescent, she would show them Holly Penn, who still stood resentfully centre stage; the bitch inside, so rarely revealed. She heard the heavy clunk of her key in its lock; it sounded remarkably loud. With it, she seemed to clunk back into place too. She pursed her mouth and opened her door. It was raining steadily, and she inhaled the damp air.

They had parked a Shogun and a Range Rover on the other side of her forecourt along the edge of the grass. There were six of them in line, half-way across her gravel, when she opened her door. They stopped when they saw her. Panqual of course was familiar to her; four of them she did know from Adam; the woman next to Panqual rang alarm bells. She was squeezed into a low-cut white dress covered in orange and red poppies, and she held up a matching umbrella, she held a walking stick too, which Holly thought she recognised by description, and she had white hair. Rachel Zimpara was not among the group. More of them could be coming at Larkspur through the wood behind the house of course, she thought, but perhaps not in Louboutin's. She felt oddly self-possessed now. She smiled to herself.

'Who are you?' She asked loudly enough for them to hear across the intervening distance. 'Have you lost your way?'

Panqual was about to step forward and speak, but the woman on her right intervened. She carried her walking stick, clutched to her body, her left hand halfway down its shaft; she wielded it and brought the upper half of it across Panqual's body, hard, with a loud smack; surprising her and abruptly ending her intention to speak.

'I'm exactly where I want us babes,' the woman with the stick replied to Holly. She smiled smugly and returned her stick to its position against her thick body; she bowed her head a fraction and tucked her chin over the sticks top, peering at Holly with bulging, gleefully mad eyes.

'I think you've lost your way sweetie.' Holly said, with a winning smile. 'Maybe missed a turning.' She heard Luca's almost silent tread behind her.

'I'm here for a little minx of a runaway called Luca Rajal; she's wanted back home, you know.'

'Yes, I'm sure I've seen a warrant. There're three days to comply.' Warrants had become increasingly more frequent since the nineteen fifties, coinciding with an increase in the numbers of demonics wanting asylum in the expanding human sphere; there was no supportive legal code, however; no twee little legislature of magicians to administer them. They were simply a spillover from another age; a courtesy, which remained a tradition; their value was subjective, but usually they were treated with respect.

'You can't have read it correctly dearie,' said the woman with the crazy eyes. Holly frowned; she had not read it at all. Who did. So, she sort of anticipated the next words. 'Luca Rajal is expected to 'deliver herself' at once.'

'Let them take me Holly,' Luca said quietly, from behind her. Holly ignored her.

'I'm Ariadne Leech, by the way,'

'I know who you are,' Holly said.

'Of course you do,' said Ariadne.

'I'll go with them, you can't stop me,' Luca said insistently.

'I can't,' Holly replied. 'But then you'll never know.'

Inquisitively, Luca came from behind Holly and stood to the side, turning round, and leaning her slim back against the wall to the right of the door, out of view of the outside. With the end of Holly's bow, she knocked over the old steel hay-hook, that Holly kept just inside the door for scraping the mud out of boot treads; she kept it wickedly sharp. Luca turned her face to Holly, she was sad, the yellow eyes were forlorn. 'Know what?' she said, with a hint of bitterness.

'If I'll forgive you,' Holly replied. She deployed Aspis and crafted elemental intent.

'She wants to play!' Ariadne announced gleefully, as she sensed intent. She deployed her own Aspis. She gasped enviously as the raging elemental energy, came gobbling over the gravel at them from a glaring Holly, in a shining, interweaving mass of tendrils, which came straight for her; it moved like a greyhound in full flow. Everyone except Panqual, deployed Aspis and threw intent. Holly slammed her front door shut. Ariadne's intent was a direct strike on the elemental form; her intention was to divert it, she knew she could not stop it. Just in case, she immediately declined time and stepped out of its intended path and stepped behind Panqual. Holly's elemental intent gobbled Ariadne's strike, but it was thrown from its course. Josh Devlin yelled in horror as it came for him; his aspis took some of its impetus, but the tendrils found him as his shiny pointed shoes slipped in the wet gravel, and it began to bind him with implacable strength. The counter was Grim intent, and he possessed some skill in that. He shrieked in pain as three of his fingers snapped, then as his right shoulder was dislocated; horrified, he wondered how much of his body would be intact by the time he managed to overthrow Holly's intent, or alternatively, it ran out of vim. 'Help me!' he yelled as he writhed and kicked in the gravel. 'Somebody, help.'

'Fuck!' Exclaimed Ariadne, as the liar reclaimed her. She laughed incredulously; her bizarre humour erupting, when she saw the albino in Holly's elemental coils. 'Cassie! Help him, before it breaks every bone in his fucking body. Sirus and Great North Jester, I'd like you round the back, fast as you can. Panqual, come with me.' Ariadne anticipated unquestioning obedience from her followers, and she got it. On thick thighed, knock-kneed legs, Ariadne marched across the gravel towards Larkspur's front door.

Holly had slammed the door shut the moment she released her elemental intent; she stepped back from it as Vis ultima rattled it on its hinges; a single depleted strike, all that had survived her Aspis.

Luca handed Holly the recurve bow she had brought for her; she had attached the rack of carbon arrows. Her knife was in her hand, the blade contained in its temporary leather sheath. She turned the key in the lock and began to slide its four, heavy bolts.

'That won't give us any more time,' Holly was already on the move. 'She will open it as quickly as you lock,' she threw over her shoulder. 'We need to get out into the garden. She'll already have people on their way there.'

'I'll catch you up,' Luca said.

'No, you come now!' Holly said fiercely.

'Alright.' Luca caught up with her as she hurried through the house; she looked cautious; worried.

'Why do we need to get to the garden?'

'Because we need to.'

'Holly, I need to know.'

'Not now.'

'But I might be taken, and I'll never find out.' Luca almost wailed the words. She followed Holly through the house and into the main lounge. The sinister, occasionally crafty looks of the Wally birds seemed to follow them as they passed their cabinet.

'Tough. You know, I should have restored my Guardian; I've had days to do it in.' Holly snapped. 'The best I could manage was to clean your fucking knife!'

'That's my fault, I distracted you.'

'Don't go guilty on me for that; You weren't there to distract me when I didn't craft more like him, and I didn't craft elemental weapons, or create a secure Place. There's plenty of other stuff for you to feel guilty about, madam.' she added unnecessarily.

Luca winced; she was hard to hurt but Holly seemed to be able to do it easily. 'Luca!' She heard Panqual's voice call through the house and went cold. They were inside; there had been no sound of them breaking in the front door, but why resort to violence, when locks could be desired open.

'Get the doors!' Holly snapped. She nocked one of the arrows to the bowstring. Luca sprang ahead of her to open the French doors. They jogged outside into the rain, at the same time Great North Jester desired the gate locks and burst through into the walled garden. He was tall, rangy, in his late twenties; he had a long, pale face and a long thin pink mouth, he wore his hair in little tufts. He saw Holly line up her bow and to her surprise desired elemental intent as she released the arrow at him. The intent formed like paint thrown from a tin, trailing greyish tendrils; it snatched the arrow from its flight before it reached him. She lowered her bow as he stepped around the arrow. He scooped up the still active intent with his right hand and dispatched it like a bowling ball at Holly. She treated him to her own, and casually dismantled his, as it reached her. She saw the massive figure of Sirus, as he jogged, panting, through the open gate. Luca and Holly were on the other side of one of the raised beds; Luca jumped up onto the low wall and pulled her knife from its sheath; she crouched preparing to test her resilience to his intent and run at him.

'Luca no!' Holly snapped. 'Any second now they'll come through those doors; you'll be cut off.'

Luca paused; she straightened; she gave Holly a searching look. She was aware of the Great North Jester grimly, gradually, overcoming the coiling tendrils of Holly's elemental intent, with his own. 'Then what can I do?' she snapped. She gasped; her body reacted, jumping like she had been shocked, as Sirus's intent struck her. 'Bastard!' she shouted towards him. She jumped down from the bed wall.

Holly checked her with a look. Luca could absorb intent, but it did not mean that it didn't hurt. 'We're heading for the stable block, to the room where I opened the portal.' Holly told her. 'You have one task. To open the door.'

'You're sending me back!' Luca said. She nodded determinedly. 'And you should.'

'Just get the door open Luca,' Holly said impatiently. She discarded Sirus's next strike, lobbing his intent at Ariadne as she appeared with Panqual through the French doors. They saved Sirus from getting an arrow in his considerable body as Holly turned her bow on them, too. Ariadne deflected the redeployed intent, destroying a swathe of potted shrubs. She jerked her stick, nudging Holly's arrow towards Panqual, who it struck ineffectively. Holly frowned; puzzling what Ariadne used to deflect the arrow, intent; probably a form of grim intent. Holly was backing away as fast as she could; to turn round and run would be offering herself for destruction. Her eyes volleyed between the four of them. She struck at Sirus with more intent; sent an arrow at Panqual in the hope of breaking skin, another at Great North Jester who had overcome her previous elemental intent and was about to dispatch his own. Holly barked with effort as she struck at Ariadne with elemental intent. Ariadne tossed her folded brolly aside and grasped her stick in both hands. She thrust it into the tendrils of Holly's elemental intent, and they began to blacken and wither, falling like ash from a burning log. Holly could not help watching in fascination. Luca barged her aside and took Sirus's intent in her face with a force like a heavyweight boxers straight punch. She cried out in pain; ignoring it, she bundled Holly through the doorway of the old tack room. Holly formed elemental intent in front of the doorway, a barrier of gleaming, ribboned tendrils, then slammed the door; with a hard look at Luca, she bolted it.

'Are you okay?' Holly peered at Luca's bleeding nose.

'Yes. I'm alright!' Luca snapped, she wiped angrily at the blood, smearing it. 'Let's get this done.'

Holly looked at her balefully. She led the way through into the other room, now cleared of her alchemy. It was the first time Luca had been in there since her arrival through the portal. Holly crafted another barrier of elemental intent in front of the doorway, then closed the door and bolted it from inside.

'We have moments,' Holly said. She began to release intent into the dormant portal; she could not see it like Saskia had seen it, but she was able to sense it. She glanced at Luca who was watching her in silence. Holly's artists eyes noted the unintentional beauty of her stance. Her knife hand hung at her side; her head hung slightly down, her chin rested on the knuckle of her free hand, one leg was straight, the other bent at the knee, her foot pointed down, rested on the toe of her shoe. Saskia was right, Holly decided, there was a look of Brigitte Bardot about her. Holly spoke to her.

'Answer me this: were you sexually involved with that creature? No lies! No, I'd rather die! The truth Luca!'

Luca inhaled a very deep breath; her expression became defiant; suddenly haughty. 'She claims anyone pretty,' she announced. 'I am her favourite. She likes that I am clever. My watch lasts three nights and three days, often she keeps me in her rooms for a day and a night, occasionally for my entire watch. Refusal is not an option. She is cruel and demanding. You do whatever she requires of you.' She held Holly's gaze, coolly, impassively. They heard the crash of the outer door, the groan of metal and the splintering of timber; someone had obviously discarded the idea of desiring. 'So...yes, I fled Pandemonium, very willingly indeed. I used you. It didn't mean that I didn't care for you.'

There were raised voices on the other side of the door. They could hear a crackling sound like melting ice; as Holly's elemental barrier began to fail.

'Luca!' It was Panqual's voice; plaintive; shouting through the door.

'It's done,' Holly announced. She turned to Luca. 'The portal's unlocked.' She stared into Luca's large, saddened eyes.

'I'm ready,' Luca said. 'Goodbye Holly.'

Holly frowned. 'Goodbye? Do you think I'm sending you back?'

'Aren't you?'

'What would you do?'

'I think I'll go on the run.'

Holly sighed. 'I said the portal was unlocked. I didn't say it was open.'

'Then what...'

'We're going between; unless you don't want to come with me.' She took hold of Lucas wrist; her eyes questioned. 'No?' she said.

'Yes,' Luca said. She had no idea what Holly was suggesting, and she realised right at that moment, that she really did not give a damn. She went with Holly to the portal; Holly still held onto her wrist. Holly thinned in front of her eyes; her substance drained away, turning her into a fading ghost. Luca peered over her shoulder as the door splintered at the lock and ripped away its bolts, crashing inwards. Ariadne and Panqual came into the room.

'Fuck me!' said Ariadne, in surprise; her mad eyes took in the fleeting remnant that remained of Holly, and Luca's fading ghost.

Luca stared into Panqual's black eyes. She felt the portal taking her. She could not feel if Holly still gripped her wrist. 'Bitch,' she said to Panqual.

'It suffered,' replied Panqual vindictively.

'What?' Luca frowned, by then barely visible, barely audible.

'Your cat.'

The rain grew heavier whilst Ariadne stood under her orange and red poppy umbrella. It pummelled, falling vertically. She felt angry; there was something amiss and she meant to find out what it was. She waited, motionless, deep in her thoughts. She was not alone in Holly's walled garden; Panqual sat on one of the raised bed walls, with her hood drawn over her head and with her long fingers making cages over the shapes of her knees under her long coat. rainwater streamed down its hood and length and dripped from her macabre face. Ariadne observed her with a cynicality that was detached from her current emotion. The constant working of Panqual's fingers making her claws bite into the leather of her habit, was not lost on Ariadne. Things were not as they had at first seemed, she decided. She often made assumptions and fuelled mistruths, it was in her nature; she was cynical and narcissistic and allowed these traits to develop her narratives. Life was no fun for her if she did not have a victim to gaslight. But fun stopped at the door of ambition, and that she had in buckets. When Panqual was introduced to her she had felt exhilarated; she sensed opportunity; a stepping stone to Pandemonium aristocracy. Princes of darkness was the label attached to one of her buckets. She had offered Panqual assistance, and put her not inconsiderable resources at her disposal, to execute the will of aristo Satran Saradina, and facilitate the capture of a runaway retainer. Something had niggled her at the beginning and now it was niggling her even more; what made a skinny arsed demonic, indentured or not, so important to Saradina, that the captain of her house should arrive in the human sphere, in Kadman, to personally bring her back. Panqual had skin in this game, she was certain of it. She broke from her train of thought as Cassie Crow emerged from the French doors and strode up to her. Cassie was one of her most trusted, one who could run very dark indeed.

'It's done Ariadne. The cars are as close to the house as I could get them,' she said. 'Baldur's laid in the back of the shogun. I suggested he laid on one of the beds, but he didn't want to. He's handling the pain. But he's out of this.'

'Okay,' Ariadne nodded. 'Make sure everyone stays inside the house, until I'm finished.'

'Okay. I checked the phone against her phone book like you told me. The last few numbers Holly Penn rang this morning after they served the warrant, all belonged to Ayesha Shah and Saskia Challoner.'

'Did they indeed!' Ariadne's face showed genuine interest.

Cassie frowned. As she watched her thoughts playing. 'Should we be concerned.'

'I'm about to do what I'm going to do, so that we don't need to be concerned,' Ariadne said. Cassie nodded and went back into the house. Great North Jester emerged from the stable block. 'No luck, just a few visuals,' he said, shaking his head. He had been trying to breach Holly's portal for twenty minutes with elemental intent. He scratched his long nose. 'Can we do this Ariadne?'

'Eventually,' she said. 'Go inside the house, while I buy us the time. Panqual!'

Panqual looked up. The black eyes fixed on her, emptily. 'I'll stay,' she said.

Ariadne regarded Panqual searchingly. She drew her thin loose lips into an uneven line. 'Please yourself,' she said; her mouth performed a quick dismissive smile. As she walked away her smiled broadened her eyes gleamed. 'Saskia Challoner, eh?' she said to herself.

As if inspired she thrust her stick into the air above her head and waved it around in a circle. She went to the edge of the path opposite the French doors. There she opened two of her centres, earth and crown, to the nature of Place; she felt it rise up through her. A swarm of black specks emerged from her stick, like myriad insects. They rose into the air above Ariadne, and when she deemed that they had risen high enough she stopped the circling of her stick. She knew that below her, under the ground an identical process would be ongoing. She crafted the basic mechanism of Place like Holly crafted elemental intent. She released her swarm; it shot in every direction at terrific speed; arching over the house, a rapidly forming yellow miasma stretching between each tiny element of the swarm, expanding and engulfing them. Place for some unknown reason, formed spheres. Abruptly, the pouring rain ceased to fall.

Nine

Larkspur was wrapped in just under an acre of wood; this was enclosed by a narrow lane through more woodland; it looped back on itself, from the lane to the nearest village, on which two cars could just squeeze past each other. The house was usually visible through the trees at several points from the loop. When Ayesha and Saskia arrived, it was raining quite hard, and the woods were dim and moody. A screen of mist hid Larkspur entirely from view. The entrance to Larkspur was on the right, about one hundred metres in, if you came at it from the direction Saskia and Ayesha came. It was only a narrow track, hidden among trees and shrubbery; unmarked too. Driving down it, the car sides brushed against briars and overhanging branches, on both sides, until it widened nearer the house and morphed into the gravel drive and forecourt, and a broad expanse of grass and shrubs. As they approached it was apparent that Larkspur was shrouded in no ordinary mist.

Ayesha stopped the car and turned off the engine. 'Reach me my jacket from the back,' she said.

Saskia gave her a look and released her seat belt; she twisted round to reach over the seats and clutched their jackets, passing Ayesha hers. They stepped out of the car and drew them on. They had both opted for dark blue jeans and lace up boots; Ayesha wore a coral-coloured sweater, Saskia's was midnight blue; her light padded jacket was charcoal grey, Ayesha's was burgundy. They reached into the door wells for umbrellas; they opened them and scrunched through the gravel to inspect the barrier. Close up they could see that it curved around and over and appeared to form a substantial dome. A substance like oily yellow smoke hung in pouches like mammatus cloud, and hundreds of tiny, shiny black particles scintillated through it, giving the impression that it fluctuated.

'Saskia!' Ayesha cautioned, as Saskia prodded it.

'It feels resistant.' She prodded harder, her finger seemed to bounce back.

'It's going to circle the house isn't it,' Ayesha said.

'Let's walk round it and see, maybe there's a way through,' Saskia suggested.

'Left, or right?' Ayesha said, meaning anticlockwise.

'Widdershins yeah?' Saskia closed her umbrella.

The paved paths on both sides of the house were inside the barrier, forcing them into the undergrowth, under the bushes and low hanging boughs of trees that bordered them. Some boughs were trapped in it. The stable block proved to be entirely contained inside it, but the far corner of the walled garden was free, cleanly dissected. They circled twice, examining every metre of ground along the way; before eventually coming to a stop at the point from which they had begun, at the front of the house.

'This is mad,' Saskia said.

'We've walked round this stupid barrier twice! I'm seriously worried,' Ayesha said.

'Let's just stay cool. I'll try phoning again,' Saskia said. She had already tried phoning Holly twice on each circuit.

'Good luck with that.'

Saskia drew a long breath and pressed the button to redial on her call menu. She listened then shook her head. 'Not available still. I'll try her mobile.' She redialled that number and again waited. 'Number not currently available,' she said after a few moments.

'Something is seriously wrong. She knew we were coming. I wonder if it's even safe out here,' Ayesha said; she looked warily into the trees that surrounded the lodge.'

'She'd have warned us somehow, surely,' Saskia said, uncertainly.

'If she had time. There's one other way we might get her attention.' Ayesha took a deep breath and yelled at the top of her lungs. 'Holly!' Saskia joined her, shouting Holly's name as loudly as she could. They alternated, shouting and listening, as their voices echoed among the trees; the only response was a startled blackbird that hurtled off to their right, keeping low. They stopped yelling Holly's name, in a sort of unspoken agreement, both sensing that it was pointless. Ayesha glowered at the barrier.

'I'm going to try something,' Saskia said. She approached the barrier again, watched dubiously by Ayesha. She pressed up against it as far as she could and rested her outspread hand on it. She opened as if accessing Place and used the Melville quote. She backed off almost instantly and came back to Ayesha, grimacing.

'Holly had nothing to do with crafting that,' Saskia said. 'It made my skin crawl. What's the plan?'

'Find coffee,' Ayesha said.

*

'The hole was crafted with elemental intent.' The voice was a deep male voice, as always, it had a sardonic edge.

'Can you breach it?' She asked.

Ariadne stood in the circle she had made, naked. A single candle burned on the floor, between the circle and the portal Holly had crafted to Pandemonium. Otherwise, the room had no light source. She had directed Sirus and Great North Jester to block out light from the small windows. They had done so with duct tape and cardboard they had found in Holly's studio. The dim candlelight extended cautiously to Ariadnes ungainly body; her white skin was partly in shadows, and the light crawled over it, almost with a degree of uncertainty. Ariadne's walking stick lay on the floor, between the candle and the circle; it was a rare physical separation from it. Ariadne shivered. There were dark scars on the floor, midway, from elemental fire; she could still smell its bitter agency in the cold air.

'It's impressively strong,' observed the voice.

Ariadne had given the portal temporary visibility, coercing it with intent into the physical spectrum. It hung there in the far half of the room, unmoving, like a large round lens of blurred grey agate, which seemed to suck at the candlelight. Defying her; she could almost sense its contempt.

'Not beyond you though?'

'It would not be beyond me,' the voice answered. 'Are you unable to, Ariadne?'

She swallowed, her mouth was as dry as sandpaper, 'Yes, but I don't have the time it would take me. Your way would be quicker.'

'Perhaps more destructive,' he told her.

'What are the best odds?' she demanded.

'I would say an even risk,' he said.

He was moving back and forth, between the walls; her eyes tracked him. He was in the darkest part of the room beyond the portal, but he seemed to be one with the dark also. It followed him. Once or twice his teeth had flashed whitely as he spoke. The meagre candlelight had caught his swarthy jaw, and the back of a black-haired hand. He was watching her too; his eyes scanning her from the dark; observing her thickset body.

She nodded. Pensive. 'The clock is ticking. I'll try my way for a bit longer,' she said.

'Very well,' he said. 'Ariadne.'

'Yes,' she said.

'The creature is duplicitous.'

'What do you mean?' she said, surprised and suddenly very on edge.

'Ariadne. The hour's up.' There was a knock on the bolted door to her left. The voice of Great North Jester. She turned her head; impatient; ready to scold. Then she sighed; he was obeying her. When she looked back the room had no other occupant but herself.

'I'll be out in a few minutes,' she called. 'Did you find me some music?'

'A portable CD player,' Great North Jester replied. 'All sorts of genres. Lots of seventies and eighties. Abba. Boney M.'

'The woman has taste,' she remarked.

Ten

Ayesha steered back onto the loop. As she straightened the car, another vehicle moved into the lane from where it had been pulled into the side, about fifty metres away.

'What's the matter with them.' Ayesha shifted her hands from the sides of the steering wheel and repositioned them at the top. Her dark brows delved in a frown. Saskia watched admiringly as her under lip came out, as she prepared to be stubborn; Ayesha sat slightly forward, peering into the rainy gloom under the trees, at the oncoming car, it's headlights flashing on and off main beam. 'There's room to squeeze by; I can't move over any further; there's no need to flash their lights like that.'

'They've stopped,' Saskia said. 'I think that's what they want us to do.'

'I wonder what they want?' Ayesha said.

'Let's find out shall we.'

'Yes let's.' Ayesha stopped the car and turned off the engine.

'Ooh, you've prepared intent,' Saskia said.

'I have, and so should you.'

They climbed out of the car; they were still in their jackets. They reached for their still wet umbrellas. As they climbed out, the occupant of the other car switched off their headlights, swung open their door and emerged. It was murky under the trees, the crash of rain sounded on the leaf canopy and dripped through in a steady downpour. Three umbrellas extended and opened; three car doors closed simultaneously. Guardedly, a petite woman in black stilettos and a dark suit with a short skirt, walked towards them. She held her umbrella aligned with her heart, in both hands.

'You're trying to get into Larkspur lodge?' she said.

'Who wants to know?' Ayesha came to an immediate halt, bringing Saskia to a stop with the touch of a hand.

The woman halted too, her Louboutin clad feet centred neatly together; she looked barely as tall as Ayesha despite them; the aggregate chip surface of the road would be unforgiving to her stiletto heels, she thought, but that could not be helped; the shoes had already suffered probable irreparable damage from their earlier misuse. She took a deep breath, resisting the very strong urge she felt to ready precautionary intent.

'My name is Rachel Zimpara.'

'Zimpara? Hang on I know who you are!' Ayesha's eyes narrowed in sudden recollection. 'You helped Nathan Xavier against us!' her voice sharpened angrily. 'Your actions almost got me killed, you little bitch!' she yapped; instinctively she fell into an aggressive crouch; like a little gunfighter, Saskia thought.

'That was not my fault! I was only doing my job.'

'That's the perennial excuse of people who haven't the courage to take responsibility!' Ayesha threw back. 'You're even contracted to the legal firm I worked for, for fucks sake!'

'That should tell you I have some integrity. I was mad as hell when I found out the truth!' Zimpara's face was animated. she looked sincere enough, Saskia thought, indignant even.

'It didn't make you mad as hell that I was going to be kidnapped, then?' Saskia growled.

'Actually, yes it did. Nathan said he was the injured party and at the time I trusted him. Now, I don't trust him. Look, I want pax. I'm here to help you, if you'll let me.' Her eyes volleyed from Ayesha to Saskia, she had chosen to take a dangerous risk with these two; they had a reputation.

'She hasn't prepared intent Ayesha,' Saskia said, softly.

'That's the only reason she's still on her feet,' Ayesha snapped. 'How do you think you can help us? You'd better be convincing.'

'I know why you can't get to Larkspur lodge.' Zimpara risked three paces, closing the gap between them to less than two metres.

'I suspect elemental intent, but at a subatomic level, witchery,' Ayesha said. 'But go on, sell it to me.'

'You're right. I'm impressed. I did the same as you before you turned up, looking for the way in. Then I watched you from the lane through the trees, you walked round twice.'

'Did you find it entertaining?' Ayesha said.

'It was stressful,' Zimpara said.

'You don't strike me as the stressed sort.'

'Appearances can be deceptive. This could still go badly wrong,' Zimpara looked cautiously from one to the other.

'Okay, we've agreed its witchery; what kind is it?'

'The coercion of Place.' Zimpara told them. 'Have you heard of Ariadne Leech?'

Saskia shook her head. The name meant nothing to her, except that it sounded rather macabre. Ayesha on the other hand recognised the name and the reputation behind it. She straightened and exhaled hard. 'I've heard of her. I've met her, briefly.'

'Gross personality yeah?'

'Gross everything. She's utterly vile.' Ayesha turned her gaze on Saskia. 'Claire's firm acts for her,' she explained. 'She's one creepy bitch! Urgh!'

At any other time, Saskia would have found Ayesha's expression of disgust amusing. She looked curiously at Zimpara. 'What has this got to do with you? why are you trying to help?'

'I want Pax first.'

Saskia shrugged, indifferently. 'Okay Pax, for today anyway,' she agreed. 'We still have issues.'

'Saskia!' Ayesha gave her a disbelieving look. 'She almost got me killed!'

'I'm scared for Holly,' Saskia reasoned. 'I want to know what's happened. When Holly phoned us, she was hiding it, but she was really worried.' She peered inscrutably at Zimpara through the falling rain. 'Was it anything to do with you?'

'I'm not going to deny it. I took a commission from a diabolical called Panqual, who works as major domo, for an individual called Saradina, who's a Satran of Pandemonium.'

'We've met,' Saskia said grimly.

'I sort of heard. The commission was to serve Luca Rajal with notice to return to Pandemonium. Which I did. It's my living, it's what I do. Usually, I have to find them too; in this case that wasn't necessary; Luca's whereabouts, were already known. This puzzled me at first, because I'm the best bloody finder there is.'

'Luca! Cat girl Luca,' Saskia blinked, surprised.

'She isn't a cat girl, but yeah, her.'

'Why is she still here?' Ayesha demanded, her voice rising, she was bewildered now, as well as angry.

'Oh, my god! You don't know do you?' Zimpara's eyes lit up with amusement.

'Know, what?' Ayesha said savagely. Zimpara caught her lower lip between her teeth and smiled, she wove her eyes about, now highly amused.

'Fucks sake! tell us,' Saskia snapped.

'W...ell, When Holly Penn answered the door this morning she was sweating and she was very flushed, and her bed-tee was on inside out. Luca was very close behind her. They had obviously been having sex, when we interrupted them. Holly was furious.'

'Bollocks!' Ayesha growled.

'Not bollocks.'

'Holly and Luca are fucking?' Saskia said, wide eyed.

'It's more than just fucking I assure you. I know an item when I see one. Holly was protective. They're in a relationship, they said as much. Holly guaranteed Luca protection. I felt genuine sympathy.'

'That is just so fucked up, aren't you ashamed?' Ayesha looked furious.

'I'm ashamed I was taken in, Panqual deceived me, she had an arrangement with Ariadne.' Zimpara said indignantly. 'They used my resources and my reputation, and I am truly fucked off about it because Holly Penn accepted my warrant giving Luca seventy-two hours to decide; that removed their focus and left them vulnerable to a surprise incursion.' Her expression became grim. 'Ariadne and Panqual actually thought I'd fucking join them. How fucking dare, they! I told them where to go. You know for a minute, when I walked away, I actually thought they might kill me.' She paused to huff. 'But how could I leave it like that. I had to come back. Oh, I'd no intention of riding up on a white charger; I was taking a risk, but I wasn't going to risk my life. I'm angry with myself that I didn't drive straight to Larkspur when I had the opportunity, but to be honest I was scared, and I don't scare easily. I came back though and that counts for something doesn't it?'

'What if we hadn't turned up when we did?' Ayesha demanded.

Zimpara tilted her head to the side. 'Well, you did,' she asserted. 'It's not all bad news.'

'It can't get much worse,' Saskia said. Ayesha contented herself with a searing glare.

Zimpara sighed. 'Don't you get it? You don't, do you? For Ariadne to craft Place means that something must have happened, to shaft her plans. I can only think that Holly Penn didn't play by Ariadne's rules. She fucked her and it's still happening. The barrier round Larkspur lodge is designed either to keep them inside or people like us, out here; because something's gone down, and they need time to sort it. Get it?'

'You're saying Ariadne created the barrier; that makes sense. I tried to access it; it felt queer,' Saskia said. 'It felt sort of distorted, repellent; my skin crawled.'

'That's Ariadne you felt,' said Zimpara. 'That's her.'

Ayesha gave her a dark look and transferred it to the barrier through the trees. The rain became heavier then, thundering down on their umbrellas and gushing in torrents from them. 'This is horrible. I'm getting back in the car.'

'Me too,' Saskia said. She looked at Zimpara. 'She thinks she hates you; I get it; your actions almost got her killed. I'm angry with you too, but you're invited.'

Zimpara hesitated, watching her walk away. 'Okay,' she called after her.

Umbrellas shaken and collapsed; they sat in silence. Ayesha scowled into the rear-view mirror with merciless persistence her eyes never leaving Zimpara; she had slammed her door closed, making a statement of it. Zimpara timed hers to close with Saskia's.

'How many of them are there? Ariadne's people,' Saskia said, turning in her seat.

'I saw three in Ariadne's shogun, two in the Range Rover, plus Panqual of course,' Zimpara replied.

'I don't like those odds; how could they overcome Holly's guardian in the first place? It's formidable; they must have used some pretty powerful craft.'

'I didn't see a guardian. I assumed there was one. If they have overcome, it; we can't say for certain th…'

'We aren't going to find out either, sitting here like this,' Ayesha stated, talking over Zimpara. She caught Zimpara's look in the mirror, but it denied her satisfaction, remaining impassive. 'We can't access Ariadne's Place in the usual way, so what's our alternative Saskia?'

'We think out of the box,' Saskia said.

'So, are you thinking what I'm thinking?'

'Probably,' Saskia replied. 'Because we're wasting our time here. Are you thinking Porta Magica?'

'That's exactly what I'm thinking.'

'You have a Porta Magica?' Zimpara said with interest.

'We, don't,' Saskia replied. 'But we know someone who does, and they'd do anything for Holly Penn.' Saskia observed Ayesha eyeballing Zimpara in the mirror. The energy was palpable, Ayesha's was full on dislike, Zimpara's was passive defiance. If the situation had been different, they would have clashed; dangerously.

'What are we going to do when we get there?' Ayesha asked. 'What is the purpose of going?'

'To do whatever we need to, of course,' Saskia said.

'I must be mad,' Zimpara said deliberately. She rolled her eyes, aware of how out of character she was behaving, though in an odd way, she did feel she had skin in the game with these two. 'If we could gain entry covertly via a Porta Magica, we could at least find what's happening in there. I'm coming with you. I'll follow, in my car.'

'We?' Ayesha rasped.

'What's the point in that? ride with us.' Saskia said. She ignored Ayesha's questioning glare. 'We can chat, and Ayesha can vibe you.'

'Okay, just let me park my car out of the way.'

'You found me for Nathan, didn't you?' Saskia said. They had travelled for several minutes in silence, permeated by Ayesha's hostility, and the fast swoosh of the windscreen wipers. 'He intended to trick me; he promised my fetter could be removed, but he intended to comply me, with thorns.'

'Did he? I wouldn't know, he didn't confide in me.'

'You'd done your job, what happened next wasn't your responsibility, yeah,' Saskia said sardonically.

'Something like that. You took a bit of running to earth if that's any consolation,' Zimpara told her.

'I'm not complaining, others might,' Saskia said, obscurely. 'You know we're not going to be friends, don't you?'

'It never crossed my mind.' Zimpara shrugged.

'She has a snake's tongue. She has cunt printed right through her like a stick of seaside rock,' Ayesha declared.

Zimpara shook her head at this; she gave Ayesha a tight smile in the mirror, it was just on the edge of mockery. 'Do I give a fuck!' she said.

'I think you do,' Saskia said. 'Otherwise, why are you here?'

'You're wrong.' Zimpara frowned; she disguised her annoyance a fraction too late. Her smile returned, gradually curving her wide mouth, her eyes not leaving Ayesha. 'Don't forget to watch the road,' she said. 'You do know I wasn't working for Nathan? My pay cheque came from Claire Bosola. They regularly do, you know that. I would never say she was unethical.'

'You took your orders straight from Nathan, on the night he used the ghost of John Pickering to come for us!' Ayesha spoke with a cold bitterness. 'Six of them took turns striking at me with intent! They intended to kill me and take Saskia.'

'That was regrettable.'

'Regrettable!' Ayesha sneered.

'I haven't had anything to do with Nathan since,' Zimpara insisted. 'I had a phone conversation with Claire Bosola to clarify my position and reassure her that I'd been misled. I have a history with her firm going back to her father's time there.'

'I'm surprised you two have never met,' Saskia said.

'We have never spoken on the phone, either,' Ayesha said. 'She was always secretive. Don't fall for her image of the respectable, responsible ethical facilitator, Saskia. It doesn't exist.'

'I never made that claim,' Zimpara said. 'I have my own set of rules, and I stick to them. I choose or reject commissions on their merits. As for ethics, there's a fine line in my business. It's not all about my ethics, however. Sometimes it's about other peoples.'

'I don't know what you mean?' Ayesha snapped.

'Was it ethical to fetter Saskia?' Zimpara said.

'Of course it wasn't! What's that got to do with it?' Ayesha frowned.

'Where are you going with this?' Saskia asked.

'Was it unethical of her mother to want her fettered?' Zimpara pressed them.

'Of course it was!'

'Was it unethical of the Bran, Tadgh Byrne to fetter Saskia?' Zimpara was not going to stop.

'Of course it was! She was never given a say; she was a young girl! He took away her birthright,' Ayesha frowned. 'How do you know all this?'

'So, it was right and proper that he was found and forced to hand over the alchemical properties of his nasty little procedure?' Zimpara continued.

'Absolutely. I'm grateful to anyone who had a hand in that,' Ayesha replied.

'Hang on a minute,' Saskia gave Zimpara an intense look.

'So, I was right to take the commission from Selene Bacchus to find him?' Zimpara said. 'Because it was my agent Max Angus that tracked him down, using information supplied by me. It wasn't just about money. I wanted to find the nasty little bastard.'

'Fuck!' said Saskia.

Ayesha stared grimly at the road ahead for a few moments, gathering herself; then she looked up and exchanged nonsmiles with Zimpara in the rear view. Hate stares, Saskia decided. She remained quiet, her thoughts felt tangled by Zimpara's reveal; to be honest, she knew Ayesha's would be too, which of course was Zimpara's intention.

'I suppose thanks are in order,' she said at last.

'You don't owe me gratitude,' Zimpara replied; there was harshness in her tone, maybe just too much to make her words that credible. There was a temporary silence. Inevitably it was Saskia who ended it.

'Tell me about this Panquil,' she said.

'Panqual,' Zimpara corrected. 'We should avoid her if we can. She's a diabolical, from Asmodeum; quite a handful, though she doesn't possess intent; believe me, that is a bonus.'

'What's she like?'

'She's as much a monster inside as she is on the outside. Need I say more?' Zimpara said.

'Is Asmodeum similar to Pandemonium?'

'Questions, questions.'

'I'm only curious.' Saskia said. 'You don't need to answer them.'

'It's okay,' Zimpara shrugged. 'The people of Asmodeum have very few human attributes, apart from maybe the worst ones. It's a less populous place, which is probably a good thing. Some of its denizens, like Panqual, live in Pandemonium.'

'Is Asmodeum further away from this world?' Saskia asked. 'It seems to me that there hasn't been the same sort of relationship between the two dimensions.'

'Further away,' Zimpara mused. 'I suppose it lies deeper than Pandemonium,' she said, mysteriously. 'Connection between our world and theirs is not as commonplace as it is with Pandemonium. Though I suppose that would depend on who you ask.'

'I think you like to be mysterious,' Saskia remarked.

'Not so much,' Zimpara said. 'It's all subjective.'

'You said 'our' world as if you belong here,' said Ayesha sardonically.

'This is my world,' Zimpara replied, her tone matter of fact. 'I wasn't spawned here, but I belong in it. I've lived in it longer than you, after all.'

Amused, Saskia turned away, to avoid one of Ayesha's dagger gazes. 'Time for chocolate,' she said. They had made a brief stop at a garage for drinks, chocolate too. Saskia retrieved the bar from the glove compartment and removed its paper slip. She snapped several of the segments with her fingers before peeling open the foil. She offered it to Zimpara who with a barely visible smile, took a piece between her long red nails. Saskia presented a segment to Ayesha, holding it just a couple of inches from her set mouth.

'Open,' Saskia encouraged. Ayesha's eyes flickered briefly to the side, glancing at the proffered chocolate between Saskia's fingers, before immediately returning to stare ahead. Saskia tilted her head to one side; she could smell the broken chocolate in the air; she knew Ayesha could too, for some reason it seemed quite intense. 'It's a double piece,' she said, tantalizing. 'And its melting in my fingers.' She waited, calmly studying the intensity in Ayesha's outwardly inexpressive face. Her ears caught the sudden hard exhalation through her nostrils. Ayesha's lips and teeth parted to receive the chocolate; Saskia inserted it between them, placing it on her moist tongue. Saskia withdrew her fingers, as Ayesha closed her mouth on the chocolate, catching Ayesha's under lip with a melted trace of it. Individually, Saskia placed her own fingertips between her lips until every trace of melted chocolate was gone, then selected her own piece from the bar, and popped it into her mouth.

'Saradina used you.' Saskia said, surprising Zimpara, who had watched the chocolate episode play out, fascinatedly. 'Why?'

'I don't think it was Saradina.' Zimpara replied thoughtfully. 'I think Panqual devised this on her own, maybe for favour, or maybe because she's evil and a control freak. I don't believe Saradina cares on the when and the how. Luca will be pretty low on her spectrum too. She may not even know.'

'What is she like, Saradina; to know?' Saskia inquired curiously.

'She's a much bigger stick of rock than me.' Zimpara said with a veiled little smile. 'I've no reason to love her and every reason to hate her.'

'Yet you do work for her,' Saskia pointed out.

Zimpara shrugged. 'Not after this, I think.'

'More chocolate?'

'Of course.' Zimpara selected a piece.

'Rachel, you said earlier you were puzzled that Luca had already been found,' Saskia said. 'But only at first; what did you mean.'

Zimpara leaned back in her seat; she made a little grimace. 'It can take weeks to find someone; they might not be found at all. I can't imagine there were many clues to finding Luca Rajal.'

'There's a portal Holly created to bring her through. She sealed it provisionally. If Luca hasn't returned to Pandemonium, Holly probably destroyed it, but she might not have.' Saskia suggested.

'I don't see how that could help to find someone in this reality,' Zimpara said. 'In the circumstances there's only one, almost certain method, and it's a pretty ghastly one.'

'How?' Saskia asked, gingerly.

Zimpara thought about it for a moment and then explained. 'By means of an extremely barbaric ritual, which involves the ghastly torture and slaughter of some poor creature, as payment to a very unpleasant variety of entity for its services. They exist in the subtle layers of this reality. Exposure to something belonging to the individual being sought, furnishes them with what they need to hunt it in the manner of a bloodhound; on the sub-astral and the etheric.'

'That's sick,' said Saskia. 'Anyone involved in that sort of magic is perverted.'

'Evil is everywhere mantis,' Ayesha said. 'As much in our world as in the ordinary world. We simply hope to avoid it. The difference is that some of our kind, are more draconian in how they deal with it, when they encounter it.'

Saskia nodded. She knew there was 'black' magic, the thought of being touched by it, even as tenuously as this, was quite ugly.

'Is Ariadne capable of that sort of sick magic?' she asked Zimpara.

'Probably,' she replied.

Ayesha's ringtone sounded, 'the Hall of the Mountain King'. They had contacted Baal house with Ayesha's phone, unable to get Felix on his own phone, and Saskia had charge of it. They had agreed she would only take a call if it was from Felix or from Baal house. She answered, switching to speaker. 'Hello Ayesha,' it was Sofia's voice.

'It's Saskia. Ayesha's driving.'

'Oh,' there was a brief hesitation. 'I've spoken to Felix. You may use of the Porta Magica.'

'That's fabulous Sofia!'

'Felix can't get back until the evening though.'

'There's nothing else we can do, we'll just have wait for him,' Saskia replied disappointedly.

'I can get you into Larkspur,' Sofia said, matter of fact. 'I can open the portal. Felix has allowed it. He'd prefer you to wait, but he understands if you can't.'

'Sofia, you're wonderful,' Saskia said. Sofia did not respond; she had ended the call. Saskia screwed up her face in thought. 'Maybe we're being Gung Ho,' she said. 'Maybe we need more people.'

'If we had to wait, I'd say yes,' Ayesha replied. 'But we can't afford to delay. Holly's life could be in danger.'

'You know I'm coming with you, don't you,' Zimpara said determinedly; she was shocked that she was even saying it.

'Oddly, I didn't think otherwise,' Ayesha replied, surprising her.

'So, tell me about this Felix,' said Zimpara. 'How come he has a Porta Magica?'

Eleven

Sofia had coffee and snack food waiting for them when they arrived, surprising them. Jyothi was there too, looking anxious, and a pretty Japanese girl called Kiera, who had brought them two antique tantos: knives for close fighting. She had inherited them from her father, she told them, and they could be seen as surplus to her needs; whatever that implied. They accepted them, because they were fine iron, or steel blades. Saskia took one, examining it closely. Ayesha took the other and after giving it a cursory look shoved it into the waist of her jeans. Kiera eyed Zimpara apologetically. 'It's okay. I have this,' Zimpara said. She unbuttoned and opened her jacket on the right, to reveal a miniature pistol, an under and over derringer, in a skeleton holster, attached to a firmly fitted, black lace bra. 'It's a working day,' she said, by way of explanation.

'I've heard of you Rachel Zimpara,' Sofia frowned. Saskia had introduced them. She stayed with them while they ate.

'Nothing good probably,' Zimpara replied sardonically.

'Little. Though I am sorry for what happened to you,' Sofia said; a statement that was not lost on Saskia. Sofia's eyes continued to drift towards Zimpara with interest as they snacked. She intrigued her.

They were hungry and they ate quickly and drank coffee. Then Sofia led the way down to the room that contained the Porta Magica. Saskia walked with Zimpara. 'What happened to you?' she asked, deeply curious.

Zimpara looked about ready to tell her to mind her own business, but she relented.

'I'm a demonic,' she replied. 'An imp, and imps have horns. Mine were removed against my will.'

'That's awful!' Saskia looked shocked. 'I thought you'd had them removed, so you could blend in.'

'They were only little. I'd have worn a baggy cap,' Zimpara said.

'Who took them from you? And what the fuck, for?'

Zimpara decided she had indulged her enough. 'Stop while you're ahead Saskia,' she advised. She glanced at her and winked, to soften the caution. Then all her attention was drawn away, to be focused on the series of fantastic mosaics that expanded before her fascinated eyes. She wanted to wander and peer, but there was no opportunity for that. Her eyes were everywhere as they descended; then they stopped roving about and focused on one thing only.

'That is some Porta Magica,' she remarked.

Saskia smiled darkly as her eyes fell on the door. There was no extreme of temperature on this occasion; the room felt ambient. The huge Olympian deity masks on the wall viewed them with indifference. Sofia walked towards the door and halted two or three steps away. She bowed her head as if she was venerating it, but almost immediately it swung open, as Saskia recalled, like the huge door to a vault, yet so impossibly thin; it revealed the implacable blackness beyond it; then Sofia raised her head again.

'My God Saskia, you looked into that, in the state you were in,' Ayesha remarked softly. 'You can be such a bloody idiot.'

'How do we get to where we want to be?' Saskia asked.

Sofia glanced over her shoulder. 'The short answer is metaphysics,' she said. 'By means of structures called devices, in this case by desiring; I'm familiar with the device to Holly Penn's home; it's been desired often. Are you ready for this?'

'No,' Ayesha said Tensely. 'But that's beside the point.'

Sofia stepped towards the Porta Magica; she inclined her head again. The portal was like a nimbus of darkness around her elegant form. The blackness began to seep away almost immediately; it disappeared becoming an opaque barrier, like a curtain of antique Vaseline glass, which shimmered in ribbons of translucent yellow.

'You have your doorway,' said Sofia. Her desiring completed she stepped aside. 'I still wish you'd wait for Felix.' She was stressed, but it was a hard show on the Gorgonesque demonic.

They approached the Porta Magica together, their faces tense. Passing through a portal wasn't an issue to any of them, any entrance to Place was a portal to an alternative environment; what they might encounter on the other side was the issue. They could see dim shapes through the barrier; they were inert though; there was no indication of movement.

'Good luck,' Sofia said.

Saskia could feel Ayesha's presence next to her. 'Prepare your intent just in case,' Ayesha told her. Saskia nodded. Her keen ears heard Zimpara detach her derringer from its holster. She drew a deep breath; she felt Ayesha's hand close around hers; she squeezed it and stepped into the Porta Magica

*

'We need to move now,' Holly said. Her voice sounded a long way off, as if she was speaking in the next room.

'Why?' Luca asked. Her voice on the other hand sounded loud, as if she was speaking directly into holly's ear. They had been through the don't speak so loud discussion; it did not seem to matter if they spoke more softly, so they had no option but go with the bizarre effect.

'If Ayesha and Saskia are coming, it will be soon,' Holly replied, though in all honesty she had no idea of the passing of time in this strange out of focus world. 'Saskia might see on our wavelength. Come on.' They had explored their environment and found it unfriendly and quite depressing. They could hear; see unclearly and breathe; there was no sense of touch. They were sat on the couch in the lounge right then, but there was no feel of the couch underneath them. When they walked, they had no sense of a solid floor under their feet. In the garden there were no plants in the beds, there were no trees around the house; there was no wildlife; no other life at all. They were surrounded by a grimly dark circular barrier through which they could not pass. Luca followed Holly upstairs.

'They will be walking into danger,' Luca said, she was finding it difficult to see more than blurry shapes; but she knew where she was in relation to her location in the house.

'They won't be alone; they'll gather lots of help,' Holly said.

'What if they don't come?'

'They will. This is the area of the house they will come to. Where the Porta Magica appears.' Holly opened the door to her dressing room and went inside. Luca delayed, straining her ears. She was sure she could hear voices. But they were indistinct, mumbling. She followed Holly into the dressing room.

'You haven't told me yet,' she said petulantly, though it was difficult to convey petulance in this environment.

'Told you what?' Holly demanded.

'If you've forgiven me.' She looked disappointed, but that was hard to convey too.

'You don't deserve to be forgiven. You played me like a fiddle.'

'It was not my intention to hurt you,' Luca said. 'So, I used your protective instincts to seduce you, and my physical attractiveness, my charm and my big sad yellow eyes. It didn't mean that I didn't fancy you like fuck!'

Holly laughed. It sounded odd. 'Thanks for being honest.'

'You want more honest?' Luca said. 'Luca Rajal is your girl. I wasn't at first, but I am now. If you can't forgive me now, I'll earn your forgiveness.'

'Luca, I don't want to talk about it now!' Holly told her. 'We'll discuss it later.'

'Holly.'

'What?' Holly said impatiently.

'I thought I heard my name spoken,' Luca said.

'Did you recognise the voice.'

'Just a voice, no inflection. Inside my head.'

'Maybe nothing, maybe something,' said Holly. I want you to stay here, I'm going to your portal.'

'I'm coming with you.'

'No, you aren't. One of us here, one of us at the portal in case that bitch breaks through. Okay?'

Luca drew a long breath. 'Okay.'

'Move between here, the bedroom and the en-suite,' Holly instructed.

'How do you know the Porta Magica will appear in this vicinity?' Luca demanded.

'Because that's how my lover visits me.' Holly grinned meanly, though the grin was wasted. She left the dressing room, heading for the back stair in the en-suite. Leaving Luca, scowling.

Twelve

There was no sense of transition like there had been in the portal between Mocking beck and the Wild. They stepped into Larkspur like passengers exiting a train on the underground. The opaque barrier was ethereal, it seemed to sigh as they passed through it; there was the sense of a hundred cool fingertips, trailing delicately over their skin. They could smell fragrance, vanilla, mingled with citrus, a stronger smell, a cleaning agent. All three of them nearly jumped out of their skins as they saw themselves emerge from the porta magica opposite, barely a couple of metres away. Saskia heard Zimpara's gasp of surprise and Ayesha's sotto voce obscenity. She chuckled softly.

'We're in Holly's en-suite,' she whispered. 'Facing her mirror wall.' She realised she could not see the portal reflected in the slightly darkened glass. She turned around to find it shimmering behind them. They looked at each other. Ayesha shrugged. 'I don't know how to conceal it. I presume it works like Place. Hidden, open or locked. But I'm not risking it,' she spoke in a soft voice.

'I can,' Zimpara said, her voice was equally soft. She rested the palm of her empty hand, her right one, fingers splayed, against the soft translucence of the portal; its light played between them. Her brows indented slightly as she concentrated briefly, and the portal dimmed out of sight, revealing Holly's large copper bath. 'Shall I lock it?' she asked.

'No. We'll chance it; in the event we need to retreat.' Ayesha replied.

'In the event that I'm down, you mean,' Zimpara said. Ayesha nodded curtly. Zimpara crossed to the part open door and cautiously checked beyond it. 'Empty.' She slipped into the bedroom. Saskia and Ayesha followed her. Their eyes took in the still disordered bed, and a scattering of playthings in it. Saskia raised her brows and felt herself smile whimsically.

'Saskia, this isn't the time or place,' Ayesha told her, catching her look.

'It's just unexpected. It's Holly.' She shrugged.

'The clock radio is off,' Ayesha said. She lifted the telephone to her ear. 'It's dead. We can assume there's no power.'

'You know what's next door?' said Saskia.

'Holly's dressing room.'

'You know what she keeps there.'

'Her clothes...oh her bows!'

'Let's see if she got to them.' Saskia led them out of the bedroom into the wide corridor, she pointed as she avoided a creaky board in the doorway, stepping over it. She kept to the wall and led them right, knowing there were less likely to be more creaks. Zimpara narrowed her eyes thoughtfully.

'Did you used to burgle houses?' She breathed sarcastically.

'Only occasionally,' Saskia replied, and Zimpara was unsure if it was only dead pan humour. Saskia came to the dressing room door and pressed down on the handle. Holly had modernised her kitchen and bathroom and en-suites, but she had retained many original features and others that had been added over the years, including the stunning art nouveau brass handles and fingerplates, that an earlier occupant had fitted to all the doors. They depicted nubile nymphettes in lily ponds. Saskia loved them and was considering trying to buy some identical ones off eBay or from a salvage yard, for her doors at Mocking beck.

They went inside. The concealed lighting was off, and it was dim inside the room. All the wall space was taken up with expensive fitted cupboards. There was a gap between the curtains in the small window. Ayesha went to peer out, cautiously keeping to the side.

'I can't see anyone; that barrier dome looks bizarre from inside,' she said, peering upwards. 'She moved aside. 'Take a look.' Saskia, then Zimpara, glanced through the gap. Saskia frowned.

'It looks weird,' she said. 'Holly says Place forms a sphere no matter what it contains. I suppose that accounts for the power outage.'

'I told you,' Zimpara said. 'It's Place but not like we're used to; it's part of Ariadne; she made it; it's quite ugly, like she is, inside.'

'She isn't overstating it,' Ayesha said, grudgingly.

'I believe you. I want to meet her, almost as much as I don't.' Saskia slid open one of the cupboards revealing a neat row of jackets. She glanced down at pairs of shoes on racks. 'Holly's a size three. I think you are too,' she said to Zimpara. 'Do you really want to do this in Louboutin's?' Zimpara nodded and shrugged, she knew it made sense. Saskia went to another cupboard. This was in the corner near the window and extended almost to the ledge. She slid open its door, this was articulated and curved smoothly and silently back. It revealed padded jackets and some drawers on one side, on the other, narrower side, a selection of bows, strings loosened. Saskia opened the top drawer to reveal racks of carbon arrows, and some with wood shafts, they were all iron tipped.

'One bow and one rack of arrows is missing,' Saskia informed them. 'I don't think she kept any enhanced arrows.

'There are none with elemental enhancement,' Ayesha said, mirroring her disappointment. All of the arrows possessed iron points, but none of them were capable of wounding a demonic, other than maybe bruising their skin.

'They'd be okay against human beings but not against that Panqual thing,' Saskia said. She sighed. Then knelt and opened the bottom drawer of the set. Inside was a long polished wooden box. She undid its catches and opened it. A pair of beautifully crafted shotguns lay in recesses, inside it.

'Purdey's,' Saskia said. 'She rarely if ever uses them, but she keeps them regularly serviced.' She lifted one of the beautiful side-by-side shotguns from its housing. She pushed the self-opener, breaking the gun.

'It's stiff to shut.' she closed the Purdey with a smooth click, pushing the but against her thigh for leverage. 'They were Holly's dads. I think they are quite beautiful, but I hate to think how much wildlife they might have murdered. There is a leather case full of cartridges behind the box.' She reached behind the gun case and pulled out the cartridge box. She opened it; there were about sixty cartridges inside. She selected eight, stuffing them in her side pocket. 'They are soft iron shot too, if you get my meaning.' She closed the box and shut the drawer and stood. 'I'm not a really good shot yet, with a bow; I'll never be Holly's standard, but I can shoot a shotgun, Roger taught me; before he became ill, he used to go clay pigeon shooting.'

'Are you sure about this?'' Ayesha asked, she frowned dubiously.

'Not really,' said Saskia. 'But I can shoot straight.'

'It's why I have this,' said Zimpara, she presented her Derringer. 'Our world can be dangerous, I know my path is, and you two seem to be set on one that's similarly hazardous, and intent isn't always enough, unless you're someone like Theo Bacchus, or Hal Bosola.' She looked so small in the trainers she had selected from Holly's shoe racks, Saskia thought; she was now several inches smaller than both her and Ayesha. Certainly, barely taller than Holly.

'Stop waving that about,' snapped Ayesha, her expression disapproving. 'Is the safety catch on?'

'Of course, at present. I'm very responsible, don't worry. I'm also a very good shot.'

'Ready?' Saskia asked, tensely. Ayesha nodded equally tense. Saskia went to open the door, her fingers had almost touched the handle, when she gasped in surprise, as Holly Penn walked straight through the closed door, dressed in black leggings and jumper. She looked like she was opening an invisible door; her eyes cast about as if she was searching for something; she was certainly not seeing them and Saskia stepped quickly to the side to allow her to pass. She watched her go by her and walk straight through Ayesha. Zimpara was peering uncertainly, as if following Holly's movements too.

'What's the matter!' Ayesha hissed. 'What are you staring at?'

'I'm staring at Holly Penn,' Saskia whispered. 'She's just walked straight through the door like a fucking ghost.'

'She can't be dead?' Ayesha said.

'I don't think so. She's not a ghost. She's Holly.'

'You're looking back at the bow cupboard, is she there?'

'Yes, but she's just standing looking about, sort of puzzled.' Saskia peered at Zimpara whose gaze was still focused on Holly. 'Do you see her?'

'I see her, she's not a ghost though,' Zimpara stated.

'What makes you so sure?' Ayesha growled softly.

'She doesn't feel like a ghost.'

'No, she doesn't,' Saskia agreed. Just then Luca stepped through the doorway and walked in front of Zimpara, who stepped back suddenly. 'Luca,' she said.

Ayesha frowned. She felt frustrated that she could not see what Saskia and Zimpara could. 'What are they doing?

'Talking, maybe arguing,' Saskia replied.

'Try saying something to them!' Ayesha suggested.

'They don't seem to be hearing us now, so what's the point?' Saskia said.

'Try anyway.'

Saskia shrugged. 'Holly!' she said, risking her normal voice. 'Holly!' She tried again, but there was no response from Holly. 'Luca!' she said. She saw a tiny movement of Luca's head in response, a little puzzled frown delved between her eyebrows. She tried again. 'Luca.' The puzzled frown remained, and Luca tilted her head as if she had heard something but was unsure about it; she did not look in Saskia's direction. She shook her head, bewildered. She said something to Holly, getting her attention.

'What are they doing now?' Ayesha said.

'Talking, maybe still arguing,' Saskia said. Holly and Luca were speaking animatedly. Abruptly Holly nodded, and turned away, leaving an unhappy looking Luca. Holly went back through the door into the corridor.

'Looks like Luca is staying, here. I think we need to follow Holly.' Zimpara said.

'I agree.' Saskia moved as quickly and as silently as she was able, opening the door and going back out into the corrido. Zimpara was on her heels. Ayesha followed, not with absolute conviction though. She threw a last curious glance back in the direction she thought Luca might be.

    Holly strode determinedly to the bedroom, she passed straight through the door which they had left partly open; though she appeared to use an invisible handle and push open an invisible door, as she had in the dressing room. She went into the en-suite; Saskia was pretty certain where she was heading. Saskia entered the bedroom as Holly went into the en-suite. Saskia went in after her; Holly walked straight past the concealed portal, apparently sensing nothing. Zimpara and Ayesha followed Saskia. Ayesha thought they were making far too many creaky noises now for comfort, even though they were being as cautious as they could. She was perplexed for a moment when Saskia led them into the en-suite, but only for a moment; then she realised where they were headed. To a tiny, cramped room, that was barely more than a cupboard, which housed a narrow back stair; this descended both to the ground floor via the kitchen and climbed to the attics, a region of Holly's house where Saskia had not been, though she had plans. Saskia opened the door and peered into the cramped little chamber. The stairs were narrow, barely shoulder width for her; a man would have had to walk slightly side on to avoid squeezing between the boarded walls. These, like the stairs, were painted white. Saskia saw the figure of Holly walking down the last few stairs of her descent. The same stairs, Saskia considered. Probably not, more likely they were an alternative version, like the doors she had opened, that were invisible to Saskia, were probably an alternative version, in whatever reality Holly and Luca were inhabiting. She began to descend the narrow, dim stairs; the only light filtering from the en-suite; she resisted the temptation to go faster, wavering between keeping Holly in sight and keeping their existence at Larkspur a secret for as long as possible. She chose caution, treading softly on the stair. Holly was alive and presently safe, and that was what really mattered. Her caution paid off; she carefully opened the door at the bottom of the stairs. There were coat hooks on the other side of the door where Holly hung a couple of kitchen aprons, and Saskia heard their soft rustle as she opened the door. There was no sign of Holly, but there was a man in the kitchen, a very large man, with long straggly black hair and a bushy beard with a central plait. He was dressed all in black; a black biker jacket, black jeans and black, 'no mean city' tee-shirt, stretched across an enormous stomach and man boobs. He had boiled water in the kettle on Holly's oil-fired Aga and was making tea for five on the work surface, on the opposite side of the central island; his attention was on what he was doing, as he sang 'Whisky in the Jar,' contentedly to himself. Saskia shot back out of view. She corkscrewed partially around, holding the shotgun against her body to stop it knocking against the walls. She found herself slightly below, and just a few inches, from Zimpara's face, and her intense gaze. A little behind and higher up the stair, Ayesha was regarding her with equal intensity. The steep stair made them all look as if they were going to tumble on top of each other at any moment, Saskia thought.

'Very big man. Long black hair and beard,' she breathed; her words were only just audible.

'What's he doing?' Ayesha asked, equally softly.

'Making tea.'

Zimpara squinted her eyes in thought. 'If he's really, really, big,' she said. 'He could be a guy called Sirus Henney. He's not the likeliest looking candidate for the wild hunt but believe me he's dangerous; I don't know him very well, but I've never liked him; think we should just walk in on him, and I should empty this into him.'

'We're not emptying anything, into anyone, unless we have to!' Saskia said, appalled, though not actually as much as she thought she should be. 'We could wait until he leaves with the tea,' she suggested. 'He's squeezing tea bags.'

'Then we miss the opportunity of getting one of them on their own and possibly taking them down without a fuss. These odds are not good, remember.'

'Saskia, just walk in, hit him in the face with intent, we'll follow,' Ayesha breathed; she leaned over Zimpara's shoulder. 'Bitch face can threaten him with her illegal firearm and hit him with intent too, if she's capable of doing both at once. I'll follow. It's got to be you; you might be skinny, but there's no way we're getting past you in this space; especially her, with her tits.'

Zimpara turned her smile of disbelief to the side. She rolled her eyes and shook her head. Her tits really were no bigger than Ayesha's perky 34Bs. 'Just do it,' she said.

Saskia nodded, her lower lip gripped firmly between her teeth, she stepped into the kitchen.

'Hello darling,' said Sirus Henney, not looking up 'I like your perfume.' Saskia froze in surprise but only for a second. Instinct kicked in. She sensed the mass of intent coming at her from the side, a great big swinging club of malice. She deployed aspis at the very last fraction of a second from the intent she had been carrying ready. She felt it absorb the Grim intent; it saved her from the worst, spreading the impact, but the blow sent her reeling across the kitchen to crash against the Scandinavian fitted units. Guiltily, she heard Holly's pots crashing around inside them.

'Hey!' she grinned sarcastically. 'You play rough! I'm only a girl!'

'Fuck off!' Sirus grinned malevolently back; he revealed intermittent, tusklike teeth. His beard wobbled over a huge chin. Saskia threw intent straight for his face. He prevented it with aspis putting up both his hands palms out and fingers spread, jerking his hands apart pretentiously. He stopped her intent in its tracks, and it bundled and twisted scattering mugs of tea and plates of biscuits everywhere until aspis dispersed it. 'That could have stung,' he told her, mockingly. Zimpara chose that moment to emerge from the stairs, distracting him; immediately levelling her Derringer; she simultaneously threw intent, continuing to move across the kitchen towards the doorway. Sirus turned on her releasing his own intent whilst he simultaneously grabbed an iron frying pan from the rack behind him; he flung it in a flat arc at Zimpara's head. He moved incredibly quickly for a very large man, Saskia thought, as she threw intent again. He was too preoccupied with deflecting Zimpara's intent and to her satisfaction it struck him in the side of the body; she saw his skin ripple under his tee-shirt as his layers of fat absorbed the impact. She had kept Zimpara in view and she saw her deflect Sirus's intent away and through the closed kitchen door, ripping out the old cat flap. Zimpara avoided the frying pan with a neat sidestep; though not totally; the handle caught her on the shoulder as it went on to crash into the units behind her. She winced at the impact and narrowed her eyes as she pointed the Derringer at Sirus's body.

'I will shoot you Sirus,' she said, as she released the safety catch and her intent at the same instant.

'Ariadne!' Sirus yelled unexpectedly at the top of his voice. 'The bitch is back!' He tilted his head in surprise as Ayesha stepped into view from the stairway. She released her intent instantly toward him, whiplike; he was engaging Zimpara's with aspis and he could only forlornly physically attempt to avoid Ayesha's strike. Her intent hit him full in the chest, making his entire body shake as if he was laughing. In the meantime, Saskia had slipped around the island. Sirus's eyes swivelled round to regard her. 'Shit,' he said. At a time like this she would have relished possessing grim intent, Saskia thought. As it was, Ayesha told her she released intent like a cobra striking at a victim, and she contented herself with that; twice. Sirus went white, even his lips seemed to go white. He groaned and slumped over the work top; only that prevented him from collapsing onto the floor. They closed in on him like three wolves. His body was pumping sweat, and his tee-shirt was soaked under his jacket. Sweat coursed down his face. Saskia wondered if she should feel guilty about her second strike, she decided not.

'What have you done to Holly and Luca?' Ayesha hissed savagely into Sirus's ear.

'Answer her!' Zimpara grabbed a fistful of his black hair, her red nails bright as they closed in it; she lifted his head out of puddles of spilled tea. His eyes rolled, then focused on her. She peered into them with very real threat present in her own. 'Clearly, concisely, tell us what happened, or I will shoot you through your eye and hope the bullet will find a brain. You know, I will.'

'Cunt,' he groaned. 'No, you won't.'

'No, I won't,' she replied. 'However, you're helpless and I will enjoy doing unspeakable things to you.'

Sirus nodded, appreciating the fact, that she probably would. 'Okay. Alright. It went tits up from the start.' He gulped air as he spoke; it was an effort, and his massive body heaved out the words.

'What happened,' said Ayesha.

'Holly did Baldur with elemental; she's broken his bones. They got into the back garden. Fucking arrows and intent everywhere.' He let out a loud groan. 'Fuck, I feel ill.'

'I don't care,' Zimpara told him. 'Get on with it.'

'Holly had a portal in one of the buildings. She cranked it up and dragged her fucking cat bitch in with her. They're between! Ariadne says. I didn't know it was possible. Panqual went apeshit, Ariadne made Place, while she figures out how to get them back and we're fucking stuck here until she does. It's a total fucking cock up! I'm gonna be sick!' He vomited copiously over the work surface. Zimpara stood back just in time, letting his head drop face down into the flowing remains of his previous meal.

'It was Holly's last resort, to go between,' Saskia said. She exchanged looks with Zimpara. 'It explains how we're seeing them as ghosts.' Zimpara nodded. She tapped Sirus's head with the end of her Derringer. 'I think those last hits took him out of play,' she said. 'As if to confirm her opinion Sirus slid down. Zimpara stepped back as he slumped with a heavy, pot rattling thump, to the floor.

'He could choke on his vomit, if we leave him like that,' Saskia pointed out.

'He might,' Zimpara agreed.

'It obviously wasn't coincidence that Holly and Luca's ghost selves came to Holly's dressing room,' Saskia said. 'Holly was probably pretty certain we'd come when we saw there was a problem; that I see as a given. It's not a massive leap to assume we'd enlist Felix's help, assuming we knew about the Porta Magica. I think Holly's spidey senses maybe sensed the Porta Magica opening, though she seemed totally unaware of it when she walked past it. I assume that is the part of the house it's usually opened in. So, they headed up there. Now Luca's staying in the proximity of the Porta Magica. Holly, I think has gone to the portal.'

'I agree,' said Ayesha. 'Holly couldn't sense us; I do think Luca might have heard you, though.'

'We need to move on.' Zimpara said. 'We've got to assume someone heard Sirus yelling for Ariadne, and we made a hell of a racket taking him down.' She cautiously opened the kitchen door and peered along the passage.

'Let's just ride our luck,' Ayesha said.

'They might be in the stable buildings,' Saskia observed.

'Sirus was making tea,' said Zimpara.

'So? Maybe he was going to call them inside or take it out to them,' Saskia said reasonably. 'Our purpose is retrieving Holly and Luca, now we know what's happened to them. Do either of you have any idea how we do that, without getting our arses kicked?'

Ayesha shrugged, she found herself looking uncertainly at Zimpara, then at Saskia. 'I know this, I think that one of us two, must reach the portal; It doesn't matter which one of us either, because we both helped to craft it; it'll only recognise us, it's my bet that's why Ariadne can't access it.'

'It's really that simple?' Saskia looked dubious.

'It's what Holly did, to access between. She's hiding in there until someone comes for her, I know she is. Maybe it needs to be opened again; maybe she needs to be summoned; I don't know, I'm as in the dark as you. So, let's be practical. The garden is too exposed. We go through the house, climb out of the library window and come into the old stable block through the rear door in Holly's lab, and hope, somehow, that we can avoid any more contact.'

'We've been lucky, so far,' said Zimpara. 'It can't last.'

'Or not,' Saskia said, glancing down at Sirus.

Ayesha gave Zimpara a dark look; she narrowed her eyes. 'What are you saying?'

'We know how things stand now,' Zimpara said. 'It's stalemate here.'

'You want us to go back through the Porta Magica, don't you' Ayesha said.

'Ariadne is formidable. We go back and get more help,' Zimpara reasoned.

Ayesha's eyes filled with dislike and contempt. Zimpara did not find it comfortable viewing. 'You're scared,' Ayesha said.

'Yes, I'm scared, aren't you?'

'Yes, I am. You go back though.' Ayesha's voice was cold. 'We can manage without you.'

Zimpara looked away, her face set. 'I'm sorry,' she said.

'Rachel, please,' Saskia said, almost whispering; she had looked on surprised at the quick turn of events. Zimpara refused to look at her and walked past her. She disappeared through the narrow door and climbed the stairs.

Ayesha grabbed Saskia by the arm. 'Come on we need to go.' Saskia nodded; suddenly she felt almost forlorn. She drew herself together. She glanced at the beautiful young woman next to her; she was the very centre of her world, but sometimes she despaired at her;

if she had made just that little effort with Zimpara, she might have stayed with them. She held her tongue though and went with Ayesha, cautiously, through the kitchen door, into the passage.

Thirteen

Zimpara reached the eighth stair before she stopped climbing. She felt her right-hand clench into a fist and her left hand tighten around the grip of her Derringer. Her sly eyes closed in self-despair, and she exhaled a long breath through her nostrils. 'Fuck you, Ayesha!' she said, through clenched teeth, as she carefully turned about and started back down. Twice in one day she had decided to fly in the face of her better judgement. What the fuck's the matter with you, Rachel, she thought. She emerged through the doorway at the bottom, as the kitchen door to the outside opened and Cassie Crow walked grinning into the kitchen. She was looking down at the wrecked cat flap.

'What did the cat do Sirus? Where's that fucking tea, man?' The grin froze on her face as she looked up and saw Zimpara. 'Zim!' she said. She went for charm, remembered too late, and turned to intent. It wasn't exactly the indecision that was her undoing. Zimpara was faster anyway; but she might have stood a chance at deflecting her intent. It hit her like the kick of a mule and threw her like a rag doll against the door frame. She looked at Zimpara almost with surprise, then her head contacted timber, with a sickening little thud. She fell to the floor and lay quite still.

Zimpara hastened to examine her; she frowned at the blood running down from a head wound. She checked the pulse in her throat. She was alive but out cold. Zimpara regarded her dispassionately; the head wound was bad, maybe a fracture, but Cassie might come round and still be a threat. She considered breaking her ankle, so she was unable to walk. She decided to postpone the action while she quickly searched the kitchen drawers. 'Lucky girl,' Zimpara said, when she found what she was looking for; cable ties in the fourth drawer she searched. She secured Cassie thoroughly with them, then as an afterthought Sirus who was beginning to show signs of returning consciousness. Then she went to find Saskia and Ayesha.

Saskia was not blind to the reality that they were risking their lives. She had been angry with Holly and Luca because they had made it a necessary action, interrupting the rhythm of their self-satisfied little world, though she kept it buried away inside. Holly would do the same for her and Ayesha without hesitation though; she had already proven herself, in Claire's Garden and in the Wild and at Mocking-beck. Both of them had. Saskia realised that there was another aspect of herself that relished the danger. She had felt it when she taunted Sirus, and she had experienced a sort of dark dry malevolence at the thought of testing herself against him.

She recalled some of the words from the ballad, whisky in the Jar, that Sirus had been singing softly to himself; she wondered if they applied to her; did she like to hear the sound of cannon balls roaring? She wondered if Holly experienced these two sides of the same coin; more importantly, did Ayesha; she decided that when the time felt right, she would ask her.

They had transited cautiously along the passage from the kitchen towards the entrance hall; they had decided to scan the dining room at the front of the house and the big main lounge at the back, for possible occupants. Saskia peered inside. There was no fire; it would not be lit until the evening anyway at this time of year. The French doors were standing open, and a draft of air blew through. Saskia did not see her at first, she supposed because she was so still, so statue still, in front of the cabinet filled with Holly's treasured Martin brothers, Wally birds. She stared at the grotesque long beaked birds, in silent fascination. Saskia froze, as her mind at last discarded the room and saw her; Saskia's breath exhaled; she forgot to inhale another. Ayesha's fingers on her shoulder reminded her; and she drew it, silently.

'I hear you,' said Panqual, in a sinister tone. 'I hear the mice under the floors and the beetles in the walls. And I can hear you.'

The diabolical had removed her heavy leather habit to allow her body to cool; she had laid it across the couch; her only covering was a creased black linen tabard. She turned round, revealing her breast and flank as she came about. Round, black, soulless eyes, as big as the palms of hands, rested on Saskia; the macabre beaked head as always, pointed down. Saskia thought she resembled a giant plucked bird with taloned feet and taloned hands, at the end of unnaturally long arms. Her skin was chicken skin, a greasy grey colour, with quill like bristles at her joints and neck. Saskia wondered if she had once been feathered, had moulted, and they had never come back. She decided it was best not to ask.

'Not my perfume then?' Saskia inquired.

'Have you loaded your gun Saskia?' Ayesha asked.

'Have you Saskia?' said Panqual. The black eyes were pitiless; Saskia thought they were the emptiest things she had ever seen. She shook her head. She felt Ayesha ready intent.

'Don't,' Saskia said. 'Not in there. There's too much that Holly loves.'

'I know,' Ayesha said gently. 'I think we'd better get the hell out of here then.' Her fingers raked at Saskia's shoulder, enforcing the imperative; they fell back; down the wide central passage. They were flanked on the walls, by Holly's collection of original prints from captain Cook's voyages; the eyes in the fascinating faces of natives from the various islands, watched them inscrutably as they retreated backwards; Panqual too, as she emerged laughing and in between laughter, issuing fake screeches, like a thing demented. She stalked towards them on her horribly long, skinny legs; she raised her arms and threw them outwards and splayed her taloned fingers; knocking prints off their hooks; they fell to the floor their glass smashing. Panqual's raised arms, revealed flaps of skin, stretched, down her sides to her thighs; She looked primeval; in her mind Saskia saw her swooping down on a terrified victim, like a pterosaur from hell. Since her death at the hands of the CaolShee Saskia had considered the possibility that she would never be capable of experiencing genuine fear again; except in her nightmares, when she relived the event in dreadful detail, but she was dealing with them. Panqual possessed that quality of nightmare; but she wasn't enhanced recycled memory, she was imminent and very real, and she caused cold fear to claw up inside Saskia. Saskia stumbled back; she whimpered in fright as Panqual emerged through the doorway. She unleashed intent as she retreated and felt Ayesha strike with Vis ultima. She heard the impact of both strikes; hers would feel like a sledgehammer, to a human; Ayesha's like a small wrecking ball. Panqual seemed unaffected, she barely reacted, jerking twice; she lacked the intent to deflect them with. Saskia heard Ayesha swear under her breath, and felt her strike again with Vis ultima, though she was no longer looking at Panqual to see the result; she was giving her attention to loading the shotgun. The entrance hall was five metres away. She broke the Purdey as she retreated and scrabbled in her pocket for cartridges; she clutched three with trembling clumsy hands; she tried to load one and dropped it. She yelled at herself, angrily. The rage seemed to calm her, and the next two cartridges slid into position. She closed the Purdey as she made it to the hall, feeling resistance until it snapped shut. She felt a surge of relief and a claw of panic; the cartridges contained death for Panqual; however, there were two negatives to consider; how quickly the iron shot would take effect, and more significantly, could it break

Panqual's skin. Briefly she met Ayesha's gaze; she looked as scared as she was. She tried to smile encouragingly.

Ayesha backed across the hall, unleashing Vis ultima as she retreated, evenly spaced strikes that thumped audibly into Panqual's body. She wished she had Grim intent like Claire, so she could drive misericords of agony into the monsters eyes. She aimed a strike at Panqual's eyes and the diabolical flinched at that; it was the first indication that she might be vulnerable. Ayesha struck again at her eyes; this time Panqual barely reacted, and Ayesha saw that two vertical milkily transparent lids had drawn across them. Saskia had tried striking at Panqual's skinny legs in the hope that they were vulnerable; that had proved useless. She almost felt it was pointless. She heard the whisper of drawn steel as Ayesha unsheathed the Tanto, Akeira had loaned her. She cast her eyes down to look doubtfully at the long barrel of the shotgun; she wished then it was Claire's elephant gun; that would stop the bitch. She struck with intent, angrily. Was Panqual breathing hard now? Was she grunting at each impact; was there the sweat of effort gleaming on her skin? Whether the strikes had begun to have an effect was irrelevant, Any of Ayesha's strikes would have killed someone. Another couple of retreating steps and Ayesha would be driven into the space under the stairs; her alternative was the doorway to the room on her right, where according to Holly her mother used to practise the saxophone. The instrument was still in there. Along with one or two others apparently. If nothing else Ayesha could hit Panqual with them. Saskia pointed the shotgun, she had almost been putting it off, a desperate last hope; she fired. She anticipated the recoil, but nothing happened. She felt a momentary surge of panic. Safety catch, safety catch, she repeated the words, hissing them, admonishing herself. She released the safety. Ayesha slashed with the tanto, keeping an eye on Panqual's huge claws; she struck her on the thigh, hoping to draw blood; failing. She stepped back, looking afraid and unleashed Vis ultima, glancing over at the pointed shotgun. Saskia discharged both barrels almost together, successfully this time, firing two loads of heavy shot into Panqual's body. Panqual staggered to the left almost thrown off her feet by the force of the shotgun blasts and Ayesha's Vis ultima, combined. She collided with and shattered the demilune table by the wall and to Saskia's horror the piece of Bernard Leach pottery that stood on it. Saskia yelled as her horror turned to glee at seeing Panqual almost go down. Her satisfaction was short lived as Panqual's macabre head swivelled to regard her, she had withdrawn her lids, and her eyes were as black as tar again. Defiantly Saskia gave her look for look. She was damaged; her skin was turning livid where Ayesha's Vis ultima's had struck her upper body repeatedly, and where Saskia's shots had struck her haunch and stomach, shredding the tabard. To Saskia's dismay none of the heavy shot had pierced her skin.

'Hit her again!' Saskia yelled. She broke the smoking barrels; with desperate fingers she clutched more cartridges from inside her pocket.

'Yes, hit her again Ayesha!' Zimpara yelled. She came stalking into the hall; her arm was stretched out in front of her, pointing her Derringer at the back of

Panqual's head. She shot her from less than a metre away and struck with Vis ultima too, coinciding with Ayesha's own strike. Panqual screamed in rage and pain. She turned, lurching, striking Zimpara who was too close to escape. Panqual hit her with a clubbing blow; knocking her off her feet and across the room; she fetched up against the wall next to the night porters chair, smacking her head and back, hard. She shook her head, bracing both hands on the floor and pushing herself up; her hair spilled down over her face, hiding whether she was angry or in pain. Saskia, re-loading both barrels of the shotgun, suspected both. She was surprised she had not been knocked out cold, or worse, she'd hit the wall with such force.

Panqual turned on Ayesha, she drove her back under the stair. Ayesha savagely struck at her arms and fingers with the tanto. She struck with Vis ultima too. She actually wondered how the bitch was still on her feet. She screamed as Panqual reached under the stair and dragged her out, her talons biting into Ayesha's shoulder. Panqual bent down to stare into Ayesha's face searching for the pain. Ayesha grimaced, then she laughed as Saskia watched in horror. 'Call that pain!' Ayesha jeered. Panqual shook her head and tossed her against the wall. She fell in a heap on the smashed demi lune and scattered pieces of Bernard Leach stoneware.

Furiously Saskia unleashed; it was a hammering blow as always. She knew it was possible to change the nature of the strike, as with grim intent; it was also possible to make it hot like flame, or burn like acid, or strike like a scorpion sting, but this was a rare skill, one she wanted. Her strike could shatter a stone birdbath and accidentally lay out a sheep with a piece of the debris; her very first deliberate unleashing of intent had done just that; yet it barely got a reaction from Panqual. The diabolical glanced at her, discarded her, determined her for next up and turned her eyes again to Zimpara who had climbed to her feet.

'I never trusted you, Rashara. You never showed respect for the dignity of my rank,' she said, almost conversationally.

'Chief thug,' said Zimpara scathingly. 'Evil murdering cunt.'

'I'm going to break your legs,' Panqual chuckled. 'Settle her, then come back to dismember you. We'll see how long I can make you scream.'

'Evil fucking bitch.' Said Saskia, she spoke softly, her voice contained no inflection; she stepped closer to Panqual, riskily close, with the shotgun levelled, and fired it at the side of Panqual's head, aiming for her ear cavity. At that distance it was more effective than she had dared to hope. Panqual screeched with a combination of pain and fury. She clutched the side of her head with her outspread hand; taloned fingers pressed into her naked bony skull. She twisted away, recoiling from the blasts; the barrels had discharged only centimetres from her head. The impact of the blasts had made her skin dark and raw. The empty eyes focused on Saskia, like they were draining her soul, and Saskia stepped away, desperately reloading, suddenly very afraid. Panqual grabbed the shotgun by the barrels as Saskia closed it and tore it out of Saskia's grasp, almost snapping her finger in the trigger guard. Zimpara came at Panqual from the side, she unleashed intent, striking at Panqual's face. Panqual swung the shotgun round at her like a club, hitting her across her upthrown arm and face with the stock. She went down, sprawling at Panqual's massively long, clawed feet. Panqual kicked her vindictively in the head; then turned on Saskia again tossing the shotgun away; it rattled across the floor. Saskia stumbled backwards and unleashed intent twice, before Panqual, who had begun to sway, reached her, and seized her around her throat in a clammy grip. Saskia yelped in pain as Panqual bore her back with brutal force against the side of the staircase, shattering several spindles with the impact of her shoulders and head, and thrusting her head back through them; a broken upright shard opened her cheek.

'I'll rip your fucking spine out through your throat you skinny little bitch!' Panqual snarled leaning over her and into her; she was breathing hard, and she shook her head and shoulders as if trying to throw something off. Saskia almost did not take her threat in; her focus was on the trickle of nearly black liquid that ran down the right side of Panqual's beak. And more subliminally the delicate whiff of a Tom Ford fragrance, indicating that Ayesha was very close.

'Close your eyes and ears little mantis,' Ayesha snarled. Saskia did as she was told, but not before she saw the barrels of shotgun come into view pointed at Panqual's head. Saskia's ears were still ringing from the mini thunderclaps of the earlier discharges; she quickly stuck her index fingers in her ears. She felt Panqual's grip tighten and heard the report of the shotgun pretty much simultaneously. She heard Panqual's muffled shriek and felt her grip slacken and release her. Saskia instinctively dropped into a crouch away from the fumes, only then drawing breath and opening her eyes. She moved quickly to the side before bobbing up. Panqual was down on her knees drawing in great gulps of air. Saskia was next to a battered and bruised Ayesha; she felt her fingertips trace against hers. Saskia's left cheek was stinging.

'Your cheeks bleeding,' Ayesha observed, she smiled, breathing hard. Saskia was not ready for the look of surprise on Ayesha's face that followed her statement. Ayesha disappeared like she had fallen through a hole as Panqual seized her and dragged her down onto the floor. Ayesha had shot her in the left eye, the black disc was oozing brownish fluid and the skin beneath it looked raw like tenderised meat. Blood was leaking from inside the eye cavity where iron shot had penetrated. There was more, trickling down the side of her face from Saskia's shots. Panqual's protective horizontal eyelid slid into place over the damaged eye. She swayed on her knees; steadied herself. Ayesha kicked and thrashed on the floor, fighting against the grip of Panqual's hand and the pressure of Panqual's weight bearing down on her ribs; her black eyes blazed hatred at Panqual as she desperately struck her with intent. Panqual gasped feeling the blows now; she was like a flagging boxer taking punishment, though still utterly dangerous. Saskia struck too and drew her own tanto and tried to stab Panqual in her ruined eye; Panqual slashed at her with her free hand, keeping her at bay.

'I'm going to rip your pretty face away,' Panqual told Ayesha, she was dripping blood and yellow saliva from her beak onto the struggling Ayesha.

Ayesha's face twisted in fear, she was unable to speak, and she could barely breathe; she wrenched at Panqual's wrist, but it was a useless effort against her abnormal strength. Saskia cried out in misery, she clasped the tanto in both hands, preparing to risk her life striking at Panqual with it. Ayesha's eyes begged her not to. Zimpara appeared behind Panqual then; she looked barely taller than the kneeling diabolical. She struck down at her neck; Saskia saw that she was wielding the hay hook that Holly kept near the door for boots. Zimpara struck with all her strength; she was demonic, with the strength of her kind. The needle-sharp hook broke the skin and buried into Panqual's flesh almost to the curve. She moaned as the bitter pain of the iron established its reaction in her blood. Zimpara heaved with all the strength she had left and dragged Panqual over backwards. She lay on her back gulping air, the hook protruding from her neck, its handle under her. She seemed suddenly spent.

Sobbing for breath, with Saskia's help, Ayesha climbed to her feet. She gave a little moan and massaged her bruised ribs as she studied Zimpara's battered and bloody face with searching eyes. 'You're a mess,' she said.

'You should see yourself,' Zimpara replied.

Groaning, Panqual rolled onto her front and slowly, painfully, pushed herself up, onto her knees; her body swayed, and she almost did not make it; she remained bent forward, supported by her arms. She could feel the iron poison threading through her blood, she knew it would eventually consume her body; it would be a painful death; a long one; she was a diabolical, it would kill her more slowly than it killed a demonic. She became still, but for her laboured, shallow breathing.

'We should finish her,' Zimpara said. She glared at Panqual with unconcealed malice and no shred of mercy. The side of her face, where she had been struck and kicked was a bruised, bloody mess. Her head felt like it had been split with an axe, and she felt dizzy and ready to fall over. The faces of her companions lacked any compassion too. Ayesha was about to speak, but someone pounded on the front door and shouted through it, startling them.

'Panqual, Cassie! I'm coming in!' His words sounded as if they were an effort. Zimpara recognised the voice.

'That's Josh Devlin,' she said to Ayesha. 'He calls himself Baldur.'

Ayesha nodded to her and stepped closer to the door; with an effort she pulled herself together. 'I strongly advise against that Mr Devlin; Baldur.' she announced in her best legal tone; she raised her voice so he could hear. 'None of your people are standing, and Panqual is dying.'

'Fuck!'

Ayesha was aware of Zimpara passing her, she swayed erratically. Ayesha reached out and bunched the shoulder of Zimpara's jacket in her fist and steadied her. Zimpara threw her a resentful look and shook herself free; she leaned almost drunkenly against the door.

'Hi Josh,' she said loudly.

'Rachel,' he sounded surprised.

'Sirus won't be taking any further part in the day. Panqual really is just clinging on. Cassie might have a fractured skull. I hear you're not too good, yourself.'

There was silence on the other side of the door for several moments; then Josh spoke again. 'I'm standing down. I'm injured.'

'Yeah, well stand down somewhere else,' Zimpara told him.

'He's walking away, well limping actually, he looks a wreck. There're two vehicles outside, he's climbing into the back of one.' Ayesha peered through the narrow window to the left of the door; she kept behind its drawn curtain. She looked at Zimpara, who looked ready to fall over. She got her by her upper arms and guided her to the night porters chair. Zimpara almost fell into it, sitting down with a bump.

'It feels quite comfy,' she said, amused. 'But I'm not staying in it.' Ayesha digested her words, then gave a little shrug. She watched Saskia go to pick the shotgun up off the floor, where she had dropped it when Panqual grabbed her. Saskia ejected the spent cartridges; she found one in her pocket. Zimpara extracted another from her pocket. She held it up. 'You dropped this,' she said.

'You were struck with the shotgun. It did damage, I saw,' Ayesha said curiously. 'Wood and steel, yet I don't think you're poisoned.'

'I've been here sixty years, Ayesha,' Zimpara said. 'I acquired immunity a long time ago.'

'I didn't know it was possible,' Ayesha said.

'Believe me it is. The means isn't pleasant, though.' Zimpara smiled darkly.

Ayesha frowned slightly; she gazed into Zimpara's face; she looked drawn under all the pinkish blood, and peering into her eyes, she could see the lights were not all switched on.

'I'm coming with you,' Zimpara stated.

'I can't really stop you.' Ayesha winced and clutched her shoulder; she seemed puzzled when her jacket felt wet to her touch and her fingertips came away red.

'Ariadne's strong,' Zimpara spoke almost conspiratorially. 'She's a monster.' Ayesha looked at her glumly.

'I've heard,' she said. 'I'm surprised she isn't on top of us.'

'She'll be waiting for us. Like a big fat spider. It's what she does.' Zimpara pushed herself out of the chair. She swayed; it apparently amused her.

Ayesha turned away and found Saskia looking amused too. 'What are you grinning at?' she demanded. Saskia shrugged. 'Because, if I don't grin, I'll probably cry,' she said.

Fourteen

'No more guns, for us, from here onward, Saskia,' Ayesha said. 'I don't care about Pearl and Amber, or Claire using a firearm. I don't want us to. We both need to acquire grim intent, and you need vis ultima, and that's just to begin with. Is that even in working order?' She eyed the shotgun. Saskia had wiped Zimpara's blood off the stock and hammers with tissues; the stock was split.

'I'm not sure about firing it with the stock like this. I'll fire it from the hip if I need to.' She looked glumly at Ayesha. 'I'm not keen either. I want to become skilled with a bow, you know that; I was going to use Holly's, but none of the arrows had been customised; they'd have been no use against Panqual and that's who I meant the gun for. We must have struck her about thirty times between us, you know.' Ayesha nodded grimly and winced.

They were grouped in the middle of the entrance hall, ready to resume their strategy. Saskia's right shoulder felt battered where Panqual had smashed it through the stair spindles, but as she looked at her companions, she seriously wondered how they were still on their feet.

'What is that music?' Ayesha frowned, as loudly played music, abruptly, began to beat along the passage.

'I think it's coming from outside,' Zimpara said. 'It has that sound to it, you know like at an outdoor concert.'

'It's a song Holly likes. From the seventies or eighties, she's into them. It's directed at us, isn't it?' Saskia said.

'I believe it is,' Zimpara said pensively.

'Is it a challenge do you think?' Ayesha asked.

'No, I rather think it's an invitation,' Zimpara replied.

Ayesha and Saskia exchanged looks. 'Shall we accept?' said Ayesha.

'It might be rude not to,' Saskia observed.

Yes Sir, I can Boogie, by seventies duo Baccara, met Saskia, Ayesha and Zimpara on full volume, through the open French doors into the lounge. It was coming from Holly's portable CD player on battery. It had been placed strategically on the terrace just outside, its speakers pointed towards the doorway. Curiously, they went out onto terrace, into the greyness of the day. The outer third of Holly's walled garden was hidden by the screening pseudo mist of Place that had been thrown over the house; it looked eerie, alien in fact as it shifted and distorted. Only light and air penetrated, excluding everything else, so they were unaware if the rain was still coming down. A woman: it could only be Ariadne, Saskia thought, appeared to be waiting for them. She was sitting on the limestone coping of one of the raised beds; this was filled with red and pink fuchsias and bougainvillea's, as her chosen backdrop. She was stressing a tight, sleeveless, low-cut summer dress; it was white, decorated with a pattern of orange and red poppies. In her left hand, rested half on her thigh and half on the coping, she held a walking stick topped with a carved head; beside her on her right lay a collapsed umbrella, which matched her dress. When she saw them, she grinned and waved them over. As they stepped from the terrace, Great Northern Jester got up from the folding chair he had brought out of the greenhouse, down by the gate. Ariadne stood him down with a gesture, and he resumed his seat, watching them curiously. As they approached Ariadne cautiously, she repositioned her stick and bizarrely placed a kiss on the carved head, before resting the tip on the ground; she set both her hands over the carved head, one on top of another, so she could lean her ungainly body forwards. Instinctively, Saskia, Ayesha and Zimpara drew apart as they walked towards her, until there was about three metres between any two of them and a single strike could not be directed at them all.

She watched them coming, with her mad, cow eyes volleying between them. Her lips parted in a rather unhinged smile; she kept her teeth clenched firmly together; they were not quite white. Saskia decided that she had an extremely creepy look, and far from in a good way. They stopped a short distance from her; they regarded each other, with equal curiosity. Oddly, Ariadne appeared to be pleased to see them.

'You are so cute! I love that battered look, or would you prefer war torn?' she said. 'My, we've been incredibly noisy; haven't we!' she spoke in a sort of husky staccato; slightly derisively. 'You all look so determined, through the blood. Take a step back, be cool, this doesn't need to end badly.' She adjusted her position, shuffling and removing one hand from the walking stick so she could tug down the hem of her dress; it had crept up past the mid-way point of her bulky thighs as she had shifted. She leaned heavily on the stick as she performed the action, when it was completed, she relaxed, and spread out her fingers, stretching them up like a cat spreading out its paw, before closing them again. In that brief moment Saskia clearly saw the head at the top of the walking stick; it was a kind of beast, but it had the features of a man, they were saturnine and sensual; it had pointed ears and horns flowing backwards and carved close to the head, through thick hair. It was not a faun. It seemed cruel, even debauched. It emerged from a collar and cravat, like a regency gentleman's. It had green hardstone eyes, which gave it an almost fiendish look. Saskia decided the carving was equal to any you could find. The stick was all one piece; it had probably been carved from a root; and it was antique, possibly from the period represented by the head. Ariadne saw Saskia's interest in her stick; she returned both hands to it, enclosing the head almost jealously.

'You didn't feel inclined to join in then?' Ayesha said, replying to Ariadne's words.

'Me?' Ariadne looked surprised. 'I'm not very hands on; especially with all those bullets flying about. You'll realise when you get to know me.' She pulled a strange facial expression, which Saskia was unable to define.

'Get to know you,' Saskia frowned, puzzled.

'It's your play, your followers,' Ayesha remarked coldly.

'Panqual's play, actually. To me it was merely another step along the path to cosying up to a Pandemonium socialite. Now I'm pretty convinced she's playing me; like she played you, Rachel. But I don't care!

Well, I do, but something more intriguing just stepped onto the stage. And everything changed. Fate just ate my peach.'

Ayesha narrowed her eyes suspiciously. 'Would you like to explain what you mean,' she said, softly. So far, the encounter was going very differently from what she had anticipated.

'Have you any idea how famous you two are in the circles that whisper? In the lodges and in the Temples, and even in the halls of the Shee?'

'Are we?' said Saskia, furrowing.

'The mysterious Saskia Challoner. Custodian of the Wild.' Ariadne shifted her eyes theatrically from side to side.

'All I did was inherit something.'

'Something!' Ariadne scoffed. 'The nAill, the Geifu Prydain, if you want, or just plain old: the gift, is what you inherited. For some reason the Shee chose one of your ancestors, way back in the time of King Stephen, to be its custodian. Any idea why?'

'I really don't know,' Saskia replied.

Ariadne drew in her under lip, thoughtfully. She nodded. 'I thought as much.'

Saskia's eyes narrowed slightly. 'I didn't realise it was that long ago.'

'The connection goes back even further than that, into the misty pagan past,' Ariadne replied mysteriously.

'You seem to know a lot about it. More than me.' Saskia was intrigued.

'I've been digging.,' Ariadne smirked. 'I like mysteries, and the legend of the gift is about as mysterious as it gets.'

'I hadn't heard it called the gift until now,' Saskia said.

'Most Millennials in the magic world will not have heard of it,' Ariadne said. 'Many of us Boomers have, but all but a tinsy, tiny few, academics mostly, understood it. They don't know it meant the Wild. They don't care either. They have ordinary little lives to lead, like the ordinaries. Only the ones who matter, give a damn.'

'How come you're so interested?' Saskia frowned. 'As one who obviously gives a damn.'

'Haven't I just told you the answer to that, on several levels.' Ariadne sighed. 'Come on you're a clever girl. Don't take me for an idiot.'

'It really is my business though, no one else's,' Saskia said reasonably.

'You know that's bollocks. Even if it's true.' She fixed her mad eyes on Saskia; they burned with intensity and an underscore of mockery. She continued. 'To the Craft, the Wild is folklore, a legend, about as vague as the gift. Just a few know the importance of that gift, without knowing the why.'

'Some must! Otherwise, how do you know so much?' Saskia reasoned.

'It depends on who you ask?' Ariadne said.

'She means the Shee, mantis,' said Ayesha.

'I know who she means.' Saskia a little sharply. She immediately glanced apologetically to Ayesha.

'You lit the blue touch paper by the simple act of having to be found. Deep, still waters were disturbed. You became a thing of value to some, an obstacle to others; Pandemonium was enlisted to seize you; the cold Shee came to murder you.' Ariadne's eyes lit up. 'That must have been so scary! You woke us up in all the dark places pretty girl. Alliances are being made, enmities strengthened, and most, still don't even know why. In a few months, the north of England will be like the Spanish Maine. Run up the black flags me hearties, Yoh Hoh Hoh! and all that. You heard it here first. You have no idea how delighted I was, when I discovered it would be you, who would be coming to help your little friend. Is anyone still alive, by the way?'

'Were not killers,' said Saskia.

'Tell that to the Shee,' Ariadne chortled. She became gleeful again. 'I've wanted a little tête-à-tête with you both since you came to my attention, and I started digging into the Wild. So, this is an opportunity not to miss.'

'A tête-à-tête is one on one, not one to two,' Ayesha pointed out deliberately.

'Let's not deal in semantics.' Ariadne wiggled her fingers like stumpy spider legs on top of her stick. 'You two come as a package, there's no ambiguity about that.'

'All we want is Holly and Luca safely back, and for all of this to stop,' said Saskia. 'What will that take?'

Ariadne sniffed; she ignored Saskia's question. 'That portal's bespoke, but you already knew that, as you probably helped to craft it. How did you bypass my defence. Anyway?'

Ayesha threw Saskia a look of caution.

'It's not that big a deal, for fuck's sake!" said Ariadne seeing the look.

'We used a porta magica,' Saskia said; she received a glare from Ayesha.

Ariadne looked pensive. 'Hmm, I only know of four in the Uk, only one is owned by someone who doesn't make me think: I really don't want you as my enemy. But it isn't him; not your style.' Ariadne licked her lips. 'How do we make this stop you asked. Perhaps Panqual can help.'

'Panqual's dying,' said Saskia.

'I admit she doesn't look well.' Ariadne swivelled her bulging eyes past them, in the direction of the house. Tentatively they followed her gaze.

Saskia tightened her grip on the shotgun as she saw Panqual lurching down the three steps from the terrace to the path. She swayed drunkenly as she came towards them. She looked ghastly; her skin was covered in yellow blotches and a film of yellowish sweat; around her ear and eye had turned black where the iron shot had penetrated. Her pigeon chest heaved as she appeared to be fighting for air.

'I must return to Pandemonium, urgently' she wheezed. 'Are these two are capable of fetching back Holly Penn? If they can...she can open the portal.'

I'm pretty certain they can,' said Ariadne. 'You really don't look well. Panqual.'

'I am very sick. In Pandemonium, I can get help. Make them fetch Holly Penn!' Panqual came to a stop, her body sagging.

'Maybe you need to rest,' Ariadne suggested.

'I don't want to rest. I need to get help!' Panqual hissed angrily. A single black eye transited them emptily.

Ariadne walked casually between Saskia and Zimpara who was on Saskia's right; she gave Zimpara a searching look. Zimpara swayed and looked as if she could fall over at any moment.

'It worked out okay in the end,' Ariadne said obscurely. Zimpara looked puzzled.

Saskia's hand was flinching nervously where it encircled the shotgun stock behind the trigger guard, she could feel the crack through the wood under her palm. Ariadne tutted deliberately.

'Guns are for ordinaries, Saskia,' she said, disappointedly. She carried her stick vertically in front of her, not quite pressed against her heavy body; her left hand was positioned a few inches above her right on its shaft. She stopped a short distance in front of Panqual. Panqual regarded her, her taloned fingers clenching and unclenching. She pointed at Saskia and Ayesha. 'Make them open the portal,' she said, her once siren voice, a wheeze.

'All this, for a little slut with fur and pointy ears,' Ariadne said, obscurely. She jerked her stick right then left, hard and fast in two short, quite vicious movements.

Panqual let out a single shriek. Her lower body snapped violently to the right, her head to the left, at the same time both twisted round with dreadful force. Saskia and Ayesha heard the cracking sounds of her bones. She crashed twitching onto the brick path, like some huge broken, ghastly marionette.

Ariadne turned to them, her teeth were clenched, showing in her wide, bizarre smile; it seemed to mimic the ghastly smile on the face of the head on the top of her stick. 'Wasn't that an unexpected turn of events?' she chortled. 'I'd say let's go to the pub,' she said, 'but I'm sure we all have other things to do.'

Saskia nodded, preparing to defend herself. She could see that Ayesha had begun to drop into her gunfighters crouch but had stopped halfway. They watched Ariadne warily, something of the look of a cornered wolf about them. Only Zimpara seemed unconcerned.

Eyes swivelling between them, Ariadne lifted her stick high above her head in her left hand. 'I don't need to say this,' she told them. 'I just like to.' She took a deep breath and making her voice as deep as she could she called out: 'Hu...La!'

'Isn't that...?'

'It doesn't matter Saskia,' Ayesha said. Saskia shrugged. Her eyes were attracted by movement; she saw Ayesha looking too. The barrier had begun to palpitate, the tiny particles that permeated it streamed from it; for a couple of minutes, the air appeared to be full of wayward particles, like swarms of black flies. They came from every direction, above and over the house, gathering above Ariadne until her stick was invisible inside their concentrated mass. Then like an inverted explosion they disappeared into it, as if they had been sucked inside it. The barrier disappeared like wisps of breath on an icy day. The garden walls appeared and the trees beyond them.

'Don't look so suspicious,' Ariadne said to them as she lowered her stick. She held it with both hands tightly against her heavy breasts; the macabre head held to her cheek, like she was snuggling a pet cat. 'Take it. It's over, no one else needs to die.'

'What do you get out of it?' Saskia demanded.

'That remains to be seen,' she said, again obscure. 'It's a gift, freely given, don't knock it. I suggest Holly Penn opens the portal to Pandemonium and throws that into it. A gift for Saradina, though she won't have a clue about it.' She jerked her head towards Panqual's body, her demented look momentarily intensifying. 'Then if I were her, I'd just close it.' She walked away. 'I'll let myself out, after I've gathered up my people. Toodle-oo.'

They watched her until she disappeared through the French doors, her large hips swinging. 'I wouldn't trust her as far as I could spit,' Ayesha growled. She watched Great Northern Jester get out of his chair and follow Ariadne inside.

'Me neither, she's batshit crazy,' Saskia said.

'We've been lucky Saskia.' Ayesha walked over to Zimpara in time to catch her, as her legs gave way beneath her.

'I don't want to trust to luck Ayesha.' Saskia broke the shotgun, unloaded it and went and laid it on the terrace next to the CD player, which was currently playing Mr Blue Sky. She reduced the volume a little, instead of turning the player off, liking the song.

Conclusion

The rain had moved on whilst Ariadne's Place had been in situ, leaving moody skies above. Holly came into the garden from the stable block, looking decidedly mean. Luca followed a few paces behind her, with Saskia, who had volunteered to activate the portal. Saskia gave Ayesha an odd look and rolled her eyes. She had already heard Holly tell Luca that she should be grateful she hadn't left her between. Luca looked upset and furious. Holly saw Zimpara sitting on the edge of the terrace, elbows on her knees, her battered face cupped in her hands.

'What's that little bitch doing here?' she demanded. She strode belligerently towards Zimpara, who eyed her warily.

Ayesha had been poking at her shoulder wounds and considering the possibility of infection; she was relieved it was on the side that would not compromise her compliance thorns. Now she pulled her jumper back over her still leaking wounds and walked between Holly and Zimpara.

Holly stopped. She frowned at Ayesha, annoyed and puzzled.

'If it wasn't for that little bitch and me and Saskia, you'd still be between,' Ayesha told her. 'She isn't the problem.'

'She brought an enemy to my door.'

'It was the other way round actually. She was duped too; by that.' She pointed towards the body of Panqual sprawled along the side of the raised bed where she had fallen. 'She duped everyone. We didn't win here Holly, we were lucky. Why are you angry with Luca? I thought you were an item.'

'I feel like an idiot,' Holly said. 'She played me. She made me fall for her, you may as well know.'

'She didn't make you,' Ayesha said. 'But that's between you and her; I hope it works out okay; if it doesn't, I'll be there for you. Some advice Holly. If I learned anything here today: it's not to be too quick to condemn.'

Holly responded with a nod; she did not trust herself to speak anymore; she felt too emotional. She walked past Ayesha casting a darkly puzzled look in the direction of Zimpara. She went inside, to inspect the damage to her house.

'I don't think she would have attacked me,' Zimpara said. 'But thanks for that.'

'We all earned our spurs today chick,' Ayesha said, surprising herself as well as Zimpara. 'I'm going to take you to Baal house.'

'Okay,' said Zimpara, nodding, feeling too unwell to resist.

'Saskia, are you coming?' Ayesha called. 'I'm taking Rachel back through the Porta Magica.'

'I'll be with you in a couple of minutes.' Saskia went up to Luca. 'Are you in love with her or is it all sham?' she inquired conversationally.

'I don't know if I can love. I'm from Pandemonium, in our tongue we don't have a word for love; when we speak it, we don't understand it. I might say I love; but do I really mean desire.' Luca said. 'I know how to desire with an intensity that burns through me, but it's not the love that your people speak about. It's passion. If you want to interpret that as love, then so be it. My kind do not'

'What have you told Holly?' Saskia asked.

'That at first, I liked and wanted her. Then I came to love her.'

'So, you're still protecting yourself?' Saskia frowned.

'No, I'm protecting Holly. I was prepared to go with Panqual. I would give my life for Holly. Now she's angry with me, and I'm aching with it.'

Saskia looked at her sympathetically. 'Holly's proud. But her anger won't last forever.' She gave Luca a friendly hug. 'I might see you later at Baal house. If Holly gives you the option, don't decline, accompany her.'

When Saskia had gone, Luca was tempted to look at Panqual's body; it was hard to believe she was dead. She realised she would rather be with Holly, no matter what mood she was in. She found her in the kitchen. In yellow washing up gloves from a newly opened packet, looking at Sirus's vomit.

'To be honest, there's less damage than I thought there'd be,' Holly remarked, conversationally. She tossed Luca an unopened pack of kitchen gloves. 'Let's see how you manage in 'marigolds'?'

*

As Ayesha and Zimpara emerged from the Porta Magica they were met by the enormous figure of Felix who was about to step through it. His face was set in a grim expression; he looked quite indomitable. He had a Caduceus in his left hand; the central shaft made of bronze with one golden snake and one silver. He looked surprised when they emerged, then relieved, but this quickly became concern.

'Ayesha, you're bleeding; you're hurt.'

'I'm okay; well, I'm not, but right now Rachel needs help more than me,' she said.

Felix's eyes fell on Zimpara; he frowned; their acquaintance went back a long way; they had not always seen eye to eye, but there was no real enmity between them; he was surprised that she had taken an active part in this business. She looked stricken and Ayesha was keeping her supported with an arm around her waist, though she looked about done in herself.

'Think I'm gonna pass out!' said Zimpara. Felix made a move towards her, but Sofia who had come to stand a little to his right and was regarding them with dismayed eyes, darted in and caught her. She glanced at Ayesha. 'You've put aside your differences then?'

'They seemed trivial, all of a sudden,' Ayesha said.

'What about Saskia?' Sofia said, concerned. She was holding Zimpara up, examining her head wounds with darting eyes and slim fingers.

'I'm sorry to announce she's still breathing,' Ayesha said, attempting humour.

'Seems harsh,' Zimpara mumbled.

Saskia chose that moment to emerge from the Porta Magica, preventing Felix's second attempt to stride into it. She smiled through the crusted blood that had leaked from her sliced cheek.

'Hello Felix.' She said, pleased to see him. 'Bet you didn't think you'd see us back here so soon.' She looked at his grim face and her eyes played over the Caduceus with interest. 'Don't worry, it's all over,' she assured him.

'I was about to tell him,' Ayesha said.

Saskia moved to Ayesha's side, she held her and kissed her bruised face. 'I should tell you more often that you're amazing,' she told her. She looked at Sofia and saw the look in her eyes.

'Fucking hell, Saskia,' she said in low voice.

'Is Holly alright?' Felix asked, worried.

'She's fine. Not even a bruise,' Saskia said.

'Felix, these two need attention,' Sofia said.

'I know,' he said, 'go on, it looks like we have guests again in Baal house tonight. Saskia I should go to Holly, please excuse me.'

She stepped into his path, again preventing him from entering the Porta Magica. 'Unless you're skilled in couples counselling, I'd leave it for now,' she said.

*

A few days later, with Felix's help, Luca and Holly brought the body of Panqual to Baal house. They had wrapped it in black polythene and duct tape. Felix closed, then re-opened the gate and they cast Panqual into the vast dark that Sofia referred to as the abyss. They threw her leather habit in after her. Luca watched them spin away into the emptiness. Holly did not even look, she watched Luca's face instead; observing that its expression encompassed loathing and relief, in equal amounts. It was hard to imagine what she had suffered at Panqual's hands; it was trite to think that Luca was a denizen of Pandemonium and therefore her experience was diminished by some sort of habitual exposure to horror. Holly did not see it that way. Neither did she blame Luca for her choices, or her actions. She embraced her deeds, generous, bad or murderous as they were; she respected her for that. She even thought that Luca was being honest about having fallen for her, after originally playing her. They had not mentioned forgiveness since their flight through the walled garden. It did not seem necessary. They had become lovers again by a mutual need, only the night before, with an intensity they had not known on previous occasions. They were returning home shortly. Probably to make love again. After which, Holly intended to destroy the portal to Pandemonium, with extreme enthusiasm.

*

'This is going to be exquisite,' said Saskia.

'I really think Holly should have put everyone in the picture,' Ayesha replied.

'I thought you'd sneakily tell Claire as it's her party...well your party...her party, to celebrate your birthday, Ayesha.' Saskia smiled brightly, emphasising the thin white trace of scar on her cheek. Medicinal alchemy had healed her wound rapidly, she had kept the scar as a badge of honour, abnormally pleased with it, though it was barely visible.

'It's just a party now,' Ayesha smiled. 'I hope there isn't a cake, you don't think there'll be a cake do you?'

'I told her you wanted a cake,' Saskia stated.

'Lying little cow... at least you'd better be.'

They were in Challenor-Shah antiques and fine art. They were closing early. Ayesha and Saskia were leaning on the counter looking through the sales book. They intended to lock up in half an hour or so and go on to Claire's dinner party. Pearl and Amber had already left and would be heading for the same destination. The buzzer sounded indicating that someone had come into the shop. They looked round and Saskia straightened and peered. 'Oh, wow!' she said softly. Curiously Ayesha straightened up and followed her gaze. She considered what she saw, then allowed a slow, warm smile to curve her mouth and fill her dark eyes. Two women approached, both chic in jeans and jackets, and stiletto heeled ankle boots.

'Look at you two,' Ayesha said.

Zimpara smiled. She looked remarkably well considering the injuries she had sustained; skilful alchemy had brought her back to health, aided by her own demonic constitution. 'We couldn't come for a day out in York without visiting you two, could we?' she said.

'This is fab,' said Sofia, looking round with keen eyes. 'We've got to come again.' She was all in black, with a stunning black and gold Indian turban, covering her snakes; a large Citrine flashing at its centre.

'I hope so,' said Saskia. Her eyes danced between them. 'This isn't just a friendly outing, is it? I hope not!' She went behind the counter and scrabbled in her bag. She kept looking up as she scribbled something out.

'We're staying in a hotel overnight,' said Sofia. 'We're going to the museum tomorrow, and the railway museum.'

'We're going on a city ghost walk tonight!' Zimpara announced, chuckling. They all laughed, amused.

'Here,' Saskia held out a cheque to Sofia. 'I've left the name blank.' Sofia looked puzzled.

'For your hijab,' said Saskia, smiling. 'It's the three hundred and fifty quid I owe you.'

'Saskia, it isn't necessary, really,' Sofia protested.

'Yes, it is. Take it.'

Sofia sighed and surrendered. 'Okay,' she smiled.

'Saskia, we've come for another reason, at least I have,' said Zimpara, becoming serious. 'I hope you both consider me a friend. As a friend I'm going to break the confidentiality of my trade.'

Ayesha and Saskia regarded her curiously. Whatever it was it sounded as if it could be interesting.

'I'm listening,' Saskia said.

'A few months ago, on a commission for Ariadne Leech, I located and bought a map. This is very relevant to the conversation had between you and Ariadne, in Holly's Garden. The map was very large and hand crafted, it was of the nAill; the Wild. She paid a great deal of money for it.'